I0742546

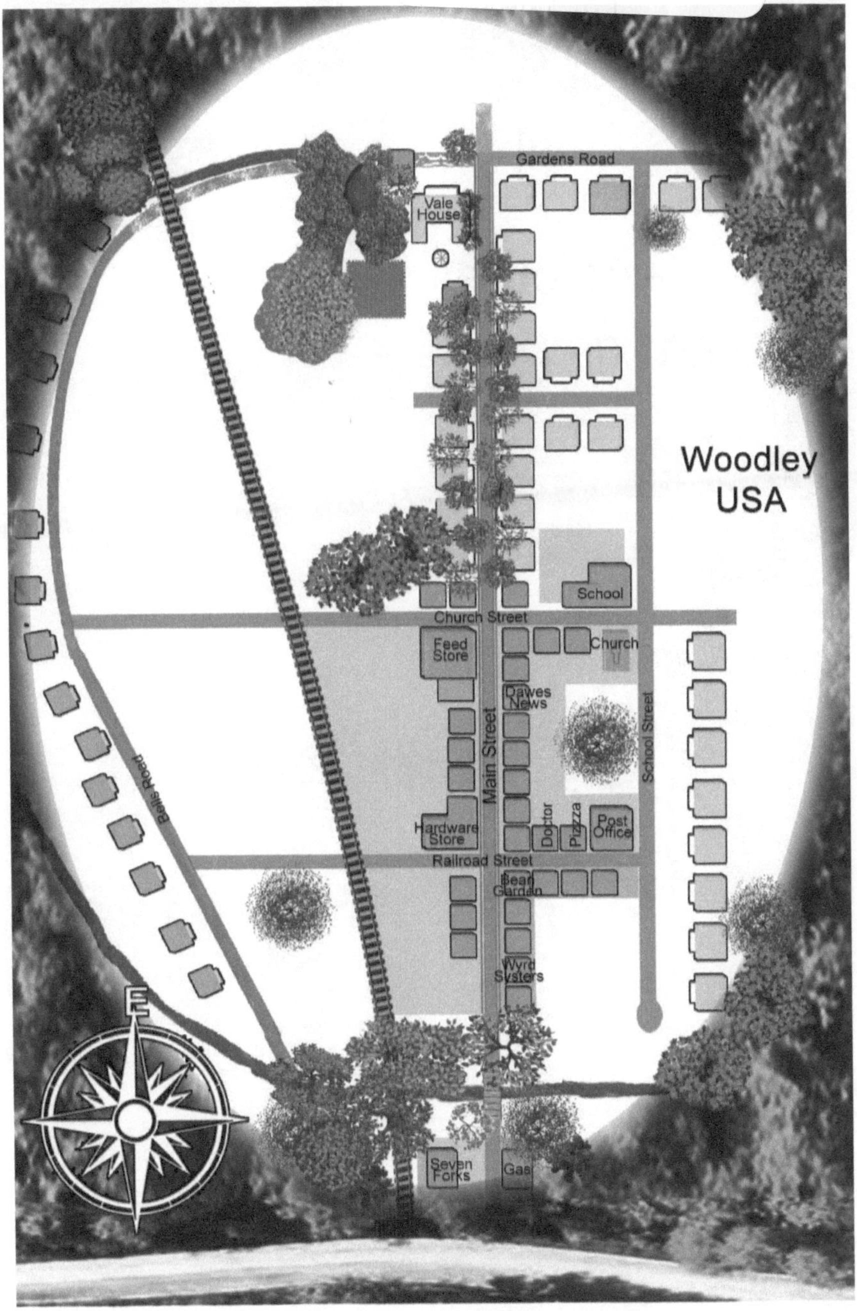

Gardens Road
Vale House
Woodley USA
School
Church Street
Feed Store
Church
Dawes News
Main Street
School Street
Bells Road
Hardware Store
Doctor
Pizza
Post Office
Railroad Street
Bear Garden
Wyrd Sisters
N
E
Seven Forks
Gas

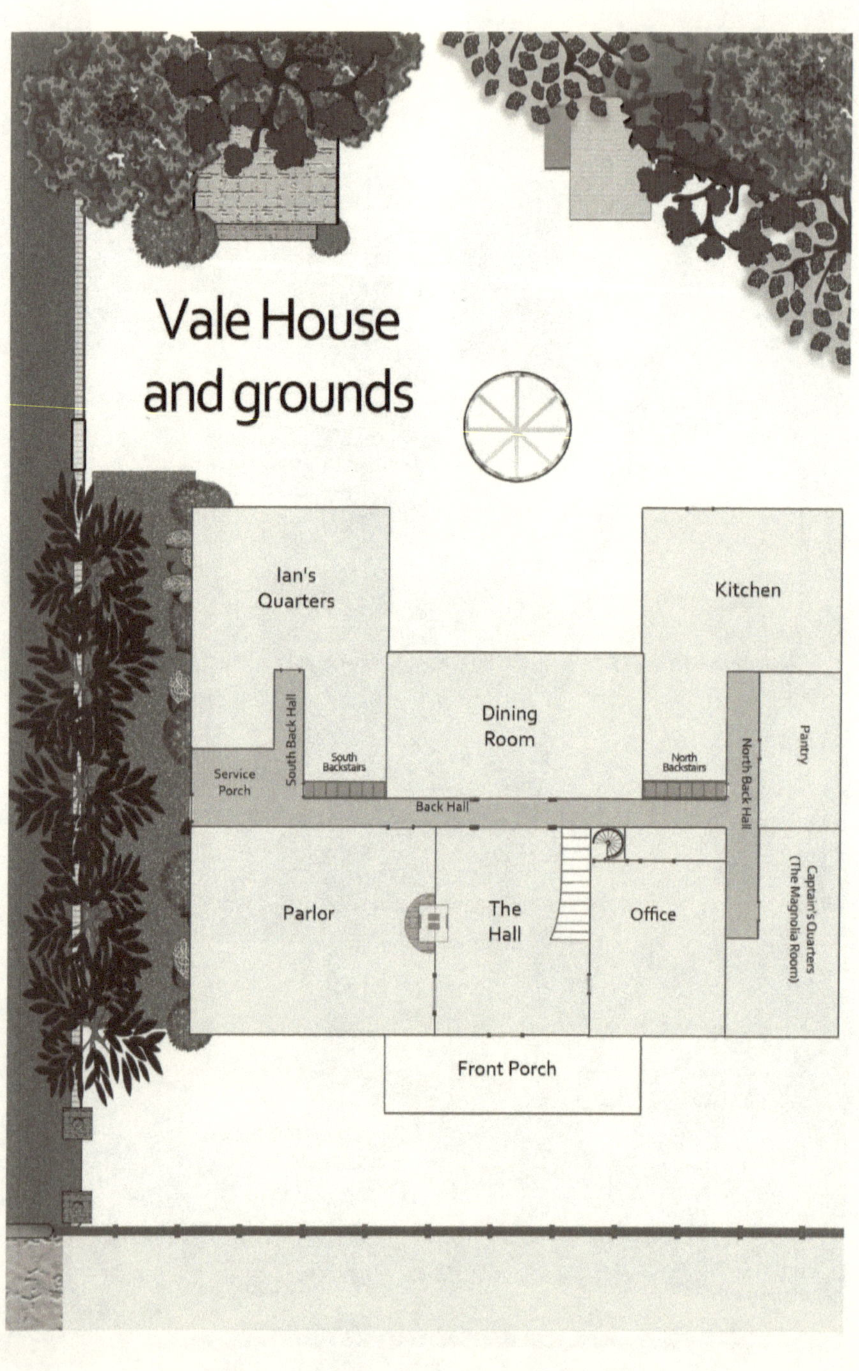

Vale House
and grounds
Ian's Quarters
Kitchen
Service Porch
South Back Hall
South Backstairs
Dining Room
North Backstairs
North Back Hall
Pantry
Back Hall
Parlor
The Hall
Office
Captain's Quarters
(The Magnolia Room)
Front Porch

Moonlight and Moss

Kim Beall

MOONLIGHT AND MOSS

Copyright 2018 by Kim Beall

First edition by KrystalRose Press 2019
krystalrose.com/Press

This is a work of fiction. All characters, places, and events described within are products of the author's imagination or are used fictitiously.

Except Doctor Boojums. He is absolutely real, and will fight anyone who says otherwise.

ISBN 978-1-7339964-0-2

Published in the United States of America

Illustrations by Kim Beall

DEDICATION

For the Franklin County Writers Guild and my critique
partners in Second Cup. Long live the Six Pack!

CONTENTS

In Which a Ghost is Pleased to Introduce the Story

In my favorite fantasy, while interviewing me Stephen Colbert breaks out his guitar and invites me to jam with him on national TV. I'm not sure what number we perform, though. "Another One Bites the Dust" has a great bass line, but I don't think Mr. Colbert can hit all the notes Freddie could. Maybe we could do XYX by Rush. That way, neither of us would have to sing.

Where my fantasy falls apart, of course, is when I remember Mr. Colbert can't see ghosts. Ironically, his television audience would be able to see and hear me perfectly well, because I am so much better at manipulating electronics than I am at manifesting myself directly to the eyes and ears of the living. Except for certain people, of course.

Callaghan McCarthy is one of the people who can see and hear me - and most other spirits - perfectly well. She has been seeing us all her life, but I was the one who finally convinced her what she was seeing was real. Now I count her among my very best friends.

What follows is the story of how Ms. Cally was instrumental (that was a pun - did you get it?) in helping to fulfill the mission of Vale House in championing the human side of the gateway, here in the Vale, though at first she had a pretty hard time choosing to accept her own role. After all, as I have learned, there really is no such thing as destiny. There is only the choice between the right path or the wrong one. Some say we each face seven such crossroads in our lives (though, in my case, I did not live long after I had encountered my first one.)

I believe this is the second of Ms. Cally's crossroads. I will leave it to you to decide whether or not she chose the right path.

Until that time when we all will know, I remain
Your faithful servant,
Guacanagarix

1 - The More You Change the Less You Fear

"I want to learn to play the bass guitar," said the ghost.

Cally continued to frown into her computer monitor, tugging her sweater around her shoulders to fend off the chill drifting through the screen door. "Why can't I get this thing to... George, what?"

"I said I want to..."

"I know what you *said*. I meant, well, for one thing, it's called a bass, not a bass guitar."

"How do you know that?"

"My son is a drummer." She looked around the antiques-decorated Reception Hall of the Vale House Bed and Breakfast, making sure nobody was nearby to hear her apparently talking to herself. Guests had been coming down the stairs for breakfast over the past half hour or so, and Bethany Chase, whom she was relieving at the reception desk, was due back any minute.

"Look, George," she said presently in a softer voice. "I admire that you love to learn, but how are you going to play the bass when you can't touch things?"

George gave her one of his angelic smiles, and she forgot about the program she was trying to update on her laptop (and about how it was refusing to cooperate.)

"Is your son as good as Neil Peart?"

"Nobody is as good as Neil Peart," she stated flatly. "But Brandon is as good as Mick Fleetwood. How's that?"

"Does he have a band? Does he need a bass player?"

"No. Yes? I don't know!" She shut her laptop a little too roughly. "Georgie, just because he's related to me doesn't mean he can see ghosts, and anyway, how are you going to play a real instrument without...hands?"

He stood up straight and took his hands out of his pockets, holding them out to her. They looked quite solid, to Cally, but she knew they weren't really. "I can learn to touch things," he insisted. "I'm getting better at it." He nodded and flicked at a pen on the old wooden desktop. It did not move. "Anyway, as you know, I am very good at electronic things. I don't have to touch those. You can just get me an electric bass."

"Can I, now?"

George was the first ghost Cally had ever met. At least, he was the first one she had ever realized was a ghost. He looked like a typical teenaged black man, tall and thin, with wide eyes and even wider cheekbones, and he spoke with an accent that could have been Jamaican or could have been Haitian but was neither. Today he wore his hair in a short, natural style and was dressed in a white button-down shirt that was not tucked in, with a red-and-yellow polka-dot tie knotted loosely outside the collar. George had always been very concerned with his appearance and liked to try a different style every day. This was easy to do, for someone whose hair and clothing were made of aether.

"Well," George said, in a voice dripping with honey, "you can afford it now. Now that you've got your check. The advance on that book you wrote. After all, it *is* about me."

"You're in it, George, but it's not about you. And anyway..." She opened her laptop again and frowned at the screen. "It looks like I'm going to have to use that money to buy a new computer. This one is so old, I can't update my word processor anymore." Ordinarily, she was proud of being a luddite and of never having adopted most of the new technology, the games and apps and all the video streaming nonsense that was so popular with young people these days but, well, she was a writer. She needed a reliable word processor.

"When you get your new computer, you can give me your old one!" George grinned and offered her a high-five. She gave him a steady look from under one raised brow. The thought of George having unlimited access to the internet made her nervous. He was over four hundred years old but, somehow, he still seemed to her to be young and naïve, and she felt protective of him.

"I had *really* hoped to use the money as a down payment on a house in town, or maybe even open a small business..."

"You don't need a house," George told her. "You live here."

The sound of footsteps on the stairs interrupted them, and George thoughtfully waited for Cally to turn her head and look away before he vanished. A slightly built man with a briefcase in his hand was just reaching the bottom stair.

"Good morning!" Cally greeted him in a voice that sounded more cheerful than she felt.

He came to the front of the desk and stood his briefcase on it, resting both hands on its handle. "Am I to understand," he said, flashing a toothy smile, "that you are the famous Callaghan McCarthy?"

Cally took a deep breath and said carefully, "I am Callaghan McCarthy, but I'm not famous."

"I would beg to differ!" he said. "I'm your biggest fan!"

"How nice." Her shoulders tightened. She always felt she had to be careful around *Biggest Fans*, as most of them tended to ask a lot of awkward questions. "Thank you for reading my book. The next one will be coming out in time for Christmas."

"Oh, I've never read your book," the man said. Cally couldn't help giving him a puzzled look. "I know you from a different fame," he explained. "I'm Eddie Tiene!"

He pronounced his surname *'teen'* and held his arms out at his sides as if he expected her to applaud.

She looked carefully at his eyes, which were greenish, and his hair, still wet and combed straight back over his head. It had apparently once been light brown or dark blond, but was now streaked with gray. None of his features triggered any memories. "I'm sorry, I don't..." She cast about in her mind trying to unearth a clue as to who Eddie Teen might be, but came up blank.

"We went to high school together." He smiled, and when understanding still did not dawn on her face he added, "I had a huge crush on you."

And then she did remember, but she didn't smile. In fact, she took care not to show what she was feeling at all. She suddenly found herself back in school, being laughed at by an entire troupe of young males who had thought it funny to send their ringleader, this Eddie, to feign romantic interest in her only so they could then ridicule her for believing anyone as popular as him could ever find her attractive. Few memories of high school were pleasant for Cally, but she had managed to relegate most of them to the cobwebs of her subconscious.

"Oh. Yes. Eddie Tiene." She pronounced his surname *'chen-a.'* "Yes. How have you been?" Her forced smile made her teeth hurt.

"Can't complain," he said, "though sometimes I still do." He threw his head back and let out a laugh so sharp, people in the dining room to put down their forks to look through the wide doorway into the Hall. "My goodness, you have become more beautiful than ever," he added in a quieter voice. "Did you ever find that Arkenstone, Kili?"

Even now, this remark tied Cally's stomach in knots, and she hated herself for that. She had read the works of J. R. R. Tolkien when she was in middle-school, and had spent the next several years trying to convince the kids around her to do the same. She'd even made up quests for them, to seek the Arkenstone in the shale hillsides around their neighborhood, or to destroy an evil artifact by questing through the corn fields, but of course none of them had ever participated. Instead, they had teased her by morphing her name to Kili, after one of the characters in *The Hobbit*. She might have actually enjoyed that, but the jokes about how she frolicked with goblins in the woods had only grown nastier as they all grew older.

Time and geographical distance had given Cally perspective on the whole thing, but she still sighed when she answered the grown man and his good-natured (she told herself) teasing.

"I'm afraid I never found the Arkenstone," she said. "But I did finally meet some Elves."

He laughed at her joke that was not a joke, then he asked, "But I don't understand: why has such a pretty girl never married?"

"I did marry." She didn't bother to point out she wasn't a girl anymore. "I married Wes Rayne. You should remember him. He was second string on the football team. I took my real name back after the divorce."

"So sorry to hear it didn't work out." He didn't sound sorry. "You must have moved away after you graduated. We... I lost track of you for a long time. And tell me, did this union result in any offspring?"

Cally frowned while he continued to peer earnestly at her. Though it was a personal question, it was a common one for people to ask of acquaintances they had not seen in many years. It was just that the way he'd worded it sounded less like friendly inquiry, to her, than like he was collecting statistics for a breeding program. She felt uncomfortable answering it, so she answered a different question instead.

"I did move away, back then. I guess I've always had a bit of wanderlust." That sounded better than, *"I've always been restless."*

"I'm alone now, too," he informed her. "Maybe it's not mere chance that we've met again. Perhaps it's fate telling us we should pick up our old friendship where we left off." He leaned over his briefcase and gave her a wide smile. He was a handsome man, by the usual criteria, but she could think only of a wolf lunging for the throat of a deer. If the way he and his cohorts had harassed her in the lunch room all those years ago had been his idea of friendship, she thought, she had been fortunate indeed he had not considered her an enemy.

"It's funny how people's memories can differ," she remarked at last. "But I believe it's always best to leave the past in the past."

"I'm sorry you feel that way." He stood back and reached into his briefcase, withdrawing a business card and a key with a picture of a white lily on the fob. The card he placed on the desk in front of Cally, but he held up the key, jiggling it in the air. "I wonder if I might extend my reservation in the Daylily Room for another night? It turns out my business in this town has gone better than I expected."

"I'll see what I can do," Cally said. "But as far as I know, we are fully booked, it being October and all."

She didn't have to lie about this. She had even relinquished her own room, the Dogwood Room, in order to make it available for paying guests, and had been sleeping on the sofa in her office for over a week.

"Ah, yes. October must be a busy month for a B&B with a reputation for being haunted. I didn't see any ghosts last night, myself, though. Do I get a discount for that?"

Cally struggled to maintain her friendly expression as she shook her head. "Sorry, hauntings are not guaranteed, but a good breakfast is. Katarina has made egg strata this morning. You go enjoy your breakfast, Mr. Teine, and I'll check about extending your stay."

"Thank you." He took his bag from the desktop and turned toward the dining room, then turned back. "I've been hoping for a very long time to catch up with you again. You..." He looked around the Hall, into the parlor at his left and up to the top of the stairs opposite it. "You seem to have landed in a place which suits you." He reached over the desk and shoved his business card closer to Cally before heading for the dining room. "But I won't let myself lose track of you again."

2 - It's Complicated

"Because that's not creepy at all!" Bethany's voice came from the parlor after Eddie had gone, and Cally turned to see the older woman shaking her head with arms crossed.

Cally laughed, sincerely this time. "He seems to remember our school days very differently from how I do," she explained as she gathered up her laptop and notebooks. "One of us apparently has a bad memory."

She stood to surrender the office chair (which was the only modern piece of furniture in the entire house) and changed the subject. "When is Ignacio going to start lighting a fire in the fireplace? It's starting to get chilly in this Hall in the mornings!"

Bethany took off her apron and sat down at the desk, adjusting the chair to its tallest setting. "Oh, this is your first autumn in the South, isn't it? Well, they say, if you don't like the weather around here, just wait five minutes!" She laughed merrily, but Cally didn't laugh, so she elaborated. "You see that fog out there?" Bethany nodded toward the door. "Ignacio says that's a sign it's going to turn out to be a warm day. He's very good at predicting the weather – I've never seen him get it wrong yet." The phone rang, and she excused herself to answer it.

Cally glanced out the open door, where fog was indeed curling like a gray ghost through the screen. It was still dark outside, she noted, which meant she still had time. But probably not enough time, she thought, turning to peer into the dining room, to eat a proper breakfast.

Katarina was dashing around the long, linen-covered table making sure everyone's coffee cups were full. Most of the guests, Cally noted, dined in couples, but Mr. Tiene sat alone, as did the strikingly tall and muscular delivery driver, Mr. Ennilangr, who had arrived an hour ago in response to Katarina's desperate plea for an emergency shipment of pancake syrup.

Almost as striking as Ennilangr's physique was the lush, blond ponytail hanging down his back. The man looked like a Norse god who could break the Vale House Bed and Breakfast with his appetite alone, if not his massive hands, but his plate lay untouched before him as he drank coffee after coffee the way some people would knock back shots of whiskey. He was laughing good naturedly at Katarina as she said, "Steady, there, Mr. Ennilangr – I'll just go and get you your own pot!"

Behind her, Bethany hung up the phone. Picking up the business card Mr. Tiene had left, she turned around and held it out toward Cally. "Huh. What kind of real estate developer uses a picture of a flaming building as his logo?"

"It's probably a reference to his surname," Cally guessed. "It's the Scotts Gaelic word for fire." She recalled having revealed this trivia tidbit to Eddie Tiene in high school, believing he would find it fascinating, but this had only earned her more nerd-bashing. The fact that she had corrected his pronunciation of his own name had probably not helped.

"Still..." Bethany tucked the card into the jar Jake Lucas from Motherboard Pizza had put on the desk. A sign taped to the jar read *'Leave your business card for a chance to win a free Gourmet Pizza!'* "I apologize for taking so long to get back from my break," she went on. "I could have saved you from having to talk to that man. I was checking on Ian and Sofie."

"No, it's no trouble at all." Cally meant this. Since becoming the Office Manager, or whatever she was here (it was still unclear to her) she actually missed working at the reception desk in the Hall. "How is Sofie today?" Her voice quavered as she asked.

"Not any worse," Bethany said with a sigh. "But not any better, either. Ian won't leave her side. He's afraid she'll die while he's not there. I wish I could just forward the phones to voicemail and sit with them awhile. But Ian May is the boss, and he says business mustn't slow down on account of an illness in the proprietor's family. To be honest I think he's showing the strain, himself. But it would probably stress him out even more to turn away business during our busiest time of year."

Cally nodded. "I'm always glad to find some way to help out," she said. "And Ian is right. The phone has been ringing all morning with people hoping to stay in a haunted Bed and Breakfast in October. Um... speaking of turning away business. One caller wanted to stay for two nights which included the twenty-fifth. I had to politely refer them to the motel in Blackthorn." This was Cally's way of trying, yet again, to get Bethany to explain why nobody was allowed to stay at Vale House on the twenty-fifth of October, at the very peak of the busiest time of year but, as usual, Bethany didn't elucidate.

"Doctor Tanahey has promised to come by later this morning," she said instead. "I hope he can talk Ian into admitting Sofie to the hospital. I'm sure it's pneumonia."

"I don't think anyone is ever going to get Sofie into a hospital again," Cally said. "Not without sedating her."

"It's Ian they'd have to sedate," Bethany corrected.

"I'll try to talk to him later about it," Cally promised. "I should be back by the time Doc arrives. I'd better get going now."

"Off you scoot, then," Bethany said, but before Cally could reach the oaken door to her office, Katarina ran in from the dining room, draping a tea-towel over her shoulder.

"You haven't had any breakfast yet!" the short, round-faced woman exclaimed breathlessly.

"I had a granola bar," Cally said, and Katarina blew her bangs out of her eyes and made *tsk*ing noises at her.

"If you are going to work at a Bed and Breakfast," she said, "you are going to have to get used to the whole 'breakfast' part of it!"

"Aw, let her go," Bethany said, giving Katarina a wink over the top of her glasses. "She mustn't keep her young prince waiting."

"Bethany means that in more ways than one!" Katarina gave Cally a friendly nudge with her elbow. Cally had often thought that if Katarina were a book, all the punctuation would be exclamation points.

"I'm not keeping him waiting," she defended. "I feel like I'm the one who spends all my time waiting for him. It's beginning to drive me crazy," she admitted. Then she added, "I mean, it's not his fault."

She didn't explain why this was so. How could one explain trying to navigate a budding relationship with a man who was obligated by some kind of faerie contract to spend his nights in a place which didn't, technically, exist? "It's complicated," was all she could say.

Katarina laughed. "There's nothing complicated about it! People have been doing it since Adam and Eve! Do you need me to draw you a picture?"

Bethany laughed, too, but came to Cally's defense. "Everything in its own good time," she said. "If it's true love, they'll find a way."

"Who said anything about love?" Cally asked, but Bethany couldn't answer because the phone rang and she had to turn away to answer it.

Katarina leaned her head closer to Cally and spoke quietly. "That's fine. Sometimes you can just have fun; it doesn't have to be love. It isn't good for you to keep depriving yourself. A healthy woman has got to have some..."

"Ugh!" Bethany grunted as she hung up the phone. "I feel that dark presence in this Hall again! Do you feel it?"

"Maybe it's the fog," Cally suggested, glancing at a dark form which had appeared in front of the desk. Bethany, as well as many guests at Vale House, tended to sense this ghost as nothing more than a presence, but Cally could clearly see a dark-suited man with such a serious face she had come to refer to him as The Preacher. He did nothing, as usual, but stare past the desk toward the framed portraits above the mantle, and he would probably keep doing it for another hour or so. Cally had no time for him this morning.

"I *also* happen to have an appointment," she told the other women, a little too defensively, "with Jud Thornton, later, to look at some real estate for sale in town. I'll be back later than usual, and not for the reasons you might think!"

She hugged Katarina and waved to Bethany, then escaped at last into her office. As she set her computer down on the desk and reached for her sweater, the computer chimed softy, letting her know an instant message had arrived. She glanced quickly as she walked out the door, determined not to let anything else slow her down this morning. The message read:

EMERALD: Cally, is everything alright?

She wondered why her old friend would ask that, but a quick

glance out the office window showed the sky in the east changing from dark gray to silver, and she knew she had to hurry if she wanted to have any time at all to spend with *him*.

3 - The Foggy Dew

There was a point, out near the horizon, where the hills were no longer part of this world. Cally couldn't see that far today, because of the fog, but as she leaned on the gate gazing out into the meadow, the sun slowly warmed the sky there from silver to palest gold. Crossing her arms to hold her sweater closed across her chest, she fixed her eyes on the place where the sky shone brightest. She sensed him before she finally saw him. He appeared to be nothing more than a dark flame dancing in the distance, through the mist, but her heart quickened and she parted her lips to take in breath as the shadow resolved into the silhouette of a man walking.

She liked the way he walked: he had a confident, purposeful stride without the slightest hint of swagger. It consumed a lot of ground with each step, and he crossed the meadow more quickly than would an ordinary man, but then, he wasn't an ordinary man.

Ben Dawes was already smiling when Cally was able to make out his face through the fog. He was almost always smiling at some thought deep inside, she mused, but this was a special smile, just for her, because he knew she would be waiting.

It had become their little ritual, over the past couple of months. At first, he had come up onto the Vale House porch in the early mornings, hoping she would be awake, and she had learned to wake up early because she loved what happened if she was there when he arrived. For the first few weeks, they would just stand side by side, talking and tormenting themselves with one another's nearby warmth. That had finally evolved into kissing, some weeks ago now, and the kisses had grown longer and longer.

Bethany and Katarina had noticed this, of course. They had taken to poking their heads out the front door to invite Ben inside for coffee, or offering some other pretense to encourage Cally to slip away to her suite with him, but he couldn't accept. He could never stay long, between his night time obligations and his day time duties, so Cally had taken to meeting him at the meadow gate, where they could at least enjoy their few minutes together in peace.

He broke into a run for the last few steps through the meadow. Grabbing the top rail of the gate, he vaulted over with an ease that was surprising for a man who appeared to be in his mid-fifties, and who was actually much older than that. Landing on the ground next to Cally, he swept her into his arms and held her tight to his chest, kissing her long and deeply. She clung to him for balance, struggling to take in enough air to satisfy her pounding heart. When he let go and stood back to look at her, she was dizzy and shaking. It was all she could do to stop her hands reaching out to start unbuttoning his shirt right there at the end of the street. She wasn't going to be able to stand much more of this; something had to give, and soon.

"How are you?" he asked. He was short of breath, too, and his grin flashed in the new sunlight breaking through the fog. "Don't answer that; that's a stupid thing to ask. Of course you're amazing."

"And you're full of shit," she said, but she smiled and put a hand up to the side of his face. The china-blue of his eyes was just a shade darker than the sky, and the silver streaks shooting throughout his hair and beard seemed to morph into the rays of sun behind him. She couldn't look long before she gave in and kissed him again. Oh, the kissing was delicious, she thought, but it had stopped being enough a long time ago. "How was your visit?" she finally asked.

He turned and put an arm around her, and they headed away from the gate, past the stately old homes along both sides of Main Street, kicking their way through the fallen leaves along the oak-lined sidewalk.

"They talked about you," Ben told her, and his smile faded a little. "I vouched for you, but they remain skeptical."

"Fair enough," Cally said. "After all, humans are skeptical about them, too."

He paused and turned again to face her. "You actually are amazing," he said. "I knew that on the first day, when I first saw you, asleep there in your car in front of the store. It was as if I recognized you from...somewhere." He gave her a look he often gave her, one which said: *I won't press you for your secret, but when you're ready to tell me, I am here and you can trust me with it.* Cally thought she might even tell him this big secret, if she could ever figure out just what, exactly, it was.

All she could do was smile and shake her head as they continued toward town. As Bethany had promised, the chill of dawn was fading with the fog, and the air was already becoming warm enough to make Cally glad she had dressed in layers. She took off her sweater, tied it around her waist, and tried to ignore the way front doors tended to open along Main Street just as she and Ben drew abreast of them. Cats came out of front doors and leapt onto porch railings to wink at them as they passed.

They reached the end of the last residential block, where the trees stopped and Woodley's downtown began. There, they could see Ben's sister, an older woman with a long, pepper-and-salt ponytail, standing in front of the News Store. Keys dangled from the lock in the shop door, and Bree's hands were on her hips.

"You're late!" she declared.

"Sorry," said Ben. He released Cally and gave his sister a hug, which she dismissed with a shrug. "You know I go by the sun, Bree, not by the clock. The sun rises later, these days."

"Thank you for mansplaining the seasons to me," Bree said. "If the sun is rising later these days, then maybe you shouldn't dally so long at the gate." She gave Cally a sharp look; Cally responded with a grin. Brigid Dawes could be acerbic – in fact there were very few other ways she could be – but Cally couldn't help liking her. No one ever had to wonder where they stood with her, in any case. "Now get this door open for me," the old woman barked at Ben. "We're burning daylight."

Ben laughed and hurried around to the alley between the News Store and the vacant storefront next door. Bree took the opportunity to tell Cally, once more, how she disapproved of Cally's relationship with Ben. "He doesn't belong to this world," she reminded Cally for at least the fortieth time. "One day he'll have to go back there, and you're not going to deal well with that. No mortal ever deals well with that. No good will come of it." She shook her head. "No good ever comes of any of this!"

Cally didn't bother to reply. She had used up all of her "Ben and I are both grownups" arguments already, and saying "Don't worry, everything will be okay" had proven to be a thing which could send Bree into a rage. Ben's sister had had a much harder time than he had, dealing with having been abandoned as a child by their faerie mother, and then by their father who had gone off to follow his lost love. In addition, her abusive husband had disappeared on her some years later (though there was speculation in the neighborhood that John Ware's disappearance might not have been entirely his own idea.) It wasn't as if Bree liked anyone else, either, so Cally couldn't really take it personally.

She made a conciliatory gesture somewhere between a nod and a shrug, then turned to look at Ben, who had appeared on the inside of the shop door. He gave the door a sharp kick from the inside to make it shudder open, and reached out a hand to help Bree up the step into the store.

"When are you going to get around to fixing that door?" Bree grumbled as she unwound her scarf, unbuttoned her coat, and assumed her place behind the counter where she started to fill the coffee maker.

"She knows I've already fixed it dozens of times," Ben said, leaning back out the door and reaching a hand out to Cally. "Come with me."

4 - The Thing

Cally stepped inside the dusty store, where the only light was that which came through the windows and from the beverage cooler at the back. Bree snapped open and began to read a copy of that day's newspaper. She didn't look up as they crossed to the back of the store, but Cally knew she was watching, in her own way, and heard her mutter, "Hmph!"

The back door was still open, and Ben led Cally out through it into the gravel parking lot shared by all the storefronts on this side of Main Street. Aside from Mr. Ennilangr's eighteen-wheeler, with its mural of leaping rams on the side of the trailer, the only vehicle parked there was the Dawes family Daimler. Ben sat down on its hood. Cally was horrified at the thought of sitting on the beautiful gray finish of the vintage car, but Ben reassuringly patted the spot beside him. Cally sat down gingerly, and then she forgot to worry about the paint when he put his arm around her and slid her across to hold her close to his side.

"So, the thing is," he said, "there's going to be a Thing."

"What kind of thing?"

He grinned and looked away over the tops of the buildings toward the eastern sky. "A Thing thing. With a capital T.

"It's kind of a big meeting of shadowland folk, and others. A sort of...United Nations summit, only of worlds, of all different sorts of People. They just call it the Thing. Boundaries are re-drawn, titles assigned and reassigned, disputes arbitrated, homages paid. I just wanted to let you know, because this means it's going to get weird around here in the next few days..." He glanced back at her smile and said, "Weirder than usual, I mean. Before a Thing, all the chickens come home to roost. It's been a long time since there's been one, and issues have arisen that need resolutions."

Something about the way he said "issues" made Cally feel like a dark hand was reaching right up out of the parking lot for her heart. She said, "I'm guessing one of the issues is you and your dual citizenship?"

"No!"

He spoke so sharply, a dog in a house somewhere on the other side of School Street began to bark. Ben's eyes became hard as flint, glaring at the sky above the buildings as if he could bring down lightning if he wished to. "No, that issue is not up for debate!"

He let out a breath and resumed his usual soft-spoken tones, but his free hand was curled into a fist on his knee. "No, but you're right, they will try. They've never been pleased that I managed to trick them into letting me spend half my life here in Woodley. They never really bought the excuse that Bree needs my help. They will try to get me to discuss it, try to trick me into agreeing to an arrangement more on their terms. They will not be able to budge me."

Cally laid a hand over his fist until it unclenched, and his palm turned upward to entwine fingers with hers.

"When is this Thing supposed to happen?" she asked.

He counted quietly to himself, looking up again as if calculating on stars she couldn't see. "Friday," he concluded. "Three days from now. It will start on Friday night, and will last for three nights. I wanted to let you know ahead of time, because I'll be gone for three days, once it starts, and I don't want you thinking I'm not coming back. I *am* coming back." This last he said as if he were already arguing with someone about it.

She looked at side of his face, at his eyes as they gazed upward. Then she said what she had once been sure she would never again say to any man.

"I believe you."

He turned his eyes to meet hers, and she felt all the tension drift out of his body. "Don't ever imagine I fail to understand what a gift that is for you to give me," he said. His smile – the smile that had always made Cally think of sunshine in a sky as blue as his eyes – returned. "I am completely humbled by it."

Cally couldn't hold herself up straight when he talked to her like that. She knew she wasn't going to be able to stand much more of this. "What would happen," she barely heard herself asking, "if you didn't go? I don't mean to the Thing – I mean, on some ordinary night, instead of going back to your mother's country, what if one night you just...didn't show up?"

She couldn't have been any clearer about what she meant, and she could see he understood, and she could see, as she had known she would, the regret in his eyes.

He said: "That night we drove to Blackthorn – you remember it wasn't really Blackthorn at all, and to Seen's Mill – I was late that night, getting back to the Faerie Court, and it didn't go down well. All hell had very nearly broken loose by the time I did arrive. It wasn't like I was a child out after curfew; the stakes are much higher than that. Some people were already ready to go to war. I made the excuse that I had technically kept my side of the bargain because we had, after all, been *partway* in my mother's country!" He let out a rather dry laugh, shaking his head. "I don't think I could get away with that again."

Then his expression became serious and he turned to sit cross-legged on the hood of the car, facing Cally and taking several slow, deep breaths before speaking. "I made a promise," he said. "Maybe I was tricked into it, at the time, because I was just a kid, but I gave my word. And there is so much more at stake than my own wishes. Bree is right: there are entire worlds hanging on how I conduct myself in this one. And there are those who would love nothing more than to revel in the chaos that would break loose if the ancient promises were broken. Someone is always trying to break them. I don't want to be the one who does that. I won't be, and I love you because I know you wouldn't want me to be that person, either."

He hesitated when Cally gulped and averted her eyes. She could tell he hadn't meant to use the "L" word out loud, and since she wasn't ready yet to deal with what she'd do if he did, she carefully pretended not to have noticed.

"Maybe, at this Thing," she suggested, speaking to the blank brick wall of the building behind him, "you can negotiate a new promise. After all, you never asked for this. It was your mother who seduced a man in order to bring some half human children into the world." She bit her lip. She hadn't meant to call his humanity into question. "Sorry, I..."

He shook his head and reached over with one finger to lift her chin. When she turned her eyes again to meet his, he nodded. "I love you," he said, and this time he spoke deliberately. "And that is how I know I am human. I wouldn't want it any other way."

He didn't wait for a reply, or even look as if he were expecting one. Instead he slid his hand through her hair and kissed her softly. "Will I see you tonight?"

Cally couldn't breathe, so she nodded. Tonight, every night, every morning, it didn't matter, just as long as she could see him again.

She excused herself awkwardly, explaining about her appointment with Jud Thornton, and walked too quickly through the parking lot past the backs of the stores toward Railroad Street. She was fairly certain she loved him, too, but she didn't trust herself enough to say so.

5 - The Gray Council

Merv Arkwright, the owner of the feed store, was sitting in a battered lawn chair on his loading dock, reading his newspaper just as he did every morning. Jud stood at the bottom of the loading dock steps, talking to Merv but glancing back occasionally toward his own store, Thornton & Son Hardware near the west end of the street. Sheriff Dunn Mahon's patrol car was parked at the curb; the sheriff himself was standing beside the car, talking with the men at the dock. Cally waved to them as she paused to let a single car pass down Main Street.

"Morning." The Sheriff nodded politely once Cally had reached their side of the street.

"Morning, Ms. McCarthy," Merv echoed. "How's that new book coming along?"

"Please call me Cally," she said futilely, knowing he never would. "If you mean my new novel, it's coming out in time for Christmas." She knew they already knew this, just as they knew everything about everyone in this town, but she was learning that small-talk was important in small towns, and she was trying to become a proper denizen. "Though I wish I'd had more input into the cover art. At least there's less cleavage than on the last one." She paused to let them laugh politely at this. "If you mean the novel I'm working on now, well, I'm behind schedule, as usual! I've been looking for a house of my own. Jud's going to show me some properties for sale this morning." She knew they already knew this, as well.

"You don't need a house," Merv pointed out. "Ian is happy to let you stay at Vale House."

"I know, and that's very sweet of him. And I do love it there, but, well, it's hard to get any privacy, living in a bed and breakfast." This last she said as Doctor Tanahey's car pulled up at the curb behind the sheriff's car.

"Morning, Doc," everyone said in unison when the doctor got out of his car.

The sheriff chuckled. "This is a small town," he said, returning his attention to Cally. "If you stay here, you're never going to have any privacy ever again!"

"You should just marry young Bennet," Merv advised over the top of his newspaper. "Then people won't bother to talk anymore." The other men all nodded, with various grins and laughs, in agreement.

Cally crossed her arms and sighed. "Guys, I hardly think it's time to start talking about marriage already, even if I did plan to do anything that stupid ever again. I barely know the man!"

Jud came to her rescue. "I thought you wanted to look at some retail properties, as well, this morning?" he asked. He continued to glance back nervously over his shoulder, and Cally realized he must have left his store unattended in order to meet with her.

"You should open up a burger joint!" Doc advised. "We need one around here." Then he addressed the men. "Sorry I can't stay long. On my way to talk to Ian. Will we be meeting up for music tonight?" The way he glanced at all of them except Cally let her know he wasn't just talking about the old-time songs the men liked to play on the loading dock on fine evenings. He was referring to their function as sort of clandestine governing council of town elders.

"I'll just wait for Jud at his store," Cally said, meaning: *'Fine, I'll give you boys your privacy,'* but a wink from Merv stopped her before she turned away.

"I was thinking," Merv said. "Well, I think it would be very good if we could persuade Ms. McCarthy to join us one of these evenings." He nodded firmly as he said the word "good," and gave Doc, Jud, and the sheriff each a level look in turn. "After all, Ian May hasn't been able to join us lately. Young Bennet assures us she has a strong alto voice."

Slowly, the sheriff and the doctor nodded in return.

"I..." Cally wasn't sure what to say. It warmed her to hear that, apparently, Ben's recommendation had garnered her the invitation, but she knew the old men talked about things during their music sessions that were not openly discussed in front of people who were Not From Around Here: things such as why Woodley was so hard for outsiders to find, and why it did not show up on maps or in GPS databases. She had long wanted answers to these questions, but she hadn't expected she would ever be told.

"I'd be happy...honored, to join your...band," she stammered. "Though I hardly think I'm capable of replacing Ian."

"Probably not!" Merv laughed. "He used to be our drummer!"

Cally's eyes widened. She knew Ian had once been a key member of what Katarina referred to as "the Gray Council," but she simply could not picture such a gentle, dignified gentleman playing drums, even in his youth.

"It's alright," said Doc. "You can sing Randy Meisner's part for us."

Cally laughed, sincerely, then. "Have mercy, Doc! Meisner could hit notes I can't even hear!"

"Why don't you stop by here tonight," Merv said. "After you see young Ben off, of course."

"I would love that," she admitted. "But I'm afraid I'll need a raincheck. I've made a commitment, this evening, to meet with a young ghost hunter from Asheboro. I don't want her just running around unsupervised through Vale House."

"I still say," Jud held forth, "you ought to make it clear those ghost stories you write actually take place right here in Woodley, and not just some fictional town. That would bring in droves of new business!"

Nobody else around the dock seemed to like this idea, and Cally liked it least of all. She shuddered at the thought of vapid tourists trampling through Vale House, making rude demands of the ghosts and trying to provoke them into manifesting themselves. "Talk about a real horror story!" she said. "Jud, my novels are works of fiction. Any resemblance to real persons or places is purely coincidental."

"Right," Merv said to the men. "So be careful, or you'll end up in the next one she writes!"

6 - The Yellow House

Cally walked with Jud the block and a half to Thornton & Son Hardware. Here, he waved her toward his car, which was parked at the curb, while he put his head inside the store and shouted something to someone standing in the shadows at the back. He looked distracted and unhappy as he turned back to Cally. "Alright, let's go, then," he muttered.

"Jud, if this isn't a good time, I can..."

"No, no, it's alright," he said. "My son Donald blew into town last night, and he can keep an eye on things for me..." He looked at his store again and shook his head, turning away with an effort.

"You must be glad to see him." Cally had not seen her own son or daughter for several months, now. "Will Donald be in town long?"

Jud shook his head. "He just needs a favor. He won't stay long. He never does." Then he reprised what Cally had heard many of Woodley's old-timers say: "Young people who grow up here, they don't stay around. They leave for bigger opportunities out in Raleigh or Charlotte. None of them are interested in sticking around and taking a hand in the family businesses that gave them their start in life."

"I understand how you must feel," Cally said perfunctorily, though she personally thought some people tended to keep the apron strings tied a bit too tight. She was proud of her children for the lives they were creating for themselves, even if it meant she didn't get to see them as often as she would have liked.

Jud opened the passenger door of his car for her.

"Do we really need to drive?" she asked. "I would prefer to find a place within walking distance."

Jud gave her a confused look. "You don't want to look at any of the properties on Bells Road?"

She looked down Railroad Street, across the tracks to where a wide, mown field ended in a colorful border of charming cottages nestled against the encircling forest. "Oh!" She realized that probably really was a long walk for someone Jud's age. "No, of course, I would love to see them." She got into the car.

Jud remained silent and broody as he drove the short distance across the tracks to where Railroad Street ended in a T at Bells Road. One of the homes for sale lay directly across this intersection, and the other was tucked partway into the trees at the east end of Bells Road where the meadow fence disappeared into the forest. Cally thought they were both quite charming. The first had a second bedroom Cally could imagine using as an office, and the other had a small, leaf-strewn front porch that seemed like a perfect place for a cat to nap.

"Neither of them is haunted, as far as anyone knows!" Jud commented, laughing a little too loudly, as if he really didn't think this was funny at all.

"They're both nice," Cally said honestly. "If it's not too much trouble, I would also like to have a look at the Yellow House."

She was pretty sure the old, gable-front home, known to everyone in town as the Yellow House, was too big for her and almost certainly too big for her budget. But, as she was gathering research for her next book, she wanted to see the inside of the house because of the many local legends about its alleged hauntings. While it wasn't really fair, manipulating Jud into showing her a property she had no intention of buying, whatever she did end up buying would help him with his dream of 'putting Woodley back on the map,' as he called it, so she swallowed her guilt as she got back into the car with him.

Jud drove back up Railroad Street and turned left onto Main. He didn't speak, glaring again at his hardware store as they passed it. At the end of Main Street, just past Vale House, the street simply ended at the meadow gate. Jud turned right, here, onto the narrow lane named Gardens Road, and pulled up in front of the third house on the right. The Yellow House had its own driveway but this, along with the front lawn, was overgrown with dog fennel, wax myrtle, and a few gumtree saplings, so Jud parked on the verge of Gardens Road.

"Merv Arkwright is the only owner now, since the Captain passed away," he explained to Cally as they got out of the car and walked through the high weeds to the front porch. "It's getting harder and harder for Merv to get over here to keep the old place up. We boys used to have a lot of fun in this house, when we were all kids!"

He paused and looked up at the yellow clapboards glowing softly in the sun, one hand resting on a white porch column as he absently picked at the flaking paint. Cally was amazed to see his face softened by what she could almost swear was an actual smile. Then Jud's gray eyes rose to the round attic window below the gabled roof, and his smile faded. He fumbled with his big ring of keys and kicked his way through the drifts of leaves covering the porch.

The breath of air that rushed out when Jud pushed the door open smelled, also, of leaves, and Cally wondered if the roof had fallen in and let the outdoors inside. There was no smell of dampness or mold, though. In fact, except for the sheets covering all the furniture, the house looked very much as it must have looked the day the Captain had left it to move in to Vale House. It looked and felt, Cally thought as she stepped into little front parlor, like it was just waiting quietly for someone to move back in. "I've been listing it for the Arkwrights ever since Doug's wife passed away," Jud was saying. "But getting people to look at properties in this little town is..." He went off on his usual rant about how difficult it was to get people to take an interest in such an out-of-the-way small town.

The Captain, when he was alive, had told Cally a story about ghostly bodies he and his siblings and cousins had sometimes seen hanging from the attic rafters. As she walked to the end of the entry hall and looked up the dark stairway, Jud correctly guessed this was what she was thinking about, and he said with a sigh, "You want to see it?"

She grinned sheepishly. "If you don't mind."

He led the way up the stairs, sending dust bunnies scattering into the corners of the creaking wooden treads. The stairs ended at a little hallway with a green paisley rug down the center, surrounded by open doorways, and one narrow wooden door at the end. Jud selected an old-fashioned skeleton key from those on his key ring and fitted it into the lock of this door.

"Did you ever see the hanging ghosts?" Cally asked him.

"No." Jud pushed the door open and stood aside to let her enter. The stairwell was so narrow her shoulders nearly touched the sides as she ascended the ladder-like steps.

The outdoorsy smell of leaves and fresh air grew stronger as her head rose above the top step, and then she saw the big, round window the Captain had described to her. It filled the wall almost from floor to ceiling, and through it she could see the blue sky above the golden meadow. Several of the window's great pie-slice shaped panes were lying whole or in shards on the floor, and an abandoned bird's nest was wedged into the angle of one empty muntin. Cally walked to the end of the gable and stood before the window – it was almost as tall as she was.

"I did see the bonfire," Jud conceded, coming up behind her and looking over her shoulder at the hills of the meadow rolling away endlessly into the east. "It was just a bonfire. Someone was camping, out there on a hill somewhere, or having a keg party or something. That's all it was. Never understood why the other boys always insisted it was a tree on fire. They were probably smoking something. Anyway, there was never a tree growing out there, on fire or not."

Cally nodded to show she understood, but said nothing. She had seen the tree, and the fire. She had been there. She had seen that the tree and the fire were one and the same, and she knew they were still out there, even though she couldn't see them at the moment. Turning, she looked up at the rafters. There were no nooses or bodies hanging from them, and no rope-marks on the rafters she could discern between more crumbling birds' nests.

"So, the story is, you only see those at the full moon." Jud snorted. "Just another crazy story. They didn't hang people in houses, even back when they did hang people around here. They used the courthouse for that. You can go and hunt some ghosts there, if you want – the old courthouse building is our post office now."

"Thank you, I will, maybe, someday." Cally changed the subject. "Did you have a retail property you wanted to show me today, too?”

As Jud pulled the front door shut behind them, Cally could swear she heard the old house sigh. She looked behind her and felt like she wanted to apologize, as if she were walking away from a friend in need.

The storefront Jud was hoping she would be interested in was on the south end of Church Street, between a sewing machine repair shop and the old stone church. As they pulled up and parked in the street, Cally found herself completely uninterested in the rather plain storefront. Instead, her eyes were drawn to the old church building.

“Is that on the market?” she asked, getting out of the car and walking toward the stone church, admiring its arched door and windows. Running her hand along the rusty pipe railing, she climbed the three wide, concrete steps and peered through one of the smeary window panes. She could see only wooden floors inside, made of wide, gray planks with dusty footprints all over them. There were no pews or other furniture.

“You don’t want that!” Jud climbed out of his car and went straight to the storefront next door, picking through the keys in his hand.

“Why not?” Cally ran a hand over the red-painted double door and traced the leaves molded into its dark iron handle. “It’s kind of cute!”

“It’s still...used. Sometimes.” Jud remained steadfastly on the sidewalk in front of the store until Cally relented and returned to join him.

The interior of the empty shop was long and narrow. Yellowed signs taped inside the windows advertised things like CD players and 25-inch color TVs for *the lowest prices anywhere!* Cally had no idea how to shop for a business location, in no small part because she didn’t know what kind of business she would open if she did open one. She walked back and forth in the space, wondering what she should be looking for. Outlets – there were certainly plenty of electrical outlets, she had to give it that.

“This would be a nice place to open a bakery,” Jud suggested, walking to the rear of the store and squinting through the small square of glass in the back door. “Or maybe a nail salon. Excuse me.” He took his phone out of his pocket and looked at it.

“Jud. A nail salon? Seriously?”

He wasn't listening – his attention was on his phone, at which he frowned and shook his head before shoving it back into his pocket. He said, "I really must apologize, Ms. McCarthy. I need to get back to my store." He looked nervously out the front door, then back at her. "Donald isn't answering. I need to find out what they're up to. What he's up to. My son, I mean..."

Cally wanted to say something along the lines of, "Show a little faith, Jud!" but he had already dashed out the door, leaving her to lock the storefront behind her and walk back to Vale House alone.

7 - Fox Tracks

It was turning out to be a very warm October day. That, everyone in Woodley assured Cally, was perfectly normal for this part of the country. At least the air felt less close, in the autumn, much less humid than it had during the summer. Still it felt strange, to Cally, to feel so warm while watching red and gold leaves falling from the trees.

Instead of walking all the way to the end of Main Street and through the main Vale House gate, Cally stopped and let herself into the grounds through the little wooden gate at the rear of the property. From here, pausing in the shade garden just inside the gate she could see, tucked into the shrubbery at the back of the lawn, the little stone cottage where Katarina lived with her husband Ignacio, who also worked at Vale House as the all-around handyman. In the center of the lawn, kept immaculate by Ignacio, stood a white gazebo. The sight of it, now, always reminded Cally of the night Ben had sat down with her and begun to tell her the truth about Woodley, USA. Crape myrtle trees arching overhead gently showered her and everything in the scene with little red leaves, giving the green lawn and the white gazebo the look of a pointillist painting in the sun. Cally breathed deeply, wishing - not for the first time - that she could paint as well as write.

A flash of gold, like a stray sunbeam that had broken off and taken on a life of its own, caught her eye just where the lawn began its slope down to the pond. She followed the streak of movement to see a fox - more yellow than red - pausing with one black foot in the air, looking over its shoulder as if it were laughing at her. At first Cally thought it made the picture all the more idyllic, until she remembered: "The chickens!" She ran onto the lawn, and the fox disappeared over the hill.

Doing a quick check of the perimeter of the yard, she spotted the chickens all scratching peacefully under the edges of the shrubbery. At least, Cally was pretty sure it was all of them. It was hard to count the crazy-quilt of red, white, and black heads milling about, but the hens all sounded calm and content. Still, she would be sure to let Ignacio know she had seen a fox in the yard.

She followed where it had gone, down the hill to the little farm pond nestled amid willows and river birches in the wide field separating Vale House from its distant neighbors along Bells Road. Here was where Ian kept his derelict old fishing boat, which B&B customers had dubbed "the Pirate Ship," half grounded on one bank. Seeing it brought a sad smile to Cally's face. Since Sofie had fallen ill, Ian had ceased almost entirely to spend his afternoons there, fishing from the tilted deck.

The fox stood on the far bank, looking back at Cally with its tongue hanging out, still looking for all the world as if it were laughing. With a toss of its black muzzle, it leaped up the bank in a flash of gold into the sunshine. From there it ran along the fence, down to where the railroad tracks crossed over a stone culvert into the meadow.

"Just you keep going!" she called after it. "These chickens belong to us!" She shielded her eyes with her hand and watched it leap between the rails of the fence into the tall grass on the other side. For the briefest moment, she could swear she could still see it, crossing the tracks and cutting a wake through the grass, but now its golden pelt looked more like the hair of a boy with his head thrown back as he ran. He looked over his shoulder again and flashed a wide grin full of white teeth bared in laughter. Cally blinked, trying to resolve what she was or was not seeing, but the creature vanished into the woods at the meadow's edge.

There had been a time - not long ago - when she would have put considerable effort into convincing herself this had been merely an illusion, a trick of sun and branches and rippling water. She didn't even bother to try, now. She supposed the fox - or whatever it was - must be some sort of relation to the old Earth spirit, Rum, who often passed through the Vale House property and who - so far, at least - had proved to be more helpful than harmful.

She followed the fence back up the hill to the front yard and saw Doctor Tanahey's car parked near the porch. The Captain's ghost sat on the porch, in the sunniest wicker chair, snoring soundlessly with the ghost of an old, gray tomcat dozing near his feet. Cally regarded them both with a smile as she crossed the porch and opened the screen door.

"Hey, Bethany," she called into the Hall. "Why don't you let me watch the phones while you go back to Ian's quarters and see if there's anything Doc needs help with?"

"Nice try!" Bethany gave her an innocent grin, but Cally could see a red flush creeping up the woman's neck.

"Just trying to return a favor," Cally smirked.

"Hah. I'm too old for that sort of thing."

"Better not let Kat catch you saying that!"

The redness had risen to Bethany's cheeks, and she shifted in her chair and cleared her throat. "Anyway, Ian was asking about you. You should go, yourself, and see him."

Cally truly did want to see Ian, but she wanted to see him at the dinner table, the way it used to be, or on the Pirate Ship, or on the porch during summer storms. Seeing him the way he was now broke her heart, but she nodded and took a shortcut through the parlor to the little service porch at the end of the back hallway. From here, she followed the dark-paneled hall that led to the proprietors' quarters.

Ian's study still smelled slightly of smoke and wet plaster from the fire which had, thanks only to a miracle, been prevented from destroying Vale house that summer. But the south wing suite looked cheerful, now, with its new coat of paint and the green leafy wallpaper Bethany had selected for it. Cally entered the study and, through the doorway at its far end, she could see Doc standing at the foot of the four-poster bed in the master bedroom. As usual, the men's voices ceased as soon as Cally stepped into the room, but this time Cally guessed it was just because they had run out of things to say to one another. Doc's gray head was bowed as he put his stethoscope away in his bag.

The bedroom, though the curtains were drawn back to frame a lovely view of the gazebo, was still full of soft shadows, as the sun had not yet come over the roof to this side of the house. Ian, impeccably dressed as always, sat in the upholstered chair next to the bed with one hand resting gently on his wife's elbow. Sofie lay with eyes closed, propped up by many pillows. She appeared to have lost an alarming amount of weight, but her color was good and her face bore a more peaceful expression than Ian's did.

Doc tore two prescriptions from his pad and placed them on the night-stand. "I'll make sure someone takes those to Blackthorn to get them filled," Cally assured him, but he gave her a sad look that seemed to say: *There's hardly any point.*

As the gray-haired doctor turned to leave the room, Cally said, "Oh! Doc, would you do me a favor? On your way out, please stop at the desk and tell Bethany I saw a fox in the back yard just now. Someone should tell Ignacio to keep a close eye on the chickens."

Doc's sagging shoulders lifted a little. Turning around, he winked at Cally. "Are you sure you should be setting this task to an old fox such as myself?"

Cally gave him a firm hug as he left, then turned to pull the carved vanity chair over to Ian's side. "How is she?" she asked as she sat down, even though she already knew the answer.

"The same," Ian said. His voice was creaky, as if he were unaccustomed to speaking. "She doesn't stir. She hardly speaks. But she's comfortable."

"She does look comfortable," Cally agreed. "I wonder..."

"Please don't."

Cally nearly burst into tears. Ordinarily Ian, the perfect Southern Gentleman, would have said something more like, "Dear Ms. McCarthy, I appreciate your concern, and please be assured that I have carefully considered everyone's well-intentioned opinions, but I know Sofie would never agree to being put into a hospital, and I will defend her wishes while she can't." But the old gentleman was exhausted, worn down from his vigil, and the best he could manage, now, was "Please don't."

Cally couldn't help it - she leaned over and put her arms around him. "Ian, it's okay," she said. "I trust you to do what's right." Sitting back, she put a hand over his. "I was only wondering, if I brought a glass with a straw, do you think Sofie might be able to enjoy some of Katarina's iced tea?"

He looked up at her and smiled for what she thought must be the first time in at least a week, and his pale blue eyes almost sparkled the way they once had. "Why, thank you, Ms. McCarthy. That's a wonderful idea. Yes. Yes, I do think she would like that."

Cally stood. "I'll bring some for you, too." Bending over the bed, she took one of Sofie's hands in hers. The old woman's skin felt like tissue-paper and Cally was afraid she could tear it if she wasn't careful. "Sofie, I'm going to bring you some sweet tea. I'll be right back."

The old woman's eyes opened, then, wide and brown and looking straight at Cally, but Sofie only said, "My, doesn't that sunshine feel good!" It was the same thing she had said in response to anything anyone had said to her for many days, now.

"I'm glad you're enjoying it," Cally said sincerely. Who was she to know for sure whether or not the room was actually filled with sunshine?

She stepped back into the study, but behind her she heard Ian say, "Ms. McCarthy, please wait." She turned back to see him reach for the polished wooden cane which had once belonged to the Captain. He used this to struggle to his feet and follow Cally into the study, where he shut the bedroom door partway behind him. "I need to tell you something in strictest confidence."

"Of course, Ian. Anything you say is safe with me."

"I have no doubt it is." He glanced through the doorway to Sofie's dozing face, then took Cally by the elbow and led her a few steps away. "My greatest fear," he said, pausing and taking a few breaths as if he were struggling to get the words out. "My greatest fear, is that I will not outlive her, and she could wake to find herself alone."

"Ian, that's..." Cally put a hand out as if to steady him, but found she was actually steadying herself. "Don't talk like that!" she admonished.

He gave a little chuckle. "No, I won't," he said. "And if you tell Doc I did, I will deny it." The conspiratorial little wink he gave her was comforting, in spite of its context. Cally experienced a tumult of emotions between shock and relief, and wished she had a cane like Ian's to lean on.

"I am at peace with it," Ian was saying. "Except for the fear of abandoning Sofie. I will hang on as long as she needs me," he said, more to the world at large than to her.

Cally took two steps back and looked at him, and his smile did indeed seem peaceful enough, though his body, now that she was looking for it, looked tense and stiff, as if he was in pain.

"Ian, what's wrong? No, I promise I won't tell Doc." She didn't promise she wouldn't implore him to tell Doc himself.

"It doesn't matter," he said. "I have no intention of dying in a hospital, either, even if Sofie does go first. I am content. My life has been very good." He glanced back through the opening in the bedroom door and smiled softly for a long time, while Cally wanted to scream. Then he pulled the door completely shut and said, "But here is what I wanted to tell you."

He limped to the desk and picked up a length of red ribbon with a tiny silver key dangling from the end of it. "This unlocks the top drawer of this desk," he said, handing it to Cally. "When I'm gone, it is my fondest wish that you might take my place as the *Armadeur* of..." He made a gesture, with one finger pointing upward, in a circle encompassing the room and everything beyond it, "of Vale House. Now, I won't pressure you about it. This is the last time I'll ever mention it. In any event, my will is in the top drawer of this desk." He nodded toward it. "And there's a copy on file with my lawyer in town, just, you know, in case." He smiled, a thin-lipped grin, at this. "I have named you executor, because I am confident you will make sure my wishes are honored."

"Ian, I'm flattered." This wasn't a conversation Cally had been prepared to have, not now, not ever, and it was making her dizzy. "Of course you can rely on me."

"It's a heavy responsibility, and I apologize for laying it on you," he said. "If I had any other choice, I would spare you. But Bethany is getting on in years, herself, and Nell is, well, you know."

Cally did know. Helen May, Ian and Sofie's daughter, suffered from a mental illness similar to her mother's. Cally disagreed that the young woman was anywhere near as disabled as others tended to think, but she didn't think this was a good time to debate that point with Ian.

"Besides," Ian continued, "she no longer lives at Vale House."

"Ian, she only lives right down the street, above the coffee shop!" Cally couldn't help arguing that point. Everyone at Vale House had been devastated when Nell had decided to leave the nest, even though she hadn't gone very far at all.

"Nell has a path of her own to follow," Ian said, and Cally was gratified to hear someone say that, at least. "Anyway, I like to entertain the idea you were sent to us for a reason."

He began to sway on his legs, and Cally escorted him back to his seat beside Sofie's bed. As she turned once more to go, she heard Sofie say, "That sunshine feels so good, doesn't it?"

8 - He's Back

Cally arrived in the bright, industrial kitchen to find Katarina preparing batter for the next morning's muffins. Katarina didn't believe in using the large, restaurant-quality mixer gathering dust on the counter; she said food always tasted better when the cook put love into it by hand. She hummed tunelessly as she worked, as if singing along with the birds outside the window. Occasionally she glanced out the window, herself, and Cally knew she was watching Ignacio, who was probably working in the garden beyond the little stone outbuilding that had once been Vale House's kitchen and was now the Munoz's own home.

"What can I get for you?" Katarina called over her shoulder as she continued to stir the huge bowl of batter.

"I can get it myself," Cally assured her, opening the refrigerator. "Ian thinks Sofie might drink some of your famous iced tea."

Kataraina's shoulders sagged at the mention of Sofie, and she stopped stirring, but she said, "Maybe that will help. Tea is full of good stuff."

Cally carried the pitcher to the wide work table in the middle of the room and said, "Jud showed me a cute cottage on Bells Road this morning."

"That's nice," Katarina said. "But I don't see why you have to move out. You are more than welcome to stay here. Ian says so – so does everyone."

"I do like it here," Cally admitted. She sat down on the stool next to the work table. "But it doesn't make sense for me to be taking up a room that could be used by paying guests. And besides, it's hard to get any privacy."

Katarina turned around to grin at Cally, and carried the bowl of batter over to the work table. "That would make more sense," she said, resuming her stirring, "if you had any intention of taking advantage of the privacy we try so hard to give you!"

"Oh, Kat, believe me. I have every intention. It's just..." She didn't like trying to explain. She had sworn she would never let herself be trapped again in a relationship for which she had to make excuses.

Kat seemed to sense her discomfort and didn't press the issue. Instead she walked to the tall, glass-fronted cabinet at the end of the room and took two tea glasses from it. Setting these down beside Cally, she said, "You know: people know. They may not act like it, but they do know."

"Know what?" Cally kicked her heels against the rungs of the stool, privately wishing there were something going on for them to know about.

"I mean, they know about Ben." Katarina spoke in a low, conspiratorial voice as she gathered a bowl of ice and a pair of ice tongs. "Where he goes at night. Well, that he goes, anyway. *Where* he goes is still open to conjecture, of course. Or, it would be if anyone would conjecture about it. It's been happening since long before you came along. People in this town, they aren't completely dim. They see how he never ages. They know things are different around here. They don't know exactly what, or how. They just kind of take it in stride. They see it, right in front of their faces all the time. They just don't talk about it."

"Sounds like you're describing me," Cally said, "before I finally admitted my marriage was a sham."

Katarina laughed. "I don't think it's a sham, around here, though. Just a little different, is all." She leaned both elbows on the work table. "To be honest with you, I actually kind of like it. I wish people would talk about it more openly, but I guess they just want to stay sane."

"So." Cally took the tongs from Katarina's hand and began dropping ice into the glasses. "If people did talk about it, what might they say?"

Katarina stood up straight and crossed herself. "I like to think

I'm a pretty good Christian," she said. "I'm not perfect, but I try. And I know we're not supposed to talk about other gods. But that doesn't mean they don't exist, along with those who serve them."

"Gods? Seriously? Kat, I think it's just faeries, or old earth spirits or something like that."

Katarina crossed herself again, more vigorously this time, and looked around nervously. "It's probably better to just call them Neighbors," she said, looking out through the back door as if she expected to see these Neighbors peering in at her disapprovingly. "They just have their own gods and kings and such, that's all."

"This is definitely an interesting Neighborhood," Cally admitted, but she didn't mean 'interesting' the same way most people meant it.

"Well, Ben, he's a good man, everyone agrees. If he goes visiting every night, we are all sure it's for a good reason. Nobody ever questions that."

"He has a job to do there," Cally confided.

"He's told you about it?"

"Sort of. He tries. It's hard to explain." Even as she said it, Cally thought this sounded an awful lot like the kinds of excuses she used to make for her cheating ex-husband. She wondered if she was letting herself fall back into the same sort of situation. A lot of people said it was nearly impossible to escape that cycle.

"Well, whatever it is, I hope they pay him well," Katarina said, nodding firmly. "You wonder when the poor guy ever gets a chance to sleep!" She looked away through the window over the sink, in the direction of downtown Woodley. "Maybe he can convince his sister to give him a day off once in a while so he can get some, you know, *sleep* during the day sometime?" She winked over her shoulder. "You should tell him about that old boyfriend of yours who's been hanging around here. That will motivate him!"

Cally made a face. "Ugh! Mr. Tiene isn't my old boyfriend! Anyway, you know how hard Bree is to deal with."

"Well, you just tell him," said Katarina. "He needs to step up! He'd better take the chance to get some good, quality sleep on this side of the fence pretty soon, before the opportunity slips away. Life is short!"

"Kat, I'm not that old. Wasn't it you who told me that?"

"Oh, all true!" she said. "But a gentleman doesn't keep a lady waiting. I'm just saying."

"And how many years did you wait all spring, summer, and fall, year after year, for Ignacio to come home from his work in another country?"

Katarina stopped working and smiled dreamily, wrapping her arms around herself and getting batter on her dress. "Sometimes, it's worth it," she admitted.

Cally started to say: "Sometimes, I wonder what would happen if I asked Ben to take me with..." but Katarina looked out the window and made a zipping motion over her lips. Katarina's husband, a tall man with a wide, gentle smile and a black ponytail much longer than Katarina's, was coming across the lawn, heading toward the kitchen door with a basket in his hands. Returning to the muffin batter, Katarina murmured so that only Cally could hear, "Anyway, for what it's worth, I think you've become much better at picking them than you were when you were younger!"

"I didn't exactly pick him," was all Cally had time to say before Ignacio opened the door and stepped into the kitchen. Setting the basket full of fresh white and brown eggs on the counter next to the sink, he swept his wife into his arms and kissed her as if they were still newlyweds. If anyone knew a good man when she saw one, Cally thought, Katarina Munoz did.

Ignacio's face, when he drew back and looked at Katarina, was serious, though. Katarina held his onto arms and demanded to know what was worrying him.

"He's back." Ignacio's voice nearly choked as he answered. "He's out on bail."

Even the birds outside the window stopped singing, and a stunned silence filled the kitchen, until Cally jumped to her feet, instinctively looking around the room for something she could press into service as a weapon. "Who?" she snapped, though they knew all too well to whom Ignacio referred. Then "How?" she corrected herself. "How could Foster Brentwood be out on bail? He tried to kill at least six people!"

"Allegedly," said Ignacio, exchanging grim looks with her and Katarina.

"Allegedly my ass," Cally said. "Pardon my French," she added to Katarina, who didn't like that sort of language. "I know! I was there! I was one of those people!"

"I'm sure he'll still be convicted," Ignacio reassured them both. "When his court date does finally come. Then he'll go back to prison where he belongs, and we won't ever have to deal with him again."

"I don't want to deal with him *now*!" said Katarina.

"Surely there's at least a restraining order to keep him out of Woodley?" Cally said.

"He's not allowed within a hundred yards of Vale House, or of Nell, regardless of where she is." Nell was one of the people Foster had attempted to kill, the night he set Vale House on fire. She had also, at the time, been his wife.

"That's 'way too close, as far as I'm concerned!" said Katarina, and they all nodded.

"How did you find out?" Cally asked Ignacio.

"Nell was just telling me. I was helping her and Andi move a pottery wheel up to her apartment above the coffee shop, and she mentioned she saw Foster going into Jud's hardware store early this morning. She says he's staying there, sleeping in Jud's store room. Apparently, she's known for days that he was out on bail. She was sent a letter by the judge, for her own safety, informing her of his release. She never told anyone because she didn't want us to worry about her."

"Didn't want us to worry! The hardware store is just across the street from the coffee shop! It's got to be less than a hundred yards!" Katarina raised her arms and looked heavenward. "*O Dios mio*! I keep saying that girl should not be living on her own like this. There's plenty of room here at the house!"

"That girl," Cally reminded her, "is thirty-five years old."

"But..."

"I know what you mean, Kat," Cally said. "I want to protect her, too. But I also want to respect her autonomy. I'm not sure what to do."

"Well..." said Ignacio, "I'm not sure, either, but I do have a sudden craving for artisanal coffee with locally-sourced organic cream." He grinned and nodded, giving Katarina a swift kiss before heading back toward the door.

Cally's shoulders unclenched, then. "Ignacio, call me," she said, "when you need a break, and I'll come relieve you. I have a feeling we're all going to be drinking a lot of artisanal coffee in the next few days."

9 - The Waiting

Cally delivered the tea, on a tray with a sandwich for Ian, to Sofie's bedside, and decided it was not a good time to tell Ian about his former son-in-law's release from prison. She watched as Ian gently pressed the drinking straw to Sofie's lips. Though Sofie licked her lips and smiled, she didn't drink very much. "I'll try again later," Ian promised Cally as she turned to go back to her office to wait for Ignacio to call.

She paused in the Hall to give Bethany the news, but Bethany was already on the phone, doing her part as a crucial branch of the Woodley grapevine, telling everyone the news and getting their opinions on the matter. She saluted Cally with one hand, nodding grimly, as Cally passed the desk and entered her office.

The old gray cat, Doctor Boojums, lay curled close to Cally's computer, but she doubted he was really asleep. The cat was, as she recalled, the second denizen of Vale House she had realized was actually a ghost. Nell had told her there were "at least six" spirits living in Vale House, but aside from the Preacher, Cally could only think of one other: Nell's friend Melissa who, supposedly, lived in the television set in the parlor, but she had not met that one yet.

Speaking of ghosts...

"Georgie, are you here?" she asked aloud. "Did you hear about this business with Foster being out of jail?"

There was no reply, which didn't surprise Cally. George had never liked this room and, to her dismay, she tended to agree with him.

It was a pleasant enough room. The golden light of early afternoon poured in through fluttering lace curtains and, through the window, blackbirds getting ready to migrate were making a cheerful racket along the meadow fence. This room had once been a parlor – the smaller of two parlors in the rambling antebellum house – and it was still filled with comfortable old sofas and armchairs. Cally's pillow and blanket were currently stacked on the arm of the sofa she'd been sleeping on since the Dogwood Room, which connected to this room via a spiral stair, had been rented out to paying guests. Since Cally had come to live at Vale House, Bethany had had the entire suite redecorated in a tasteful dogwood theme, all creams and whites and light greens.

Somehow, though, the office always felt dark to her. She attributed this to her memories of its previous occupant. She sometimes wondered if this was how ghosts got their start, even though Joan was still very much alive and, thankfully, living somewhere else now.

At least now she understood what Emerald's message, earlier that morning, had meant. She sat down at her desk and reached carefully past the sleeping ghost cat to open the antique (as computer programs go) instant messaging application.

Emerald: Cally, is everything alright?

Cally: Foster is out on bail. But I guess you already knew that?

Cally sent the reply, though she wasn't sure whether or not Emerald was even online at this time of day. Apparently, however, she was hovering over...whatever she hovered over, waiting to hear from Cally, because she responded almost immediately.

Emerald: Are you OK? Is everyone OK?

Cally: Everyone is fine. Though of course we're all pretty upset.

Emerald: Understandable! Please be careful!

Cally: You don't need to tell me that! I'm more worried about Nell. How did you find out?

Emerald: Melissa told me.

Cally: Melissa – the ghost in the old TV set, right?

Emerald: Yes. I don't think you've met her yet.

Cally: Not yet. Apparently only Nell can make her appear. How do you know her?

Emerald: She hangs around here a lot.

Cally: "Here" being…?

There was a long pause. Cally had been internet-friended to Emerald for years, long before she had come to Vale House, but they had never met in person. Cally had her suspicions that Emerald was also a ghost, but she had never quite been able to get Emerald to admit this. This was probably because Emerald didn't want to know it, herself, and Cally had learned not to pester her about it. Whatever she was or was not, one thing Cally could be certain of was that Emerald was her friend.

Cally: Sorry.

Emerald: It's OK, I understand. How are things going with Ben?

Cally: Speaking of artfully changing the subject…

Emerald: :)

Cally: Look, Em, the thing is, I'm having trouble with this computer. I might have to get a new one. Would we still be able to chat if I can't get this old chat app to run on a new platform?

Emerald: Have you tried turning it off and back on again?

Cally: Haha. But yes. Multiple times.

Emerald: I guess I could always text you on your phone, but ugh.

Cally: I hate that tiny text window thing too. But I don't want to lose touch with you. Or "u" as they say in textspeak. I'd be willing, is all I'm saying.

Emerald: Hint taken.

Cally: No! I meant, well, that's all I meant. Really.

Emerald: Hint still taken. I will keep trying to find a way for us to meet in "real life."

Cally: I look forward to that.

Emerald: And meanwhile, you take care. And look out for our Nell.

Cally: We all will.

Emerald: And you'd better back your files up to the Cloud while you still can.

Cally: Right. Oh! The Cloud! Is that where you live?

Emerald: Aha, you guessed it. Cloud Cuckoo Land, yep!

Cally ended the chat by sending a string of "wink" and "laugh" emoticons, then checked one more time to see if her word processor had managed to finish updating yet. It was still frozen halfway through the update, no further than it had been last night, and because of this she couldn't get any of her files to open. With a heavy sigh, she followed Emerald's advice and began uploading her work in progress to her online storage account. That wouldn't take long, even with the slow WiFi at Vale House; she had been unable to get much written, lately, anyway. She had a sinking feeling this trend would continue for the foreseeable future.

While she waited for the upload to complete, she watched the gray cat snoozing on the desk, resisting her natural instinct to reach out and pet him. His eyes were closed, his paws tucked under his chest which rose and fell as he snored soundlessly, but Cally was certain, somehow, that he was watching her. *Do ghosts even sleep, anyway?* she wondered.

The phone on her desk rang, and the cat did not budge, which convinced her beyond doubt that Doctor Boojums was faking it. She shook her head and reached to answer the phone, hoping it was Ignacio calling to tell her to come take over his watch at the coffee shop.

"This is Callaghan McCarthy," she informed the caller, in case it wasn't Ignacio.

"Hey!"

The shadows hanging over her heart parted like clouds when she recognized the voice of her youngest child. "Brandon! How are you?"

She didn't get calls from him very often. Since he'd graduated from college, he had drifted from job to job, none of them having much to do with his fresh, new engineering degree.

"I'm fine," he said simply.

"It's so good to hear your voice!" She filled him in on news about the publication of her new novel. Finally, she asked, "So what's new with you?" hoping he wouldn't take that as nagging about his job status.

After an awkward silence, he said, "Well, um, I was just thinking about paying you a little visit there in Small Town USA." Before Cally could exclaim in delight, he went on. "I've met someone. Her name is Rosheen and she plays cello in a little ensemble I'm in. I was wondering if you'd like to meet her?"

Cally could hear the murmur of another voice on the end of the line, and had a clear vision of a young woman standing behind Brandon, not letting him back out of asking this question.

"Of course I would love to meet her! Oh, but sweetie, we have no vacancies here right now. You might have to stay at the Motel Nine in Blackthorn. It's a short drive from here and..." She knew this was probably not something Brandon could afford, and if Rosheen was also a starving young musician fresh out of college, she probably couldn't afford it, either. "Hang on. Let me think for a second."

While she made mental calculations, wondering if it was a good idea to offer to take money out of her savings to pay for their motel (and probably food and gas for the couple, as well, and for how many days?) she heard muffled conversation on the other end of the connection. At length, Brandon's voice returned and he said, "Don't worry about it, Mom. Rosheen says she thinks she has an idea. Love you! See you soon!"

The line went dead before Cally could say "But when?" She sighed and said, "Bye, Son. Love you, too," into the silent handset and hung it up.

Sometime during her conversation, the ghost cat had decided to vanish. Cally looked down at her computer and saw that her upload was complete. Resignedly, she powered down the laptop and then leaned back in her chair, spinning it from side to side and wishing

Ignacio would call so she could just go on down to the coffee shop to pretend she wasn't being overprotective of a woman who was fully capable of taking care of herself.

Then an idea occurred to her. The pizza parlor, Motherboard Pizza, was just around the corner from the coffee shop, and it was run by a young man who also happened to be adept at repairing computers. She could take her computer there, and just wait in the coffee shop while Luke looked it over. She agreed with Katarina that the hardware store was too close to Nell's apartment above the coffee shop; if she could determine that Foster was in violation of his restraining order, she could get the sheriff to haul him right back to prison. And, who knew: maybe Luke could even actually fix her word processor?

Making up her mind, she closed the computer and stood, tucking it under her arm. Just as she reached for the door knob, however, George appeared in front of her and she had to swerve to avoid walking through him.

"Take me with you!" he said.

"What?" Cally took two steps back. George was standing, literally, just inside the door. Part of him was still outside it, in the Hall. He was looking around him nervously, reluctant to enter any further.

"I'm on my way downtown," she told him. "You can't go that far. Anyway, I'm in a hurry."

"Just take my zemi with you. I can go where it goes. Cally, you promised you'd try, one day."

"Really, Georgie, this isn't a good time..."

"Bethany is talking about Nellie's ex-husband being out of jail!"

Cally sighed. Even the ghosts at Vale House were concerned about Nell. "Fine. Fine. Give me a minute."

Satisfied with this, George vanished. Cally wished she could simply take the spiral stairs up to the Dogwood room and slip into the upstairs hallway to retrieve George's little wooden idol from the butler's desk, but she couldn't remember whether the guest in that room had checked out this morning or not. She sighed and went out through the Hall instead.

Bethany was still on the phone, talking in strident tones, and she took no notice of Cally as she went up the grand staircase. "I know! Can you believe it?" she was saying to the person on the other end of the line. "No, he's not, and anyway where did he get that kind of money? His bail was set very high, because of the seriousness of his crimes. Alleged crimes. Whatever – you know there's nothing alleged about..."

Cally reached gallery at the top of the stairs and turned toward the right end of the upstairs hallway. Closed doors lined this hall on both sides, each identified by a different botanical print in an oval frame. She paused beside a door with a vintage rose on it and sighed wistfully. This had been her room, when she had first come to Vale House. So much had happened since then and, Cally had to admit, she missed the cozy Rose Room in spite of all Bethany's fussy rose-themed decorations.

George was already waiting for her at the end of the hall where a small, green lamp on an antique butler's desk illuminated the blotter, as well as Doctor Boojums, who had arrived before either of them and settled back down to pretending to sleep. George pointed past him impatiently, unable himself to open the tiny door in the desk that held his zemi.

Cally looked around quickly before opening the little door and retrieving a small, triangular carving from its nest of rubber bands and bent paperclips. This she slipped into her purse as she shut the door, straightening quickly and hoping she didn't look as guilty as she felt. George gave a little leap of joy, clapping soundlessly before vanishing.

"No, I don't think he'd do that," Bethany was saying when Cally passed her again at the desk. "Jud's a funny duck, but he's an honest man. His son, though, well he's..." Cally paused and waited for Bethany to notice her.

"I'll just be heading down to Luke's computer repair," she said when Bethany looked up.

Bethany covered the mouthpiece of the phone. "If you see Foster," she said, "clock him one for me!"

10 - Coffee and Sliced Bread

She took the mulched path through the shade garden which ran along the south side of Vale House, her footsteps loud in all the crunchy gold and orange leaves underfoot. George bounded around her like an excited puppy being taken for a walk, but his footsteps were soundless. Cally found herself wishing George could still experience the joy of kicking through autumn leaves. Then she wondered if he had ever experienced this anyway, having grown up and spent his short life in the tropics. She didn't think it was a good idea to try talking with him about it just then, though, as they were in sight of all the front doors along Main Street.

They passed through the little white gate at the rear of the property, he literally, and she by opening the gate. Turning westward onto the sidewalk along Main Street, Cally wished George would just vanish as he followed her but, she had to admit, she didn't feel quite as much like she was being watched through all the front doors, this time. Everyone's attention was focused elsewhere today.

Ahead of her, where the tunnel of oaks opened onto the business district, she could see Merv sitting in his lawn chair on his loading dock. The chair was turned to face toward the hardware store, and he was not reading his newspaper. The brim of his baseball cap was pulled down low, and it occurred to Cally he must have been a formidable figure in his youth. He didn't appear to be trying to make any secret of the fact that his gaze was fixed firmly on Jud's store.

"Has he come out yet?" Cally asked rhetorically as she came abreast of the loading dock and into Merv's peripheral vision.

"What could they be doing in there?" Merv replied, equally rhetorically.

"I'll just be over at the coffee shop." Cally waved and stepped off the curb to cross Main Street.

She paused to peer through the window of the News Store to see if she could get a glimpse of Ben. He was standing on a ladder, placing packages of paper towels on a high shelf. All she could see were his legs and backside, which were worth looking at, but she didn't stand there long. She could feel more than see Bree's sharp gaze on her from inside the store.

Turning the corner, she continued to the bright red and yellow storefront – just across Railroad Street from the Law Offices of Johnston and Reid, Attorneys at Law – of Motherboard Pizza. Signs in the windows advertised this week's specials: butternut squash pizza and pumpkin-spice breadsticks, as well as low, low rates for computer repair and malware removal. Unfortunately, there was also a sign taped to the door that said *"Back in 5 Minutes!"*

"Damn," said Cally. But she was pretty sure she knew where Luke had gone, and it was where she really wanted to go anyway. "Okay, George, are you ready to meet the rest of Woodley?" She couldn't see him, at the moment, but she knew he couldn't be far away.

The Bean Garden was busier than Cally had ever seen it before. Several cars were parked in the street nearby, and she could hear the hubbub of voices even before she smelled the aroma of coffee wafting out the open door. Andi Kilmarten, a cheerful, dark-skinned woman about Cally's age, was running back and forth behind the counter, monitoring brightly colored beverages in blenders and steaming espresso spouts, but she took a moment to smile and wave to Cally as she entered. "The usual?" she called, reaching toward the bank of gleaming white coffee mugs. George appeared behind the counter, peering curiously at all the machinery. Cally nodded to Andi, then looked around for Ignacio.

He had positioned himself at the table nearest the front window, facing diagonally across the street toward the hardware store. His feet were up on the chair across from him and an empty mug sat at his elbow. Cally followed his stare out the window to the hardware store. She had never been good at estimating distances, but she definitely thought the front door of the storefront diagonally across the street looked less than a hundred yards away. However, the door to the store room at the rear of the building, where Foster was reputed to be crashing, was around the far corner of the building. Ignacio's eyes were fixed on that corner.

The inside of the coffee shop sounded much merrier than Cally felt. The three local "homeschooled" teens, Errin, Mima, and Zenbe, were hanging around one of the counter-height tables near the rear of the shop with a tall, young black man Cally had never seen before. A beat-up old acoustic guitar lay on the table between them. Luke was there also, wearing his pizza delivery hat, closely watching something the newcomer was demonstrating on his smartphone. Two out-of-town couples, whom Cally recognized from that morning as Vale House guests from Kentucky, stood at the rear of the store looking at the artwork displayed on the walls. Nell was with them, chatting charmingly about the art as her little calico cat wound around everyone's ankles. Some of the art for sale in the Bean Garden was Nell's own work, but she was gushing just as enthusiastically about paintings by other artists displayed there. She looked poised and confident, and Cally smiled to see her so happy.

Finally, Cally bent to speak into Ignacio's ear. "Can I get you another coffee?" she offered.

He jumped, then looked up at her and grinned sheepishly. "Maybe not," he said. "I've had three already. And the coffee Andi serves here is, well, it's real!"

Andi appeared at Cally's side with a deep mug of plain black coffee. "Coffee flavored coffee for my favorite author!" she said, handing it to Cally.

"I don't know how you do it," Cally told her.

"It's easy when someone orders the same thing every time." Andi laughed, giving her a quick side-hug before dashing back to the gleaming banks of beverage machines.

Cally sat down at Ignacio's table and put her laptop down in front of her. With half an eye, she watched George moving around the shop, smiling at Nell's art, which was familiar to him, and at all the other art he had never seen before. He bent to pet Cyndi Lauper, the skinny calico cat, and the cat arched her back delightedly at this attention. Little Cyndi had used to live at Vale House, before Nell moved out, and the only thing that had ever frightened her there had been some of the living humans.

Then Cally watched, with some chagrin, as George walked through the front door and halfway across the street toward the hardware store before he stopped suddenly, having reached his apparent maximum distance from his zemi. She forced herself to look away and stop acting like a hovering mother.

"Ignacio, you can go ahead home now if you want," she said. "I'll be here for a while – I've got it covered."

He shook his head. "Now I have to stay here and keep an eye on you. Have to make sure you don't do anything illegal if Foster comes out of that store!"

Cally laughed. "I promise to behave. Go on. Kat could use your help. She has to change every single bed in the place today – we've got a full house again tonight."

That convinced him. He got up stiffly and carried his empty mug to the counter, and Cally moved over to take his seat with its view of the hardware store's far corner. From there, she could also see Merv sitting in his lawn chair. Sheriff Dunn would be proud, Cally thought, of the way Woodley had visual surveillance of Main Street covered.

Cally watched George stop in the middle of the street to pet the ghost dog that frequented that spot. The dog looked like it might have been a collie, once, but the predominantly gray color of its shaggy ghost-coat made it look more like a wolf, now. It seemed very happy to meet George, and neither of them were fazed when a car came down the street and drove through both of them. Cally imagined that must have been what had happened to the dog in the first place.

While she waited for Luke to stop talking to the young man with the smartphone, Cally decided she could at least check her email, which was an old-fashioned application and therefore still worked. Keeping one eye on the street over the top of the screen, she connected to the coffee shop's WiFi. Her email inbox promptly filled up with offers for bargain-priced pharmaceuticals and celebrity videos promising to shock her. These she deleted, keeping only one message from her agent (which she filed under "Later") and another from Danya Barry of the Greater Asheboro Area Scientific Paranormal Society, titled "Looking forward to Vale House investigation tonight!"

She swore under her breath as she clicked to open the message.

G.A.A.S.P.S., an amateur paranormal study group, had conducted an investigation of Vale House over the past summer, and George had deliberately photo-bombed one of Danya's recording sessions. Danya had been pestering Cally ever since, asking for a chance to come back to investigate further. Cally had finally agreed to this on the condition that Danya come alone, but now she wished she had known tonight would turn out to be such an incredibly inconvenient time.

She sighed and hit "reply."

"Danya: Please remember, as we discussed previously, that October is our busiest month and we currently have no vacancies at Vale House. I hope you've remembered to book a room at the motel in Blackthorn just down the road.

"Here's great idea: I am currently researching a local legend about a haunted railroad crossing, here in Woodley, for my next novel. The locals say you can hear screaming there at night. We can check it out together."

Well, she thought as she clicked "send" and closed her computer, she had always meant to research the railroad crossing anyway. Maybe that would keep Danya busy and she would forget about wanting to expose George to the media.

"Or the media to George," she muttered, watching him walk past the coffee shop and go as close as he could get to the Wyrd Systers book store two doors down. She wondered what he would have to say about the New Age paraphernalia they sold there, and she wondered if the flighty proprietors, for all their professed expertise on metaphysical subjects, would even see him at all. If they did, they would probably try to give him a free tarot reading, she thought, and laughed.

There was still no sign of Foster, and she wasn't sure whether to be glad or disappointed.

"This is for you!" Cally looked up to see Nell sitting down at the table next to her. The younger woman's long, auburn hair obscured half her face, as usual, but Cally could see that her dark eyes were sparkling with happiness. Though Cally was gratified to see this, she felt Nell should be looking a lot more worried than she seemed at the moment.

Nell had placed a small ornament on the table and was pushing it across to Cally. "Keep this on you," she said. Cally picked it up and held it up to the light in the window. It was a small square of fired clay, just over an inch from corner to corner, painted with a sprinkling of moons and stars. Narrow blue and purple ribbons had been strung through a hole in one corner and Cally tried to hold the ornament up by these, at first. Then she realized the ribbons were meant to hang downward, because they were strung with beads and tiny silver bells that chimed softly when she finally held it the right way up.

"Did you make this?" Cally asked. "It's lovely." She meant it.

"Yes. Keep it in your pocket, in case you need it."

Cally didn't ask why she might need such a thing, but she carefully folded the ribbons behind it and tucked it into her jeans pocket. "I see you had some potential customers," she said to Nell as the two couples from Kentucky waved and left the shop.

"Oh, they were just being nice," Nell said. "Unicorns and flowers aren't really their thing."

"I'm sure they agree with everyone that your work is wonderful," Cally said. "How are you doing?" She gave Nell a serious look to let her know she didn't mean this in a perfunctory way, and wanted a serious answer.

Nell gave her a serious answer, though not the one Cally was looking for. She explained, instead, in great detail how the adjustments made in her medication since Foster had gone to jail had helped her become more clear-minded and let her focus better, but how they had also dampened her creativity somewhat. "I am in the process of eliminating one compound at a time so I can learn how to determine what is real and what isn't, based on which voices I hear or do not hear under what circumstances."

Cally thought that sounded very ambitious but said, "Nell, you should never make any changes in your medication unless your doctor tells you to."

"Don't worry – all this is being done under Doc's strict supervision. I am keeping a detailed log. For instance, I have now ascertained that Georgie is real and has been all along." She nodded toward the back of the shop, where George was standing behind the group of teenagers and looking very closely at the guitar, which the newcomer had picked up and begun to play, demonstrating some complex rhythms.

"Well, I could have told you that," Cally said with a quiet little laugh.

"And you did." Nell nodded, her expression serious. "But for all I knew, I only imagined that, too."

Cally kept her face under control so she would not appear to be pitying Nell. She knew very little about schizoaffective disorder, and she couldn't even imagine what it must be like to live never knowing for sure if anything she saw or heard was real. She searched for a way to express her admiration of how Nell managed all this while keeping such a cheerful outlook, but she was afraid she might sound patronizing. She broached a different subject.

"Doc has also prescribed something new for your mom. We haven't found out yet whether it's going to help or not. You should come and see her." She did not add: *While you still can.*

"Oh, Mama's fine!" Nell smiled reassuringly and patted Cally's hand. "She's just on a journey."

Cally didn't press the issue. Forcing Nell to worry about Sofie wouldn't help either of them, in any case.

"I'll come and see her when she gets back," Nell promised, then turned to greet Andi, who was coming toward them.

"Phew!" Andi dropped herself heavily into the chair across from Cally. "I've never had such a busy morning." The clamor in the shop had died down, as everyone but the teenagers had left, but Andi was still in busy mode, wiping the table with a bar towel as she spoke.

"Well," Cally said, "you're always saying you want to help save Woodley by bringing in more business. Be careful what you wish for!"

"Hah! No, it's alright. Just that I've been busy at home, too. My son is home on school break, and he brought all his laundry with him." She flicked the towel over her shoulder toward the table full of teenagers. "Kurtis, come and say hello!" she called.

The young man put his guitar down on the table and stood up – and up and up. Cally had to tilt her head back to look into his wide, thoughtful eyes, and it took all the tact she possessed not to ask him how the weather was up there.

"I know, right?" said Andi. "Callaghan McCarthy, this is my son Kurtis 'Sliced Bread' Kilmarten. He's going to be famous someday. Kurtis, this is Callaghan McCarthy and she's already famous. She's an author.”

“I’m not famous. Please call me Cally.”

“Pleased to meet you, ma’am.” Kurtis hurried to offer Cally his hand before his mother could remind him to. Cally was surprised at how gentle his grip was. The calluses on his fingertips were thick, however, letting Cally know he really was a serious guitarist. “So, your music is the best thing since sliced bread?” she guessed.

Kurtis looked at his mother. “See? She gets it!”

Andi waved a hand dismissively. “I think Kurtis Kilmarten is a perfectly good stage name, without the sliced bread part.”

“It does have a certain rock vibe to it,” Cally had to agree, and added, “Do you ever play with Merv and the guys on the loading dock in the evenings?”

“Mr. Arkwright taught me the first riffs I ever learned,” he said. “In fact, he gave me my first guitar.” He gazed fondly at the old acoustic on the table. “But he doesn’t get the whole grunge thing.”

The thought of Merv and the other town elders playing grunge music made Cally grin.

“Kurtis wants to put together a band,” Andi said, “and use one of these empty storefronts as a kind of music venue. I think Jud put the idea into his head.”

“Jud would,” Cally agreed. “But who would you recruit for a band, in this town?”

Kurtis tilted his head toward the table at which he’d been sitting. “Luke plays keyboards, and Zenbe is an awesome guitarist, better than me, in my opinion. He already has a regular gig with a retro band at the Fountain in Blackthorn, but he says he’ll jam with us sometimes.”

Cally smiled inwardly at her memory of the band at The Fountain, and didn’t say what she was thinking about how kids today used the word “retro” to refer to music that had been cutting-edge when she was growing up. She did say, “All you need now is a good drummer and a bass player.” Then she shut her mouth quickly, hoping George had not heard her.

Andi huffed. “You don’t need anyone with much talent to play that grunge stuff.”

Cally and Kurtis both looked at her and said “Yes you do!” Then they laughed simultaneously as well. Cally explained, mostly for Andi’s benefit, “My own kids have dragged me kicking and screaming into the world of modern music. I mean, it will always be old school rock for me, but I have to admit, that grunge stuff does take a lot of work. Mr. Bread, I wish you all the luck in the world."

"Call me Slice." He reached to shake her hand again. The young people at the other table had got up and were walking toward him.

"We're going down to Blackthorn for a while," said a girl with masses of red curls. "The long way around," she added, nodding and giving Cally a pointed look. "Cally you still owe me a driving lesson, remember!"

Cally closed her eyes and tried not to think about it. "Maybe when I'm a little less busy, Errin." The young people all filed out the door, and then the coffee shop was finally truly quiet inside.

"Well," said Cally.

"Well," Andi concurred, turning her head to look out the window toward the hardware store. There had been no sign of anyone going in or out the whole time they'd been sitting there.

"He's probably sleeping so he can be up prowling around town at night," Andi supposed.

"I hope his court date is set soon, so we can put this whole mess behind us," Cally said.

"You're all too hard on him," said Nell. Cally and Andi turned to look open-mouthed at her. She continued in a level voice, "No, I don't miss him any more than anyone else does. But he had such big dreams, and now he's lost everything."

"Threw everything away, more like!" Andi said.

"Nell, I would say you are too kind," Cally said, "but maybe your kindness is part of your strength."

Nell smiled and looked down at the table. Then she looked back up again and brushed her hair out of her eyes. "Anyway, don't worry. He won't be around long."

"You can't know that," Andi warned, but Cally said nothing, remembering that Nell often knew things nobody else could know. She just hoped Nell was right about this one.

Suddenly, Cally said, "Oh, damn it!"

"What!" Andi jumped up from her seat and looked out the window, but nothing was still going on at the hardware store.

"No, I'm sorry," said Cally. "It's just that I completely forgot to ask Luke, while he was here, to look at my computer."

11 - Old Stories and Agreements

Sheriff Dunn arrived at the Bean Garden later that afternoon and took over Cally's post at the table in the front window. She just had time to run over to Motherboard Pizza and hand over her computer while wolfing down the prosciutto and mozzarella focaccia Luke had already prepared for her. The sun was setting – it was time for Ben to leave Woodley, again, and return to his mother's court beyond the meadow.

She arrived out of breath where he was waiting for her at the gate at the end of Main Street. He took her breath away some more with a kiss, but she could tell by his expression that Bree had already filled him in about what was going on with Foster.

"Now I have even more reason to hate leaving," he said.

"I'll be fine," she assured him. "We all will. We've got it covered."

"No, I know you do," he said. "You did fine without me before, after all." He turned to lean on the metal gate, facing out into the meadow.

Cally didn't know quite what to say to that. She stood next to him with her hands on the gate.

"I mean, you handled Foster's villainy before just fine without anyone's help. But I still hate always being on the other side of the fence while you're going through these things."

They stood shoulder to shoulder while the sun set at the other end of Main Street behind them. Cally wanted to fill the silence with kisses and heart-thumping embraces while they still had their few minutes left, but Ben seemed distracted.

"I'm going to tell them to invite you to the Thing," he said at last. "As the Armadeur of Vale House, you are entitled to a seat at the table."

This alarmed her far more than the idea of Foster Brentwood lurking in the hardware store a few blocks away.

"But I'm not the Armadeur yet!" She turned her head to look toward Vale House, hoping this would remain true for a long time, but fully aware that hope was fading. "I don't even know what an Armadeur does! Has Ian ever attended a Thing?"

"I think the only May that ever did was Lionel, back during the Civil War. He wasn't actually the Armadeur yet, but I am told he kind of insisted. He's why Vale House is still standing."

Cally closed her eyes and took a deep breath, pushing with both hands against the top rail of the gate, as if trying to stop the world from changing before she could even get used to it as it was, which was already hard enough. "I'm afraid the opposite would happen if I went," she said. "I have too much to learn, just to bring myself up to speed, and diplomacy has never been my strong suit. I would be sure to put my foot in it." *Also, I am terrified of meeting your mother,* she did not add.

"I could help bring you up to speed," he offered. "But I don't want to sound like I'm mansplaining."

She couldn't help but laugh at that. "It's not mansplaining if you tell me things I don't already know."

He looked at her carefully. At least, his expression was careful at first but, as always, his face soon melted into that soft look – the one with the crinkles around his eyes – that it always took on whenever he looked at her. She watched him watch her face, as if he would be content to never do anything else ever again, for a long while. When he still didn't speak, she cleared her throat. He let out a little laugh and shook his head.

"Maybe you could start by telling me what you do know," he suggested.

"I know just enough to get myself into trouble." She pulled her hands off the gate and flexed them to work out the stiffness, then leaned forward and rested her elbows on the top rail. Gazing out toward the darkening horizon, she went on. "I mean, I know a lot of the old legends and tales. I was once a Celtic mythology nerd. It's how I met Emerald, in an online discussion about the Mabinogion and such. I don't know how much of it is based on fact, though. Until recently, I was blissfully unaware that any of it was."

"A lot more of it is based on fact than most people realize," he replied. He moved to stand behind her, resting his own hands on the gate on either side of hers as he followed her gaze out across the meadow to the horizon. "But most of the stories have become terribly conflated over time," he went on. "Well, 'fact' is a pretty relative concept, anyway."

"Hm." Cally nodded. She certainly couldn't argue with that – not anymore. "Okay well, I'll tell you what I've seen to date. Would that help? Or, I can tell you what I thought I saw, and you can tell me if I interpreted it correctly or not."

"Again..."

"Yes, I'm sure 'correct' is also a relative term." She attempted to continue her story without letting his nearness distract her. "Well, you know I've met Rum. I think I understand, now, that he is an old Earth spirit of some sort, and Jerome, who makes 'the best barbequed spareribs east and west of the Appalachians,' is just one of his personae. Sometimes when I'm looking at what I think is a stump or a scraggly little tree, it waves and winks at me. But he never looks the same from one instance to another. He has this endearing quaintness about him, but Emerald says he's a Big Deal in these parts."

"He is most definitely a Big Deal," Ben confirmed. "He's the local land wight. This entire *bhaille* is under his purview." He waved his arm to indicate everything around them: the meadow, the woods bordering it to the north, Gardens Road where it wound away to parts south, and all of Woodley behind them. "He is the one who originally made the bargain with Ian's great, great grandfather so many years ago, to protect this land – this gateway – in exchange for protection and prosperity for the May family. Even the Queen of Faerie wouldn't confront Rum lightly."

"I would certainly never mess with him," Cally admitted. "He seems to be on our side, and I trust him, but I wouldn't ever want to cross him."

Ben nodded. "That's probably the best approach to dealing with most of the spirits you run into around here. And you're not wrong to feel cautious about going into Faerie. At the very least, it's never a good idea to try to go there alone."

"You mean, like you didn't do?" She turned her head enough to give him a sly look, remembering stories he had told her of his determined efforts, in his youth, to find the Faerie Court on his own.

He laughed. "Which other spirits have you met? So far. Who is Emerald?"

Cally was disappointed he had to ask.

"I was hoping you could tell me," she said. "I've known Emerald for years, over the internet. Long before I came here. Even she doesn't seem to understand who or what she actually is. She wrote me a little story about her life, but it's all disjointed and doesn't make any sense, and she gets confused and upset when I try to get her to discuss it. She does identify strongly with this Vale...this *bhaille*... in any case."

"And you trust her."

"I trust her."

"Good. Then I trust her, too." His arms tightened around her in a brief, reassuring squeeze. "Tell me about the tree you've seen."

Cally raised her arm to point across the meadow, to the farthest hill visible on the horizon. The sun was gone, in the west behind them, and out across the meadow the sky had faded from blue to slate. A chill breeze was rising from that direction. There wasn't much time left to talk or do anything else tonight.

"I've seen it twice," she said. "The first time, it was Rum who egged me on to walk toward it. It looked like a far-off fire, that night, a bonfire, or so I thought at first. Then, as I got closer, it looked more like a city, full of lights, or made of light, or maybe the light came from the people walking in its streets. Streets, or branches – it was hard to tell. Rum wanted me to get closer to it, maybe even walk in those...streets. But I chickened out." She felt Ben's chest rumble as he chuckled softly behind her. "Is that where you go every night?" she asked.

He sighed. "I have been there, a time or two." A star (probably a planet, but Cally wasn't sure which one) flickered into view above the hill they were talking about. "The people who live there just call themselves 'the People.' They call the city Shannish. My mother considers it to be part of her domain, but the People don't necessarily agree." He laughed again at this. "Mostly I go to the Sidhe court. It appears to be in the same place, from here." He pointed. "But you have to use completely different roads to get to it. It took me years to find them all, and sometimes they still change."

As he spoke, gesturing with his hands to describe the different places, she was able to add new segments to the mental map forming in her head, a twisting knotwork of roads like the after-images of headlights on a dark night, curling across the hills, sometimes overlapping one another but seldom intersecting.

This didn't confuse her as much as she would have expected. What she had the most trouble getting used was the fact that, no matter what she asked Ben, he always answered her. Just answered her. All she had to do was keep reminding herself it was alright to ask. He never showed any need to keep anything from her, which was more than she could say for most of the men who had been in her life and, more recently, for the denizens of Woodley. Every word he said, she realized, could well have been complete and utter bull. But it seemed to her more like he had been waiting a long time to have someone to whom he could tell all these things. Or maybe it was just that, as he had once told her: *When you've lived as long as I have, you lose the heart to lie.*

She resumed telling him what she'd seen of the tree beyond the meadow. "The other time I saw it was the night Vale House caught fire, the night Foster was arrested. Mima took me there."

"Mima? So you know who she really is." He sounded impressed.

Cally looked around the meadow, but didn't see any sign of the three horses who often grazed there. "I'm guessing she's the same thing Errin is. I have no idea what they are, though. Errin once told me she's a unicorn, but she gets a kick out of winding me up."

"Have you ever heard of a kelpie?"

Cally had read old legends about horses able to transform into sea monsters. "I guess that would make sense, sort of."

"They're something like that, anyway. Those stories are awfully convoluted, too," he admitted. "All I know is, Errin and her friends are very old, and very wild, and answer to no one. Much to my mother's consternation."

"I like them better and better all the time," Cally admitted grudgingly. "Anyway, Mima took me to the tree that night. Straight to it, like a shot. I saw you there – I think it was you – dancing with people around a fire. I wasn't sure. She didn't stop; there was no time. Mima ran straight at the tree and...*up* it, as if it were a hill.

Which it did turn out to be, once we reached the top. It was that hill, that one right out there." There was, at the moment, no tree visible. "I know I'm not making much sense." She turned her head to look apologetically at Ben, but he was nodding solemnly.

"You are making perfect sense." He took his hands off the gate and wrapped his arms around her. The air was definitely chilly, now, the sky dark.

"My mother's people are not originally from around here." He nodded toward the dark hills in the distance. "That is to say, they are not native to this continent. But their legends claim they were the first people to arrive anywhere on this Earth. As far as they are concerned, all other people are invaders, and not very impressive ones, at that."

"Impressive enough to have love affairs with, though!" Cally laughed, referring to Ben's mother and father, then realizing with embarrassment that he might have mistakenly thought she'd been talking about their own relationship.

He answered frankly, though. "Well, once the Sidhe had achieved immortality, they lost the ability to procreate, so the advent of ever-so-fertile humanity was a mixed blessing."

"Why would they need to procreate if they're immortal?"

"They are immortal, but that doesn't mean they can't be killed. And they are almost as prone to warlike behavior as humans are. More so, some would say. You've read the stories. This stuff has been going on since the dawn of time. They claim there was no war before humans came along and forced them to defend themselves, but I have a strong feeling that's not strictly true.

"One of the upshots of all this warring was that some bands of Faerie, with *Daoine Sidhe* to oversee them, came to this continent. Some say they got here before humans did, but the People who already lived here, such as the People who live in Shannish..." He tilted his head toward the place, without taking his arms from around her. "They claim to have already been living here for millennia, and they say the faerie and human races arrived at pretty much the same time.

"By 'humans arriving,' I mean the People say they were already here even when the Native Americans arrived. In any case, the Native people acknowledged them and treated them with respect and did a decent job of coexisting with them. The same can't be said of the Sidhe and the European humans who arrived later, each believing themselves to be the rightful lords of these lands."

Cally shook her head. They were pushing the limits of Ben's contract, now, and he was absolutely "out after curfew," but she had one more question. "How does the Sidhe version of the story end?"

She felt him shrug. "It hasn't ended," he said. "Not yet, anyway. The warring ended, at least. Mostly. For now. Ostensibly, the humans won. The fae all around the world have gone underground, figuratively, and literally for some. A tenuous truce has been maintained for thousands of years. Of course, there are always those who want to overturn this truce. The Fomorians, for instance, and others like them, don't like having to coexist with what they consider to be inferiors and usurpers.

"Humans have short memories because they have short lives, so the little they remember of this is only snatches of legend, now. But the immortals remember as if it were yesterday. My mother's mother was sent here with her court ten thousand years ago, to oversee the maintenance of the truce and to rule over the faerie people who live here, guarding this gateway. She did a good job of it by all accounts. But she missed the land from which she'd sprung. This is a condition which affects all faerie folk. When I was a child on the verge of manhood, and Avwynn felt secure in the knowledge that the family line would continue, she returned to what is now called Ireland, leaving my mother in charge. And, say what you will about Rianwynn, she is keeping the peace, with an iron fist, despite all the resistance over the years. But the resentment is growing. Things are changing."

"Changing how?"

"Nobody's sure. You can feel it, but so far Mother and her people have been unable to pin down the source. They say your presence here is one of the signs." He turned her so he could look at her, and smoothed her hair back from her face. "Whatever it all turns out to be, I'm thankful it's brought you to me.

"I'll see you in the morning."

12 - On the Fence

"Why don't you ever go with him? Scared?"

"No!" Cally answered, a little too quickly. She wrenched her eyes away from the darkness in the east into which Ben had disappeared. Turning around, she gave Errin a stern look. "It's none of your business anyway." The girl stood in her bare feet in the crossroads at the end of Main Street and Cally could see, even in the dimness, that her green eyes danced with amusement.

"I think you're just commitment-phobic," Errin said. "Not ready to meet Mother-in-Law yet." Errin shook her cloud of brilliant crimson curls.

"Errin! Seriously! Why does everyone have me married off to him already?" Cally let out an exasperated sigh and stepped away from the gate. "But you're right that we're not yet at the 'hey, meet my family' stage of the relationship, and frankly we may never get there. Not all relationships do, you know. Can't anyone around here just let things go at their natural pace?"

"Suit yourself," Errin said. "But knowing someone on the inside would be a great way to find out things you'll never find out otherwise."

She had a point. Ben was in a position to introduce her to wonders most people would never even know existed. He had already shown her some of them, if only in the form of great hamburgers and old music in an anachronistic town halfway inside Faerie. And she really did want to go back there someday. Maybe even further.

"I just don't believe women should expect men to lead them around all the time," she said at last, and this was also true. "Maybe you can show me the way, yourself, sometime. Girl power, and all that."

"True," said Errin. "You do still owe me a driving lesson."

"You know, I think I can find it myself," Cally said. "Someday. I wouldn't be the first human to do so."

"Good luck with that!" Errin laughed and turned away toward Gardens Road.

"Anyway, George's zemi is still in my purse. I don't want to drag him along with me into a place I'm not familiar with."

Errin waved the back of her hand dismissively and laughed. "That thing is just a Dumbo's feather!" she called over her shoulder as she disappeared into the darkening distance.

Cally shook her head and walked the other way, back to the main gate of the Vale House grounds, passing through the masonry pillars decorated with finial lanterns in the shape of pineapples. The grassy space between the front porch and the meadow fence was filled with cars. Cally's own red Corolla stood in a patch of tall grass, having forced Ignacio to mow around it ever since she'd "lost" her keys. She paused to pat its fender and promise she hadn't forgotten it, then looked around to see if she could spot Rum passing through. Aside from a troupe of barred owls chuckling in the oak tree next to the barn, however, the yard was silent and empty of life.

Bethany had turned on the porch light before leaving for the evening and Cally, as she ascended the wooden stairs, could see the Captain's ghost asleep in the wicker chair next to the door. A phantom flask dangled precariously from his spectral hand, and Cally wondered what it would be like to drink ghost whiskey. She paused a moment and gazed tenderly down at the spirit of the old man as he snored inaudibly. "Why are you still here, Captain?" she asked softly. "You should be on the Other Side, wherever that is, with your wife and your old army buddies."

If he heard her, he didn't reply.

A few guests were sitting in the parlor trying to watch the old television set. Cally dashed past the parlor doorway and up the stairs, looking around to make sure the guest room doors were all shut, before she slipped George's zemi back into the butler's desk. She turned around and let out her breath, relieved that she had accomplished her mission without being detected.

She hadn't seen George since she'd left the coffee shop but, in case he was listening, she said: "Thank you for having been on your best behavior, today. I promise to take you to some other interesting places someday. But tonight, I think it's best I deal with Ms. Barry by myself."

"What?" came a voice from the top of the stairs. It was Eddie Tiene, carrying a heavy suitcase as he turned toward her end of the hallway.

"Oh!" she said. "Sorry, I was thinking out loud. I see you managed to extend your reservation?" She tried not to let her disappointment show.

"Yes, though I did have to move to a different room which became available. I'm in the Dogwood Room now." He smiled broadly, showing her the key fob.

Cally glanced sadly at the freshly painted door with the botanical print of a blooming dogwood branch on it. The room – "her" room – would seem even more unpleasant to her, now, once she finally got to use it again. She looked forward ever more eagerly to the possibility of buying a small cottage of her own.

"I'm glad everything is going well for you," she said to Eddie. "If you'll excuse me, I have some business to attend to. Feel free to help yourself to anything on the sideboard in the dining room." She gestured toward the lighted cabinet just visible below the gallery railing. "If you need anything, my cell number and the housekeeper's number are on the speed dial of the phone in my... your room," she finished as she headed for the stair landing.

"Wait!" he called after her. "Perhaps I can go with you? You can show me around your charming, small town!"

She ran down the stairs, pretending she hadn't heard.

She had meant to stop in her office and check her voicemail to see if Danya Barry had arrived in town yet, as Woodley was notoriously hard to find. But the paranormal investigator had already arrived. She was standing just inside the front door, looking up at Cally with wide eyes, when Cally reached the bottom stair.

"Do you see that?" she asked breathlessly.

Ordinarily, Cally would have rolled her eyes at this sort of drama but, she had to admit, maybe Danya really could see the Preacher, who happened just then to be standing in front of the desk, gazing as usual at the portraits of Lionel and Isbel May.

"What do you see?" Cally asked carefully.

"It's kind of a..." The dark-haired young woman gestured with both hands, drawing the outline of a tall shape in front of her. "A shadow – a sort of zone where the air doesn't look right."

Cally could see Danya was trembling. It may well have been her first real ghost, for all she knew. "It's one of the sightings most often reported here," she concurred. She didn't elaborate about how the Preacher's ghost appeared as a fully resolved apparition to her.

Though her hands were still shaking, Danya fumbled in her bag to withdraw a small video camera. With this, she recorded several minutes of video of the front of the desk, narrating in a tremulous voice, noting the date and time. "Maybe it's a demon!" she remarked for the benefit of the soundtrack.

"I doubt it," Cally snorted. She wondered why ghost hunters always insisted on conflating ghosts with demons. "Ghosts are people, too," she reminded, sharing one of Nell's favorite quotes.

Danya lowered the camera but kept her eyes on the shadow she perceived before her. "Well, it feels evil to me," she observed.

Cally tended to agree, but she didn't say so. "Many people do say it feels oppressive, when it's around. But all it ever does is stand there." This last she directed, along with a scowl, toward the Preacher, which probably did not account for his happening to vanish just then.

"I'll let you know if it shows up on the video," Danya said. She tucked the camera back into her bag and crossed the Hall to extend a hand to Cally. "Anyway, hello, I'm Danya Barry, from the Greater..."

Cally shook the young woman's hand. "I remember you. I'm sorry you had such an unpleasant experience last time you were here."

Most people who claimed to have had unpleasant experiences at Vale House spoke of unexplained noises or mysterious chills, but Danya's unpleasant experience had been at the hands of a living human. "I'm just glad to see that...woman...isn't here anymore," Danya said, and Cally laughed to show she completely agreed with that sentiment. Danya went on. "I was the one who took the photo of that African American ghost. I just have a feeling about it..." She gave Cally a look that clearly asked, *"Are you going to tell me the truth about this?"*

Cally knew more about George than anyone currently alive, but she didn't know why she felt so reluctant to talk to this woman about him. The fact that Danya had just referred to him as "it" didn't help. Still, Danya had made a good faith showing of forgiving and forgetting the previous fiasco, and though that had not even been Cally's fault, she felt she owed her something to make up for it.

"I know he is neither African nor American," she offered. "But most of the details are unclear."

Danya waited for her to elaborate, but Cally walked to the door instead. "I'm excited to investigate the local railroad crossing phenomenon with you." She paused to retrieve her denim jacket from the coat rack next to the door. "It's a nice night. Let's walk."

Cally offered to help Danya with her equipment bag, which looked heavy, but Danya insisted she was used to it. As they crossed the parking lot toward the gate, what looked like an animated tree stump, walking along the fence line toward Gardens Road, paused to salute Cally with the stick it carried like a cane. Cally was careful not to call Danya's attention to Rum. Instead, she gestured out through the gate and told Danya the local legend of the Crossroads Banshee who was rumored to appear on stormy nights at the intersection of Main Street and Gardens road. She didn't include her own private theory that this banshee was probably not a ghost at all, but more likely some kind of ancient earth goddess.

Danya recorded some video footage of the intersection, and may or may not have caught an image of Rum just exiting the field of view. Then the two women turned right, onto the residential part of Main Street, where Cally could already hear drifts of music coming along the breeze from town as the men on the loading dock tuned up their instruments.

"Listen, Danya," she tried to explain. "We still aren't sure whether or not it would be a good idea to advertise Vale House as an authentic Haunted Attraction. Some say it would bring more money into the local economy, and it might, but..." She gestured around to all the peaceful, older homes with their porch lights shining out to illuminate their way as they passed. "Sometimes it's not just about the money. This is a small town, and we need to consider our neighbors' feelings. I hope you understand."

Danya nodded, but Cally wasn't convinced she did understand.

As they reached the end of the residential district, Cally could see that the sheriff, Doc and Jud had joined Merv on the loading dock at the feed store. An empty personal-size pizza box lay at Merv's feet. To all appearances, he had not moved from his seat all day but, at some point, he must have at least got up to fetch his guitar from inside the store.

Cally introduced Danya to the men. "Merv sings Glenn Frey's part," she added, eliciting a blank look.

They were ostensibly there for their customary evening music session, but everyone was facing the hardware store, except for Jud, who was facing everyone else and looking defensive.

"Mr. Arkwright," said Cally, "Ms. Barry and I are on our way to check out the haunted railroad crossing. I wonder if you would you be so kind as to fill her in on the details of that legend while I run inside the News Store for a minute?"

Merv said he would be happy to do so, and Cally stepped into the street, waving to Luke, who was carrying a pizza warming envelope toward the loading dock.

It took her several tries to yank open the door of Dawes News.

"Hey, Bree!" she called into the dimness. Bree had already shut off the lights, leaving only the drinks cooler glowing at the back of the store. The old woman was pulling on her coat as she headed for the door. "Maybe someone should walk you home tonight," Cally suggested.

"I'm not that old yet!" Bree said. She pushed past Cally and stepped out onto the sidewalk, yanking the door shut behind her.

"No, well, I didn't mean that." Cally waited while Bree fiddled with the key in the lock. "Just, you know, it's probably not safe for you to be walking around alone tonight."

"You're referring to that lanky weasel." The old woman's glare shifted toward the hardware store as she put her keys into her bag and stepped off the curb. "I can handle *him*. Thank you for your concern," she snorted. She crossed the street, waving to Merv and the other men. "'Night, Mervyn!" she called as she turned the corner around the side of the feed store onto Church Street.

"'Night, Brigid," Merv responded. He didn't appear to be concerned about her walking down that dark stretch of street at night, so Cally supposed she was worrying needlessly.

Danya was putting away her voice recorder, and Doc was opening the pizza box on top of an overturned milk crate. As Luke tucked the empty warming envelope under his arm, Sheriff Mahon called out in a loud stage-whisper, "Hey, Doc, what do you call a sleeping pizza?"

"I don't know," Doc played along. "What *do* you call a sleeping pizza?"

"A pizzzza!"

Luke's face was patient as he paused to grin at the men. "Ha. Ha," he said.

"OK, I guess it works better as a joke when you read it," the sheriff admitted.

"That's okay," said Luke. "What's the difference between pizza and Eagles music?"

The men all furrowed their brows in thought. Cally grinned because she thought she knew the answer. Finally, Merv asked, "Okay, what's the difference between pizza and Eagles music?"

"Pizza is good!" Luke laughed and took the money Doc handed him. "Goodnight, guys. I'll put the change toward your outstanding tab."

"That was supposed to be your tip!" Merv called after his retreating back. "All nineteen cents of it!"

Merv strummed the first few chords of "Take It Easy," and Cally gestured for Danya to follow as she headed away toward Railroad Street.

14 - Ghost Hunters

Her entire body tingled with nerves as they turned right, under the street light, passing by the length of the east wall of the hardware store. Somewhere beyond that unassuming cinder-block and glass exterior, Cally knew, lurked a man who had tried to kill her and several people she loved, and there was nothing she could do about it. She wondered if he was watching her passing by, and she was thankful Danya was there to distract her.

They went on into the darkness, down a gentle slope to where the sidewalk ended at the railroad tracks. "So, this is where they say it happens," Cally said, stopping at the edge of the gravel berm. "I've never experienced the phenomenon myself. Not yet, anyway. If anything happens, it'll be a first for me, too." She gazed across the dark field, on the other side of the tracks, to where the lights of the cottages along Bells Road twinkled warmly.

A cool breeze was rising as Danya put down her bag and began extracting her ghost-hunting equipment. She set up a slender tripod and mounted her camera on top of it.

"Here," she said, handing an instrument like a chunky plastic pistol to Cally. "You just point this at things, and it will read the temperature." She pressed the trigger and the digital readout glowed red, informing them the air temperature had dropped to 59 degrees Fahrenheit, dropping further to 58 as she watched. When she pointed it at Danya it read 97. "When it's pointing at a ghost or other otherworldly phenomenon," Danya explained, "the temperature will read much cooler than it should."

"I don't know if that will be much use, tonight!" Cally said. Zipping her jacket and turning up the collar, she revised her previous assessment of the night from "nice" to "getting chilly."

Danya selected an EMF detector for herself and set a large instrument on the ground. "This is a top of the line Electronic Voice Phenomenon recorder. It's much more reliable than this one," she explained, showing Cally an EVP app on her phone which she confessed often gave false positives. Even as she held it out to demonstrate, Cally saw the readout display the words "picture" and "who," then "train."

"Well, at least that's relevant," Cally remarked. She was glad George was stuck back at Vale House. She could only imagine the mischief he would enjoy creating through these instruments.

The two women settled in to wait. Local legends spoke of screams heard at this intersection at night, and attributed these to old stories – almost certainly apocryphal – about stuck cars and trapped children. Cally didn't know any more than Danya what to expect, or whether to expect anything at all. She considered turning on her own phone's audio recording app; she was sure it had recorded some interesting "voices" at least once before.

The air grew noticeably cooler and Cally grudgingly gave Danya credit. Though she had once pegged everyone in G.A.A.S.P.S. as ridiculous purveyors of supernatural drama, Danya was serious about her work, silently enduring the chill as she patiently watched her instruments and made notes of their readings. Cally's fingers and toes grew cold, and she marveled at how the younger woman could stand there so silently, gazing at instruments while it was all Cally could do not to pace about and stomp her feet to keep warm.

Suddenly a loud, screeching noise erupted from the woods beyond the cottages, and Danya spun around to point her instruments toward it. "Oh my god!" she exclaimed as her arm shook. "What was that?"

Cally burst into laughter at this, and Danya turned to glare at her. "What's so funny?"

"I'm sorry," said Cally, struggling to master her mirth. "It's just owls. Barred owls. They can be real jerks sometimes." She didn't add that the tendency for paranormal hunters to utter "Oh my god what was that?" was a favorite joke among Vale House staff, and had even been made into a drinking game at one point.

The whooping and screeching in the woods simmered down into cackling as several owls called in a disjointed chorus, "WHO got got got got?" Cally pointed to Danya's EVP translator, which currently read "who," and stifled another chuckle. "Sometimes they sound like a bunch of drunken teenagers having a loud party in the woods. They've fooled me more than once."

Danya accepted this turn of events philosophically and resumed her silent vigil over her instruments. That was when Cally began to notice a soft, high-pitched noise just on the edge of her hearing. Danya appeared to have noticed it too, and turned her head toward the tracks, from whence it seemed to be arising. It grew louder as they both walked closer, turning their heads from side to side in an attempt to pinpoint the source of the sound. They both had to agree it was coming from the steel rails themselves. Danya didn't exclaim this time, but quickly moved her tripod from the tracks to the grass, asking, "When does the last train go?"

"It already has, at five thirty." Cally stepped closer to the rail and cocked her head, listening. She guessed the high, ringing sound, emanating directly from the cold steel, was what people were talking about whenever they repeated the urban legend about screaming sometimes heard here. It didn't sound much like a scream, to her, but it was growing louder.

Danya returned to join her with a voice recorder and her EMF detector, but the needle didn't register anything as she pointed it at the rails. Cally looked up, then grabbed Danya's hand and pointed the instrument toward a spot a little to the east along the tracks.

"Hey, what are you...oh!" Danya's eyes grew wide as the EMF needle jumped to the red side of the gauge. "Oh my god! What the hell is that?"

She moved the instrument right and left, pointing it into the darkness, but Cally gently moved her hand back. "No, right there. Don't you see them?"

Danya didn't appear to see the small, bluish shapes Cally could see, but she was able to zero her instrument in on them by the motion of the gauge's needle.

The screeching sound continued to grow louder. It was definitely not screaming, as it had a metallic edge to it, a high metallic whistle that was beginning to hurt Cally's ears. She knew Danya must hear it too, by the way she cocked her head uncomfortably, hunching her shoulders.

"They look like upside-down blue flames," Cally reported to Danya. "Three or four of them, just above the tracks. About the size of, say, grapefruits. Not too bright, just kind of glowing softly like an old-fashioned TV after you would turn it off in a dark room." She wasn't sure Danya had ever seen an old-fashioned TV.

"Do they have faces?"

Cally squinted. "Not that I can make out." The harder she looked, the more elusive they were. The way they twitched back and forth made Cally think they were in pain, but she found herself not wanting to say so out loud.

Cally finally had to put her hands up to her ears and Danya, also, though she took the time to set her instruments down carefully first, covered her ears and crouched down saying, "Oh my god!"

Then the noise stopped abruptly, as if it had been switched off. The two women next to the tracks carefully uncovered their ears, though they kept their hands raised just in case they needed to cover them again. Again, Danya said, "What the hell was that?"

Cally didn't laugh this time; she could only shrug. "It was certainly not screaming children trapped in a car as a train roars toward it, or whatever other legend people repeat about it here." She looked south along Railroad Street toward Main Street and wondered if the men on the loading dock had heard it as well. "How about we go back and talk to the town elders?"

Danya walked back to her tripod and took the camera down from it. "You go ahead. I'll join you in a bit. I just want to keep recording a little longer, maybe walk down the tracks a little way."

Cally had to admire the woman's dedication in the face of her obvious uneasiness. "Okay then." She headed back up Railroad Street toward the street lights and human company. "Be careful, Danya." She meant it.

The men were still on the loading dock, but Cally realized she wasn't going to get a chance to ask them if they'd heard the sound. A sizeable crowd of the local citizenry had gathered in the street around the feed store, and Foster Brentwood stood in the midst of them.

15 - Friend of the Devil

"I just needed someplace stay," he was saying. "I'm not '*up to something.*' I'm literally sleeping on the floor in a store-room!" Foster spoke defensively as he turned slowly to face all the people surrounding him. Cally was momentarily dismayed to see that Eddie Tiene was one of them, but not nearly as dismayed as she was by the sight of Foster himself.

"I'm not hurting anyone," he was insisting. "Don't worry, I'll only need to stay here a few days longer, and then I'll be out of everyone's way for good."

"You already had a place to stay," said Merv. "All expenses paid by the state. Three meals a day."

The people gathered around the loading dock laughed at this, and Foster pushed up his glasses and tried to respond. His voice was drowned out by the ongoing outrage.

"You're a generous man, Jud," Luke snorted. He had his pizza delivery hat gripped tight in his fists, and it didn't look like it was ever going to be able to resume its original shape. "But you better keep an eye on your stock for the next few days, I think."

"Now that's not fair," Jud replied. "Foster and my boy grew up together. He wouldn't do anything to hurt me or my business."

"Better keep an eye on your boy, too," said Doc.

"When you step out that door, you pass too close to my coffee shop!" Andi complained. "I'm sure it's in violation of the restraining order."

"I checked," Jud said. "Well, my son did. On Google Earth. The door of my storage room is three hundred and nineteen feet away from the foot of the stairs to Ms. May's apartment. I think that addresses the restraining order more than adequately."

"Now, I *am* sorry about that," Foster said, putting his hands into his pockets and taking them out again to push up his glasses. "I didn't know Nell was living there. I had no idea she was starting a business of her own. She never takes my calls. I would have been happy to help her set up her studio, too. I'm a successful business man and..."

"That's not what I'd call you," muttered Ignacio, who had just emerged from under the oak trees of the residential district to join them.

"Look, I'm sorry to have bothered you all so much," said Foster. "I'll just go back inside. I thought I could reason with my former neighbors about what I'm supposedly accused of." He threw Ignacio a particularly dark look. "But I can see nobody wants to hear my side of the story. Everyone just automatically assumes I'm guilty!"

Cally's jaw dropped. She didn't need to hear his story. She'd been there, with his hands around her throat. "Foster," she said, "I think those last two words: 'I'm guilty,' are the only true words I've ever heard you speak."

He hung his head as if crushed by the harshness of her words, but the sideways glance he cast at her was like a dagger and sent a chill through her heart.

"Goodnight, former friends," he said. Pushing up his glasses with a sigh, he turned away and started down the street toward the hardware store.

Sheriff Mahon cleared his throat. "No, that takes you too close to the coffee shop," he said. "Go around the back way."

Foster turned around and passed through them again so he could follow Church Street to the railroad yard behind the feed store. He had to walk by Ignacio, who did not step aside to let him pass. As Foster went around him, Ignacio said in an uncharacteristically harsh voice, "If you go near Nell – if you go near anyone I care about – I swear to you, nobody will ever find your body."

"Not that anyone would bother to look!" Merv added, strumming a minor chord. Foster didn't look back, but continued into the darkness between the buildings.

Silence fell on the crowd around the loading dock. Presently

Andi stirred. "Well, I'd better get back," she said. "Need to lock up my shop for the night. I'll make sure Nell has locked her door, too, before I go home."

"I'll walk with you." Luke followed her, and everyone was glad Andi's son was in town and waiting for her at home.

When they felt enough time had passed that Foster was probably safely back inside the store room, the crowd began to disperse.

When only a handful remained, the sheriff said, "Um, Ignacio, just a hint. Maybe you shouldn't threaten to kill people when an officer of the law is standing right beside you."

That broke the tension. Merv laughed and strummed a chord on his guitar, and Doc sat down, lifting his mandolin into his lap. They played a few bars of "Friend of the Devil" and everyone nodded at the appropriateness of the title. When the men began to sing, Cally thought they harmonized as well as the Grateful Dead ever had, but Ignacio headed home stating, to her amazement, that singing wasn't one of his myriad talents.

Cally tried to sing along, attempting to pick out a harmony somewhere between Phil Lesh's and Bob Weir's, but a discordant high note from somewhere threw her off. Merv paused his playing, pressing a hand against the guitar strings to silence them. Sheriff Mahon held up a forefinger and said "Listen!"

It came again – a high-pitched screech that Cally at first took to be more of the phantom railroad-track noises she and Danya had heard earlier. Then the screaming began to form words: "Oh my god! Oh my god!"

Cally let out her breath and rolled her eyes. "Ghost hunters," she said. "Am I right? I'll go see what she's on about." Turning the corner around the side of the building, she hurried along Church Street toward the tracks. Danya's screaming rose in pitch, and Cally grew alarmed as she remembered that Foster had just gone this way. "Hang on, Danya!" she called. "I'm coming!" She broke into a run.

As she neared the end of the alley, she could see the young woman on her knees in the moonlight just beyond the railroad tracks. Danya's hands covered her face and she rocked back and forth as she frantically screamed, "Oh my god!"

Keeping her eyes on Danya as she ran, Cally tripped over something in the dark street and went sprawling to the pavement. She jumped up again quickly as other footsteps joined behind her, but the ground was wet, and she slipped again. She landed on something soft, and the sheriff appeared at her side to lift her up. Wiping her wet hands on her jacket, Cally glanced down to see what had tripped her.

It was Foster. He was covered in blood.

That wasn't what Danya was screaming about, though. She was screaming because Foster's head was lying beside her on the other side of the tracks.

16 - Dark Morning

"I think we're just going to have to declare your jeans a loss," said Katarina, meeting Cally as she shambled out of her office into the Hall. The Hall was filled with sunshine and bird song. It was well past breakfast time, and all the guests had already checked out. "But I think I've managed to salvage this, at least," Katarina was saying. She held up Cally's denim jacket. It looked much better than it had the night before, Cally had to admit, but she thought she could still see rusty red stains lingering in the seams.

"We could try dying it red?" she suggested.

Behind the desk, Bethany laughed uneasily, until the phone rang and she pounced to answer it. "Oh, I know!" she exclaimed to the person on the other end. "It's so shocking! I won't say there's any love lost, there, but still, it's always sad when a man dies." She didn't sound very sad.

Katarina draped the jacket over her arm and put a gentle hand under Cally's elbow. "Come get some coffee," she urged, giving her a little tug toward the kitchen. "We'll see if Ignacio can think of a way to save your jacket. After all, he is good at everything! He's just popped in to town for a minute, to see if the sheriff has found out anything new. But don't worry..."

Cally followed in a daze, not really listening. She hadn't slept well, having dreamed all night about trying to run through the meadow and tripping over dead bodies at every turn. She hoped the breakfast guests had left plenty of coffee.

From the aroma in the kitchen, she could tell Katarina had put on a completely fresh pot. She filled a blue mug from the drain board and handed it to Cally; Cally tried to ignore the fact that her hands were shaking as she took it. She carried it to the work table and sat on the stool.

"I slept in," she said. "I didn't get to meet Ben at the gate this morning."

"Bree told him what happened. He came by here a couple hours ago, to check on you and make sure you're alright."

"Oh, you should have wakened me!" Cally wondered if Ben had come calling with or without Bree's permission.

"You needed the sleep!" Katarina insisted. "You can go down to the store later to let him know you're okay." Her eyes flicked to the window over the sink. "Oh! Look, Ignacio is back!"

Cally abandoned her coffee and followed Katarina out the back door. Ignacio had paused to open the chicken coop and let the hens out to scratch in the garden. Both women hurried across the lawn to meet him.

He put out his hands to slow them down. "There's not much to tell," he said, to their disappointment, but he told them what he did know. "The police report says they can't even figure out how it was done. All they know is his head was torn off – just torn right off his shoulders. They have no theories as to how. They got poor Ms. Barry's statement last night but she was mostly incoherent. Apparently, she did see someone, but it was pretty dark, and she doesn't know anyone's names around here anyway."

"Poor thing! I hope she's okay," said Katarina.

"Did anyone tell Nell yet?" Cally wondered.

Ignacio told them he had stopped in the coffee shop, where Andi had already posted the police report on the wall for everyone in town to peruse. "Nell seems to be taking it in stride," he said. "Well, she never reacts to anything the way you'd expect someone to."

The first item on Cally's agenda that morning, even before stopping to see Ben, was to visit Nell and make sure she really was okay. After that, she didn't care what Bree might think: she intended to hang around at the News Store for a good, long time today.

"Okay," Ignacio said. "I'd better go report to Bethany, or she'll never forgive me. Even though she's probably already heard it all anyway!" He turned and headed toward the house, but then paused as they all heard the click of the latch on the back gate. It was Sheriff

Mahon, walking slowly with his eyes cast down as he crossed the lawn toward them.

"Morning, Dunn! Haven't seen you in at least an hour!" Katarina laughed. The sheriff had been at Vale House until the wee hours, that morning. "There's fresh coffee if you want!"

The sheriff declined the coffee with a wave of his hand, not looking at Katarina. He stood for a long time with his hands in his pockets, staring at the ground while the radio in his car crackled incoherently and the chickens milled around his feet, hoping he might drop some donut crumbs.

"Any news?" Cally prompted.

Dunn Mahon shook his head as if trying to rouse himself from a dream. Taking his hands from his pockets, he said: "I'm afraid I'm not here on a social call."

They heard Bethany's voice, then, calling "Wait! Sheriff, please wait!" She came from the shade garden beside the house, with Ian leaning heavily on her arm. Ian's face was drawn with pain as he hobbled as quickly as he could toward them. Stopping just short of the little group, he spread his hands in a pleading gesture.

"Dunn..."

"Don't worry, Ian," said the sheriff. "I'm sure we'll have this all straightened out by the end of the day." He looked up at Ignacio, and the smile disappeared from Ignacio's face as understanding dawned in his eyes. "Ignacio Munoz, I'm afraid I have to place you under arrest in the matter of the death of Foster Brentwood."

He did not move toward Ignacio, and Ignacio did not step away. The silence that filled the yard lasted a full minute. It was finally broken by Katarina's voice.

"Sheriff, have you gone loco or something?"

"He's just following orders," Ian said. "The detectives' office in Blackthorn called me a few minutes ago to make sure Ignacio was still here. Apparently, he fits the description of the man Danya Barry saw last night. That and, well, what everyone overheard him saying. They sent Dunn because he knows us all and..."

"That's bullshit!" Katarina burst out. It was a word Cally was willing to bet the woman had never uttered before in her life. *"Es pendejada! Mas te vale callarte..."*

Ignacio moved to put his arms around her. "It's alright," he said gently. "It's going to be alright. He's just doing his job."

The sheriff sighed and looked back at the ground, probably wishing he had chosen a different career, Cally thought, while Katarina burst into fresh shouts of "Just doing his job! I've got your job right here, Dunn Mahon!" Her fists were beating the air and probably would have landed on the sheriff if Ignacio had not been holding her back.

Cally finally found her voice and put a hand on the woman's shoulder, saying, "It's just a formality, Kat. I'm sure they'll have it all straightened out soon. They can't hold him on circumstantial evidence." She looked at the sheriff. "Can they?"

"It's called 'probable cause.' Mr. Munoz will be held for questioning, and will probably stand in a lineup to give Ms. Barry a chance to positively identify him. But she's had to be sedated, and won't be able to do that until..."

"Es un montón de mierda!" Katarina erupted again, nearly breaking free of Ignacio's grasp. "If my husband had done it, they never would have found the body!"

"That's not helping, Kat," Cally whispered urgently. As Sheriff Mahon read Ignacio's rights to him, enunciating the "right to remain silent" part in an extra loud voice for Katarina's benefit, Cally felt dizzy and sick, not certain she was even in the real world anymore. Perhaps she was still trapped in her nightmares from last night. How had Foster, such a petty, mean, ineffectual excuse for a man, managed to reach beyond his jail cell, and now even beyond death itself, to continue hurting people she cared about?

Ignacio gently pushed Katarina into Cally's arms and turned to the sheriff, holding up his hands with his wrists together, waiting for the handcuffs.

"There's no need for that," Sheriff Mahon said. "Let's just ride into Blackthorn and see what they have to say. I'm so sorry to put you though this, Mr. Munoz. You deserve better."

He turned and walked back to the gate, holding it open for Ignacio, who followed him through. Ian hurried as best he could to join them. As Ignacio got into the back seat of the patrol car, Ian bent down and said through the window, "I'll be coming right behind you to post your bail. We'll have you back here by lunchtime." Bethany, the only one of them other than Ignacio who could drive a manual shift, already had the keys to the red truck in her hand.

"It's generous of you, Ian," said the sheriff. "We would all do the same if we could, but this is going to take a long time. There's a mountain of paperwork to get through, and the questioning and lineup procedures will most likely take more than a day. Bail won't be necessary unless he's actually charged. I'll be the first to let you know if that happens. There's still plenty of hope that it won't."

Cally didn't think the sheriff sounded very hopeful at all as he looked away down the street, then sighed and got behind the wheel of his car.

Ignacio smiled for his wife from the back seat of the patrol car. "Don't worry, *mi carina*," he said through the narrow opening at the top of the window. "We've been through worse. God is in control. I will see you soon."

Cally tightened her grip on Katarina as the car pulled away from the curb, but all the fight seemed to have gone out of the woman's body. Her face had become expressionless, her eyes unreadable as she said softly, "My Ignacio and I have not had to sleep apart for over twenty years. We thought we had left those days behind us." She didn't weep, though, as she drew herself up and walked back to the house while Cally stood watching helplessly.

17 - Fresh Questions

"But what did Ms. Barry see, exactly?" Ben asked. "I don't understand how anyone could, physically, have done it anyway. Not anyone human."

For the first time since she'd met him, Ben had no insights to offer. He only raised fresh questions, and that was more unnerving to Cally than any of the strange things he had ever told her before.

It was no comfort at all when he resumed being knowledgeable. "To remove someone's head from their shoulders would take an incredible amount of strength," he said. "Even with an adequate edged tool."

They stood together inside Dawes News, looking out the front window toward the yellow tape, with the words "Police Line Do Not Cross" repeating all along it in red, barricading access to Church Street from Main Street. Merv Arkwright wasn't sitting on his loading dock this morning, for the first time Cally could remember since she had arrived in Woodley.

Cally quoted the police report, which she had stood in line to read on the coffee shop wall. "The exact words were: 'Ms. Barry observed a figure standing over the victim. The figure appeared to be a tall, muscular male with dark hair worn in a ponytail. Barry reports the victim fell over and his head landed at her feet in the same moment.'

"By the time I came along," Cally continued, "there was nobody in the alley except Foster, or, well, what was left of him."

"There are lots of tall people in this town," Ben mused. "And lots of people with ponytails." He glanced at Bree, who stood in sullen silence behind the counter with her eyes fixed firmly on her newspaper. "But only one person with both those features, and that's Ignacio."

"What does Jud's son look like?" Cally wondered.

Ben shrugged. "I haven't seen him since he was a teen," he said. "But I'm sure the sheriff questioned Donald, too, before he left town again this morning. He never stays long anyway, but since people found out he was harboring Foster, he's kind of *persona non grata* around here."

The phone on the counter rang, and Bree put down her paper to answer it. "Good morning, Ms. Chase. Yes. Pretty awful. So, what do you want *me* to do about it?" Bree, though she knew everything about everyone in Woodley, had never been one to revel in gossip.

"It had to be someone from out of town, then," Cally continued as she and Ben turned their attention away from Bree. "But the sheriff was at Vale House until late last night, interviewing all the guests. They could all account for their whereabouts, and anyway none of them matched the description Danya gave." Cally's first thought, at the time, had been that it must have been the musclebound, ponytailed delivery driver, Mr. Ennilangr, but he was blond, and anyway his rig, with its conspicuous mural of rams on the trailer, had not been seen by any of the sharp-eyed denizens of Woodley since breakfast on Tuesday morning.

"I wish I had been there," Ben said, brushing Cally's hair back from her face. "I hate this. I wish I didn't have to go, tonight. I wish I could think of a way to get out of it, for just one night. I wish I could at least get out of attending the Thing..."

"There's nothing you can do, anyway." Cally said, putting a hand over his. "And there was nothing you could have done last night, either, even if you had been here."

"I could have just been here for you," he said, and turned to face the window again, squeezing her against him with one arm while they continued to stare silently across the street at the fluttering crime scene tape. Cally knew she should say something more. She should tell him she loved him, she thought, but then thought better of it. This wasn't exactly a romantic setting, after all, and anyway she still wasn't sure what she was so unsure of.

"It's just," Ben was continuing, "there hasn't been a murder in this town in such a long time. Even I wasn't born yet, the last time anything like this happened." He shook his head as he spoke. "And whoever did do it – because it was *not* Ignacio – is still out there, walking around in Woodley, and that doesn't feel right at all...

"What does Nell say?" he asked, suddenly turning to look at Cally.

Cally glanced down the street toward the coffee shop and sighed. "She says she's painting a mural of waterfalls and stars, and that she won't be available for comment until it's done. I think she's probably protecting herself from having to think about it."

"That's too bad," Ben said, as if he thought Nell were the one person who would be able to offer useful insight into the problem.

Bree hung up the phone. "Hey!" she called across the store.

"Whatever it is, dear sister," said Ben, "I've already done it."

Cally smiled up at him and whispered, "I'd better go, before I get you into trouble."

"More trouble, you mean." The sorrow in his face gave way to his brilliant, blue-eyed grin for a moment, and Cally smiled to see it, in spite of herself, as she kicked the door open.

18 - Adam

Cally used her own key to let herself into Vale House through the side door into the service porch, so that she could take the shortcut to Ian and Sofie's quarters. Sofie seemed unchanged, but Ian, slumped beside her in his chair, didn't look anything near as positive as he tried to sound. He carefully assured Cally everything would be worked out by the end of the day, or by morning at latest. Cally didn't feel it would do him any good if she were to belabor the point that even if Ignacio's name were cleared, there would still be a murderer freely walking around in Woodley.

"Do you need anything, Sofie?" she asked as she turned to leave the room.

The old woman smiled, but didn't say anything, not even about the sunshine. "I'll be nearby," Cally assured her and Ian as she turned to leave.

As she crossed the service porch between the south wing and the parlor, she paused. Instead of going straight through the parlor to the Hall, she walked to the corner of the room where the walls were composed mainly of tall windows meeting at the southeast corner. Here, the big console television sat mostly unused, its old broadcast-type system unable to receive modern digital signals.

Glancing around to make sure nobody was watching, she stooped in front of the set and powered it on. As the screen crackled to staticky life, she sat on the edge one of the sofas and picked up the control box, switching channels slowly, as she had seen Nell do. The quality of the static on the screen sometimes changed, from channel to channel, and occasionally organized itself into diagonal bands, but nothing like a face appeared in the gray snow.

"Melissa?" Cally asked in a low whisper, feeling foolish and self-conscious, hoping Bethany couldn't hear her. She stared, and cocked her head, and squinted, but she couldn't make out anything resembling a woman's face. "Melissa, it's me, Cally. I'm Emerald's friend, and Nell's."

There was no reply she could discern amid the hissing of the static. She tried switching to a few other channels but, though she did find one broadcasting the hazy image and voice of a televangelist, she didn't manage to raise anyone named Melissa.

"I'll try again later," she promised the spirit Nell had often assured her did indeed exist within the old device, then she reached out to switch the power off. The static on the screen dimmed down to a tiny square which slowly shrank to a point as she turned to leave the room. Melissa probably wouldn't have any answers to the kinds of questions she had at the moment, anyway.

As she left the parlor and stepped into the Hall, she thought she heard a tiny, birdlike voice behind her say something that sounded very much like, "You must head him off at the portal!" When she turned back, though, she saw only the white dot of light in the middle of the screen winking out at last.

She took her phone out onto the porch with her and sat on the bottom step. Here she attempted to text the news to Emerald from her phone, swearing every time the tiny keyboard made her have to go back and un-correct something. Behind her, the Captain's ghost snored, while Doctor Boojums sat companionably on the top step with his gray paws tucked under his chest.

"Do you miss little Cyndi?" she asked the ghost cat. He flicked an ear in her direction but didn't look up. "I do. Porches aren't the same without cats to sit on their railings. Living cats, I mean. No offense," she added, but Boo showed no sign of having been offended.

Movement in the meadow drew her eye and she looked up, expecting to see the three horses, white, black and chestnut, grazing in the golden autumn grass. Instead, a blond-haired boy stood there, leaning on the fence, grinning at her.

As soon as their eyes met he ran, in a flash of gold, to her left along the fence, down the hill toward the pond, and that was when

Cally realized he was the fox she had seen the morning before. She jumped off the step and followed him, though she didn't know why she would do such a thing or how any human on foot could ever catch up with even a normal fox, let alone one that was apparently some sort of shapeshifting, faerie fox.

He had stopped at the bottom of the hill, where the stream ran out from the pond to the culvert under the railroad trestle. There, he turned and waited, smiling at her as she crashed through the undergrowth of young birches surrounding the pond. He did not, as she half expected, turn back into a fox and dash away.

He could have been anywhere between nine and twelve, and he was nearly naked, Cally observed, clothed in strips of rags that looked more like moss. Maybe they were moss? He didn't seem at all self-conscious about this. Just like a fox, he was poised lightly on his toes, ready to disappear in a blur at any moment, and Cally thought again that he looked like he was laughing at her. Or, she thought now, maybe not at her, but with her, as if they were sharing some incredibly amusing secret. She wished she knew what it was. She slowed down as the ground leveled out, and paused just opposite him on her own side of the fence, standing amid the clasper burrs and browned stems of summer's jewelweed.

"Hello..." she panted. How did one strike up a conversation with a fox-boy on the edge of a faerie meadow in the middle of the day? He stood still, gazing at her with laughing green eyes, and Cally wondered if he could speak at all. "Have you lived around here long?" she finally asked. It was a trite question, but it was better than standing there staring.

His grin grew even wider, if that was possible. Square, white teeth flashed in the sun and Cally thought it looked like his head might split at the ears if he smiled any harder. Yet, for all that, he was a strikingly handsome young man. His face was perfectly symmetrical with large, emerald green eyes and halo of golden curls backlit by the sun.

"I have not lived around here long at all," he said. "Not yet!" He threw back his head and laughed out loud at this, a rippling sound like silver bells under water. It echoed in the woods at the north edge of the meadow, causing a cloud of blackbirds to fly out into the sunlight. "Call me Adam," he added, nodding.

"Very pleased to meet you, Adam." Cally extended a hand, but not quite all the way. Her elbow remained bent, as if prepared to jerk her hand back should need arise suddenly. "You can call me Cally," she added.

He glanced at her hand but didn't make any move to reach back, himself. "'Tis a good Irish name," he said.

She wondered how he knew that, but only briefly. Everyone around here knew her full name and everything else about her, so why not the...Neighbors, as well?

"You don't have to worry," he went on. "I'm a vegetarian."

She looked at her still-extended hand, embarrassed that he seemed to have sensed her instinctive fear of being bitten by a wild creature. But he clarified: "I won't hurt Ignacio's chickens."

"Oh!" She withdrew her hand slowly, trying to make it look like offering a handclasp and then rescinding it unclaimed was a perfectly normal thing everyone did every day. "A vegetarian fox?" she asked before realizing that probably sounded rude. She tried out other questions in her mind: "Are there others like you?" "What are you, exactly?" but she thought these questions might be too intrusive to ask of a complete stranger.

Adam saved her the awkwardness of having to carry the conversation. "I'm one of the chickens!" he declared. He laughed again, then stopped when she gave him a puzzled look. "Sorry, was that a bad joke? I was referring to what Ben said: how the chickens come home to roost before a Thing."

Cally laughed, too, then, because it was a pretty good joke, in a topical sort of way, but she had to ask: "Have you been eavesdropping on my personal conversations?"

"I've been watching you!" he said enthusiastically and not apologetically at all. "You're amazing! I really hope you are going to stay here." He nodded toward Vale House. "I need you to. Please say you will!" He thrust his square-toothed grin closer to her face, very nearly causing her to step back and fall over into the weeds and muck.

"Well, Adam, I ... that is, I wasn't planning on going anywhere any time soon..."

Suddenly he swiveled his head around, as if he had heard something, and looked down the hill. His nostrils flared and Cally could swear his ears even twitched as he gazed into the culvert under the railroad trestle.

"I have to go!" he said then. "I can't let them see me yet. We will meet again!" He stepped backwards, turned away, and in three steps had blended into the ripples in the yellow grass.

Cally stood for a long time listening to the water gurgling between the rocks. "O...kay?" she said. "Adam."

19 - The Katarina Conspiracy

She picked burrs from her socks and the cuffs of her jeans as she returned up the hill, and as she came near the house, Cally was sure she could hear Ben's voice in the Hall. She ran up the porch steps to see him standing at the desk in the Hall, talking to Bethany. "But," he was saying, "Bree said you need some help today."

"Nonsense," said Bethany. "Why would she say that?"

"Might it be," he continued as Cally quietly entered the Hall, "because you telephoned her and said that, what with Ian being sick and Ignacio being incarcerated, you don't have enough hands to get all the work done during this busiest of seasons?"

Katarina stood in the dining room doorway with a large basket cradled in her arms. "Ignacio will be home tonight," she stated firmly. "They've got that Ms. Barry coming in, in a few hours, and she's going to look at Ignacio in the lineup and tell them he's not the person she saw in the alley at all."

Bethany nodded her agreement. "We merely asked Bree if we could borrow you for a few hours. We didn't tell her what we needed you for. In fact, I don't remember what we needed him for, do you, Katarina?"

"I do not," Katarina affirmed.

"So, Mr. Dawes, I guess you're free for a few hours to do whatever you want to do."

Ben shuffled his feet awkwardly, and Cally shook her head as she came to the front of the desk and put an arm through his. "I sense a conspiracy," she said.

"I've made you a picnic basket," Katarina said. "Pasta salad from last night, and pickles and cheese and some of the yellow apples from Ignacio's tree."

"Thank you, Kat," said Ben. "But you actually are short-handed, today, and I would be more than happy to..."

"I'll get you a blanket to take with you," Bethany interrupted, jumping up from her seat. "So grass and bugs won't get...everywhere!"

Cally sighed in exasperation as Bethany disappeared, giggling, into the parlor. "I believe you are right," Ben said, turning to Cally and smiling until the corners of his eyes crinkled. "We are caught in the midst of a conspiracy."

Katarina held the big willow basket out to him. He accepted it with a bow, and Cally gave Katarina a grateful smile. That was when she noticed the red and puffy rims around Katarina's eyes. She had been crying, and she knew Cally could see it, but a quick, dark look let Cally know that if she were to mention it, Katarina would not reply.

Bethany reappeared with one of the crocheted throws from the back of the sofa, and Ben held out his other arm for her to drape it over. "You ladies are too kind," he said. Bethany sat back down, and Katarina straightened her apron.

"Off with you, then," she said. "I have bread dough to get back to!"

Bethany answered the phone, even though it hadn't rung, and Ben held the door open for Cally.

"There actually is something I was hoping I could show you," he said as they crossed the porch. Cally looked across the lawn to the fence, and out into the meadow beyond it. The shadows of afternoon were beginning to stretch across the golden grass that swayed there in the breeze, and the three horses stood a long way off, not grazing but just standing, swishing their tails and looking toward the most distant of the hills.

Misreading the worry in Cally's expression, Ben explained quickly, "I'm not going to take you across to my mother's court or anything like that. I just wanted to show you a couple of turns in the road. Like that time when we went to Blackthorn-that-isn't-really-Blackthorn."

Any lingering traces of worry faded from Cally's face as she remembered that evening. She led the way down the steps and crossed to the fence. Slipping between the rails into the meadow, she turned to take the basket and blanket from Ben's hands so he could do the same.

"I would like to go back there again," she confessed, "and have another one of those wonderful hamburgers. But then we'd waste the nice picnic lunch Kat and Bethany so thoughtfully made for us." She laughed, quietly, to herself, because she knew the two conspirators had been hoping they were going to waste it.

Ben took the basket from Cally's hands and forged a wake through the tall grass. He headed east, or perhaps, Cally thought, maybe just a little north of east, through the open, sunny hills of the meadow. Showing the way through nods and gestures, he led her to the crest of a hill and pointed toward the horizon. "I think you can see that. Am I right?"

A little north of where the sun had risen that morning, one of the distant hills seemed just a little odd, sharper and more jagged than a hill should be. Squinting, Cally began to think it looked more like a city skyline. She thought it might have been the City she had seen on that strange summer night with Rum, except now it lay piled like translucent jewels in the sun atop the hill. The longer she looked, the brighter it shone, and she had to blink to stop it from starting to look like it was on fire.

"The City – the one the People call Shannish. Is that where we're going?"

Ben shook his head. "It's too early. Some roads only come out after the sun goes down. Like stars, I guess. Shannish lies across the second bridge, but you can see it now. That is, some people can, and I had a feeling you were one of them."

She shaded her eyes with her hand and gazed across to where it grew more vivid, the longer she looked. "I have always regretted chickening out, that night Rum tried to show me the way there. I still hope to try again someday."

He raised an eyebrow. "It's... well, I'm sure you already know this but, it's not a good idea to try that sort of thing alone."

"I absolutely do know that," said Cally. "Who would ever do anything that foolish?" She winked and walked past him.

"I wasn't trying to advise you against it," he said, catching up. "I know better than that! I just felt obligated to share my experience, is all."

"I thank you for that, and I promise I will keep it in mind. Now what was it you did want to show me?"

"Something a lot closer than Shannish."

Cally turned around and looked behind her. She could still see Vale House in the distance, but it stood alone in the midst of a wide, empty field. The fence, the barn, the oak trees and all the rest of Woodley had vanished. "I'm sorry," she said. "I didn't pay attention to how we got here."

"No, I'm sorry," Ben said. "I should have been pointing out landmarks. I'm afraid I'm not as good a teacher as Errin."

Cally laughed. "You're a much better teacher than Errin! You have not taken any years off my life yet with your teaching methods!"

"It's just a little further." He was looking around at the ground behind him, then up toward the sky. Cally followed his gaze but didn't see anything aside from yellow grass and blue sky. Finally, cocking his head to one side, he placed his hands on Cally's shoulders as if they were going to dance. "If it's okay with you, maybe we can take a little shortcut." When she nodded, he said "Stay close to me," and stepped backward.

She did her best to follow him as he turned around, and then turned again. She almost thought she could see the path his feet were tracking, a pale pattern under the grass atop the hill, flowing underfoot like a letter in an unfamiliar alphabet. The landscape around them seemed to shift in her peripheral vision. Some of the hills grew taller and others moved further away, though Cally was sure she and Ben never moved more than a few feet from where they had started.

He stopped suddenly, and Cally bumped into him, something she did not mind doing. "You might want to close your eyes for this part," he advised, preparing to take one more step.

She looked up at him. "I don't want to close my eyes."

He put his arms around her, swinging them both in a wide circle. Cally saw the sky above his face grow impossibly close overhead, and the ground reared up all around them like a tawny wave. She lost her balance completely and saw her feet go flying from under her. Then she landed in cool, green grass, with the contents of the basket tumbling around her knees. Ben was kneeling beside her, supporting her as best he could while he laughed and apologized.

"Okay, I should have closed my eyes," she admitted.

"You did fine." He stopped laughing and gathered up the little plastic containers, putting them back into the basket while Cally looked around. They appeared to be on the same hilltop they had started on – the city, Shannish, was still visible in the same spot, and just as distant. The hills around them, however, were no longer covered in dry autumn grass. Now they were green, with occasional drifts of color where wildflowers sprung up through them, just as they had when Cally had first arrived in Woodley. A semi-circle of myrtle trees, covered in ivy and jasmine, crowned the hill and blocked her view of the direction from which they had come.

Ben spread the blanket on the ground at the feet of the myrtles so that their branches, dripping with jasmine blossoms, overhung it. Sitting down, he reached a hand up to her. "What do you think?"

She sat beside him and looked around.

"It looks like..." She searched for words. "It looks like it's not October anymore. Did we move somewhere else in time?" This would not have surprised her.

"Not really," he said. "It's just that it's always spring, here." He stretched one hand out toward the sky. "Can you feel it?"

She wasn't sure what he meant by that. All she felt was that the air was warmer and the wind gentler than it had been. Different birds were singing different songs.

He withdrew his hand and hugged his knees. Looking toward the distant city on the hill, he said: "I used to come here all the time. Back when I first started to learn the roads. It was the first place I ever found. There's a stream at the foot of this hill, but..."

"But don't drink the water," she finished for him, smiling.

He laughed and drew her in front of him, so that she sat with her back leaning against his chest. Putting his arms around her and pressing a cheek against her hair, he gestured out toward the land surrounding them.

"This is the *bhaille*, before us, all around us. The *bhaille*, the vale – the homeland, it means, the familiar place. The stomping grounds. And heavens know I've stomped over every inch it since I was a younger man."

"I wish I could have known you then," Cally said. "I imagine you were quite the handsome rake."

"I was a rake, certainly. It's probably just as well. You would not have liked me very much, then. I was still very angry. I still had a lot of growing up to do.

"Beyond Shannish," he went on, "sheer cliffs plunge down to the sea, and at the base of them is a harbor where ships made of beech and ash lie at anchor, waiting to set sail to other ... *bhailles*. Along one arm of that harbor is a truly beautiful forest, and this is where my mother holds her Court. At the end of the other arm of the harbor is Thingol, the Thing Hill, where everyone will meet two nights from now."

Cally thought about Ian's fishing boat, now grounded on the bank of his pond. She wondered if he knew there was actually a sea so close at hand, into which he could launch it to do some real fishing.

"Are we in the shadow lands, then? In Faerie?"

"Not quite. This is a special place, separate from either world. I'm not sure whether I found it, or actually created it for myself. Nobody else ever comes here. Just me – and now you.

"And, Cally, as you already know, it's not safe to eat food you find in Faerie. But here, at least, it's perfectly safe for us to eat the food we brought with us."

Cally nodded, but she wasn't especially interested in food at the moment. Neither, apparently, was he. She nestled back into his arms and closed her eyes, feeling the warmth of the sun on them and listening to the breeze in the branches above. With her eyes shut, she could almost see the path they'd taken to get here. "You know," she said, "I think I could find this place again on my own. It feels familiar. Is that what you meant when you asked me if I could feel it?" He didn't answer, but she was content with his silence. Eyes still shut, she took in a deep breath of the jasmine scented air. "This isn't nearly as scary as it was when Errin showed me how to do it in a vehicle traveling sixty miles per hour."

She loved the way it felt when he laughed. She wanted very much to turn around and face him, but she didn't want to break the magic of this moment.

"It's not for me to tell you what to do," he finally said. "But please believe I know what I'm talking about when I say it would be perilous for you to try to go to the City without someone else who has been there before. Me, or Rum, or whoever." When she didn't reply, he added, "I know better than to ask you to promise me you won't. But at least please be very careful if you do. They are tricky and manipulative. They will pull all kinds of tricks to try to get you to stay."

"It never worked on you," she pointed out.

"No. No, it never worked on me."

"Would it really be so bad? To get stuck and have to stay there, I mean."

He thought a moment before he answered. "You'll feel the difference. When we go back from here, you'll notice it. You'll feel the difference between here and... home. This." He swept his arms open, gesturing out toward the green fields in front of them, to the City and all that lay beyond it. "This is very pretty, very magical. But it isn't home."

Cally opened her eyes and she was sure the City had definitely grown closer – she could clearly make out individual doors and windows on all the buildings, but their shapes were oddly distorted. The way they didn't quite square up made her feel queasy if she looked at them too long.

"Can they see us from there?" she asked.

"They can't see us," he said, definitively. "They can't see this place at all. This is my place. And yours, now."

She did turn around to face him, then. She laid her hands on his shoulders, meaning to kiss him, but he didn't move any closer to her. His face had grown serious.

"Cally," he said, and turned his eyes away, looking past her over the hills.

He said nothing further, and didn't move.

"Ben?"

He shook himself as if waking from a dream, turning back to look into her eyes. "I hate this," he said. "No, not this! Just that I know I'm starting something I can't finish. That's dastardly; I hate myself for it."

She drew back from him. This was a song she had heard before. "Is this the 'it's not you, it's me' speech?" she asked. "Are you dumping me now, or something?"

"What? No!" he reached for her with both hands, pulling her tight into his arms. "Oh, no, no, no!" He spoke into her hair. "My god, I could never get away from you now, even if I tried. But I hate what I'm going to put you through, someday..."

She lifted her arms to encircle him, and felt his ribs expanding and contracting in deep gulps of breath.

"What *we're* going to put me through," she corrected, pulling back so she could make him look at her. "We're in this together. I mean, it's not as if you've ever told me anything but the truth. My eyes are open." She paused so he could see that they were, both literally and figuratively. "I am fully aware that you are going to have to go away and break my heart one day. It's already broken, so let's just enjoy the time we have together. And whatever Bree may say about it be damned, too."

The serious look melted out of his face, at that, and he laughed. "I don't care what Bree, or anyone but you, thinks. As far as I'm concerned, you *are* the Queen of Faerie. Of everything else, too."

"I think the actual Queen of Faerie might have something to say about that..." Cally began, but he stopped her lips with his own, and neither of them said anything more for a long while after that.

—

The sun was setting behind the sheltering half-circle of trees. Cally sat up and watched Ben sleeping, carefully reaching out to gather her clothes without disturbing him. He always had an easy grace about him, she thought, but she had never seen him so peaceful as he was then in his sleep. She knew they would have to leave, soon, and go back to the ordinary world, but she wanted to stay longer, just watching him, and she wondered if there was a place, maybe a place he knew how to find, where time never passed at all. Maybe she would look into that herself, one day soon. She took one of Katarina's brownies from the basket and bit into it contemplatively.

Then she saw he was awake and watching her. His eyes looked like reflections of the darkening sky overhead.

"I'm sorry," he said. "I haven't done that in a long time."

She laughed. "You have nothing to be sorry about!"

He sat up, laughing as well. "No, I mean, well, that too. But I meant sleep. I don't often get a chance to."

"You never sleep? My god." Katarina had joked about it, but Cally had never truly understood that, between putting in his appearance in the Faerie Court at night and working in Bree's shop during the day, Ben not only never had time for a personal life, but also literally had no time to sleep. She put the brownie down. "That's...appalling!"

"It's okay," he assured her. "When you spend as much time in Faerie as I do, you don't really need sleep."

"But you do," she insisted, remembering how peaceful he had looked. "I'm glad we gave you a chance to sleep today, anyway."

"I am, too." The way he smiled as he reached across the blanket to retrieve his shirt made her think he wasn't talking about sleep. "I should have taken the opportunity to eat, as well," he added. "But it's getting late."

"No, you eat." Cally opened one of the little plastic containers. It contained a serving of Katarina's excellent pasta salad. "We can't have you going into Faerie hungry." She handed him a fork.

She sat close to him, watching him eat as the air grew cooler around them and the sun sank lower.

"I have just about enough time to walk you home, before I go," he said at last.

She looked over her shoulder at the lowering sun. "No," she said. "You know what? I think I can find it on my own."

Standing, she turned and squinted through the trees behind them. "I'm sure I can." She felt, more than saw, where Vale House lay. She felt it the way one could feel their way around in the dark in a familiar house. It wasn't very far at all.

"Let's consider this practice," she said, making up her mind. "I'll go this way, and you go that way. If I get lost, and I don't think I will, I'll call to Rum for help. He's always told me he'll help me if I just call, and he's made good on his word at least once." She gathered up the basket and blanket as he stood, giving her one of his careful looks. "I'm sure Katarina and Bethany are not expecting me back tonight anyway." She handed him a yellow apple to take with him on his way. "Ben. We'll both be okay. You'll see."

"Yes," he said, shaking his head with a smile. "We will."

She couldn't tell, from his voice, whether he was certain of this or had merely decided it wasn't worth trying to argue with her about it. He sounded as certain as he ever did, though, when he took her in his arms and said, "I'll see you in the morning."

He gave her a long kiss before he released her to turn away, heading outward into the darkening, grassy hills just as he did every evening. The only difference, this time, was that there was no fence standing between them.

It was practice, alright, Cally thought. She would have to walk away from him for good, one day, and she would make herself practice every day until then, else she might not be able to do it at all when the time came. She headed in the opposite direction, through the crescent of myrtles and down the hill toward where the sky still glowed dull red in the west – toward where she was certain Vale House lay. When she got to the bottom of the hill, she looked back and could no longer see the springtime trees at the top. The grass around her feet was tall and brown. When she crested the next hill, she could see Vale House's porch light, already on and twinkling welcomingly against the backdrop of the street lights of Woodley. A chill autumn breeze dried the tears on her face.

21 - Horror Movies

Cally braced herself for some good-natured "walk of shame" ribbing as she entered Vale House, but this changed immediately to concern as she passed through the empty Hall. A low susurrus of chatting guests drifted in from the parlor, but neither Bethany nor Katarina could be seen peeping from around any corners at her return.

She supposed Bethany had already gone home for the evening, and she felt a pang of sorrow that Katarina would probably be eating her dinner alone tonight. Cally had to return the picnic basket to the kitchen anyway – she made up her mind to keep Katarina company for as long as she needed that night.

She paused at the desk, on her way to the dining room, to make sure the phones had been switched into night mode. They had not been, and she reached to correct this, then swore out loud when she looked up from the console to see Eddie Tiene leering at her.

"Hi, Kili! I wonder if I can ask you something!"

"Mr. Tiene, only you know what you can and cannot do."

He gave her a blank look, then rolled his eyes. "Ah. Ha ha. Always the English nerd," he said. "Well, if I *may* ask you, then. Why do you keep such an old TV in that room there?" He pointed back toward the parlor. "It isn't internet ready – it's hardly any use to any of your customers anymore. Why don't you replace it with something more modern?"

Cally had to admit he had a point. The old television had only been kept around at Nell's insistence, but Nell didn't live at Vale

House anymore. Cally still hoped she could figure out how to talk to Melissa through the old TV herself someday, but to Eddie she just said, "It's more in keeping with Vale House's rustic aesthetic." She smiled as congenially as she could.

"Well." He nodded, reaching into his pocket. "It just so happens, I also deal in electronics." He handed her yet another of his business cards. "I would be happy to provide this establishment with a brand-new high definition, internet-ready home theater system at my wholesale cost. Your guests would be able to stream horror movies in Full Splatter! And, for no additional fee, my delivery men will also haul away that old hulk of yours and dispose of it."

Cally took the card and said, "Thank you for offering. I'll ask my boss about it."

The smile disappeared from his face and he glared at her, as if he could tell she was lying. She put the card in the desk drawer and, for good measure, so she really wouldn't be lying, she promised she would give it to Ian at her earliest opportunity. She knew his response would be to trash the card himself.

Eddie Tiene seemed satisfied with this and went upstairs to the Dogwood Room. Cally put her head inside the parlor to remind the guests there to feel free to help themselves to anything on the sideboard. She laughed when she saw Katarina at the other end of the room, where she had just come through the doorway from the service porch to remind them of the same thing.

Katarina did not laugh, however. Instead she silently beckoned Cally to follow her. Leaving the picnic basket on the settle in the service porch, Cally followed the woman down the back hall to Ian's quarters.

"Is Ian alright?" she whispered anxiously as they went. "Is Sofie getting worse?"

"No, no, Ian is fine and so is Sofie," Katarina said. "Well, as fine as can be expected, anyway. No, it's just, the sheriff called while you were gone."

"Oh..." Cally peered past Katarina into the proprietor's study. Bethany had not gone home, after all. She was seated opposite Ian in one of the wingback chairs near the fireplace. Cally stepped into the room, dreading what she knew he was about to say.

Ian looked up at her. "Ignacio has been formally charged with Foster's murder," he said, not even waiting for her to sit down in one of the other chairs. When she did sit, she nearly missed the chair. Bethany leaned over and put a hand over hers. "Ms. Danya Barry from the ghost hunting outfit positively identified Ignacio in the lineup," Ian continued. "The detectives also say other evidence has come to light, but Dunn isn't at liberty to tell me what it is. He suggests we engage a lawyer."

Cally swore softly and repeatedly. "I am so sorry." She looked at Katarina, who still stood in the doorway, her face expressionless. "I should never have told that woman it was alright for her to come back to this house. Damn all ghost hunters to..."

"We mustn't blame her," Ian insisted in his usual gentle tone. "Ms. Barry is merely cooperating with authorities, as any good citizen would do. We know it could not have been Ignacio, but she must report what she saw, to the best of her ability. The poor young lady has been through a very traumatic experience."

"Traumatic!" Bethany jumped to her feet. "Not as traumatic as what Katarina and Ignacio are going through! Ian, I hope you are going to send your own lawyer to help him!"

"Mr. Reid's practice on Railroad Street only handles family law and real-estate," Ian explained patiently. "But I'm sure he can recommend a criminal defense lawyer. First, however, we must post Ignacio's bail and get him home where he belongs. I was told the bail has been set very high. It's going to tie up all the available funds I have, but I have complete faith Ignacio's good name will be cleared. Bethany, if you would be so good as to drive me down to Blackthorn first thing in the morning, I will talk to my bank manager about pulling the funds together."

"Speaking of what Katarina is going through," Cally asked, "Where did she go?"

—

Katarina was not in the kitchen, where Bethany had supposed she must be. Cally almost ran out the back door to the little stone cottage, but she paused and turned back. On the way to the kitchen, she had noticed the narrow door to the backstairs was open. She turned and went back to this.

She could hear the sobbing before she even reached the top of the narrow stairs, as the stairwell shared a wall with the Wisteria room. Usually it was guests in this room who would report hearing "mysterious noises" in the wall, as most people were unaware the backstairs even existed. This time, truly haunting sounds came through the wall in the opposite direction.

She stepped into the upstairs hallway and shut the backstairs door, turning to put a hand on the knob of the next door over, the one with a botanical print of a blooming wisteria vine in an oval frame. She wasn't sure whether she should disturb Katarina or let her have her privacy. After a moment's hesitation, she opened the door and stepped softly inside.

Katarina was kneeling, her back to Cally, beside the freshly-made bed, used sheets piled in a basket beside her. Her arms stretched across the coverlet, one hand clutching a rosary, and her face was pressed into the mattress as her body convulsed with sobs that shook the whole bed.

"Kat..." Cally stepped partway into the room. "I'm so sorry."

Katarina didn't look up, but she drew in her arms and pressed the rosary to her breast. "It's going to be alright," she said into the mattress. "God is in control."

Cally waited long enough to realize Katarina was holding her breath, holding in her sobs until she could release them unwatched. Leaving behind just one caring touch on the Katarina's shoulder, she backed out the door and shut it behind her. As she descended the main stairs down to the Hall, she couldn't help wondering just which god was in control, and whose side it was on.

22 - Lights

The guests in the parlor, having given up on the old television, had retreated to their rooms. Cally switched off the parlor lights and went into her office.

Sitting down on the sofa she had been using as a makeshift bed, she glared up at the ceiling, uncomfortably aware that Eddie Tiene was up there, separated from her only by the locked door to the spiral stairs. Maybe it was just her general mood at the moment, but she could swear she felt his presence, like some kind of dark electrical field, right through the joists and plaster as he moved about the room above her. She didn't think she would ever be able to feel at home in the Dogwood Room again. She sighed and wished she at least had her computer back so she could chat with Emerald until she grew drowsy.

Digging her phone out of her purse, she started to compose a text message to Emerald, but after the third time the auto-correct function changed "arraignment" to "arrangement" she gave up in disgust and threw the device back into its nest of crumpled receipts and dried-out pens. Then, hanging her purse on the closet doorknob, she went back out into the Hall and locked the office door behind her. The key to the office she hid under the mulch in one of the potted ficus trees beside the door as she slipped out onto the porch.

The Captain's ghost was there, as usual, dozing in the wicker chair next to the door, but she didn't pause to speak to him. She had no idea what she was doing, or why, but she did not hesitate once her feet hit the porch steps. She walked straight to the fence, ducked between the railings and set out across the meadow into the night.

She came first to the myrtle bower atop the hill, where she and Ben had so recently been. She was surprised at how easy it was for her to find, having expected to make several false starts, and she couldn't wait to tell Ben she had done it. By the light of the waxing moon, she could still see the impression in the spring grass where they had spread their blanket. She knelt and pressed her palms against the ground there, thinking maybe she could spend the night here, blanket or no. It was peaceful, here, and warm. She could sleep in a place where no creepy former bully was pacing back and forth above her head, where nobody she loved was dying or weeping over injustices she was helpless to rectify.

As soon as her gaze drifted across to the flamelike glow atop the furthest hill, though, she knew she would not be staying anywhere that night. The feeling of warmth and peace fell from her like a discarded garment, and when she heard the swishing of the dry autumn grasses passing beneath her feet, she realized she had already begun to walk toward the City.

She didn't understand why, and she didn't pause to wonder. She certainly knew better than to expect she would find Ben, out here, and in fact she hoped she wouldn't encounter him, after all his warnings to her not to try this alone. All she knew was that, despite all the excuses she had been giving herself ever since she had arrived in Woodley, she had always been meant to go there. She was fed up with making excuses and with watching things happen over which she had no control. She was going to make some things happen, herself, for a change, even if she had no idea what.

As it always did, the City seemed to grow nearer and clearer the longer she looked at it. She had a feeling it would do so even if she weren't walking toward it. It was the only landmark she knew, out here; she visualized a beeline across the hilltops, with Shannish at its end. It occurred to her she really could – and probably should – have asked Rum to come with her, but she didn't want to turn around to go back for him now.

She paused at the crest of the second hill, careful not to turn and look behind her. A hollow sensation between her shoulder blades let her know she would not see the reassuring glow of the Vale House porch lights, now, if she did turn, and this might cause her to panic and run aimlessly back into the darkness, never to be found again.

The moon had moved higher into the sky. It was full enough to cast her shadow in the grass, like the shadow of a sun dial gnomon pointing west, but a scattering of stars was still visible in spite of its brightness. The night noises were different, this time of year. Nighthawks no longer called from hilltop to hilltop, but the grass was alive with the ringing buzz of crickets and katydids and other insects whose species Cally had never learned. They had been growing louder and louder every night, lately, as if they knew this was their last chance to be heard before the frost arrived to silence them.

Ahead, she could see the City clearly now, warm yellows and oranges glowing in the individual windows of the oddly rounded buildings whose walls appeared to possess their own luminescence. Even though this whole scenario still lay a long way ahead, Cally thought she could make out individual figures, passing by inside the windows or walking between the buildings. The little valleys were filling up with figures holding candles or torches.

Without taking her eyes from the lights, she stepped off the hilltop, but the far slope was much steeper than she was expecting. Her foot landed on empty air and she stumbled, sliding down over the crackling grass, bumping over the lumps in the ground. She finally came to a halt near the bottom where the ground began to level out at the edge of a narrow, dark stream.

She stood slowly. The water chuckled softly over the rocks at her feet and she understood instinctively that she should not touch it or attempt to jump across it, narrow as it seemed. This, she reminded herself, was a fairy stream. She stood teetering on the bank, shaking with relief that she had not fallen in. Maybe she should have waited for Ben to show her the way, after all, or Rum, or even Errin.

But she had never been good at doing things the way she had been told to. She brushed the torn grass and earth from clothes and turned to follow the whispering water downstream. This brought her ever closer to the lights of the City, and by the time she reached a bridge, the lights were almost directly across the stream from her. Shannish sparkled on the hill above and she could see its reflection wavering weirdly in the water.

The bridge was little more than three rough boards cobbled together and thrown across from bank to bank. She hesitated, wishing there were a hand-rail.

"Don't be ridiculous," she told herself. "It can't be more than six inches above the ground, and anyway it's only one step. Two, at most."

Still, she had to hold her breath and keep her eyes carefully fastened on the lighted buildings at the top of the hill as she steeled herself to step quickly over. It occurred to her that it still might not be too late to call to Rum for help.

When her feet touched the ground on the other side, the People walking in the City stopped whatever they had been doing and turned their glittering rainbow eyes to Cally, all moving as one toward her now. They did not look, Cally thought, like the same people she had seen that night, long ago, dancing with Ben. They were not nearly so terribly beautiful, or beautifully terrible, though they were still graceful as deer as they stepped away from their glowing streets and flowed toward her through the high, dry grass.

She let go of the handrail. There was a handrail. There was a handrail? She turned and saw a beautifully carved railing, like the one on the grand staircase at Vale House, running along one edge of a white bridge which leaped, in a single, graceful arch, back over a dark canyon to where it landed on the opposite bank many yards away. It glimmered like bone against the dark bulk of the hills. Water roared through the depths of the darkness beneath it, and Cally grasped again for the railing, feeling as if she were already falling down and down between the stone walls toward the roaring dark waters below.

"Here, hang on!"

The People had reached the slope of the hill just above her, and one of them, much shorter than all the others and clad all in white, had run from the crowd to her side. He took her hand and tugged her away from the edge. His hand felt thin and raspy in hers.

"There you are. Just look at us, now." The little man winked at her, and Cally thought he resembled Rum. He didn't look like him, physically, being paler and much less rough around the edges, but his voice was similar, and he did have a white beard that reached nearly to his feet.

The People continued to gather closer until they surrounded her on all sides, blocking her view of the bridge and the bank on the other side. They were not carrying candles and torches. The light she had seen, at a distance, came from their faces.

They all looked very much alike, to Cally, mostly androgynous, and all about the same height. Their garments were also all similar, long and flowing in myriad pale colors, though to Cally they didn't appear to be garments made of cloth so much as extensions of these People's bodies. It was impossible to tell their age - they all had smooth, youthful skin the color of moonlight and deep, ancient eyes. Those eyes silently scanned every detail of Cally's being: her clothes, her expression, her breath - nothing escaped their notice. The only individual she could distinguish among them was her small companion. He must be Rum, she thought. She was almost sure of it. If it was him, though, she didn't want to admit she didn't recognize him, so she refrained from asking.

They stood silently, waiting for her to say something, she guessed, but she had failed to think this far ahead. Her first words to them would be important - she should have had something prepared. She sensed they already knew her name. She would have told them her business, if she knew what it was. Finally, she said "Your City is beautiful." At least that came from her heart.

In response, they murmured all at once in words she couldn't quite make out, closing in around her, to her growing alarm. But their touch was gentle as they laid hands on her arms and clothes and hair, and the press of their bodies began to move her up the hill with them toward the lights. Somewhere behind her she thought the Little Man Who Might Be Rum said, "Got your back."

She had read Biblical references to a City of Gold, with walls made of gemstones. This City's streets resembled gold, but when she stepped onto them, the surface yielded under her feet almost like flesh. She felt like she was committing some kind of gross sacrilege by walking on it with shoes, and thought she should stop and take them off, to go barefoot as they did. Then she thought better of it. She might discover it really was flesh, and then she didn't know what she might do.

The walls between which they passed glowed from within as if the buildings themselves were gigantic lanterns of colored glass or flower petals. All the corners were softly rounded, and no seams or joints were visible. The buildings arose directly from the golden streets as if they had sprouted there.

Turning a corner, Cally and her escorts arrived at the wide, well-lit doorway of a broad building whose walls glowed deep red like garnet. Here she was drawn inside by dozens of hands, with the little man going on ahead of her. A long, sapphire-colored table filled most of the interior, and Cally was ushered to a seat at the center of this.

Lanterns were lit, and candles were brought, and light was layered upon light as People dashed back and forth with cups and plates. A platter of colorful little cakes was set before Cally, and a golden mug of something with a creamy head. Cally looked up to see Probably Rum sitting across the table from her. He winked and popped a couple of the cakes into his mouth, then washed them down with a long gulp from his own gem-studded goblet. He never took his gaze off Cally, and his eyes danced with mischief as if he were saying, "I dare you."

Cally wrapped her hands around her mug, but she didn't drink. As the People all settled into their seats and into some semblance of silence, she remembered to say, "I've brought you a present."

The voices grew silent, then, and all eyes turned to watch her reach into her pocket. She felt self-conscious when she withdrew Nell's little clay ornament and placed it on the table. It looked terribly dull and mundane amid these bright and fantastic surroundings. But it was meaningful to Cally, made by someone she loved, and she understood now that this was why Nell had given it to her. One must never, both Nell and Emerald had often reminded her, enter Faerie without a gift to give.

The People around her reacted as if it were a very good gift indeed. They gasped in awe, and a young man (at least, he seemed vaguely male to Cally) snatched it up and held it aloft. Others took it from him and it disappeared into the crowd; Cally could track its movement though the room by its tinkling and by the gasps of delight wherever it went.

Someone on the other side of the table spoke up, then. "But what we were really hoping for was a story!" Cally thought this Person might, perhaps, be a woman, and older than most of the others present, though she wasn't sure why as she looked carefully at the luminous features.

"Don't worry," laughed the old woman. "You humans all look the same to us, too!" Those around her laughed.

Cally had a feeling she was the butt of a joke, so she chose not to address this. She asked, "What kind of story would you like?"

while she mentally sorted through all the stories she had read over the years. She wondered if some part of *The Hobbit* could be boiled down into a ten-minute yarn.

"Oh, we've heard all those already," said a younger Person behind her. "What we would really enjoy would be a story from your own life. Something that really makes you feel something - something that will make us cry."

Cally could think of a lot of stories about her life that made her feel things, and especially ones that had made her cry or were going to make her cry someday, but the main thing that had been keeping her on the verge of tears lately was Ignacio, jailed for a crime he hadn't committed, and Katarina alone and weeping silently behind her brave face. She didn't think it made a very entertaining story, though, especially since she couldn't think of an ending that wouldn't be just plain dismal.

"Oh, yes, that one!" said several People. "That's the one we want to hear. Tell us!"

She turned her hands palm upward and shrugged. "I'll do my best," was all she could promise. Then she told them.

She told them the story of a pair of young lovers, poor but very much in love, who were unable to be together because of the necessity for the young man to travel to another country in order to make money to send home to his family. Their tale had a happy arc in the middle, wherein the couple's fortunes changed and they were able to travel to a new land and earn an honest living together. They were unable to have children of their own, but they loved and cared for the child of their wealthy benefactor. Their happiness was cut short, however, by a selfish villain whose greedy, grasping machinations could not even, in the end, be stopped by his own death.

Cally admitted she didn't know how the story ended but, she told her rapt audience, she did know one thing: "Their love, and the happiness they have shared with everyone around them, are more powerful than any evil, and in the end, love will conquer all."

She choked out the last few words and hoped they were true. The room erupted into cheering and applause. Fists pounded the table; glasses were raised and drained amid calls for more drinks all around. Cally felt this was a rather inappropriate response to her story, but she was relieved that she had, apparently, passed the test.

The People's attention turned away from her as some of them, on the far side of the room, began to play music while others got up to dance. Rum - if it was Rum - sat silently opposite Cally, grinning his approval.

Cally met his gaze and took a deep breath, gulping past the lump in her throat. She didn't look away as she grasped the mug in front of her and raised it to her lips.

In a movement so fast she couldn't see it, he jumped across the table and knocked her from her chair. The crowd around them became even more raucous, laughing and pointing. He grasped her by the collar with one hand and dragged her effortlessly out the door and into the street, where he stood over her glowering and shaking his fist. "Don't you ever!" he said. "Don't you ever do that...!"

Cally laughed and sat up, brushing leaves and twigs (she had no idea where they had come from, as the street was immaculate) from her clothes. "Don't worry," she said. "I wouldn't really have drunk it. But oh, you should have seen your face!" She stood up and straightened her clothing. "I needed that. Thank you!"

He growled under his breath, glaring at her and stroking his beard thoughtfully, and as he did, he began more and more to resemble the old black man in dingy overalls, the Rum, or Jerome, with whom Cally was more familiar. She thought how ironic it was that this bizarre old earth spirit, of all things, now felt to her like a welcome touch of home. As if she even had a home.

Finally, he said, "Understand me, Callaghan McCarthy. You can drink of the draught if you choose to. And those little cakes are not half bad, for something made of moonlight and moss. But if you ever eat or drink here, be sure you have made your choice well, for you can never un-make it. I do not believe in interfering with a mortal's free will, and this is the last time I will ever try to stop you from being stupid."

"Oh, Rum, I know. I know." She looked at him standing in the light spilling from the noisy doorway, and she wanted to hug him. Something about the dark street reminded her of the old-time version of Blackthorn outside The Fountain, and that made her think of Ben. She looked forward to telling Ben how she had tricked the great Trickster Rum, if only for a second.

Then she did hug the little old man. He felt like a bag of sticks, and he smelt of barbecue sauce. Behind him, from within the crowded room they had just left, she heard the People's voices rise in a cheer.

Rum turned to squint into the brightness. "That," he told Cally, "was the People all coming to a consensus. They have decided to champion Ignacio's cause."

Cally was gratified to hear this, though she couldn't imagine what these gentle People could do for Ignacio, across so many borders and in such a completely different world. It was enough to know they cared and, as she gazed along the glowing street into the darkness of what she was not sure was the west, she wondered how she, herself would find her way back to that world. Woodley was, she remembered, always difficult to find from the outside, even under ordinary circumstances.

"I don't know what I set out to accomplish tonight," she said to Rum, "but maybe I accomplished it. Um... now would you be so good as to show me how to get back to Vale House?"

"I?" He seemed to come out of very deep thought as his eyes focused on her. "You don't need my help with that. Don't go playing stupid with me, now. You can't pretend, anymore."

"But..." Cally knew she had got herself into this and that Rum didn't owe it to her to get her out of it. "Well, it's just that Woodley doesn't glow like Shannish does." She gave him her best disarming smile. "If you could just point me in the right direction."

He took her by the hand, but he still shook his head. "Not me. There's someplace else I need to be, tonight, and anyway there is someone you must meet, now that you're here." He led her down a dark side street, heading in the one direction she was sure was not the right one. "He can show you the way."

He drew her along a narrow lane illuminated only by the flickering lights inside topaz and sapphire walls. The noise of partying People faded behind them, until they emerged into the grass of the rolling dark hills. Rum stopped just outside the reach of the City's lights and looked up, pointing, to where Cally could see a fire burning at the top of the next hill over.

"Go there," he said, releasing her hand and putting up a finger to silence her protest. "I can't go with you. You'll be alright. You don't even have to keep your wits about you, this time, though you've never been very good at that anyway." He turned away, saluted her with the walking stick that appeared in his hand as if sprouting from it, then set off back toward Shannish.

As Cally watched him disappear into the dark valleys, she saw that the City looked very far away, now, growing more distant the longer she looked. She sighed and turned back toward the fire.

23 - Eyes to See

She had seen this fire before. Ages ago, it seemed to her now. So much had changed since then, though really it had only been a few months. That night, the tall flames had been surrounded by a celebrating crowd of beautifully terrible, or terribly beautiful, people. The flames were much smaller tonight, quieter, Cally thought, and she didn't see anyone dancing. It looked for all the world like any ordinary campfire, but Cally had learned better than to assume anything was ordinary, here.

She craned her head back, looking up at the glittering stars overhead. The moon had begun to track westward, now, and since the air had grown cooler, the crickets had grown quieter. As she looked to the sky, she began to discern lines and spaces where the stars were not visible, where they were blocked by dark branches. Once she noticed this, the outline of a tree became clear to her. Its bole and the undersides of its few remaining leaves reflected the firelight, glowing softly almost as if they, too, burned from within, quietly, and waiting.

A man sat alone on one of the logs seats that circled the fire. He faced away from the fire, hunched forward with his shaggy head bowed over hands he held clasped in front of him. An empty golden cup lay on its side at his feet. Cally stopped just outside the circle of firelight, but the man had heard her approach. He raised his head.

"I was told to expect you," he said, standing and running his hands through his rough hair. Cally thought his voice sounded familiar, but she couldn't quite see his face, silhouetted as it was against the fire behind him. He stepped forward and put out a hand. "I am so pleased to meet you," he said, and his tone was more than merely polite. He sounded like he truly meant it.

Cally stepped into the light and took his hand. It was rough, and he did not clasp hers, but just stood holding her hand in his and staring at her. She stared back. He was a clear foot taller than she was, dressed in soft, flowing garments resembling those of the People of Shannish, only much darker in color, and he was definitely not one of them. He was far too coarse and dense and mortal. Cally felt goosebumps rise on her skin when he turned his head so she could see his face more clearly. It was lined deeply with years and care, but his eyes still shone clear china blue. "My name is Michael," he said.

She gazed a while longer and finally said, "I had always assumed Ben got his amazing eyes from his mother. But now I see he actually got them from you."

Michael finally released her hand. "What can I do for you?" he asked. "I will do anything for you, Callaghan McCarthy."

The intensity of his words - almost a vow - made Cally take a step backward. He stood quietly, waiting for her to tell him how he could help her.

"I..." She wanted to say, "Talk to me. Tell me more. Tell me all about Ben. Tell me about your life and why you left," but she knew these kinds of questions would be painful topics for him. He didn't look like a man who had ever found the happiness he had once sought. Much as Ben had often professed anger toward his father for leaving in pursuit of his faerie beloved, Cally couldn't bring herself to feel anger when she looked at this man's sad, gentle face.

"I wonder if you would be so kind as to walk me home?" she finally said, stepping forward to stand beside him, putting her hand through the crook of his arm.

He smiled and put a hand over hers. "It's not far," he said. "But first I would like to show you something."

He turned toward the log he had been sitting on and reached down into a lumpy duffle bag slumped there. Standing, he withdrew something that gleamed, reflecting the moonlight, silver with glints of the reds and yellows of the fire. It appeared to be a pendant in the shape of a crescent moon, hanging from a fine silver chain. This he held up at eye level so he could look between the arms of the crescent, and turned so that he was looking back toward the City from which Cally had just come. "Look. If you want to."

Cally stepped to where she could look at the City framed by the silver moon, and almost wished she hadn't. She was dismayed to see that it no longer appeared to shine with warm, colorful light, though it was heart wrenchingly beautiful in a completely different way. It seemed tiny and fragile, now, like a cluster of mushrooms nestled in moss at the top of the hill. Cally thought it looked impossibly vulnerable, and the People... the People. "They look like... what do you call them?" She struggled to remember the word, from science documentaries she had seen years ago. "Water bears," she said at last. "Tardigrades. They look... They're so very beautiful," she had to conclude breathlessly.

Michael let out a breath, himself, and turned back to replace the pendant in his bag. Straightening, he looked carefully at Cally's face, just the way Ben often did. "I think you already know the way home, from here," he said. "But if you would humor an old man..."

He left his bag and cup lying by the fire, looking like the detritus of some kind of wilderness hobo camp. Cally wondered if he actually lived there. As he stepped away from the fire his gait was stiff, as if he had not walked, or even moved, for a very long time.

Cally glanced over her shoulder as they started down the hill, and saw that Shannish had completely disappeared from view. Only the Tree remained, glowing like a citadel in the firelight until, as they reached the bottom of the hill it, too, winked out of sight like a ship passing over the horizon.

Michael Dawes led Cally over a little plank bridge, and she allowed him to support her by the elbow so she would not succumb to vertigo and pitch herself into the dark, shallow water bubbling softly over the stones. He said, as they started up the next hill, "There's so much to talk about, but it's already so late."

Cally was sure it couldn't be very much past midnight, so she assumed he meant "late" in a more lyrical way. But, as they crested the hill, she could see the sky growing silver, and beneath it the green-roofed white square of Vale House ahead, the barn and the ancient oak and the red pickup truck next to it. The porch lights were switched off, and the Captain's ghost had finally gone to bed. The wind at their backs had grown brisk.

Michael led Cally to the point along the fence where she had last seen Adam standing and staring at her, such a short while ago and so long ago, now. He put a hand on the top rail and turned to face south, to where Woodley's Main Street ended at the metal gate. Cally turned to see what he was looking at and, together, they watched Ben walk across the meadow, many yards to the south of them. He didn't notice them as he put his hands on the top of the gate and vaulted over it.

He was gazing toward Vale House – looking for her, Cally thought. She wanted to assure him she had, indeed, made it back from the bower, but she had a feeling Michael would prefer to get out of sight first.

"Love him well." She heard Michael's voice call softly from far behind her. "You are the only woman he will ever love."

She turned, wanting to say something along the lines of "You Dawes men all seem to have that trait in common," but he was already gone.

24 - The Chickens Come Home to Roost

When she looked again, Ben had already headed away, his back disappearing down Main Street toward the News Store. She would follow in a minute, Cally thought, squeezing through the fence. But first, she crossed the yard and sat down on the Vale House porch steps to collect her thoughts.

Doctor Boojums came out from under the shrubbery to join her. She found his presence comforting, but she did wish she could pet him. It would have soothed her nerves.

The lack of fog over the meadow, according to Ignacio's weather theories, meant that this chilly morning probably had no intention of turning into a warm day later. Cally hugged herself for warmth, but she didn't feel tired. She thought this odd, considering she had been gone the entire night and had not slept at all.

This, she mused, must be what it felt like all the time to Ben, with time passing in the "real" world while she herself had experienced none at all for several hours. It occurred to her that she was now eight hours less near the end of her mortal life than she would have been if she had stayed on this side of reality. The thought made her shudder. The gray ghost cat looked up at her and slowly blinked his pale eyes. "No, I'm not sure how I feel about it," she admitted to him. "I have logged some immortality – that should make me feel good, like some kind of privileged individual! But it doesn't, really. It feels...empty."

Doctor Boojums looked away and began washing his paws. "I'm not ungrateful," Cally assured him. "It was beautiful there. And very mind-expanding. But I think I know, now, what he meant."

She stood up and turned around to look at Vale House. The slanting rays of the sun rising behind her showed up the cracks in the paint, and the difference in the color of the tin sheeting on the porch roof where it had had to be repaired after a lightning strike. The aroma of the coffee someone had begun brewing inside the house drifted out onto the cold air. Cally spread her arms wide toward the house. "Faerie is beautiful and amazing," she said. "At least, parts of it are. And I'm glad I got up the nerve to go there. But now I think I know what Ben meant. I do feel it, now that I'm back. This – *this* – feels like home." She put her arms down and turned back to the cat, who had stuck his phantom hind leg up in the air so he could wash his bottom. "I think I understand now why you hang around here, too. I like this feeling of being home. Of belonging and..."

She should tell Ben she loved him, she thought. She had been telling herself for years that she didn't even know how to love, anymore, if she ever had. She had once believed, after all, that she'd been in love with the father of her children, but the intervening years had taught her to dismiss that as mere biology and youthful hormones tricking her into perpetuating the species.

But, damn it, she thought, there really was such a thing as love in this world. She loved her son and daughter; she was sure of that. And she loved Katarina and Bethany, and Ian May and Sofie, and Ignacio, and Nell and even George. "I even love you, you stupid old cat," she told the fuzzy ghost at her feet. He stopped washing and looked up at her with his gray tongue still sticking out. She thought the look on his face seemed to say: *"Well?"*

She would tell him. She felt much warmer, now, and she smiled and swung her arms as she walked across the parking lot to the gate. She would tell Ben she loved him, and she would go quickly, before he risked Bree's ire by coming to look for her.

By the time she emerged from under the oaks into downtown Woodley, the chilly sunlight was giving color back to the tops of the brick buildings. It was still too early for Merv Arkwright ("I love him, too!" Cally thought) to be on the loading dock of the feed store, but she knew the Bean Garden would be open. She also knew the back door of Dawes News would be unlocked, and Ben would be inside.

A car was parked in the street already, an unfamiliar one, which would have been unusual for this town if not for the fact that it was October. The car was a classy-looking Dodge Charger, gleaming black and sleek in the early light, and it was parked directly in front of the News Store. This reminded Cally of her own first morning in Woodley, waking up in her car where she had fallen asleep parked in the exact same spot. Nobody was sleeping, or sitting, in this car, however.

Hearing a noise behind her, she turned to look across the street toward the crime scene tape, sagging, now, down onto the pavement of Church Street, and saw Bree Dawes stepping over it, keys dangling from her hand.

"Good morning!" Cally called to her. She meant it. Maybe she loved Bree, too? She decided to reserve judgement on that for now.

Bree was actually smiling when she stepped around the black car and up onto the curb. She grinned at Cally. "Why don't you go around back and ask Ben to give this door a kick for me?" she suggested sweetly.

Cally was puzzled by the uncharacteristic friendly tone in the old woman's voice, but she was glad to have an opportunity to get on Bree's good side. "I'd be happy to," she said.

"I bet you would."

Cally ducked around the side of the building and followed the narrow alley to the parking lot in back. The silver Daimler was the only car in the lot, as usual, and Cally smiled to see it. The steel rear door of the News Store had been propped open with a case of canned chili, so Cally went inside. No lights were on yet and she watched the floor carefully to make sure she didn't trip over any other as-yet-unshelved stock.

The first thing she saw was a pair of heels. Ladies heels, tall black ones, and the backs of a pair of stockinged legs as she looked up. A woman stood with her back to Cally, long, black hair curling all the way down to her hips, and someone's hands were tangled in it. Ben's hands. His arms were around the woman, and his face was buried in her hair as he held her tightly.

Cally stopped so suddenly the thought it must have made a crashing sound, but it was only the sound of her heartbeat crashing in her ears. She could not move, she could not breathe. She wanted very much to back away, to back out of this moment and out of this entire morning, out of her whole life, but she could not move. All she could feel was fire creeping over her flesh as ice coursed through her veins.

Ben released the woman and stood back to look at her. He smiled his wide, beautiful smile and the love in his face shone like a beacon upon the woman's absolutely beautiful upturned features. He laughed and embraced her again.

It was the woman who sensed Cally's presence first. She turned her head slightly and, when she caught sight of Cally, her eyes glittered. She stood on the tips of her toes and stretched her beautiful, perfect legs to return Ben's embrace. Then she laughed and released him to turn and face Cally.

She was utterly beautiful, with the wideset eyes and cheekbones and full bosom and thick, perfect hair every woman coveted. She was at least ten years younger than Cally.

Cally could feel herself trembling and wished she could vanish. She still couldn't move, but she did manage to muster herself enough, at least, to keep her face expressionless. She would rather die than let this woman or Ben see how she was feeling, and she prayed they couldn't see her shaking.

The woman saw it, though, judging by the way she threw her head back and laughed. Her hair swung like rippling silk and her laughter was like cruel and beautiful music.

Turning to face Cally, she put an arm around Ben and kissed his cheek, saying, "Well, aren't you going to introduce me to your little girlfriend, Dad?"

25 - Family Matters

"I would be happy to." Ben embraced the woman, quickly, one more time. Then, putting an arm around her and turning her toward Cally he added, "If you would just please tell me what you are calling yourself these days?"

The woman's cruel smile lingered as she watched Cally's body begin to thaw. Ben was apparently oblivious of what she had just gone though, and Cally did her best to keep it that way.

"I guess we can just refer to me as Ana, for now," said Ben's daughter, and as she stepped out of the shadows Cally thought maybe her smile wasn't so cruel, after all, as merely mischievous.

Ben drew Ana with him as he stepped forward to put his other arm around Cally. The last of the trembling in Cally's bones melted away at his touch. "Callaghan McCarthy, please meet my eldest," he said. "You'll have to forgive me – I'm kind of blown away. I haven't seen... Ana ...in a very long time. I had honestly thought I would never see her again." His voice cracked when he said this last.

"You can't get rid of me that easily," Ana said with a little, birdlike laugh, but her eyes were on Cally, not Ben, when she said it.

"Um, excuse me..." Ben left them and ran to the front of the store, where he kicked the bottom of the door to force it open. Bree grumbled as usual when he helped her up the step.

"Morning, Auntie!" Ana called as Bree hobbled across the store to the counter. The old woman grunted and began to fill the coffee maker.

Cally left Ben and Ana quietly catching up near the magazine rack while she went to the register. There she stood silently glaring at Bree, who deliberately avoided looking up and meeting her eyes. Finally she whispered, as harshly as she could while keeping her voice down, "That was just plain mean!"

"What was?" Bree asked brightly, but Cally could tell by the little smile playing on her lips that she knew exactly what Cally meant.

"You knew who that car belonged to," she replied quietly. "And you knew what I would walk into the middle of when you sent me back there."

Bree chuckled, and then she did look up at Cally, china-blue eyes aglitter. "Well," she said, "Now at least you know for sure how you feel about him."

Cally opened her mouth to retort, but she wasn't sure what to say. Bree was right, of course, but how had she even known about the emotional issues with which Cally had been wrestling?

She turned away from the counter to rejoin Ben and Ana, who were talking about how long Ana would be around this time. Ana was being noncommittal, and Ben appeared resigned to this.

"So.... have you heard anything from my half-sister?" Ana asked Ben.

Ben winced as if she had punched him in the solar-plexus. "You know I've never met her," he answered quietly. Cally found herself transferring her anger from Bree to the younger woman.

Ana's ebony locks swung in a circle as she laughed and said, "Well, I've been away. I thought maybe *something* new might have happened in this pathetic little village, in all this time."

Cally did her best to offer Ben some comfort, standing close beside him with a hand on his shoulder. She felt him take a deep breath. "Well, yes," he said. "Some things *have* happened." He put an arm around Cally and sighed as he turned to look at her. "I'm glad you're here," he said, and she could feel tension leave his body. "I missed you this morning. I should have known you'd made it back okay." He glanced quickly at his daughter and changed the subject. "How is everything at Vale House today? Have you come bearing news?"

"I have," Cally said, and she made sure she was speaking loudly enough for Bree to hear, also. "I came to tell you I love you."

Not exactly the romantic moment she had imagined for her first confession of love for him, but she needed to let both Bree and Ana know she wasn't intimidated by them.

Ana snorted. "Get a room!"

Cally wished she could. The other women in Ben's life were proving to be a royal nuisance.

—

"I'm sorry," Ben said, waving at the tail lights of Ana's car as it roared away up Main Street toward Gardens Road. "I'm afraid Ana got her personality from the distaff side of the family."

"You mean the faerie side?" Cally asked.

Ben looked confused for a second, and then said, "Oh! No, no, I mean my grandmother on my father's side. The human side. All the women are like that, all the way back, or so they told me when I was a kid. Very...strong-willed. Like Bree."

Cally glanced over her shoulder, back through the front window of Dawes News, where Bree Dawes stood as always behind the counter, behind her newspaper. *'Strong-willed'* was not the term she would have used. "Okay, yes, I think I understand."

The sun had come up over the tops of the buildings. Main Street filled slowly with cool light and yellow leaves spinning as they drifted down onto the pavement. Cally was itching to tell Ben about where she had been last night, but the emotional shock he had just experienced with Ana's unexpected appearance made her think maybe she needed to spend some time listening to him, instead (and anyway she wasn't sure whether she should tell him, at all, about meeting his father.)

Ben took Cally's hand and led her to where they could lean against the front wall of the store, between the window and door, out of Bree's line of sight.

"I was very young," he said.

"You don't owe me an explanation," she assured him. "My own marriage was a train wreck, too, but I'm still grateful it gave me my children."

"I was never married to Ana's mother," he explained anyway. "Or to the mother of...my other daughter. They seldom marry, there in that land." He was gazing away down the street toward the meadow gate. Ana's car had turned south on Gardens Road and the sound of its engine had faded into the distance. "Marriage, there, is a ceremonial thing done for political reasons.

"When I was younger and still very angry, I once asked my mother if she had ever loved my father. She didn't have any real answer to give me that made much sense. I know *he* loved *her* but, well, he was human."

He still is, Cally thought as he continued.

"They don't really have such a concept as love. Not the way we have it. Sometimes they do feel it, but it's more for things than for one another. For lands, stars, beauty. They can have very strong feelings for one another. Pride, loyalty, all that, but seldom actual love."

"Well, it's a different culture," Cally said. "Who are we to judge?"

He gave her his "you're amazing" smile again and kissed her swiftly. "It's just another reason why I have chosen my human half. I like the love thing.

"I mean." He put his head back against the bricks and closed his eyes. "I thought it was great, at the time, all that freedom from messy emotions. Back when I was young, just a kid, really. I was a big deal, among my mother's people. All the women wanted me. I was a young man in a garden of earthly delights; I thought I'd found paradise!" He laughed, but it was a bitter laugh. "Ana's birth changed all that for me. I fell in love, then, alright. I fell in love with that beautiful faerie child, the first moment I saw her little face..." He stopped, taking several deep breaths, and if they hadn't been standing in view of the street, Cally would have wrapped her arms around him. "But, once her mother's people had got what they wanted from me, they had very little further use for me."

"I'm so sorry." Cally stopped herself from asking about the half-sister Ana had mentioned, but he seemed to want to tell her.

He said, "Apparently in my wild youth, back in those days, I also fathered another child, another daughter. No one even told me about her until after her mother had already whisked her away to parts unknown. I will probably never see her. I don't even know who her mother was... that sounds terrible, doesn't it?" He lifted his head and looked at her. "It's what they say every young human male wishes for, isn't it? Or thinks he does: unfettered passion with unlimited bevies of beautiful women, unencumbered by emotional or material responsibility. Be careful what you wish for, right?"

Cally was trying very hard to not feel inadequate as she pictured Ben with unlimited bevies of immortal faerie beauties, but she saw the pain in his eyes, and it reminded her how fortunate she was to have a good relationship with her own children. "Well, Ana is here, now," was all she could think of to say. "It must mean something. Maybe she hopes to get to know you after all."

"She's here for the Thing." He nodded pragmatically. "One of the chickens coming home to roost. There's no way of knowing whether or not she'll stay. My guess is: probably not."

"Speaking of chickens..." Cally had a sudden thought, and she described for him the fox she had first encountered in the chicken yard, and about the boy it could morph into. "He calls himself Adam."

She was wondering, privately, whether this shapeshifting being might have had something to do with Foster's inexplicable death, but she asked Ben: "Do you suppose he is also on his way to the Thing?"

He considered this for a moment. "It seems likely," he said. "But I have no knowledge of the kind of person you're describing. They say my grandmother – you know, the one from whom Bree inherited her charm – was able to turn into a wolf, or maybe it was a bear. But that was a purely human legend. Native American."

Cally smiled, easily imagining Bree as a wolf, or at least a wolverine.

"Maybe," she suggested, "your other daughter might also attend the Thing. Maybe you'll get to meet her after all."

Ben turned his head as the sound of an engine again arose from the residential end of the street, but this time it was Ian May's old red pickup truck. Bethany was driving, and Ian, in the passenger seat, stuck his arm out the window and waved to them as the truck passed the News Store.

They both straightened and walked to the curb, waving and smiling as they watched the truck heading toward the highway. "He's on his way to post Ignacio's bail!" Cally said happily.

"It'll be nice to see Katarina smile again," said Ben. "I mean, to see her smile for real."

Cally agreed, as she kissed him and watched him go back inside the store. She tried very hard not to think about how Ignacio's freedom might be short-lived if they didn't figure out who really had murdered Foster and, as she walked back to Vale House, she also tried not to think about how that person could be watching her from any of the doors or side-yards she passed.

26 - A Thief in Plain Sight

Katarina wiped her eyes. *"Oh, Dios mio!"* she laughed. Folding a dish-towel into a small bundle, then unfolding it again, she struggled to compose herself, only to end up bursting into laughter again. "I'm sorry, I shouldn't be laughing! That Ana, what a brat! It must have been so terrible for you. But you gave back as good as you got!"

Cally sat beside her on the top step of the porch, happy to see Katarina laughing. They were both in a much more positive mood now that they knew Ignacio would soon be home.

"I guess I'd forgotten," Cally said, "that when you get involved with someone, you get involved with their family, too."

"Well, it's too late now," said Katarina. "You don't back out of a commitment just because you hit a bump on Reality Road."

"I never said anything about a commitment," Cally said. "I only said I loved him. It's not the same thing."

"Isn't it?" Katarina mastered her mirth and put a friendly arm around Cally. "He's a good man. You have nothing to fear."

"Oh, I know, Kat. Well, at least, I think I know. Only, it reminded me so much of my marriage. I mean, I was right back there again, in that house, seeing all those things I used to pretend not to see. Trying to trick myself into trusting someone who couldn't be trusted." She wrapped her arms around herself and took a deep breath.

"I'm so sorry," said Katarina. "That anyone should have to go through that. I shouldn't have laughed. I really am such a lucky woman."

Cally transferred her embrace to Katarina. "Don't feel bad," she said. "I guess it really is funny, when you think about it. Someday I'll probably look back on it and laugh."

"You both will, together."

"Oh! No, no. I don't want him to ever find out what I was thinking!"

They both jumped when they heard the engine of the pickup truck through trees along Main Street. Katarina was already down the steps and running along the walk by the time Cally could get up to follow her.

A shadow fell over her heart when the truck rolled across the yard and stopped in front of the barn. Bethany was in the driver's seat. Katarina let out a sharp cry of dismay. "Why isn't Ignacio driving?"

It was because Ignacio wasn't in the truck at all. Katarina remained silent, hands clasped over her heart, while Bethany got out of the truck and went around to help Ian out of the passenger seat. As he climbed, wincing in pain, down from the truck and accepted the Captain's old cane from Bethany's hand, even the birds on the fence fell silent. The three horses stopped grazing and turned toward the fence, watching silently with grass hanging from their lips.

The unspoken question resounded in the air as Ian limped toward the porch. Bethany looked up at Katarina when they reached the walkway; her eyes brimmed with tears and she shook her head. It was Cally who finally mustered the courage to ask the question out loud. "Where is Ignacio?"

"We couldn't post his bail," Bethany said in a choked voice. She helped Ian up the steps, and Cally ran to open the screen door for them.

"Why not?" Katarina cried. "Why wouldn't they let you? This isn't right!"

"No, they would have let us," Bethany said as they all gathered around the reception desk. "But something has happened. Ian's money..."

"It's all gone," said the old gentleman, dropping the cane to the floor and leaning with both hands on the desk. "All of it."

Bethany took her accustomed seat behind the desk and stared at the ringing phone as if it were an alien spacecraft, not answering it. When it finally stopped ringing, she said, "Ian's accounts have been completely wiped out. All of them.”

“How?” Cally’s mind refused to grasp what Bethany was saying.

“I did it myself,” said Ian. “At least, that’s what the bank’s records show.”

Katarina spread her hands in disbelief, but Cally suddenly understood.

“Identity theft,” she said. She had a fairly certain idea who had done it, as well. She and Bethany locked eyes, and Bethany nodded. There were few people who had enough knowledge of Ian’s private affairs to be able to impersonate him, but only one of them would stoop low enough to actually do it.

“That explains where Foster got the money to bail himself out of jail,” Cally said.

“*El Bastardo*,” said Katarina in a low, hissing voice. “*El Diablo.* He’s still able to hurt us, even from beyond the grave.”

“They said I have been withdrawing large amounts of money once a week for several weeks now,” Ian explained. “They say they contacted me about it several times and were assured that I was using the money to invest in land deals.”

“But we can prove that was all fraud,” Cally was sure. “The bank will reinstate your funds if...”

Ian waved a limp hand toward them. “Yes, of course, they will. They were very sympathetic, and said they would start right away to set things right.”

Bethany continued. “But they warned us it will take weeks to get everything straightened out. Months, for some accounts.”

“And until then, Ignacio will have to stay in jail,” Katarina realized. She bowed her head and stared silently at her hands clasped in front of her.

“I’m so sorry,” Ian said. “I’m so very sorry.”

“No!” said Bethany. “No, Ian this isn’t your fault!”

He was too worn down to raise his head and acknowledge her. “I never should have trusted him,” he said. He swayed on his feet, looking much older than he was.

“None of us should have,” Cally agreed. “But it is what it is. We’ll get this straightened out.” She put a reassuring arm around Katarina. The woman didn’t yield to her embrace, but held herself rigid. Cally would have felt better if she would swear and shout, or at least cry, but it was as if Katarina had turned to stone.

"I've been gone too long," Ian finally said. "I need to make sure Sofie knows I haven't abandoned her."

"Ian," Cally said gently. "If anyone knows that, Sofie does."

He looked up at her suddenly. "I might need to sell off some land," he said. "Ms. McCarthy, I might need your help with that."

While Cally tried to think of how she could possibly help Ian with such a task, Katarina suddenly came back to life.

"You'll do no such thing, Mr. May!" she said sharply. She swooped down to pick up Ian's cane, as well as the dish towel she had dropped to the floor. "Everything is going to be alright. You'll see! You do *not* want Ignacio to get back only to find out you've sold off half the meadow!"

She pressed the dish towel into Ian's hand, realized what she had done and exchanged it for the cane, then turned on her heel and strode out through the dining room, back toward the kitchen, calling over her shoulder, "I'll bring you some lunch and a good cup of tea!"

Bethany stood up and helped Ian make his way to the back hall while Cally took her place, staring at the ringing phones but not answering them. Someone came down the stairs and stood beside the desk, and Cally roused herself to look up expecting, or at least hoping, to see George. She was disappointed to see Eddie Tiene standing there, but her dismay was tempered by the fact that he had his luggage with him. He was, apparently, finally checking out.

"Did I overhear somebody talking about selling land?" he asked, fishing another business card out of his pocket. "I'd be happy to help with that!"

Katarina reappeared like a djinn in the dining room doorway, holding a tea tray in her hands. "Shoo!" she yelled at the man. "There will be no land sold around here today, thank you!"

Cally struggled to hide her amusement as Eddie dropped the business card hurriedly on the desk, nodded, and carried his luggage out to the porch, letting the screen door bang shut behind him.

—

By the time Bethany returned from Ian's quarters, Cally had come up with an idea.

"Do you think you can spare Katarina for a few hours this afternoon? I'd like to take her into town to visit Ignacio."

"Oh!" said Bethany. "You've found your car keys!"

"No," Cally said. "I'm going to call a... locksmith."

"That's so sweet of you. I'm sure it will be no problem. Things are going to slow down for the rest of the week, now, anyway since we're going to be closed on Sunday. Cally, have you thought about where you're going to stay on October the twenty-fifth? You're welcome to come home with me that night, though all I have to offer you is a couch. Maybe you can stay with Ben!"

Cally didn't try to explain to her why she couldn't stay with Ben. She still didn't understand why she couldn't stay at Vale House on the twenty-fifth of October, but she didn't have time to think about that right now. She pointed to the telephone console.

"You get 'hold of Kat and tell her to meet me on the front porch when she's ready."

Cally went back into her office and glared at the empty spot on her desk where her computer should have been. Resignedly, she dug her phone out of her purse again and gave it a murderous glare. Then, cursing the miniscule keyboard, she typed with her thumbs: "Emerald, are you there?" At least it didn't try to change "there" to "their."

She paced the room waiting for a reply. Outside the window, she could see the three horses in the meadow standing with their heads extended over the fence almost as if, Cally fancied, they were trying to eavesdrop.

Finally, a soft beep drew her eyes back to the tiny screen.

Emerald: I'm always here for you, my friend!

Cally: How can I get my car back?

Emerald: Oh, hello to you too. I'm fine, thank you for asking.

Cally: Sorry. I'm in a bit of a hurry.

Emerald: You're not thinking of leaving us, are you?

Cally: I'm not planning to, but I need my car. What do I have to do?

Emerald: You mean, besides making another deal with an old earth goddess and digging yourself in even deeper?

Cally: Which is how I lost my car in the first place, yes, I know. But it was for a good cause, and so is this.

Emerald: Cally, you really need to be more careful. Why do you need your car?

Cally didn't feel she had the time or the patience to explain everything with just two thumbs but, typing furiously, re-typing all the words the auto-correct tried to help her with, and swearing in frustration the entire time, she ended up typing quite a long rant into the tiny window.

Cally: I can't just sit here waiting for everything to work itself out. Katarina is going to pieces and so am I. I don't know what to do, but I want to help. A good place to start would be to go see Ignition. I meant Ignacio. Maybe I can talk to someone there, or maybe he can remember something that will help us figure out who really did kill Foster.

Emerald: I understand how you feel Cally, but don't let it make you do anything stupid.

Cally: I have never been very good at not doing anything stupid.

Emerald: LOL that is true. OK, there is one thing you can try, to at least borrow your car for a while.

Cally: Anything!

Emerald: You can give Errin some driving lessons.

Cally: Anything within reason.

Emerald: . . .

Cally: I'll let you know how it goes.

When Cally stepped off the porch she saw, as she knew she would, that the three horses were nowhere to be seen. Sighing impatiently, she said out loud to the grass and trees and sky, "Errin, I need my car!"

The teenage girl with her mane of red curls walked into the yard from between the fence and the barn. "I keep telling you," she said. "It's not your car anymore!"

"I know that," said Cally. "And it's such a shame. Because, if it were, I could give you those driving lessons you keep asking me for."

Errin gave Cally a sideways look, but Cally could tell she was intrigued. The girl walked across the yard, looking at the ground and saying, "Hmm. Hmm..." Stopping suddenly beside Cally's car, she stooped over. "What's this?" She reached down into the tall weeds around the front tire and then, straightening, held out a jingling ring of keys. "Why, look, they must have been here all along!"

Cally looked at the shiny bundle of keys and stopped herself from saying "bullshit" out loud.

Errin swung the keys from one finger. "Let's go to Seen's Mill!" she suggested, reaching down to driver's side door handle.

"Well, there's just one thing," Cally said. "I, um, don't have time, right now. I mean, I'd love to see Seen's Mill, but at night, maybe. You know, when all the music starts. How about we go to modern-day Blackthorn, instead? There's a Dairy Queen there."

"Oh, I can walk there," said Errin, starting to pocket the keys.

"You can walk to Seen's Mill," Cally pointed out. "You can walk anywhere. But driving there. Showing up with your hair flying out the window, that would be cool, wouldn't it? This car even matches your hair. Sort of."

Errin gave her a big, freckle-splattered smile. "Oh, you're good!" she said. "You've learned a lot about dealing with fey folk! You're not as good as I am, though." She turned and started to walk away.

"Errin, please!" Cally implored. "Could I... borrow? Those keys, for just a little while? Just for today, I promise. It's important. Please..."

Cally didn't know if Errin and people like her had any sense of empathy or compassion, but the girl did turn around and consider her words. "Okay," she said at last. "I guess you should make sure the poor car even still runs, after all this time. And gas it up and get it washed before we get started on our adventures."

"Adventures?"

Errin turned and patted the hood of the car and told it she would see it soon, then tossed the keys to Cally.

27 - Visiting Hours

The car didn't want to start, at first, and Cally's first thought was to go back inside and ask Ignacio to take a look at it, since he was as good at mechanics as he was at everything else to which he set his hand. Then she remembered she couldn't just go and get Ignacio, now. She bent over the steering wheel and let a few frustrated tears fall into her lap.

Composing herself, she sat up and gave the key another turn. The engine whined and spluttered reluctantly, but eventually it found its will to live. Cally patted the dashboard. "Good girl," she said. "I'm sorry I've neglected you for so long, but I think we're back in the saddle now." She glanced up to see if the horses in the meadow appreciated this metaphor, but they were far across the field, grazing in a wide, loose group.

Putting the car gently into gear, she backed around and stopped in front of the porch, where Katarina was running down the steps with her purse swinging from her hand. "Thank you so much for this!" she cried, opening the passenger door and flinging herself into the seat. "I'm so glad you have your wheels back!"

Cally said nothing about this as she drove out through the gate and turned onto Main Street. She was glad to have Katarina along, on her first foray in months to the outskirts of Woodley. Maybe, she thought, having Katarina with her would mean she wouldn't have trouble getting back in, this time.

Though she seemed tense and distracted, Katarina still didn't miss the opportunity to tease Cally about the way she slowed down to look through the front window of the News Store as they passed it. Ben could be seen – at least, his legs could – halfway up a wooden ladder placing canned goods on a high shelf. Katarina winked and said, "You should be there holding that ladder for him."

"He's fine," Cally replied, setting herself up.

"I'm sure he is!" Katarina quipped.

It made Cally feel even worse to see Katarina trying to be lighthearted in spite of herself. The two women fell silent again as they reached the end of Main Street, passing under the roof of trees once more. Here the road curved gently downhill until it crossed a little bridge over the stream at the bottom. Emerging again at the top of the next hill, Cally turned left past the Seven Forks Diner onto Interstate 85.

The lonely highway unwound between rows of pine trees, and would, Cally remembered, continue to do so for several miles. Katarina pulled out her phone and began fiddling with it, but there was no signal here, and Cally noticed out of the corner of her eye that Katarina's expression grew darker and darker as she slumped lower in her seat. Finally, she sat up and jammed the phone back into her purse.

"So, who do you think really did it?" she said, glaring out the window.

"Killed Foster, you mean?" Cally asked. "No, I am sure it was not Ignacio. Everyone is, don't worry."

"I'm not worried about that! But unless we can prove it, by finding the real killer, Ignacio will still have to go back to prison, even if we ever do manage to get him bailed out!"

Cally knew Katarina was probably right about that, but she didn't think it would make her feel any better to tell her so.

"Well, I have several theories, of course," she answered, "but I'm afraid none of them hold much water. There's Mr. Ennilangr who drives the delivery truck. He's tall, and strong, and has a ponytail, but it's blond, though I can imagine Danya Barry could have been mistaken in the dark. But, they say, his rig wasn't seen anywhere in town that night. Anyway, everyone says he's a pretty decent guy.

"So then, I find myself wondering, where was Jud's son all this time? What does he even look like?"

Katarina shrugged. "He looked like a younger version of Jud, only much bigger around, last time I saw him. But that was years ago.

"Andi's son is very tall, and dark, like the person that Barry woman described," Katarina offered.

"Kurtis? Oh, no, he's such a sweet kid. I couldn't imagine he would ever hurt anyone. No more than I can imagine Ignacio hurting someone."

"True..." Katarina said.

"And besides, he wears his hair short." Cally searched for the right words to tell Katarina her final theory, the one she was leaning toward most heavily at the moment: that whoever had killed Foster had not been human at all.

"I blame that old boyfriend of yours!" Katarina blurted out.

"What? Eddie Teine?" Cally didn't bother to insist he wasn't her old boyfriend. "He's tall-ish, I guess, but his hair is short, and he's, well, really, he's kind of a lightweight."

Katarina dismissed this with a snort. "He's too interested in buying and selling land in and around Woodley. Just like Foster was. I don't think Foster could have made all those calls to the bank himself, to steal Ian's identity. Not from jail. Someone must have been helping him. I bet they were working together!"

"But if they were, why would Mr. Teine kill his own business partner?"

"Maybe the deal went south," Katarina suggested. "Or maybe once Foster got all of Ian's money out of the bank, Mr. Teine decided he didn't need Foster anymore."

Cally started to say she thought Katarina had been watching too many mob movies, but she had to admit she had a point.

The green sign for the Blackthorn exit appeared ahead, and Katarina got her phone back out. There was a signal again and, as Cally turned onto the exit, Katarina opened her phone's GPS app. Near the interstate, this iteration of Blackthorn consisted mostly of fast food restaurants, big-box stores, and motels all crowded amidst a tangled nest of busy four-lane streets. Cally found them nerve-wracking, and wondered how she had ever survived living and driving in a large city before she'd come to Woodley. Small town life had spoiled her.

The GPS guided them through many twists and turns until at last a plain gray building, the tallest in the town at four stories, appeared on their left. Katarina craned her head out the window and looked up at the slit-shaped windows. *"Mi pobre cariño,"* she muttered softly as Cally searched for a parking spot. There were plenty of visitors' spots available near the black glass doors which appeared to be the only way in or out of the building.

Empty wooden benches lined the walls of the granite-floored room inside. The top of a woman's head could just be seen through the wire reinforced window at the far end. Cally spoke through the little hole in the window, giving her information and Katarina's to the woman seated inside. Checking their identification, the woman informed them they were both indeed on the Visitors List for Ignacio, but that only one of them could visit him at a time.

"You go first," Cally insisted to Katarina. "I'll hold your things for you." She took Katarina's purse and jacket from her. The woman at the desk pushed a button and the heavy steel door at the side of the room opened with a loud, buzzing clang.

Katarina approached the door with wide eyes, clasping her hands together in front of her as if she, herself, were about to be incarcerated. The young guard who appeared in the doorway smiled reassuringly and said "This way, ma'am." Leading her away by the elbow, he let the door slam shut with a hollow boom.

Cally spoke through the hole in the window to the woman typing furiously at her computer. "Are the detectives handling this case in the building, by any chance?"

In reply, the woman pushed a folded pamphlet through the window toward her. Cally sat down on one of the benches. The only information the pamphlet contained was a list of phone numbers one could call for more information. She shoved it into her purse and sighed.

"Is this an unusually slow day for visitors, or is it always this quiet here?" she asked the top of the woman's head.

"It's always this quiet."

"That's a shame."

The sound of clacking computer keys let Cally know the conversation was over.

She tried to check her email on her phone to pass the time, but the building was cell-signal proof. It seemed like an hour, but was probably only several minutes, before the door at the side of the room clanged open again.

Katarina's eyes were wet when she reached out to receive her things back from Cally. "They let me hug him!" she said, giving Cally a hug as well.

"I won't be long," Cally promised Katarina, handing her own purse to her and turning to follow the young man into a narrow passageway. The long, windowless hall was lined with heavy doors, all closed, similar to the one through which they'd entered.

At the end of this hall, the young guard swiped his key card to let her through a pair of glass doors into a wide room filled with long tables and plastic chairs. He paused here to explain the rules to her.

"You may hug the inmate in greeting," he said, "but afterward please sit on the opposite side of the table and do not touch him. Do not give him any items, and do not accept any items from him. Your conversation will not be recorded or monitored in any way, but I will be remaining in the room in case you need me for anything."

The chairs lining the long tables were all empty, except for Ignacio seated at a table at the far end of the room. He stood when Cally crossed the room to him, and she saw that his ponytail had been unbound. A most impressive cloak of long, black hair fell around his shoulders, and across Cally's arms as she reached up to hug him. He returned her hug gently, and didn't let go until the guard said "That's enough."

Then the guard gestured toward a chair standing alone at the opposite end of the room. "I'll be right here if you need me for anything," he reminded Cally, giving her a pointed look before turning away to take his seat.

Cally sat down in the hard, plastic chair opposite Ignacio and muttered, "I hate the way they act like you're a violent criminal I need protection from!"

Ignacio sat down, too, and shrugged. "Well, I am accused of a violent crime, after all."

"Your hair looks amazing," she couldn't help adding.

He gave her a wry grin. "They took my scrunchies away."

Cally spread her hands palm down on the table, as close to the center as she dared without appearing to try to touch him. "I'm so sorry you have to go through this, Ignacio."

"I'm fine," he said. "I'm mostly worried about Kat. And about all the work I need to be doing. It's our busiest season and..."

"Ignacio, we are far more worried about you than we are about work getting done!"

"It's not so bad here." He mustered a brave and patient smile for her benefit.

"I guess it could be worse," she admitted. "But we love you and we miss you. And, we have to prove you didn't kill anyone. If you're convicted, they'll move you to a place that isn't nearly so...nice." She looked around the quiet room. The young guard was sitting with one foot on his knee, writing in the pad on his clipboard. "This is nuts, Ignacio. There's no way they would be able to convict you on the very spurious bits of evidence they have, is there?" She didn't expect him to be able to answer that, and he didn't try. "We're still working on bailing you out," she went on. "We won't give up. I guess Kat told you what happened with Ian's money?"

He nodded. "It looks like Foster acquired it and used it for his own bail," he said. "Though my bail is set much higher than his was, so Ian's money may not have been enough anyway."

"Why would your bail be higher than Foster's?" Cally wondered. "He tried to kill at least six people!"

"Allegedly," Ignacio reminded, and put up a hand to stop her before she could utter any choice words to protest this technicality. "It's not just about the number of people involved," he explained patiently. "The rate is also based on the likelihood that I might try to jump bail. I am considered a risk for running because I was not born inside this country. There's a concern that if I get out, I could high-tail it back to Mexico."

"That's insane!" Cally said far too loudly, standing up and knocking her chair over behind her. The hollow plastic boom as it tumbled on the floor echoed throughout the big, empty room, causing the guard to look up from his clipboard and put his foot down on the ground. Leaning forward, he fixed his gaze on Cally.

She gave the guard a sheepish grin and picked up the chair. He nodded and sat back, but he did not resume whatever he had been doing in his clipboard. When Cally returned to her seat, she struggled to keep her voice low, but her words came out in an angry, hissing whisper and she couldn't stop herself gesturing with both arms.

"It isn't right!" she said. "You've lived here for over twenty years. You're a naturalized citizen. Katarina is here. Your whole life is here – this is your home! Why would you leave the country?"

"They don't know me like you do," he reasoned gently.

"Their loss," she said. It was true, but it was no help.

"Unfortunately, there's more," Ignacio said. "They've uncovered another motive, making it seem more likely I did it."

"Another motive? The original one was bogus enough to begin with."

"Apparently, part of the defense Foster was working on, to get out of his own murder charges, was to prove that it had been me, not him, who set Vale House on fire. Now some of the detectives he was working with are saying it looks like I could have killed him to shut him up about that."

Cally couldn't keep her voice down, then. "God damn it!" She slammed her palm against the table, uttering a long string of very unladylike language. "I was there – I saw everything!"

"Ma'am." The guard had appeared at her side. "You are going to have to calm down, or I will be forced to remove you from the room." He spoke calmly, but his hand rested on the holstered gun at his side. Cally stared at him as if he were an apparition, until Ignacio's voice gently called her back to reality.

"Ms. McCarthy, it's alright. *Todo va a estar bien.*"

She let out her breath. "I apologize," she said to the guard in a choked voice. He returned to his end of the room, but he didn't sit down.

Cally's shoulders sagged as she turned back to Ignacio. "I'm not making things any easier on you, am I?"

He shook his head gently, but Cally saw no blame in his eyes – only his concern for her, and for Katarina, and probably for everyone in Woodley.

"I am going to find out who really did kill Foster," she promised him, "so we can get you out of here." She had no idea how she was going to keep this promise. "Ignacio, I'm no detective, but is there anything you can remember about that night that might help? "

Ignacio sighed, and the smile faded from his face. "Listen, Cally," he said. He put his hands in his lap and leaned over the tabletop, staring straight down at it and speaking in a low voice that wasn't quite a whisper. "Cally, I'm not so sure I didn't do it."

That was absolutely the last thing Cally had expected to hear him say, but she did manage to keep her voice down. "No," she said, "that's impossible. You wouldn't do such a thing, and anyway you had already gone home when it happened. I was there, remember?"

"I *saw* myself," he said. He was speaking feverishly, now, and his shoulders were trembling. "I was walking home, and I saw someone who looked just like me, tall, like me, and built like I am with black hair in a ponytail. I saw him standing in Church Street, just where the street light doesn't reach. He was looking at me but turned away when I saw him. Woodley is a strange town – sometimes you see things like this. Doppelgangers and things like that. I crossed myself." He sat up and did so again, then looked at her with eyes wide and shining with tears that threatened to brim over. "Then I kept on going. I didn't look back. I was already home and getting into bed when the sheriff came and told me to come over to Vale House, where he was questioning everyone. That's all I remember. But Cally, when that young woman, that girl from the ghost hunting place, when she identified me, she wasn't lying. Nobody else in town looks like I do. Not even in the dark. Did I really do it, and just blocked the memory of it out of my mind?" He laid his hands, palms up, on the table and looked at her as if he thought she could provide the answer.

"Ignacio, don't even talk like that!" She wished with all her heart she could take his hands. "Don't even think it! You are the gentlest person I know! You could never have done anything like..." Her memory of Foster's headless, blood-covered body filled her vision. "Like *that*. I don't believe it. I won't! Just dismiss the entire idea!"

He looked back down at the table. "I won't speak of it again," he promised. "And in any case please don't tell Katarina I said this."

Cally promised. That, at least, was a promise she knew she would be able to keep.

28 - Different Kinds of Horror Movies

When Cally met Ben at the gate that evening, she told him about her visit with Ignacio. Then, though she would have preferred to do something besides talking after that, she got up the courage to also tell him about her foray over the fence into Shannish. She wasn't yet able to bring herself to mention having met his father, but she promised herself she would do so someday. Maybe after the Thing.

She could tell he had to put deliberate effort into not letting her see how concerned he was about her having struck out on her own. But he congratulated her on making it to Shannish, and he laughed at her tale of freaking Rum out by pretending to drink faerie wine.

She had thought their little afternoon escape, the day before, would take some of the edge off her yearning for him – for a little while, at least. But, as he said, "I'll see you in the morning," and released her from his arms to disappear, once again, into the darkness in the east, she found it had only made it harder for her to watch him walk away. She stood for a long time at the gate, letting the chill of the air seep into her bones, and then turned away, back toward the welcoming lights of Vale House.

"What are you doing?"

The harsh voice assaulted her as soon as she emerged from between the masonry columns into the yard, and she jumped, spinning to look around for the source of the voice. She spotted Eddie Tiene standing between two of the parked cars in front of the house.

"Damn it!" she shouted back. "You nearly scared me out of my skin!" She didn't bother putting any effort into civility, this time.

He stepped out from between the cars, glowering at her. "What are you doing consorting with him?" he demanded again.

Various choice words went through her head along the lines of what he could do with his assumption it was any of his business in the first place, but she let them go by because his own choice of words was so puzzling.

"Consorting?" she asked. It was the kind of word he and his pack had once teased her for even knowing, let alone using.

He clenched his fists at his sides and closed his eyes, turning his face away. When he looked back at her, he appeared to have got control of himself. He produced a weak and tired semblance of his usual toothy smile. "I apologize," he said. "I was only concerned for your safety. Callaghan McCarthy, that guy is bad news!"

Cally struggled not to let herself be dragged any further into this ludicrous conversation. She failed. "How would you even know anything about him?" she wondered.

"Don't you hear the things people around here say about him?" he asked. "He isn't normal! What are you doing con...hanging around with him? Is this why you get back so late every night? Is that where you were all day yesterday?"

She could think of someone else who was also definitely not normal. "Mr. Tiene, I am sure none of that is any of your business. What are you doing here anyway? I thought you checked out this morning."

"I didn't mean to alarm you, Kili. I had to come back to retrieve my wallet, which I accidentally left on the desk when I checked out." He dug it out of his pocket and waggled it at her as evidence. "I'm going now, see?" He nodded and turned toward one of the parked cars.

She didn't wait to see him off, but hurried up the porch steps and into the house. Bethany was just taking her purse out of the desk drawer, saying goodnight to Katarina. They both stopped suddenly when they saw the expression on Cally's face.

"You look like you've seen a ghost!" Bethany said.

Cally had to laugh at the irony of that. "I only wish," she said. "Different kind of horror movie. It appears I have a stalker."

"That Mr. Tiene!" Katarina didn't even have to ask. "I never liked the looks of him!"

"I'll call the sheriff to escort him out of town!" Bethany put her purse back in the drawer and reached for the phone.

Cally shook her head. "Don't bother. He's gone, now. Hopefully he won't be back."

"He certainly won't!" Bethany said. "If I ever hear his voice on the phone again, I won't be able to find any vacancies for him!"

Katarina laughed at that and said, "Speaking of vacancies, your room is available for the next several nights! I've given it an extra good cleaning and even changed the rugs and comforter for you. You should invite Mr. Dawes..."

Cally didn't want to explain why she couldn't invite Ben to Vale House for a sleepover, but she turned her head away for a different reason. She heard Eddie Tiene's car starting in front of the house, and she found herself wanting to make sure he really was leaving.

She slipped out onto the porch in time to see tail lights disappear through the main gate, and dashed down the steps into the shade garden so she could follow the car's progress along Main Street. To her complete lack of surprise, she noted that Tiene was exceeding the speed limit, and by the time she reached the back gate, the car was already halfway through the business district. She stepped out onto the sidewalk so she could watch the twin red lights fade into the distance, disappearing into the trees on its way to I 85. The lights finally winked out, and sound of the car's engine faded until the only sound she could hear was Merv Arkwright's guitar as he tuned it on the loading dock of the feed store.

—

Katarina really had freshened the Dogwood Room so that even if it didn't feel to Cally like "her own room" as much as she would have liked, it didn't retain any traces of ever having been anyone else's, either. She slept more soundly that night than she had in many days, though she dreamt several times of a dark-haired girl with violet eyes and a lavender gown who called herself Emerald.

29 - George's Story

Katarina fumbled with tinder and matches, trying to light the fireplace in the Hall. "Just another reason to miss Ignacio," she muttered, giving up. She returned to the dining room to see if anyone needed more coffee.

Cally put her arms into the sleeves of the sweater around her shoulders and did her best to ignore the chill, and the Preacher. Bethany had warned it was going to take longer than usual to give Ian his breakfast this morning, as she intended to try to talk him into admitting Sofie to a hospital. In her absence, Cally fielded three different phone calls from quests who wished to stay the whole upcoming weekend. She had to politely decline these, as the weekend would include the twenty-fifth, the night when Vale House would be closed. She wished she could at least give them a better explanation.

"Can we go to the coffee shop again today?" she heard George call down from the top of the stairs.

"Sure," she muttered under the susurrus of chatter and clinking silverware from the dining room. "If you can carry the old television set up to Nell's apartment for me."

"Oh. I don't think I could do that."

Cally sometimes forgot that sarcasm went right over George's head.

She looked around to make sure Bethany wasn't yet on her way back, then asked, "Georgie, do you know anything about this Preacher ghost? Could you talk to him for me and find out what he wants?"

George slowly came the rest of the way down the stairs, looking tenderly at the specter of the dark-clad man, but he didn't go any closer. "He can't hear me," he said. "He can't hear anything."

"Who do you suppose he is? What is he doing here?"

"He is the man who killed me."

Cally nearly knocked the chair over in her haste to stand up and back away from the desk. "George, what?" She stared in horror at the ghost that continued to gaze blankly at the pictures behind her.

"He's just waiting for me to forgive him," George explained calmly. "He doesn't understand I forgave him a long time ago."

Cally had never liked this ghost, and now she liked him far less. "You told me you were killed in a barroom brawl, George!"

"Yes."

"Well, how did he get here? And why is he always staring at those pictures of Ian's grandparents?"

"He's not looking at Isbel and Lionel," George said. "He's looking at the picture frames. They were brought here from the tavern, before it was destroyed, along with the desk upstairs, and my zemi. Isbel bought all these things at auction many years later. I guess the frames are kind of a zemi, for him. He doesn't understand what's going on." He explained all this as matter-of-factly as one might explain to a child how the earth revolves around the sun.

"George, I... I think I owe you an apology. You started to tell me this story a long time ago and I let myself get distracted. I never did give you a chance to finish. Can you please tell me now?"

He smiled generously. "You were very busy, at the time. You had just arrived here." He turned and pointed toward the top of the stairs. "So, I wrote the story all down, myself, in the e-book reader you gave me. It's still in the desk. You can read it any time you want to." Then he nodded toward the parlor to let her know Bethany was back.

"Who were you talking to?" Bethany asked, looking toward where the Preacher was just vanishing.

Cally came, as that moment, closer than she ever had to telling Bethany about George, but she shelved that conversation for later. She muttered vaguely about having to look something up for her next book and excused herself back to her office.

Once there, she raced up the spiral stairs to the Dogwood Room, and then straight through the door into the upstairs hallway.

The e-book reader she had given George was still in the butler's desk with his zemi, concealed under several sheets of Vale House stationery. Cally slipped this silently out of the drawer and cradled it in her arms, carrying it back down to her office. There, she wrapped a blanket around herself and sat on the end of the sofa nearest the window to read George's story, which she found inserted into the e-reader between "Moby Dick" and "The Mysterious Stranger."

—

My Story – A Tale of Action and Adventure
by Guacanagarix

I have always been very good at being invisible, even when I was living.

I realized very young that I was not like the other boys. I became reclusive, knowing I was never going to belong among my people, and eventually I decided to leave my village. I thought at first that I might find a place for myself in the city. My mother disapproved of this, but not as much as she would have disapproved if she were to find out who I truly am. So, I left my family and made my way down the mountains to the coast.

The world had changed. The trees were almost all gone, and the ground was very dry. The Spanish had built plantations everywhere, and the land looked sickly. They grew a plant that made a sticky sap, and from this they made a fiery drink that made them act like fools (and made some of them act like monsters) but even so, it did not give them any visions. I did not have a chance to try this drink at this time – I was only observing, at this point. I was advised by workers in the fields to keep myself hidden from the plantation lords, as they would be inclined to capture me, if they saw me, and force me to work in the fields. I did not think field work was a suitable job for me, so I passed by stealthily and continued on to the town on the coast.

The town was under the control – mostly – of the British in those days. Many boats lay at harbor in the bay. Huge boats; they called them ships. I saw right away that many of the men working on these ships were like me, and this made me feel safe, so I allowed myself to be seen by them. They greeted me in a brotherly way, but I could tell they had also been enjoying the fiery drink made at the plantations. They did not force me to work on the ships but, even though we did not speak the same language, they made it clear to me that I was welcome to join them if I liked, so I did.

I worked hard for many days helping them to unload boxes and barrels from the ship, and transport them by wagons to merchants in the town. Our boss handled the sales, and he held the money on his own person, but he was generous in spending it on meals for us in the evenings. We worked hard during the day, and in the evenings, we would eat and drink at the many taverns in the town until late into the night. That is where I first tasted the fiery drink, which they called rum, and I can't say I liked it very much. It did not give me any visions, and in fact it dulled my connection to the spirits of the land and air. But the worst part was that it caused my crewmates, who were normally decent men, to become foolish and sometimes violent. Our boss was very good, however, at keeping us in hand, even when we were soaked in this drink, and many owed their lives and continued freedom to him!

Our boss, the captain of the ship, was the first person to call me George. He could not pronounce my real name. My real name is Guacanagarix – I was named after an ancestor who is said to have been a great prophet. My boss would try until he laughed, and finally he said "I'll just call you George, George!" I have gone by that name ever since.

The ship also had a name: *Satisfaction.* I didn't know what that meant at the time, but I was very satisfied with my new job and it was easy for me to make the decision to stay with it one morning when the ship rode high in the water, ready to set sail. I would not have been able to bear watching these fine men go, these who had so openly accepted me as I am without question or judgment.

I did, however, have to undergo an initiation. I was made to wash my body all over in frigid salt water and rum, then to put on a new pair of boots. I had never worn shoes before and I found them very uncomfortable. Wearing only these new boots and nothing else, I was made to climb to the top of the tallest mast, where I was told to remain the entire night as the ship left port and headed out into the open sea. I had some incredible visions that night, I can tell you! But by morning my cold, stiff fingers were unable to let go of the lines I had clung to all night, and my new brethren had to cut them to lower me to the deck. I did not know enough of their language yet to tell them about the visions I had seen. I don't think they even wanted to know. Maybe someday I'll tell you about them.

It is true I missed my home sometimes, after that, and I never did see it, or my people or my family, ever again. But at sea I was free. We were all free, to be who we were, where the wind and the waves did not judge.

Our job was to stop ships – certain ships, only – which the King of England had instructed must not reach the shore behind us. We would take their stores and goods, and usually we would let their crews go back to their ship and return with only enough food and water to return to the lands from which they had come. What we took from them we were free to keep or sell, as our captain decided, once we returned to port.

Sometimes the crews of the other ships would not willingly surrender to us, and then we were obligated to board their ships and take them by force. This did not happen often, and I did not like it when it did, as many good men – or men who seemed to me to be good men, anyway – had to be killed, and jokes were made that there was not even any point in giving me a sword as I was more likely to accidentally injure myself with it than I was to kill any enemies. I was eventually assigned the task, instead, of bearing fire and torches to the other ships to set in their holds, hastening their crews' eventual decision to surrender. Sometimes we lost some of our own crew in this fighting, but other times, members of the other ships' crews would join us. At sea, all ships were the best ship, and all men were sailors.

One day we encountered a ship in the employ of a different king, the king of France, and they expected us to do the surrendering. My boss of course could not tolerate this kind of disrespect and a battle was joined that still gives me nightmares, even though I don't sleep anymore. Some of my dearest friends were killed, and I am ashamed to say I killed two of the other ship's crew that day, myself. I have often asked their spirits for forgiveness, but I have received no word back. I hope this means they are at peace now.

It was when this battle was over and the French ship was sinking in flames into the bloody water, that I first thought maybe life at sea was not really for me after all.

There was a city in the land of Jamaica, called Port Royal, where we often went to sell our goods when they became so heavy our hull hung low in the water. I liked these sojourns on land. Everyone was always festive, though they were often sick as well from the rum. We earned so much money selling our plunder that, even eating and drinking night and day, we could not manage to spend it all. There was so much excess that we began to share it with the monkeys and parrots which had learned the benefits of living near taverns. A few of my brethren decided to spend some of our money on houses and land. They tried to settle down as farmers, but most of them were still not able to stop drinking the plentiful rum, and so did not succeed at this.

I considered taking up farming, myself, but my English was still very poor, my Spanish and French even more so, so I did not know how to start or where to find information about how to go about buying land.

A gentleman took me under his wing. He was an English missionary from the American colonies, where he believed his god had directed him to convert the native peoples to Christianity, and he did not drink the rum. It was he who showed me my first book, the Holy Bible. He slowly and gently taught me to read my first written words, and I will forever be indebted to him for this. We spent much time alone together in the study he kept in the back of the tavern, and in time we fell in love. He insisted we must keep this a secret, and many times he told me we must end our relationship all together aside from the task of learning about his Bible. This never worked, however, and he became very distraught about this, to the point that he began drinking the rum in order to stop himself thinking.

One night we were dining as always in the hall of the tavern, and he was, unfortunately, once again deep in his cups. He began to talk with the other men about the sins of Sodom, how it must not be allowed, how it must be stopped. He and the other men grew more and more agitated about this and I realized I should leave. I slipped out of the building and down to the docks, but they caught up with me, shouting and waving weapons. That was the night I was killed.

I was very confused, at first. It took me a long time to understand what had happened. I saw very clearly that my body was in such a state that I should not be alive, and yet there I was, still watching the fight going on all around me, and I didn't understand how that could be. I saw him... my beloved...

He had told me about a Heaven, where his people go after they die. But I didn't go there. Maybe because I am not one of his people, or maybe because I didn't worship his god. But then, neither did I go to the Hell to which he said those who do not worship his god are doomed. My own people spoke of a shadow land where the spirits of our ancestors and those of beasts go, but if that is where I have ended up, it doesn't look at all like I expected it to!

After the bloody mess at the docks was cleaned up, I found myself back in the tavern, back in the room we had shared, and I was drawn very strongly to my zemi lying on the little table there. I tried to pick it up, but of course I couldn't. Eventually the woman who kept the tavern came and took away all our personal effects. She put my zemi into her desk in the office, and I never did see what happened to my brethren after that, for I was unable to move more than a few yards away from my zemi. I was able to continue learning, though, there in that office. It was frequented by many learned and wealthy men over the next few years. And that is how my love of learning began, and continued even after the desk was put on a ship and carried to new lands.

I understand the city of Port Royal was completely destroyed soon after that.

30 – Banding Together

Cally wiped her eyes and looked up as Bethany knocked softly and then let herself in to the office.

"Sorry to disturb you," she said. "The sheriff is here, asking if he can talk to you."

Standing stiffly, Cally draped the blanket over the arm of the couch and laid the e-book reader on top of it. When Sheriff Mahon stepped into the room, he brought someone else with him. She recognized Mr. Ennilangr easily, just from his massive frame, as the sheriff introduced him to her.

"Oh, we know Mr. Ennilangr, around here," Cally smiled, extending her hand to the modern-day Jötunn. "Are you looking for accommodations for tonight, Mr. Ennilangr?" So much for sleeping in her own room, she thought.

His hand completely engulfed hers when he shook it warmly. "I'm not," he said. His ice-blue eyes sparkled as he nodded his wide head. "I just wanted to talk to you, if I may."

"In addition to being our town's favorite over-the-road trucker," the Sheriff explained, "Mr. Ennilangr is a bail bondsman. Specifically, he is the one who holds the security on Foster's bail."

Cally drew her hand back quickly. "You helped Foster get out of jail!" The words came out of her mouth before she realized how confrontational they sounded.

"There's no need to be upset, Ms. McCarthy," said the sheriff. "There was no way he could have known what was going to happen. He was just doing..." His voice trailed off and he looked at the floor.

"I do deeply apologize for all that has happened," Mr. Ennilangr said.

"There's nothing to apologize for," Cally stammered. She hoped this was true, and then another thought occurred to her. "Is there any way you could help Ignacio arrange bail? It's been set very high, and..."

"Ms. McCarthy, I'll tell you the truth. I drive a truck because it amuses me. I get to see a lot of fascinating places. But the fact is, I don't need a day job. I have considerable holdings, back where I come from. Instead of just letting it sit around in a vault while I play golf, I like to put my money to work. Right now, I'm here to guard the investment I made in Mr. Brentwood. A large portion of my holdings are tied up in legal red tape until his murder is solved, and until then I'm afraid I won't be able to secure bail for anyone else."

Cally's hopes for getting Ignacio out of jail fell as quickly as they had risen.

"Well, then, I guess you have a vested interest in finding the real killer," she said.

He shook his head. "It's not just that. I do feel I am partly to blame for what happened. Please assure everyone: I absolutely *will* find the real perpetrator."

The sheriff stepped forward to insert his body between Ennilangr and Cally. "I've already questioned everyone at Vale House," he reminded the man who stood head and shoulders above him. Turning to Cally, he said, "Mr. Ennilangr has had full access to the police report and the detectives' notes, but he wishes to conduct an investigation of his own. I have agreed to let him do this, since he has agreed to cooperate fully with my office."

Ennilangr smiled at him and then at Cally. "That's his way of saying: don't feel pressured into talking to me if you don't feel comfortable about it. He's right, of course."

Cally thought that if Mr. Ennilangr did find whoever or whatever had killed Foster, he would probably be able to handle him (or it) more efficiently than the sheriff and his deputies could. On the other hand, she was just certain that if anyone could have bodily torn a man's head from his shoulders, it would have been this blue-eyed giant. She gave her head a shake to dismiss this thought. The killer, Danya had said, was tall and had a dark ponytail. This man was tall and had a blond ponytail. At least, it looked blond in the daylight...

"You see," Ennilangr went on, "it was a third party who came to me on Mr. Brentwood's behalf, with the funds to secure his bond. That person has failed to respond to my attempts to contact him, recently, and *that* is the person I am hunting. I have a feeling they will know quite a lot about what happened, if you know what I mean. I'll be around for the next few days. If you happen to think of anything that might help me with this, do not hesitate to...let the sheriff know, so he can pass it on to me." He smiled warmly down at Cally. "Enjoy the rest of your day."

———

Cally did enjoy the rest of the day, despite everything. Her son, and his girlfriend, arrived at Vale House less than an hour later.

She was filling in again at the reception desk when they arrived, and she didn't realize who they were, at first. This was the time of day when most new guests normally arrived to check in. Her first reflex had been to call out to the couple, through the screen door as they came up the front porch stairs, "Let me get Ignacio to help you with your luggage!" but she stopped herself in time. They weren't carrying any luggage, anyway, though the woman was carrying a cello case. That was when Cally looked closer and recognized her son.

She left the desk and ran to meet them on the porch. "It's so good to see you!" She had to reach up to wrap her arms around Brandon's shoulders. He had his father's dark, curly hair and tall frame, but he had Cally's changeable hazel eyes. Today they were a bit on the green side. "Oh, you should have called!" she told him. "I wasn't expecting you so soon!" Looking across the parking lot at their heavily packed sedan, she saw a vision of herself the day she had arrived in Woodley with everything she owned in the back seat of her car.

"I did call!" Brandon reminded her. "I just failed to mention, Rosheen and I were already on the road when we talked on the phone the other day." He stood back and reached a hand out toward the young woman accompanying him. "Mom, this is Rosheen Byrne. Rosheen, this is my mom, Callaghan McCarthy."

"Please call me Cally." Cally released her son and turned to the thin, quiet woman, not sure whether she should offer a hand or a hug. "It's nice to finally meet you. I've heard so much about you." She didn't mention most of it had been from Brandon's sister rather than from Brandon himself.

The young woman regarded her with wide, green eyes that were dappled and dark like the leaves of a forest in summer. She was far too thin for her height, Cally thought, and her voice sounded even thinner when she said, "It's nice to meet you, too, Mom." Long, light brown curls reached almost to the woman's hips, swinging out softly when she bent to set down the cello case. She put her long-fingered hand in Cally's, and her shy smile made her eyes sparkle as if a wind were blowing in the leaves. She turned and gazed through the front door, her mouth set in a wide, thin smile.

"Well," Cally said, smoothing her hair and clothing, which suddenly seemed rumpled and scraggly in the presence of Rosheen's pulled-together grace, "I'm so glad you're here, but the truth is, we literally have no vacancies at the moment. Maybe I can give you my own room and..."

"It's alright," said Brandon. "A man from around here – his name is Jud Thornton – he's set us up with a rental place nearby. He says you'll be able to show us where it is. Says everyone calls it the Yellow House." He held up a set of keys with a yellow plastic tag.

"Oh! Um, Yes." Cally was confused about what Jud was doing, renting out a house he was trying to sell, but maybe he figured a little income off the property was better than none at all. He had probably also figured, she thought cynically, if the tenants defaulted on the rent, he could come after Cally for it.

Looking at Rosheen, though, she was more worried what might happen if the Yellow House's reputed spooks should show themselves while she was there. She looked like the type who would crumble at the touch of a feather. "How long will you be staying?" Cally asked them.

"Well, Mom, we need to talk about that," said Brandon, using the same voice he always used to say things he feared would disappoint her. Cally made a deliberate effort not to let this bother her. It was simply wonderful to see her son, and she was glad he had found someone who seemed to care for him.

"When was the last time you two ate?" Cally asked. "I'll treat you to some locally made artisanal pizza." Rosheen, at least, definitely looked like she could stand a good meal. "It's just down the street. We can walk."

"May I just put my cello inside?" Rosheen asked. "I don't want to leave it in the car."

Cally followed her into the house and opened her office door. While Rosheen went into the office to put down the cello, Cally dialed Bethany's cell phone.

"I'm taking my son and his girlfriend down to Luke's for lunch. Don't hurry – I'll forward the phones to voicemail until you can get here."

She hung up the phone and looked up to see Rosheen, standing at the bottom of the stairs, looking up toward the gallery and smiling.

"She's pretty!" came George's voice from the top of the stairs.

Cally carefully did not turn her head to look at him. She couldn't tell whether Rosheen was looking at George or at the grand staircase itself, and she didn't want to ask. When the girl turned away and walked back to the front door, Cally looked up and saw George waving. Was he waving at her, Cally wondered, or at Rosheen? And why did that thought make her feel a little jealous?

Brandon and Rosheen ordered Motherboard Pizza's special of the day: gouda, wild mushroom and locally-grown spinach on a ciabatta crust. Luke slid it directly from the pizza peel onto the paper-covered table and handed out paper plates. Brandon and the proprietor of Motherboard Pizza had hit it off the moment Cally introduced them. Apparently, Luke could tell a drummer just by looking at one.

"Won't you join us, Luke?" Cally offered. Luke set down the fourth paper plate he just happened to have brought, and used the side of his pizza cutter as a spatula to serve large slices to all of them. Brandon and Luke continued to talk about modern rock music while Rosheen gazed gently at Brandon and devoured her pizza in short, sharp bites. It had been Rosheen who had requested extra mushrooms and, despite her waiflike frame, she had already nearly finished her first slice by the time the others started theirs.

"So, Rosheen," Cally said, looking for a way to include her in the conversation. "Is playing the cello very different from playing the bass?"

"Well," she said, wiping her lips, "the tuning is different. The bass is in fourths and the cello is in fifths. But you can bow a bass, and you can pick a cello..."

Luke and Brandon joined enthusiastically in on this line of conversation, which immediately went completely over Cally's head, making her the odd-man-out now. She didn't mind, but ate her gourmet pizza in silence, enjoying watching the two young men geek out about music theory. Rosheen gazed at Brandon while she ate, her wide, thin lips turned up at the corners in a loving smile even as she devoured a fourth slice.

Talk inevitably turned to the band Kurtis Kilmarten was trying to form, and they joked about getting Rosheen to provide the bass line on her cello. Cally thought about how George would enthusiastically have offered to play bass for them, if he could, and smiled quietly to herself. Looking up, she saw Rosheen looking at her and also smiling, as if they shared some private joke between them.

"Okay, I need to get back to work," said Luke, taking away his own plate and most of the paper napkins that had been balled up on the table. "I'll be in touch about jamming with you guys sometime! Can't let Gray Sabbath dominate the entire music scene in this town."

"Luke!" Cally laughed, trying not to choke on her food. "Gray Sabbath? Really?"

"You're right," he said. "I need to come up with a better name for them. How about The Elderly Brothers?" He laughed and ducked behind the counter, turning to the cooler to remove several plastic-wrapped balls of dough.

While Luke sliced pepperoni in advance of what would serve as that evening's dinner "rush," Brandon turned the conversation back to the one Cally had been anticipating.

"So..." he said. "My last job didn't work out so well."

Cally put a hand over one of his. "I know, Brandon. Your sister already ratted you out."

He grinned and glanced at Rosheen. "Well," he said, "I've decided. We've decided. To pursue other options. I'm so sorry to let you down, Mom, but I really don't think I was cut out to be an engineer."

She had already figured that out. "You aren't letting me down, Son," she assured him. "I'm proud of you no matter what you do with your life. Only you can discover what that is meant to be." Who was she, after all, to criticize someone for not knowing what they wanted to be when they grew up, when she had only resolved that question for herself a few months ago?

Brandon opened his mouth to speak further, but seemed to be having trouble finding words. Rosheen jumped in for him. "We've decided to come and live in Woodley for a while," she said, "and see what opportunities arise."

That explained why they had rented an entire house, anyway, Cally thought. She still felt concerned, though, about the reputation of the particular house they'd rented.

"After all," Brandon defended, "Coming here seems to have done the trick for you!"

Cally remembered what both Ben and Merv had told her: Those who found Woodley were there for a reason, for better or worse. She looked from Brandon to Rosheen and back again. Finally, she said, "Son, you know you always have my support, no matter what you choose to do. Even if all I can offer at the moment is emotional support." She hoped he got this hint. "But are you sure that big, old yellow barn of a house is such a good place to start?"

"Well," said Brandon, "in fact, I'm not. So, let's go and have a look at it." He balled up his napkin and dropped it on his plate. Rosheen grabbed the last slice of pizza as they all stood to go.

31 - Leaving for the Thing

Rosheen loved the Yellow House. From the moment her eyes fell on the overgrown lawn and leaf-covered porch, she beamed like a sunny afternoon. Brandon, also, seemed excited about it, but Cally guessed that was mostly because he was happy with anything that made Rosheen happy.

Cally helped them carry their belongings from their car, noting sadly that Brandon's drums were not among them. Of course not, she thought. They would not have fit in such a small car – not with all their other belongings. She knew the drums were probably stashed safely in Brandon's sister's house, but she also knew how much he was going to miss them. His decision to come to Woodley to make a new start must have been as desperate as the one that had driven her.

She left the young couple uncovering furniture and piling the dusty sheets in the cellar (Brandon was certain he could get the old wringer-washer to work again) and went back to the crossroads where Ben stood waiting at the gate. She wished there were time to introduce him to Brandon and Rosheen. After all, she had met his family – part of it, anyway – but there wasn't time. She wanted to spend these few evening moments alone with him, especially on this evening. The Thing began tonight, and it would be her last chance to see him for three days.

"It looks like Bree let you off work early!" she called as she reached the crossroads.

He didn't waste time with answering, but drew her into his arms and kissed her like he might never stop. When at last they stood back and regarded one another, though, he had not forgotten her words.

"Bree really is on our side, you know," he said.

"She has a funny way of showing it!"

"Yes. She does." He kissed her again, and then she kissed him, taking as much advantage as she could of the extra few minutes they had.

"I *will* be back," he reminded her, and anyone else who might have been listening.

"I know you will," she told him, pulling her collar up against the growing chill. She glanced back toward the Yellow House, feeling like someone actually was listening to them, but she couldn't see anyone on any of the porches along Gardens Road.

"In an ideal world, I could at least take a cell phone with me," Ben was saying. "This is just the worst possible time to leave you here."

"You could take one," Cally said. "I wouldn't work, but..." She laughed. "Maybe you could leave it as one of those gifts we have to leave."

He didn't laugh. "The Crown Prince of Faerie does not have to leave gifts," he said, his voice more dismayed than amused. "He only has to give himself." Then he shook his head, and laid his hands on Cally's shoulders.

"I know you're a strong woman," he said. "You'll be alright. You're always alright." He did smile at this, and gave her a squeeze. "It's just, all these things going on in Woodley now, it seems like something we should be going through together."

His words made Cally feel like she was going to die right there on the spot. She pressed her face against his chest so he wouldn't see the tears leaking from the corners of her eyes.

"I'm sorry," he said quickly. "I didn't mean to make you feel worse."

"No, no," she said. "I'm just not used to this being loved business, and..." She didn't know how to explain to him that she had had lovers, and she had had a husband, but she had never before had a partner, and she didn't know how to act around someone who was trying to be one.

"You could still come with me."

Cally was moved that he would even suggest this, but she dried her tears on his shirt and looked up at him. "If all this stuff weren't going on," she said, "I do believe I would hop over this fence with you right now." She sighed and looked to where the moon, just a few days short of full, was rising above the meadow. "I guess my job right now is to handle things on this side of the fence, and yours is on the other side of the fence."

By the way he closed his eyes and turned his head away, she could see he knew she was right.

She shivered. She still felt like they were being watched; she looked out over the meadow and saw only the moon and the high, flying cirrus clouds. Even the horses were nowhere to be seen.

She looked back at Ben. "It doesn't mean we aren't working together, though," she said. "Would it be inappropriate of me to ask you to carry a message to the Thing for me? In Ian's name, perhaps. To ask them if they can do anything for Ignacio. To help us find who killed Foster, or to at least, I don't know, help us post bail..." She stopped, grimacing. How tacky was it to even think of asking the Queen of Faerie to use her people's treasure to bail an ordinary mortal out of prison?

Ben held her at arms' length so he could fix her with a level look. "It would not be inappropriate of you to ask. I would do anything for you, Cally."

She couldn't breathe, for a moment, looking up at him standing against the moonlit clouds. He reminded her so much of his father, she felt like she had slipped a little way backward in time. She had to stop herself telling him so, because she was fairly certain he would not take it as a compliment.

"Please just..." She brought herself back to the present. "Just tell them what's going on here. If the arrangement is supposed to be that Vale House is protected in exchange for guarding the Vale, well, it can't very well do that if a murderer gets to walk away with the title to the property. They need to step up. Tell them the ball has been kicked into their court. The Seelie Court, as it were, ahah..."

He looked at her for a long time without saying anything, and she imagined he was trying to think of a gentle way to tell her how severely she was overstepping her bounds, to perhaps suggest a more diplomatic way to state her case. But, as the clouds passed over the moon and the light faded behind him, Cally could almost swear his expression was one of awe.

"I will tell them," was all he said. He took her face between his hands and kissed her softly. "I will see you in three days."

Ever since their love affair had begun, even before their first kiss, Cally had stayed to watch him go. She had always watched him walking (loving the way he walked) as his back retreated, fading into the shadows, and she had memorized the spot where he would reappear the next day. She didn't let herself watch him this time. She was afraid that if she did, she might start to wonder if this could be the time he would never reappear.

Bethany had left the porch light on for her. She walked back through the masonry gate into the parking area in front of Vale House, and she still felt like someone was watching her. Looking over the hoods of all the parked cars, she braced herself in case she spotted Eddie Tiene inexplicably lurking there again. She saw nothing. Perhaps it was Rum, passing along the fence line? But, she guessed, he was probably already on his way to the Thing tonight, too.

It was not until she reached the top porch step that the feeling of being watched lifted from the backs of her shoulders. She paused to nod her regards to the Captain's ghost, and that was when she heard footsteps behind her.

She spun around, one hand cocked and ready behind her. If her old high-school nemesis had come back to obsess further about her and her personal life, he had made a huge mistake: she was in no mood for it. But the figure she saw, running across the parking lot, wasn't Eddie Teine, and wasn't running toward her. This person was tall, and muscular, and a long ponytail hung down his back. Even in the moonlight, Cally could see that it was distinctly blond.

Ennilangr slowed as he neared the fence, and here he dropped to all fours, continuing to run until he leaped like a gazelle over the fence. Where he landed, a gigantic ram now ran, blindingly fast, through the rustling meadow grass, toward the moon until the sound of his passing vanished into the hills.

"Son of a bitch," said Cally.

32 - Vintage Technology

"I don't need any help, thank you."

Bree didn't look up from her paper as Cally crossed the store toward her.

"I didn't come to offer my help," Cally said, looking around at the racks of snacks and magazines. The store was always dusty inside, but without Ben, it seemed dustier than ever, and deathly silent. She stopped at the counter, directly in front of Bree, and took a white foam cup from the stack beside the coffee maker. "I came to talk."

"And what could we possibly have to talk about?"

Cally filled the cup from a pot that had probably been sitting on the warmer for hours now. She winced when she took the first sip. Andi's coffee at the Bean Garden had thoroughly spoiled her.

"You're the only person I can talk to, around here, about these things," she said to Bree. "I don't mean about Ben. I mean, about people who are not absolutely, one hundred percent, bona-fide human."

"I don't make racial remarks about your Irish background, do I?"

Cally couldn't help but laugh at that. It was a clever burn.

"Look, Bree. Whatever killed Foster..."

She stopped, because someone was yanking on the door, trying to enter the store. Cally recognized the giggly voices of the two young women who owned the Wyrd Systers Books and Gifts store, several doors down the street. She turned back to the door to kick it open, and they piled into the store like an entire school bus full of children on a field trip.

"Good morning, Brigid!" called the tall blonde. Cally recalled that the woman went by some new age moniker she had chosen for herself: Sister Earthstar or Raven Moon or something like that. She could never keep those sorts of names straight – they all sounded alike to her.

"Did you know that 'Brigid" is the name of a great, ancient Celtic goddess?" the other woman, short and round with raven-black hair, called across the store. (Cally had forgotten her name, as well.)

"You don't say?" Bree called back, then muttered, as Cally returned to the counter. "She's only told me twenty times. As if *they* know anything about ancient goddesses. Or anything else!"

Cally sipped her sour coffee silently, thinking maybe their mutual disdain for the Wyrd Systers' arcane "knowledge" could, conceivably, become something they could bond over.

The two women gushed, as they went to the back of the store, about how happy they were to see Cally, and how much they were looking forward to her new book coming out. "What do you think about this murder in town?" one of them called out as she opened the door of the drink cooler. Willow. That was what she called herself, Cally remembered (or thought she did.)

Cally wasn't sure whether the woman was addressing her or Bree but, knowing Bree would probably not answer, she called back, "It's really sad."

"Seriously?" The other woman reappeared, carrying a tall energy drink and a plastic packet of snack cakes.

"No, I don't mean the murder itself." There was no point, around here, in pretending to be sorry Foster was gone. "I mean that Ignacio Munoz has been falsely accused of it."

The woman put her purchases down on the counter while her friend turned to the newspaper rack. "Ms. McCallaghan," she said solemnly, "we would be totally flattered if you would join us in a reading tonight to try to figure out who really did it."

Cally was so desperate, she was almost willing to join the two women for a tarot session. Almost. "I'll think about it," she said. She hoped it wouldn't come to that.

The taller of the two women had selected a small stack of

tabloids from the rack. Cally suspected Bree kept them in stock just for these two customers. As she counted out bills to pay for their purchases, the shorter of the two said to Cally, "Good. We'll see you tonight, then."

"I didn't..."

A sudden shuddering noise erupted from the door as someone pulled it open with a single yank. Luke dashed in, his pizza-delivery hat askew, grinning widely. "Hey, Willow! Hi, Raven!" he called to each of the Wyrd Systers in turn.

Then he walked across the store to Cally. "Glad I caught you!" he declared happily. He held her laptop out to her. "Here! Fixed!"

"Oh!" Everything else that was going on had completely pushed any thoughts of her computer from her mind, but she said, "This is wonderful," as she took it from Luke's hands. "How much do I owe you?"

"Nothing," he said. "It just needed a faster processor, is all. I took one out of the old PC Tom Mitchell left for me to trash, after he fried his motherboard trying to delete a bunch of por... spam. Well, it's faster than the one in your antique lappy was, anyway."

"Baby bro," said the one he had called Willow. "I keep telling you, your business isn't going to survive if you don't start charging your customers for your labor and expertise."

"She's right." Cally reached into her purse for her checkbook. "That used part may not have cost you anything, but I know putting it in my computer was not just a simple matter of plug-and-play."

He gave her a sly smile. "OK, here is how you can repay me: just keep reminding Brandon we need a drummer for this band we're trying to start. Alliances are sometimes more valuable than cash," he said sagely, winking at her.

Cally agreed to do this, not bothering to belabor the point that a drummer without drums wouldn't do him much good.

Once everyone had finally left the store and it had regained its dusty silence, Cally put the laptop down on the counter, determined to resume her attempted conversation with Bree. Bree had put down her newspaper, as well, and folded her arms in front of her on the countertop. Apparently, she was now ready to talk but not, Cally perceived, to listen.

"Look," the old woman said. "It's not that I dislike you any more than I dislike everyone else. It's just that I love my brother." She fixed Cally with a wolf-like glare.

"Bree, I am not going to hurt your brother!" Cally spoke more sharply than she had meant to or than, she suspected, was advisable with Bree, but she wasn't sorry. This wasn't what she had come here to discuss, and she had already had this "conversation" too many times. But, maybe, with Ben out of town for a few days, they could finally have it out once and for all.

"I know you aren't going to hurt him," the old woman said. "It isn't about you, or your feelings, or your intentions or integrity. Or his! This is bigger than any of us. You are both fools, and you are both playing with fire, and you could bring entire worlds crashing down on everyone, and all for what? *'True Love?'*" She made air-quotes, then threw her hands up in exasperation.

"Bree." Cally took a deep breath, turning her palms up on the countertop. "I know this is bigger than us, and that a couple's desire to be together is insignificant in the grand scheme of things."

Bree's face had already twisted in disgust at the mention of "a couple's desire to be together." She turned her head away and looked out the front window. "You know he'll have to go, someday," she said in a quieter voice. "Back to his mother's court, after I die."

"I do know that."

"So, you better pray for my health, eh? You'll want me to live a good, long time."

"I already care about you, Bree, regardless." It was true.

"And he's going to live forever. You know this. Once he goes...there, he will never age again."

"I understand," she told Bree. "I have made my peace with the fact that someday I will have to let him go. You don't have to be afraid I'll bring on the apocalypse by trying to hang onto him or something."

"You understand nothing!" Bree's voice suddenly filled the entire store, sharp and loud. Cally could swear a gust of wind hit the door from the inside, jamming it shut harder than it already was. She tried to step backward, but she couldn't move. The old woman's face loomed huge before her, bony fingers crooked like claws just inches in front of her face. "You understand nothing! You stupid girl! You stupid, selfish girl!"

Frozen where she stood, Cally could swear the old woman stood straighter and much taller than she thought was physically possible. Her hunched shoulders seemed to expand to fill all of Cally's vision, and her breath sounded like a growl from the depths of a cave.

Then she turned away, releasing Cally from her invisible grip, and continued to speak to the wall behind her. "He is going to live forever! Do you even know what that means? No! You only think of yourself! He is going to live forever! *He is going to love you, forever!* You're lucky. You will die, one day. But he won't. He is going to love you forever, and…"

Bree's voice suddenly choked off as if a hand had closed around her throat, and she seemed to shrink. She sank down and down until Cally had to look over the counter to see her, crouched almost to her knees on the dusty floor, sobbing with grief.

Cally instinctively wanted to go around the counter and put her arm around Bree's shaking shoulders, but she knew better than to try anything like that. Only Ben could get away with that sort of thing, and he wasn't here.

And anyway, she still couldn't move, except for the trembling that had started somewhere near the base of her heart and was now slowly spreading throughout her entire body. As she gazed at Bree, the realization slowly dawned on Cally that the old woman was right. Cally had not been thinking of anyone but herself. It had not occurred to her that Ben, also, would lose her. And that, unlike her, he was doomed to spend unending years enduring that loss. Maybe she had just never believed anyone could ever love her enough to miss her, not even for a mortal lifetime let alone for eternity, but she knew Ben was the type of person who could love like that. She should never have allowed herself to get involved with him in the first place.

"But I have never been very good at not getting involved in things I shouldn't get involved in," she muttered, not having meant to say it out loud.

Bree's sobbing ceased suddenly, as if someone had turned off a tap, and silence filled the room as Bree put a hand down on the floor to push herself back up into a standing position. Brushing dust off her clothes with both hands, the bent and trembling old woman looked up at Cally from the side of one eye and said, "No! No, you haven't, have you?"

Cally was dumbfounded to watch a smile slowly spread across

Bree's face - a genuine smile, not the cynical smirk to which Cally was more accustomed. "Maybe there's hope after all!" she, inexplicably, said.

Bree turned away again and disappeared behind an old, wooden cabinet that had once, judging by the faded tin sign attached to it, displayed chewing tobacco. Cally heard drawers opening and shutting, until she heard Bree bark, "Here!"

The old woman returned to the counter, waving something in her hand. "Now that you have your computer back, see what you can do with this."

She set the object on the counter in front of Cally. It was an old, black computer disk of the sort that Cally had not seen since her daughter had been in diapers.

"Bree, my computer is old, but not this old. It can't do anything with this." She picked it up gently, as if she thought it might crumble at her touch. "Maybe you can give it to Luke, and he can send it out to see if any data can be recovered from it?"

"No!" Bree's tone resumed its sharpness. "Don't send it anywhere! Don't show it to anyone else!"

"Sorry! Okay, I won't!" If it was that important to Bree, Cally realized, having given it to her must have been a tremendous vote of confidence. She promised to do some research and find out what she could do.

She picked up the disc, tucked her computer under her arm, and left the store never having learned anything she had gone there to learn. She figured she probably wouldn't have got a straight answer from Bree, in any event.

As she stepped out onto the sidewalk, she saw Ben's daughter and Rosheen, laughing together and walking toward her.

"No, I'm sure you won't find any fresh produce in Auntie's store!" Ana was saying. "Dry rice, maybe, or canned beans. You might have to beg Jacob Lucas for some celery."

"It's alright..." Rosheen said, then, "Oh, hello, Mom!" when she spotted Cally.

Cally looked back through the store window to where Bree glowered behind the counter, and cringed inwardly at the thought of what frail Rosheen was about to encounter. Well, at least she had Ana with her for backup, and the two young women were apparently already on friendly terms.

"Nice to see you both," she said to them.

"Mom, I'm gathering some ingredients for Brandon to cook for lunch. Why don't you join us? He's a really great cook!"

As Ana effortlessly opened the door and entered the News Store, Cally agreed to meet Rosheen and Brandon at the Yellow House at lunch time. Waving behind her, she stepped into the street to cross to the other side and looked down at the floppy disk in her hand. Turning it over, she glanced at the yellowed paper label that had been stuck to it. She stopped in the middle of the street, staring at it.

Written on the label, in neat, square letters, was simply the word "Emerald."

33 - Announcement

Cally dropped the floppy-disk on top of the pile of notebooks in her desk drawer, then eagerly powered up her newly repaired computer. She was amazed at how quickly it started up, now. Ordinarily she would have had time to run to the kitchen for a cup of coffee while waiting for all the startup routines to resolve themselves, but this time she barely had time to get comfortable in her chair.

The first thing she did was send a chat message to Emerald to let her know she was back in business. Then, holding her breath, she opened her word processor. It, too, started faster than she had ever believed it could, and Luke had already installed the update with which she had been having so much trouble. She realized she owed the young man a great debt of gratitude, and promised herself she would sincerely try to talk Brandon into joining his band, drums or no drums.

Emerald replied, in the chat window, just as Cally was looking through the list of files in her folder named "Work in Progress." She abandoned all thought of getting any writing done that day, then, and instead filled Emerald in on all the things she had been wishing she could talk to her about over the past several days.

It was wonderful to be able to chat with all ten fingers again, and the morning flew away. Emerald expressed sympathy and hope about the situation with Ignacio, but didn't have any more insight than anyone else had on that topic. To Cally's consternation, Emerald seemed already to know that Cally had gone over the fence into Shannish. She tried to get her enigmatic internet friend to explain clearly how she was able to know this sort of thing, but nothing Emerald said in reply to this made much sense, other than "Melissa told me," and that didn't make any sense, to Cally, either.

Emerald didn't already know that Brandon had arrived in Woodley, but she was pleased to hear it, which Cally somehow found deeply reassuring. As she started to type in her description of having watched Ennilangr transform into a goat the previous night, the phone on her desk rang.

It was Bethany. "Your future daughter-in-law called and asked me to let you know lunch will be served in twenty minutes."

Holding the phone between her chin and shoulder as she typed, Cally apologized to Emerald for having to cut their chat short, and promised she would only be gone a couple of hours.

"Rosheen is a very nice young woman," Bethany was saying. "And that son of yours is so sweet. He reminds me of you! You must be very proud."

Cally hung up the phone and went out into the Hall. "Thank you for saying I'm sweet," she said, retrieving her jacket from the coat rack. "And yes, I am proud, but I'll be a lot happier for them when they both get jobs."

Bethany shook her head and made clucking noises in her cheek. "We always worry about them, but they always turn out fine in the end."

"I guess so." Cally sighed and wondered if she had 'turned out fine in the end' yet, herself.

She could smell the aroma of good cooking before she even reached the other side of Main Street. It seemed to involve curry, and other herbal aromas she couldn't quite place. Turning onto the walkway in front of the Yellow House, she was pleased to see the path and the porch had been swept clean of leaves. In fact, the entire front yard had been mowed and raked, and the space between the house and its neighbor had been cleared of weeds so that Brandon could park his car there. Cally thought: "The Captain would be glad to see someone taking proper care of his old home."

Rosheen met Cally at the door just as she raised a hand to knock. The aroma of food was overwhelming. In the dining room beyond the living room, she could see Brandon rushing back and forth setting plates on the table. "Hullo, Mom!" he called, flinging a dishtowel into the kitchen behind him. "We just want to show you one thing before we sit down, okay?"

He hugged her quickly in the entryway, then turned toward the stairs at the side of the narrow room. "It'll just take a minute," he promised, leading her to the upper floor. Rosheen brought up the rear.

When they reached the narrow hallway at the top, Brandon led them straight to the little door at the end, and Cally's heart sank. What had they seen in the attic? She looked back to Rosheen behind her, but the young woman's wide, quiet smile had not changed.

Something felt different, right away, about the atmosphere of the attic room, and it didn't take long for Cally to understand what it was. Brandon was gesturing excitedly toward the big, round window as he crossed the room to stand in front of it. The glass had been replaced. The broken panes had been artfully reconstructed with colorful grout holding the shards together, and rebuilt panes now alternated with whole ones in the window frame to form an altogether pleasing pattern. Everything was held in place with a complex armature of lath and shims.

"The glazing compound is still drying," Brandon said. "I found a whole gallon of it in the basement. It was Rosheen's idea to tint it. When it cures, I'll remove the bracing. It's going to look really nice!"

"Yes," Cally had to admit. "It really is." It occurred to her that, even if Brandon didn't intend to pursue a career as an engineer, he was certainly able to put his innate engineering skills to good use in everyday life. "And maybe the Arkwright estate will give you a break on your rent, in return for all the work you've been doing around here."

She didn't mean to, but Cally turned her head and looked up at the rafters where she still did not see any hanged ghosts swinging. When she looked back, she saw Rosheen looking at her. The young woman's large, green eyes had grown even larger in surprise, but the usual mellow smile quickly returned to her face. She nodded to Cally and said, "Let's eat before the food gets cold."

Cally couldn't have agreed more. Her mouth was watering as Brandon showed them to their seats and sat down, himself, to pass around a steaming bowl of rice. "Rosheen is allergic to iron," he explained, "so I've been learning to cook, since most cooking utensils are made of iron or steel."

"I'm also a vegetarian," Rosheen added. "Brandon has been so sweet, taking my diet into consideration."

"You have certainly mastered the art of making food smell good without meat," Cally said as she spooned, from another bowl, an amazingly fragrant mixture of beans, celery, and herbs that he offered as a topping for the rice.

"I don't know what I call it," said Brandon. "It comes out different every time."

Cally laughed, and they enjoyed their meal and one another's company in silence for a few minutes. "Maybe you could open a gourmet restaurant in Woodley," Cally suggested. "I don't think Luke would mind a little competition."

"He'd mind it even less if I would join this band he keeps going on about," said Brandon. "We could get Rosheen to play bass."

Rosheen let out a laugh no louder than her usual speaking voice. "Maybe!" she said. "We'll see!"

"Mom," Brandon said. He reached a hand across the table to cover Cally's left hand with his own. He spoke in what was almost, but not quite, his "my last job didn't work out" voice.

Cally finished chewing and swallowed carefully. "Yes, Son?" She steeled herself to be supportive no matter what he was going to say next.

He put down his fork and took Rosheen's hand with his other hand. "There's something Rosheen and I want to tell you."

"Well, if you two are planning to get married, you certainly have my blessing," she said. "I'm very happy for both of you."

She nodded to Rosheen, but the young woman's smile, though it grew broader, turned downward toward her plate and Cally could see her squeeze Brandon's hand. "Well, maybe someday we'll do that," she said. "But that's not quite it."

That was when Cally began to feel dizzy. She forgot to breathe, and through the ringing in her ears she could barely hear Brandon saying, "There's a reason we're fixing up the upstairs room, you see. Rosheen and I are expecting a baby."

Cally struggled to keep her face neutral while her mind shouted, "No! You're both too young! You don't have any money, and neither of you even has a job!" She couldn't speak, however, and on a deeper level she realized this was probably a good thing.

She forced herself to inhale. She put down her fork to take

Rosheen's free hand.

"Everything is going to be okay," Rosheen said in an uncharacteristically assertive tone.

The three of them sat for a long while with hands clasped around the table in silence. At some point, there were hugs all around, and Cally watched herself telling Rosheen what a wonderful mother she would be, telling Brandon she was always proud of him. It was as if she were watching all of this on a television in another room with the sound turned low. Brandon packed up leftovers for Cally to take back to Vale House for Bethany and Katarina to try, and they all made arrangements to get together sometime in the next couple of days – Cally couldn't remember when or where.

She found herself coming out of her daze halfway down the hill behind the Vale House barn, walking through the birches along the fence toward the railroad culvert. When she realized where she was, she sank to her knees in the cool moss and let the plastic grocery bag of leftovers fall from her hands. Sitting with her back against a fence post, she closed her eyes and tried to stop her head spinning. If she could even remember her own name, it might be a good start.

"Hi!" said a voice behind her. "You aren't happy?"

"Oh, Adam, not now. I can't deal with this right now." At least she remembered *his* name.

"Is that for me?"

She opened her eyes to see him climbing over the fence, leering at the bag of leftovers with his foxy nostrils flaring.

"It's all yours," she said, letting her head fall back against the fence rail. "One hundred percent vegetarian fox friendly."

He jumped down to the ground beside her and picked up the bag. Cally hoped he wasn't going to eat it right in front of her. She wasn't sure if he would be likely to eat like a human or like a canine, and she lacked the fortitude at the moment to be curious about that.

He squatted in front of her with the bag balanced on his knees. "You know," he said, pushing his face close to hers. "Most people are happy about the advent of new life in the world."

"How did you know about that?" It was a rhetorical question and she didn't expect an answer. Of course he knew. Everybody knew everything, around here, except for her. She sat up and struggled to explain, as much to herself as to him. Gazing down the hill into the culvert, she thought the stone archway seemed to have grown much bigger and darker than she remembered. The gurgle of the stream running through it sounded like her life draining away in a fading trickle down a dark tunnel. She shook her head to clear it of this morbid illusion.

"I'm not unhappy, Adam. It's wonderful. It is. I just feel so... It makes me so... I haven't felt like this since my father died. It reminds me that I am mortal. So very mortal. Someone like you wouldn't understand."

He threw back his head and laughed at that. Cally would not have been surprised if the laugh had morphed into a howl, but it did not. "Okay, Grandma!" he said, still laughing, and somehow that made her feel a little better, even though she didn't feel ready to be a grandmother. No, she corrected herself: she didn't feel ready to be old enough to be a grandmother. That was it.

Adam opened the bag on his knees and sniffed at the contents. "Oh, this is perfect!" he said. Then he looked back up at Cally. "You need advice," he said. "And my advice is to get some advice."

She shook her head. "I don't know where on earth I could find the kind of advice I need, right now."

"Yes, you do," said Adam. "You remember Willow and Raven from the diner out by the highway. They always give you good advice."

"No, I don't..." Cally squeezed her eyes shut, trying to capture a brief memory that flitted across her vision like an illusion. "No, Willow and... wait. Maybe I do remember them."

34 - A Free Reading

A heavily customized motorcycle was the only other vehicle in the parking lot when Cally arrived at the Seven Forks Diner on the westernmost edge of the Woodley town limits. Its heavily tattooed owner was just leaving, and he held the door open for Cally. "Those two ladies sure do know how to fix some chili cheese fries!" he declared.

"Maybe I'll try them," Cally said, though she wasn't hungry at all. She would have to think of something to order, she thought. The two old women who ran the diner loved to give "free" readings, but she didn't think it would be good form to accept one without at least buying an appetizer.

The diner's interior was decorated with murals on three walls depicting ancient oak trees dripping with Spanish moss. Red-topped tables and round stools gave the whole place the look of a forest dotted with mushroom seating. Cally selected one of the booths near the kitchen, and by the time she sat down, the proprietors had noticed her.

An older woman with long, white hair bustled toward her, already pulling a deck of cards from her checkered apron. Cally struggled to remember her name. Was it Willow? Maybe it was Raven. Cally had never been able to keep their names straight, but she was starting to think of their faces as familiar.

"So good to see you, Ms. McCarthy!" the woman said, sliding into the seat across from Cally. "How is our town's favorite famous author today?" She had not brought a menu with her.

"Not very famous yet, I'm afraid," said Cally, trying to remember the woman's name. Maybe it was Raven – Willow was the taller one. Or was it the other way around?

The other proprietor came through the double kitchen doors, carrying a tray laden with glasses and a pitcher. She was short, with a round head of soft, silver curls.

"My, goodness, Ms. McCarthy, your aura looks positively wobbly today!" she said. She placed a sweating glass of iced tea in front of Cally, but also did not offer her a menu. Instead, she slid in to sit down beside Cally.

"And how are you...Raven?" Cally asked self-consciously as the other woman began to shuffle the cards.

"I'm Willow. She's Raven," said the little woman, nodding toward her tall friend and folding her hands on the tabletop. "So, Cally, what question is preying on your mind today?"

Cally felt relieved that she, apparently, was not going to be required to eat anything. But, now that she came right down to it, she couldn't narrow down the things on her mind to just one question.

"Do I only get one?" She watched as...Raven. It was Raven who pushed the deck across the table for her to cut.

"I'll tell you what," she said. "You list out the things that are troubling you, and I'll tell you what the question is."

"Cut the deck once for each one," Willow suggested, and Raven nodded her agreement.

"Okay." Cally lifted a few cards from the top of the deck and set them to one side. "Well, I'm in love with a man I can't ever really be with, but that's not as bad as it sounds. I've never been so happy in my life." She lifted and set another small pile of cards on the other side of the deck. "Here's the serious problem: a murderer is running around loose in Woodley, and an innocent man is paying for it." The two women nodded gravely at her. She knew she didn't need to elaborate on what everyone in Woodley was talking about, these days, and they were waiting for her to continue.

She cut the deck again, picking up and holding a small stack of cards in her hands, close to her heart. "I am about to become a grandmother."

Willow, the short woman beside her, placed an arm around her and said, "That's quite a list. And congratulations."

"Thank you," said Cally, not sure why this made her squeeze her eyes shut to stop the sudden sting of tears. "It's just... What on Earth am I supposed to do?" She realized she was about to cry in front of people and, for the first time in decades, she didn't even try to stop herself. The gentle gazes of the women watching made her feel absolutely nurtured, and she poured out her heart to them.

"You know, I had been entertaining notions of running off with him. Just leaving it all behind and running off to...Faerieland or whatever they call it there where he goes. Even though I love it here. I really do love it here and I had thought, for a little while, that I had finally found my home and I had thought I would never go running again like I always used to do but... Well it just seems like this town needs me, and Vale House needs me, and my kids are still in *this* world and, sure, they don't actually need me anymore but I do love them and I would miss them and that was kind of holding me back but I was still..." Willow pulled a stack of paper napkins out of her apron pocket and set them in front of Cally. "And now this. I can't leave, now that I have a grandchild on the way. I would miss all the..."

She looked down and realized she had been shuffling the cards she held in her hands. Sniffling, she said, "Oh, sorry, I..." She tried to put them back in the order they'd been in when she picked them up, but Raven put a hand over hers and pressed them gently down to the table.

"It's okay. It's fine," she said, taking the cards out of Cally's hands and putting them back on the top of the stack without rearranging them.

Cally used the napkins to dry her tears and blow her nose while Raven re-stacked the rest of the small piles, in their new order, on top of the main deck. Raven drew the cards closer to herself, patting the sides of the stack to trim the edges. Then she turned over the top card. "How is your book coming along?" she inquired, regarding the card and setting it in the middle of the table.

The cards themselves were remarkable. They were perfectly square, for one thing, unlike any tarot deck Cally had ever seen, and the one Raven had put down depicted, as many of them did, a segment of a dirt path. This one showed a sharp curve, which certainly seemed appropriate to Cally at the moment.

"My next book should be out in time for Christmas," she said in answer to Raven's question.

"That's nice, but I mean the book you're working on now. The third volume." She turned over the next card.

"Oh! Well, I..." Cally watched as Raven aligned the card next to the first one. This one extended the path and showed it crossing a little stream with flowers growing beside it. "I have to confess, I've been very distracted lately. I haven't got much writing done."

"That's a shame," said Raven. "Your fans hate the wait between sequels." She continued to draw cards from the top of the pile, arranging them next to one another on the table.

Cally wasn't even sure she had any fans left, anymore, after already having neglected them for so long, but she didn't say so. Suddenly she put a finger on one of the cards. It depicted a meadow very much like the one in front of Vale House, bordered by a similar forest, only this forest had a unicorn peering out of it. She hadn't noticed it at first because it was black. "These cards," she said, "Who is the artist? The style reminds me very much of our Nell's."

"Very good!" said Willow. "They were indeed originally designed by Doctor May, long ago."

"Doctor?" Cally asked, but Raven drew her attention back to the task at hand, setting the remainder of the deck aside and drawing her finger along the path wandering through the picture they formed.

"I don't know, Cally," said Raven. "It looks like you still have not yet met your friend Emerald. Why is that?"

"I..." Cally couldn't think of how to answer that. "I guess I haven't been trying very hard lately," she admitted. "But in my defense, a lot of other things have been going on..."

"Maybe you should be thinking about it," said Willow. "Maybe the answer to that, holds the answers to all the other questions."

"Is that what the cards say?"

"They say you need to pay more attention to the portal," said Raven and, to Cally's dismay, she began to gather the cards up and shuffle them back into the deck.

"Wait, what? Is that it? What does that even mean?"

"It means you finally know which question you should be asking."

Cally opened her mouth and started to shout something, but then closed her eyes and counted to ten.

"Well, you did start by telling me to list the problems so you could find the question," Cally admitted. She clenched her jaw to stop herself adding, "Thanks for nothing."

After all, she thought, *their readings are free, and you get what you pay for.* At least she did feel a little better for having been able to pour out her heart to two mother-figures.

Willow stood to let Cally out of the booth. Raven stood as well and both women wrapped Cally in a warm hug. "We know you'll figure it out," said Raven. "You always do."

Cally sighed and tried to remember the last time she had ever "figured it out."

"Thank you," she said. "Thank you both." She meant it, mostly, even though she felt no clearer than she had when she'd arrived.

35 - Drums in the Dark

"Everything is all set for breakfast," Cally said, setting the tray bearing Ian's dinner, along with a selection of treats with which to attempt to coax Sofie's appetite, on the night stand. He regarded his meal much more eagerly than she had seen him do in a long time. Before he picked up his napkin, however, he leaned over to offer Sofie a few sips of tea. She sipped and smiled and nodded, but didn't open her eyes.

"Ms. McCarthy," Ian asked, turning back to her, "have you decided what you're going to do on the twenty-fifth?"

"Bethany has invited me to her house. After all, I'm used to sleeping on sofas, lately!" Cally laughed and didn't mention that she had not yet given Bethany an answer.

"Just please do not entertain any ideas of staying here on that night," Ian said, giving her a serious look while pressing far too large a chunk of butter into his mashed potatoes.

"And what will you do that night, Ian?" She looked meaningfully at Sofie, peacefully reposing on her pillows and comfortable, but definitely not in any condition to go couch-surfing at a neighbor's house any time soon.

Instead of answering, Ian wiped his butter knife on his napkin, which he folded and laid down on the edge of the tray. "I want to show you something," he said.

Cally hoped he wasn't going to show her anything else that indicated incipient bad news. He grasped the cane, which he kept beside him at all times, now, and struggled to stand. Cally put a hand under his elbow to assist him, but he really did seem to be in much less pain, today. She entertained a hope that this might be because the medicine Doc had prescribed was working.

He led the way into his study but didn't go to his to his desk, as Cally. Instead, he went to the closet and, opening it, right on through it to the door at the back.

"Ignacio was supposed to have boarded that up!" Cally said as Ian felt for the latch concealed behind hanging coats and umbrellas.

"Ignacio still answers to me," he reminded her, flashing a grin that made Cally smile in spite of her dismay. A dank smell of charred wood and kerosene wafted out as Ian opened a narrow door made of drywall. He reached into the dark opening and found a flashlight hanging on a peg just inside. This he tried to juggle, along with his cane, as he stepped into the dark opening.

"Ian, you shouldn't..." Cally took the flashlight from Ian's hand. "Okay, but let me go first, in case you fall."

She stepped nervously down the narrow stair into the dark. Trying to keep the flashlight focused on the steps in front of her, she saw the beam of light wobbling in her shaking hand. The stench of char and kerosene, along with the sound of her footsteps echoing in the dark space, brought all the terrifying memories of that night rushing back into her mind.

"Normally," Ian was saying behind her, "this is where I used to stay on the night of the twenty-fifth. With Sofie. He never came down here."

"He?" Cally turned to shine the light on the bottom step for Ian. "But you can't stay here now! This room is far too unhealthy!" Anyway, she noted, scanning the room with the flashlight, it was completely empty, now. The charred remains of the bed and book shelves had been cleared out and disposed of months ago. Several damaged joists had been replaced, but charcoal and a smoky film remained in many corners.

Ian laughed and limped past her into the darkness. "Don't worry," he said. "I don't plan to stay here. Come." He was heading, apparently by memory without the aid of the flashlight, across the room to the other door at its far end. Cally turned the light to the door for him and followed, taking tiny steps as if she expected to stumble and fall over rubble that was not there anymore. In her mind, she kept seeing her foot slipping on some broken knickknack and herself falling, down into the darkness while hands closed around her throat.

"Ian, wait for me!"

She caught up with him as he opened the other door and reached out to pull the string that switched on a bare bulb overhead. For the first time, Cally saw the cellar under Vale House flooded with light.

Ahead of her rose the rickety wooden stairway leading up to the kitchen, which she had only ever stumbled up and down in darkness, before. The rest of the cellar was punctuated by masonry columns and bearing-walls, and filled with the usual detritus of old cellars. Tables covered with rusty tools, dusty chests, precariously balanced stacks of crumbling cardboard boxes, and window screens forever awaiting repair filled most of the space under what Cally guessed was probably the dining room and the north wing.

Ian pointed with his cane to a little space in a far corner where the light barely reached. There, a small room with no door lay approximately, Cally guessed, under the Vale House grand staircase. The objects inside it were covered with a plastic tarp.

"Go on," he said. "Take a look!"

She wove her way between two stacks of boxes, one of which had been knocked over to spill dozens of empty cookie tins across the floor. She could see the gray tarp had been tucked carefully around whatever it was protecting inside the little room, and also that it was hopping with camel crickets. Ian continued to smile encouragingly at her, so she put out a hesitant hand. Camel crickets exploded into the air like mud-colored popcorn, many of them landing in her hair.

"Ugh!" She brushed them off and muttered unladylike words at them as they scattered into the shadows, scurrying under other objects in the cellar. If she disliked anything about living in the South, it was camel crickets. "Okay," she said at last, and began to un-tuck the tarp from around the objects in the little room.

Dragging the crackling mass of gray plastic out into the main cellar, she turned back to look and saw a complete drum kit gleaming dully in the light of the electric bulb. Stacked one on top of another she recognized a large bass drum, a snare drum, a floor tom and even a set of cymbals and hi-hats.

"I'm afraid my drum sticks were all misplaced a long time ago," Ian said. "But I'm sure your boy brought his own with him. I know

I never went anywhere without a pair of sticks, back in the day." Cally glanced back to see him gazing at the jumbled pile of instruments with a dreamy smile that made him look at least ten years younger.

"Oh, Ian, this is...!" Cally didn't know quite what to say. She knew Brandon would be thrilled to see these, and she understood Ian was offering them for his use, but "Thank you," didn't seem like nearly enough.

"It would make me very happy to see someone use them and give them the care they deserve," Ian assured her.

Thanking him over and over, Cally helped the old gentleman back up the stairs, saw him settled into his chair with his dinner, and turned back to close and lock the door on the kerosene-smelling secret stair. Ian would wait for Cally to leave before he would start eating, she knew, so she excused herself and backed out of the room, hoping his food was still warm.

She had got all the way back to her office before remembered she still hadn't got him to tell her what he planned to do on the twenty-fifth of October.

36 - Rosheen's Plan

Cally: How is the Thing going?

Emerald: You're assuming I know.

Cally: I guess I am. Do you? Know, I mean.

Emerald: I understand Ben Dawes is dancing with all the gorgeous faerie women day and night, now.

Cally: That wasn't what I was concerned about.

Emerald: Good, because you shouldn't be. :)

Cally: Good, because I'm not. I had sent a question with him, though. I was wondering if it has been addressed yet.

Emerald: Seriously, I will probably be filled in on the outcome of everything at about the same time you will. I wasn't invited. But you were. Why didn't you go?

Cally: There's just too much going on right here, right now. Anyway, I wouldn't have the first idea what to do or how to act.

Emerald: Right.

Cally: No, really. I am not afraid to go over the fence. I thought I proved that when I went to Shannish! You're worse than Errin!

Emerald: Ow! OK now that really hurts!

Cally: :) Seriously. The main thing I'm wondering right now is about this Mr. Ennilangr, who I thought was an ordinary human. OK rather an extraordinary human, but he turned out not to be a human at all and I think he's at the Thing, right now. And I think he had something to do with Foster's death, and if I can figure out what...

Cally looked up as someone knocked on her office door. Before she could answer, the door opened and her son entered.

"Hi!" said Brandon. Rosheen, as well as Andi's son Kurtis, stood in the Hall behind him. "We're just here to get the drums!" Brandon was grinning every bit as widely as Ian had when he'd shown the drums to Cally.

"Okay," said Cally. "It will be easiest if you take them out through the kitchen. Please ask Bethany to show you the way - I'll join you all as soon as I'm done with this."

She resumed her chat session with Emerald, but Emerald was saying she had never heard of a Mr. Ennilangr. She was, however, as intrigued as Cally about the old floppy-disc with the word "Emerald" written on the label. She promised to ask around the Extremely Wide Area Network to match Cally up with someone in possession of an older computer that could read such an old form of data storage.

Cally stood, stretched, and went out into the Hall. Bethany was not yet back at the desk, and Cally could see through the screen door that the parking lot was nearly empty, as well, except for the red pickup truck, which had been moved to the bottom of the porch stairs. As she watched, Katarina came around from the north side of the house, showing the way for Brandon and Kurtis, who were carrying the bass drum between them. They loaded it into the back of the truck and went back for more.

Behind her, at the top of the stairs, she heard a woman's voice say, "Great, I'll do my best!" Cally assumed this must be a late-departing breakfast guest, and went to the desk to find their checkout paperwork.

Then she heard another person speaking.

"This is so exciting!" said a voice in George's distinctive accent.

Cally paused, feeling a sudden and completely irrational stab of jealousy. How could someone else be talking with George? But that was silly, she told herself. Of course she could not possibly be the only person who could see or understand him, and why should she be? Maybe it was Nell, home for a visit. She started up the stairs.

"All we have to do now," George was saying, "is get Cally to go, and bring my zemi with her."

"Why can't I bring it?" The woman who was speaking turned around as Cally emerged into the upstairs hallway. It was Rosheen.

Beyond her, George stood smiling, and his smile grew even wider when he saw Cally.

"I've been invited to join the band!" he declared happily.

"That's...terrific, George," said Cally, and then turned to Rosheen. "May I speak with you in my office please?"

Rosheen was already trying to reassure Cally as they went down the stairs. "Don't worry, I won't let anything happen to him."

Cally didn't say anything until they were safely inside the office, where she could be reasonably certain George wouldn't follow. She closed the door behind them and led the young woman to the sofa.

"I know I tend to be overprotective of him," she admitted, sitting down and patting the seat beside her. "I know it's nuts. He did fine for four hundred years before I came along! But, well, he's lived pretty much in isolation most of that time. I worry about what would happen if the world in general got wind of him."

Even as she said this, she found herself reveling in how good it felt to talk to another, living human being about her relationship with a ghost, as if it were a perfectly normal thing everyone talked about every day. She was still concerned about the subject at hand, though. "I just wish you hadn't put this idea into his head. I'll never be able to talk him out of it now."

Rosheen's quiet smile showed she had no intention of helping Cally try to talk George out of anything.

"You're worried about what would happen if word got out that the hottest new band on the scene has a member who is a ghost." She reflected Cally's words back to her to show she understood. "I agree. Don't worry, the plan is that I will play the bass. Well, I'll be playing one that isn't plugged in. The one George will be playing will be out of sight, behind the amps. George isn't interested in becoming famous – he just wants to play!"

"The other band members know about all of this, too?"

Rosheen nodded. "They're on board with it. Zenbe is the one who told us George wanted to play bass in the first place. Zenbe's already in another band, himself, but he's going to be our soundguy. And Brandon, well, he knows I'm a little different. I never hide anything from him."

Cally found herself wondering how Brandon might react if he should find out his own mother was also "a little different." She wondered if Rosheen had already told him.

"Luke also talks to ghosts, did he ever tell you?" Rosheen was saying. "And other things as well. As for Kurtis, well, we're just taking it on a need-to-know basis with him. He is likely to figure out I'm not really playing that bass, though. I'm guessing it won't be too weird a concept for someone who went to high school in this town, after all."

Cally was beginning to think she was the only person who had to work to absorb this sort of thing as perfectly normal but, after all, younger people did tend to be more flexible. She supposed she should be grateful for that.

"Okay, but." She struggled to find the words to voice her real concern. "I just feel uncomfortable with the idea of too many people knowing about George's zemi. What it is and where it is. It would just make him too vulnerable."

"You're absolutely right," Rosheen said, to Cally's surprise. "That's what George says, too. See? He's no dummy! I guess that's why he wants you to come with us when we play. Mom, will you be our roadie in charge of the zemi?"

Cally sighed and looked around the room, tapping her fingers on the arm of the sofa. At length, she said, "Okay, I guess we can do it that way." She had always tried to attend Brandon's performances before, whenever she could, and she wanted to be there to support him at this one, as well. "But please, Rosheen. Please, do not let anyone else know about the zemi. I mean, not even Brandon. Please."

"Fair enough!" said Rosheen, jumping up from the sofa. "Excuse me, I have to go let the folks at the Fountain know the gig is on!"

"The Fountain in Blackthorn?" Cally asked her retreating back. "When is this gig?"

Rosheen paused halfway out the door and turned to answer. "Tomorrow night. October the twenty-fifth!"

37 - The Pizza Delivery Boy's Tale

"What do you do on the twenty-fifth of October, George?"

"I'm going to rock!" he said, raising his air-bass over his head and leaping down the last couple of stairs to do a rock-star slide into the Hall. He was wearing blue sneakers, torn jeans and a Rush t-shirt with an owl on it.

"Of course you are but, I mean, what do you normally do?" Cally asked. "Have you ever seen whatever it is everyone is so afraid of? I assume you stay here, despite the rules. You can't exactly go somewhere else."

"I can. Watch." He vanished. Then, laughing, he reappeared halfway up the stairs. "Don't worry. All us ghosts will be okay."

"What about those of you who are not ghosts?" she asked, remembering he often reminded her that not every anomalous manifestation around Vale House was caused by a ghost. He didn't answer, but flashed a grin and danced his way, headbanging to unheard music, the rest of the way up the stairs.

Only a handful of guests were scheduled to arrive tonight, as very few people had been interested in staying on a Saturday if they could not also stay on Sunday, October the twenty-fifth. Bethany and Katarina had taken advantage of this slowdown to take the red truck into Blackthorn to visit Ignacio. While she procrastinated about writing at the reception desk, Cally made up her mind that tonight she would take advantage of temporarily having her own room back by taking a long, luxurious bath in the antique tub in the Dogwood Suite's tiny bathroom.

When Bethany and Katarina returned, she went into her office and carried her computer, along with an armful of notebooks and the anachronistic floppy disc, up the spiral stair. Moving aside a half-dozen of Bethany's dogwood-themed decorations, she dumped her belongings on the dresser and thought it really was starting to look more like her room again, after all.

"Maybe I'll even bring some brandy up from the sideboard later," she thought.

First, however, she needed supper. She stuck her head out the door of the Dogwood Room into the upstairs hallway.

"Hey, Georgie! Want to come with me to get some pizza?"

George couldn't eat, of course, but he would enjoy the trip and, from what Rosheen had told her, he might enjoy chatting with Luke, as well. He didn't reply to her question, though. She tried again a few more times, calling softly so the few guests in the house wouldn't hear her, but she couldn't get his attention. "He's probably practicing some killer riffs," she supposed. It was just as well. He'd get to jam with Luke tomorrow night, anyway.

She left the house through the service porch and passed under the now mostly bare crape myrtles to the little wooden gate that opened onto Main Street. It was becoming a decidedly chilly night, and the katydids in the branches above, though valiantly trying to keep up their night songs until first frost, sounded like mere memories of their summer selves. When she reached the business district, Cally noted sadly that Merv Arkwright wasn't on his loading dock. In fact, no sign of life, except a few leaves tumbling along in the cooling wind, disturbed the lonely length of Main Street. Cally considered stopping in the News Store to check on Bree, but thought better of it, especially since she had no progress to report with regard to the mysterious floppy disc.

She took a shortcut between the News Store and the vacant storefront next to it. Besides the Dawes family Daimler, Ennilangr's eighteen-wheeler, with its murals of leaping rams, was parked across about ten spaces in the lot behind the shops.

Eyeing the rig sideways, she made a huffing noise and cut across the parking lot to the back of the pizza parlor. When she went around the brightly lit yellow and green front of the shop on Railroad Street, however, she found Motherboard Pizza absent its proprietor. She called Luke's name toward the back of the shop several times, but received no reply, and figured he must have gone to deliver a pizza.

"Pls call me when you get back, thx," she wrote on a napkin, along with her cell number, and went to the coffee shop to await his return.

The door of the Bean Garden stood open, emitting aromas of coffee and chai spices into the chilly evening air. Andi had already put most of the chairs up on tables, in preparation for closing, and she and Nell were sitting at the only table that still had its chairs on the floor. As Cally stepped inside, she looked around to see if Luke was there, but he was not.

Andi stood and said "Coffee-flavored coffee, coming right up!"

"Please make it decaf," Cally said. "I plan to get a decent night's sleep tonight." She sat down next to Nell. "How are you doing?" she asked.

"I've decided to go to medical school."

It was sometimes hard to tell whether what Nell was saying was real, or a reference to something that was going on only inside her own head. While Cally was considering how to reply, Andi returned with Cally's coffee.

"Nellie, you'll be forty-five years old before you finish!" Andi pointed out, setting the coffee down in front of Cally and resuming her own seat at the table.

Nell laughed. "I'm going to be forty-five either way!"

Cally had to admit she had a point. "Doctor Helen May," she said. "It has a nice ring to it." She also thought it sounded vaguely familiar, but couldn't recall where she'd heard it before.

"I'm glad you're here." Nell reached under the table to her lap. "I have a present for you." She lifted and began to unfold a bundle of cloth. Cally was already smiling, fairly certain she knew what it would turn out to be.

"Another one of your amazing hand-painted t-shirts!" She reached out to trace with her finger the artfully intertwined musical notes painted in oranges and browns on the bright blue shirt. Amid the notes and a few flowers were letters, in a splattery font that stood out loudly from all the other details, spelling out *"Don't You Dare Turn Down That Bass!"*

Cally winked at Nell. "I know someone who would love this."

Nell handed it to her. "You can wear it to the show tomorrow night."

"Everyone in the band will love it." Andi nodded her approval. "Kurtis is so stoked! He's done nothing but practice since this morning."

Cally checked the time on her cell phone. "Have either of you seen Luke lately?"

Her answer came in the form of someone calling her name from outside in the street. It was Luke's voice, and his shout was accompanied by the sound of running feet coming nearer.

"*Cally!*" His call was more urgent than Cally would have expected, regarding a mere pizza order. "Ms. McCarthy!" They all turned as Luke appeared in the open doorway, stopping so suddenly he nearly fell over. His face was white and his eyes were wide.

"I'm right here, Luke," Cally said. "What's the matter?"

He was panting in deep gulps as he grabbed the door and wrenched it shut behind him, making the little bell attached to the top jangle like an alarm clock. He had the note she'd written on the napkin balled up in his fist, and he threw this on the table in front of Cally.

"You have to get out of sight!" He shouted, looking around at the windows and up at the short café curtains along their tops. "Andi, how does this door lock? Where's the key?"

As he turned, Cally noticed that, though his face was white as a sheet, a dark bruise was spreading across one of his cheekbones. She stood up in alarm, but when she reached a hand toward his bruise, he grabbed her by the arm.

"Jacob Lucas!" Andi stood, also, as Luke began dragging Cally toward the counter. "What is *wrong* with you?" She looked toward the counter, herself, and Cally suspected this might be because she kept a baseball bat behind it.

"He's looking for her," Luke said, not pausing. "You need to get out of sight. All of you!" He continued tugging until Cally, now alarmed, herself, followed him, but she stopped just short of letting him push her down to the floor behind the counter.

Nell stood and said, "Maybe we should all continue this conversation upstairs in my apartment."

Luke let go of Cally and let out his breath. "Duh," he said. Before he could grab her and start tugging again, Cally walked past him and started up the narrow wooden stairs at the back of the shop. Luke and Nell followed, and Andi promised she'd be with them in a minute as she went to get the key out of the register.

Cally had not seen Nell's apartment since she had helped move in Nell's many boxes of books. The studio consisted mostly of a long, narrow room with windows along the street end. As soon as Luke saw these, he ran to tug the curtains shut across them, nearly yanking the curtain rod down in his haste. He relaxed at last, then, and turned to say "Sorry!"

Andi came into the room holding something wrapped in a white bar-towel. She paused to turn the deadbolt on the door behind her.

"Now are you going to tell us what this is all about?" Andi asked.

"Yes, yes, sorry." He paused to take several deep breaths, and Cally could see his hands were shaking.

The only furniture in the room that wasn't easels and art equipment was Nell's bed, along the wall farthest from the street, and a small table currently covered with cups and jars of colored liquid with paint brushes soaking in them. Nell pulled a paint-stained folding chair out from the table and offered it to Luke, but he stared at it as if he had forgotten what sitting was. Nell sat down, instead, and stirred a few brushes around in their jars.

"Sorry," Luke said again, "but I just didn't want him to see you." He looked, wide-eyed, at Cally. "He really, really wanted to find you!"

"Who is 'he'?" Cally pressed.

"Inferno dude. The General," said Luke. "Of the Fomorians. Eladha. You know him as Eddie Teine, but he..."

Cally threw back her head and raised her arms in a wide gesture of exasperation. "Him again!" she said. "Just let him find me! I'll..."

"No!" Luke looked like he was going to start trying to shove her under the bed, so Cally settled for growling epithets under her breath.

"You're hurt, Luke," Andi said. "Did Eddie do that?"

"No. Well, yes but, he's not Eddie, he's..."

"El – a – dha," said Nell in a musing sort of way. "Yes, Eladha, Eddie Teine. It makes sense."

Andi took Luke by the arm and made Cyndi Lauper, who had been sleeping in the middle of the bed, move over so he could sit down. She held the towel against the bruise on his face. He winced at its touch, at first, but then put up a hand to press the ice inside more firmly against his cheek.

Cally was ready to leave the room and go hunting for Eddie Teine herself. She took her cell phone from her purse. "I'm calling the sheriff," she said.

"Dunn won't be able to do anything," Nell said. "Eladha has gone. His presence is required at the Thing. He's probably in a lot of trouble, now, for not being there earlier."

Everyone in the room (except the cat) stared at the young woman with varying degrees of incomprehension, but then Luke lowered the ice pack from his face.

"Okay, here is what happened," he said.

Cally lifted Cyndi Lauper from the bed and sat down next to Luke, transferring the cat to her lap. She instinctively scratched under its chin, earning purrs that soothed her nerves in return, while Luke explained.

"I was delivering Merv's pizza. He's eating at home tonight, since it's getting chilly out and anyway Woodley is so *empty* these days." He gave Cally a meaningful look, here, but she didn't understand what subtext he meant to convey. She waited for him to go on.

"Okay, well, I was walking back, coming along Railroad Street, and it was so quiet, because even the Watchers have all gone away, these past couple of days."

Cally did want to ask him, then, what "the Watchers" were, but he was staring away past the curtained windows, and she didn't interrupt as he went on. "Because it was so silent, I heard the footsteps behind me while they were still a long way away. I normally wouldn't have given it a second thought but, you know, with a murderer running around town, I was kind of jumpy. I turned to see who it was. It was that creepy dude, that old boyfriend of yours."

"He isn't my old boyfriend!" Cally growled. Cyndi Lauper stopped purring and poked her claws gently into Cally's thigh until she resumed petting her.

"That's a relief, anyway," Luke said. "Well, he's a wussy looking ratbag, anyway. I thought I could mop the floor with him, if I had to." He paused to replace the ice pack on his cheek, and Cally guessed Luke hadn't done any floor-mopping that evening.

"When he saw me looking at him, he started running toward me. He kept yelling 'Where is she? Where is she?'

"I said 'Who?' even though I was pretty sure he meant Cally.

"He said, 'That girl! Callaghan McCarthy!'

"I said 'How would I know?' and got ready to hit him if he did try to grab me. I didn't even bother to tell him Cally isn't a girl. I mean, she's got kids older than me!"

Cally ignored this while Andi grinned at her.

"Well, he got really ugly with me, then," Luke went on. "He started yelling, 'Don't play stupid with me! You saw them! I saw you watching them. You saw everyone leaving for the Thing!' Sorry, Cally," he added as an aside. "I wasn't spying on you and Ben. I just thought it was such an amazing parade, that night, all the wood spirits and Watchers and things all marching down Main Street."

Cally's eyes widened. She had certainly not seen this, and she knew she would have to ask Luke for more details at a better time.

"So this guy was going on, and at the time I thought he sounded scared and desperate. 'She should have been with them. She should have gone to the Thing. But she's not there! And she's not at Vale House, either! So where is she?' as if I would know."

"He's been at Vale House?" Cally forgot all about the cat and stood up in alarm.

Luke sidled closer to the door in case he needed to intercept her. "He had already left there when I saw him," he assured her. "He was looking for *you*. I didn't think it was any of his business where you might or might not be, so I said, 'Who the fuck are you to be asking anyway?'

"And that was when he..." Lowering the towel, Luke gazed toward the window as if he could see through the curtains. The bruise on his face was still spreading, in muddy shades of blue and purple. "That was when he laughed at me and said 'Oh, that's right, smart-boy. I guess even you can't see through glamour.'

"And then he, sort of, wiped his hands across his eyes, and when he did, they smeared under his fingers until they dripped down his cheeks. Where they had been, these big, wide, yellow slits looked out. They were like snake's eyes, looking right out through the ripped skin, and I could see whatever was underneath was as red as blood. And his mouth was..." he held up his hands to either side of his own mouth, but two or three inches wider on either side. "Full of teeth. Lots and lots of needle-sharp teeth. He didn't sound like a human anymore, either. His voice was like a thousand voices calling right out from hell!

"He said: 'I am fucking Eladha, the fucking General of the fucking Fomorian army and now you will fucking tell me where Callaghan Fucking McCarthy is!'"

Luke turned his eyes, wide and moist, back to them. "Honest to god, Cally. I was so scared, if I had known where you were, I would have told him right then. I'm glad I didn't know.

"I guess he could tell by my big stupid stare that I really didn't know, so he made this disgusted noise and smacked me out of the way and headed off, down along the side of the tracks, toward the crossing into the meadow. I think if he hadn't been in so much of a hurry, he would have stopped to finish me."

"I don't understand a single word you're saying," Andi said, putting her arms around Luke. "But I'm glad you're okay."

"Eladha," Cally was murmuring. "Eddie Teine." When she spoke them, she could almost hear how the names sounded similar. "How long has he been... was he ever just some stupid high-school kid? Were those other morons in his gang even human, themselves? Was he always stalking me?"

"And why?" Luke looked like he had some ideas about that, but Nell spoke up calmly.

"He probably disposed of the real Eddie Tiene a long time ago," she said. She stirred a paintbrush around in a cup as she gazed up at the unfinished mural of a waterfall on the wall behind the table. "I think Foster was also one of his disposable pawns, for a time, before he..." She let out a sigh and put the brush down. Cally thought she saw a tear forming in Nell's eye, the first she'd seen since Foster had been sent to jail.

Then Nell put her hands together in her lap and turned in her seat to address them all levelly. "There are rules, in Faerie, against interfering with the human world, and faeries are a very rules-bound people." Cally nodded. Ben had often tried to explain this to her. "But Eladha has been able to get around those rules by indebting humans into doing things for him, instead. Keeping an eye on Cally was one of those things, for instance. But after she got married and left her hometown, the real Eddie Tiene lost track of her. That probably upset Eladha – he doesn't like to lose."

Cally never normally questioned Nell about all the "facts" of which she had such a store inside her head, but this time she couldn't hold her tongue. "How do you know all this?"

"Melissa used to tell me about it. She used to talk about you all the time, even before you came to Woodley. It's part of the reason we brought you here..."

"But why?" Cally stood up, fists clenched, looking toward the curtained window. "Why would he want to keep track of me?"

In answer, Nell tuned back to her painting, reaching up to dab a few yellow flowers into her mural. A magnificent ram stood amidst the flowers on a jutting rock halfway up the side of the falls. "Don't worry," she said. "He's at the Thing now. The queen will be very angry at him for arriving so late. You're the least of his worries, right now."

"Why does that not make me feel any better?" Cally asked.

Cally attempted to take her planned leisurely bath in the Dogwood Room, but after her unnerving visit to the coffee shop, she couldn't enjoy it, even with the help of the best brandy from the sideboard. She jumped at every noise, and found herself wishing for a waterproof computer so she could chat with Emerald in the tub. Finally, she got out of the water, dried off, and took her computer into bed with her. There she let her old friend say reassuring things to her until she finally fell asleep.

She woke before sunrise to find the laptop wedged under her elbow, still running and complaining that its battery was low. Dragging herself out of bed, she looked out the window at the perfectly framed view of the horizon over the meadow, where the dawn was breaking and where Ben would, again, not be appearing today. She sighed and, placing the computer on top of her pile of notebooks on the dresser, plugged in its charger

Before shutting the device down, she reviewed the text of the chat from the night before. It had consisted mostly of Emerald explaining to her who Eladha was (a legendary leader of the Daoine Sidhe who had ultimately sided with their enemies, the Fomorians, for reasons of general principle) and promising to inquire among her friends about why such a person should be interested in Cally. Then, as Cally's replies had become less and less coherent, Emerald's messages had become mostly urgings to Cally to just let Ben handle it from his side of the fence, shut off the computer, and get some sleep.

Now Cally typed a quick line into the chat window, not needing a reply, to reassure Emerald that she had slept at last. Before she closed the program, she added:

"There was a time, not long ago, when I was finally okay with the idea of waking up alone for the rest of my life. Ben had to go and ruin that for me, didn't he?"

In spite of herself, even as she typed this and turned off the computer, she couldn't help smiling.

Vale House was eerily silent on the morning of the twenty-fifth of October. As she descended the stairs, it seemed to Cally that even the few lingering breakfast guests spoke in whispers, and the loudest sound to be heard from the dining room was someone stirring their coffee. Bethany's voice echoed through the Hall when she answered the phone.

"I'm sorry, I'm afraid we have no vacancies for the rest of October. We do have openings again in early November...yes, I understand! Well, just try calling earlier next year. Say, in June or so. Thank you – you too!" She hung up and looked over at Cally. "I hope you slept well!"

"I did," Cally said. "At least, I slept."

"Have you decided what you're going to do tonight? My invitation is still open, you know."

"Thank you, Bethany, it's sweet of you. Well, I plan to go and see the kids play in their show tonight. I'll be out late with them, so I think I'll just crash at their house afterward."

Bethany nodded her satisfaction with this plan. "I'm too old for that kind of music," she said, "but they really are very nice young people."

"Yes. They are. Bethany, are you certain Ian and Sofie are going to be alright?"

Bethany didn't look certain at all as she answered Cally in a philosophical tone, as if she had rehearsed the same answer to herself every year. "Well, they always have been, before. Maybe Ian uses his storm-calming skills on this thing, too. Or maybe whatever it is doesn't affect the south wing of the house."

"Have you taken their breakfast to them yet?" Cally offered. "I can do it, and I'll ask him about it."

"You can try," said Bethany. "But I can tell you from experience, he won't answer."

Cally nodded and turned toward the kitchen, feeling a little bad for having lied to Bethany. She had no real intention of spending the night of the twenty-fifth at the Yellow House. She would, she had decided, return once again to Ben's springtime bower – Ben's and hers, she reminded herself – on the hill in the meadow. She would spend the night there, gazing at the stars and the City on the horizon, trying to figure out why, every time she thought she had figured out what she was going to do with her life, everything would change and she would have to figure it out all over again.

Katarina appeared to be bustling busily about the kitchen when Cally arrived, but Cally couldn't tell, for the life of her, what the woman was actually accomplishing.

"You should just take the day off," she suggested as she accepted the cup of coffee Katarina pressed into her hands. "I'll clean up after breakfast."

"No, no," she said. "Keeping busy helps me keep my mind off things." She swiped a towel vigorously over the already immaculate work table.

Cally gazed through the window over the sink to the little stone cottage at the back of the garden. "Have you and Ignacio ever seen...you know, from your house, have you ever seen what goes on here on the night of the twenty-fifth?"

Katarina followed Cally's gaze. "We did. Once. We noticed a blue light inside this house, like someone was carrying a flashlight with a blue lens. Ignacio thought it might be a burglar, and he started out the door to come over here, but both of us were suddenly so afraid. As soon as he opened the door. We were so afraid, we couldn't move, and we couldn't even understand why. I've never seen Ignacio afraid, not before and not since. But, that night, he came back inside and we closed the door and drew the curtains and turned off the lights and hid under the covers, and we have done the same every year since. Except this year I guess I'll do it alone..."

"Oh, Kat..." Cally reached for her. "Maybe you should come with me tonight to see the kids' show?"

Katarina avoided Cally's embrace. "No. I'm going to have to get used to this. Ignacio taught me to be strong. He'll be home soon enough. I'll just be upstairs changing the beds..." she added and quickly left the kitchen. Cally could hear her opening the little door to the backstairs and running up the narrow stairwell.

Sighing, Cally loaded a tray with muffins, Danish, and hot tea and honey, then carried it to the south wing. She found Ian, as always, in his chair beside Sofie. Without speaking, she placed the tray on the night stand and, taking the chair from the vanity, turned it around to face Ian. Here she sat down and leaned forward, with her hands on her knees, and looked at him squarely until he met her eyes.

"Now, are you going to tell me what you plan to do tonight to keep yourself and Sofie safe?"

He smiled and let out a breath. "Your concern is touching," he said. "It means a lot to me."

"That doesn't answer my question."

He opened his mouth to speak, but to Cally's surprise, it was Sofie who answered.

"We'll be in the barn," she said in a cheerful voice. Cally saw that the old woman had turned her head on the pillow. She was looking, perfectly lucidly, at Cally and smiling gently. "Don't worry, Ian has already put blankets in the hay for us. We'll be very comfortable."

"This is all Sofie's idea," Ian said.

Shocked at having been spoken to so clearly by someone who rarely spoke clearly under the best of circumstances, Cally had to stammer for a few seconds until she found her own voice.

"But how will you..." She looked back to Ian. "Ignacio won't be here to help you, remember."

"I'll get the wheelchair out of the closet under the stairs in the Hall," Ian said. "We'll exit the house through the Captain's old suite, which is universally accessible. I will do this after everyone else is gone, so I would appreciate it if you would encourage Katarina and Bethany to go home early." He winked at her. "Does this plan meet with your approval?"

"I loved playing in that barn when I was a little girl," Sofie informed them. "I love horses so much." Then she closed her eyes and nestled her head back in the pillows. "Oh, look at the sunshine!" she said.

"Ian, I absolutely do not like this. Oh, god, I'm sorry – I didn't mean to say that out loud."

He reached over to pat her knee. "It'll be alright. Sofie says she's just too busy with visiting the queen, calling in a few favors. She won't accept any other arrangement. I did try, but I will never, ever again resort to telling her she's delusional. All that has ever resulted from that has been harm."

Cally supposed that was probably true, but she still didn't like it. She decided, privately, that she would come back to Vale House after the show, long enough to at least peek into the barn and make sure Ian and Sofie had made it there safely. She didn't know what she would do if they hadn't, but she suspected it would probably involve breaking some rules and doing something stupid.

"Alright," she said at last. "But I'll check on you after the show, tonight, to make sure you're both comfortable. Is that okay?"

"You are an angel," Ian said.

Cally shook her head. "Bless my heart."

She stopped on her way back through the parlor, once again, to try to raise Melissa on the old television set. The voice from the television had said something, she now recalled, about a portal, and for some reason she also had a vague memory of someone else having encouraged her recently to pay more attention to "the portal."

She did finally manage to twiddle enough of the controls see the vague outline of a face in the snow on the screen, but all she could hear was static.

"Melissa?" she asked. "What can you tell me about a portal?"

She thought she could discern movement where the staticky figure's mouth should be, but she realized that was probably only pareidolia. After trying a few more adjustments, she reached to switch the power off, but she said, "Don't worry, I won't give up. And I promise I won't let Eddie Teine – Eladha – haul you out of here in an appliance truck."

39 - Time Will Be Your Key

Cally, Katarina and Bethany shared a quick, early dinner of cold friend chicken in the kitchen that evening, and mostly avoided speaking about the things on their minds. Afterward, Cally went back to the Dogwood Room and dressed for a rock show in a burger joint: sneakers, jeans, her trusty denim jacket and Nell's *Don't You Dare Turn Down That Bass!* t-shirt. Slipping out into the upstairs hall, she retrieved the zemi from the butler's desk, nearly walking through George as she turned around to head for the stairs.

"I wish I could help load the equipment!" he told her.

"I'm sure Kurtis and Luke can handle it," Cally assured him. Brandon and Rosheen had already left a few hours ago, to drive to Blackthorn (though Cally wasn't sure, now, which iteration of Blackthorn they were talking about) for Rosheen's ultrasound appointment. They would be going directly to The Fountain from there in time for the load-in.

"It's the whole rocker experience!" George was explaining. "Being a musician means *'loading five thousand dollars' worth of equipment into a five-hundred-dollar car to drive fifty miles to earn five dollars.'* I'm missing out on that part of it!"

"You're missing out on much less than you would be if Rosheen had not stepped up for you. So be grateful."

George smiled and bowed and vanished.

Bethany had put the phones into night mode and was tidying the desk by the time Cally reached the bottom of the stairs.

"Oh! That's an interesting shirt," Bethany remarked. "I hope you and Mr. Dawes are going to have a nice time.”

Bethany and Katarina were both thoroughly convinced Cally would be spending the night with Ben, and she made no effort to disabuse them of this notion.

“Now, when you leave, please be sure to leave the porch light off,” Bethany continued as she stood and took her purse from the desk drawer. “We don’t want to inadvertently welcome any stray travelers to try to stay the night.” She paused and looked back at Cally as she went out the door. “Tomorrow will be a very slow day; I’ll be taking the morning off. You make sure you don’t come back inside the house, yourself, until the sun is up. Everything will be back to normal, then. Have a nice date!”

Cally certainly hoped everything would be back to normal in the morning. Ben would return from the Thing then, at least, and maybe he would bring an answer to the problem of how to bring Ignacio home. That would return everything to close enough to normal for her, anyway.

She switched off the rest of the house lights as she watched Bethany drive out of the parking lot, and then her own car was the only one left in front of Vale House.

“George, have you ever been in a car before?” She locked the door behind her and went down the porch steps.

Errin was already there, waiting with one hand on the driver’s side door handle. Her other hand she held out, expectantly, toward Cally.

“This is going to be the best!” Errin declared.

“I don’t know, Errin.” Cally gritted her teeth. “It’s breaking the law. You should get a learner’s permit first. What if we get pulled over?”

“And what would I use as a birth certificate, in order to get a permit?” Errin asked. She straightened and planted her feet, standing with one palm up. “Besides, the law can’t follow us where we’re going.”

Cally shut her eyes and groaned, trying not to envision a high-speed chase with Errin at the wheel as she evaded a patrol car by steering on to a road that didn’t, conventionally speaking, exist.

“Come on, Cally. You made a promise.” Errin’s voice had taken on an edge that reminded Cally how dangerous it could be to trifle with immortals.

"Okay..." Gritting her teeth, Cally fished the keys out of her purse and dropped them into Errin's hand. Errin's giddy cheerfulness returned instantly and she opened the car door. Cally sighed and went around to the passenger side. George suddenly appeared in the back seat, grinning and tuning an air-guitar.

"Seatbelt," she said to Errin, fastening her own. Errin complied happily, snapping the seatbelt at her shoulder as if it were a cool fashion accessory. George took the hint and somehow managed to find himself an aethereal seat belt, the same way he found any of his other items of clothing, Cally guessed.

"Good. Right," Cally sighed. "Now you need to..." She cringed as Errin put the key into the ignition and turned it, then turned it again, causing the already started engine to grind and shriek in protest. "Only turn it once!"

"Gotcha." Errin stepped on the gas pedal. The engine roared but the car did not move. As patiently as she could, Cally walked Errin through keeping her foot on the brake, releasing the parking brake, and putting the car into gear, while George watched eagerly over the back of the seat.

"Now take your foot off the brake. Slowly!"

The car rolled forward a few feet, and Errin turned her head to grin broadly at Cally. "Keep your eyes on the road," Cally reminded her.

Then Errin stepped on the gas. The car rocketed through the gate, narrowly missing one of the masonry gateposts, and shot across Main Street onto Gardens Road.

"Errin I swear to you," Cally muttered between clenched teeth as she clutched at the dashboard in front of her. "If you don't slow down *right now* I am going to take my keys back, promise or no promise."

Errin laughed, but she eased up on the gas and smiled at Cally.

"And keep your eyes on the road."

Errin turned her head the other way and looked across the meadow as she, somehow, managed to steer the car along Gardens Road past the last few houses of Woodley. The driveway in front of the Yellow House was empty, but the house looked cheerful and lived-in, with a lamp glowing in the front window. On the meadow side of the road, the sky was already fading from gray to black, and Cally gazed wistfully, thinking of Ben and wondering how things were going at the Thing.

A tall, pale figure came into view ahead, walking along the grass verge between the road and the meadow fence. Errin stepped on the brake so fast Cally's seatbelt locked up. Putting her head out the window, Errin called "Hey, Mima!"

The blond girl stopped and rolled her eyes at Errin.

"Want a ride?" Errin offered.

"Showoff!" Mima laughed. "No, thanks. I'm sure I'll get there before you do."

"Suit yourself!" Errin stepped on the gas again, waving with arm and head out the window, absolutely not keeping her eyes on the road.

The road curved westward away from the meadow, though an open field, and then entered a scrubby regrowth wood. Cally relaxed. Errin did seem to have an aptitude for navigating this road, even without actually looking at it. That may well have been because she knew how to steer the roads themselves. Settling back in her seat, Cally watched as the wood thickened into an old-growth forest she was pretty sure did not exist on any conventional map.

The car rattled over a narrow bridge as the road curved broadly to the right again, and then again. Errin drove with one hand, her cloud of red hair filling half the car in the wind blowing through the driver's side window. Seeing her happy smile made Cally smile, too. Maybe this girl – this being – was thousands of years old but, in many ways, she was still a child at heart, and Cally found herself hoping Errin would never lose that.

She lost count of all the turns and bridges. The turns were always to the right. Cally couldn't understand how they didn't end up back where they had started, or cross over a stretch of road they had just come along, but she had learned, by now, not to even bother asking. Somewhere along the way, George stopped manifesting himself visibly, but Cally knew he couldn't be far away.

Finally, they crossed a narrow asphalt bridge with a concrete guard rail, much more quickly than Cally would have preferred. As the car climbed the next hill, Cally saw the shabby old gas station, under a lone street light, which meant Blackthorn was just ahead. To her relief, Errin slowed down without having to be told.

The road leveled out as it became the main street of a little town that somewhat resembled Woodley, or Woodley as it might have looked if it had a busier business district and a night life. Cars were parked along both sides of the street, under quite a lot more street lights than Woodley could afford, and most of the shops were still open, with people coming and going everywhere. Cally kept her eyes open for a vacant parking spot. "There," she said to Errin as they drew near an open doorway though which light and music spilled. "Now, I'm not very good at parallel parking, myself, but what you need to do is..."

Errin stepped on the brake and jerked the car to the right. Cally yelped and squeezed her eyes shut. When she dared to look again, Errin was getting out of the car. Cally opened her own door and looked down. Errin had managed to park perfectly, four inches from the curb.

"That was cheating," she said, giving Errin a look as she got out of the car.

"Hey, look at that!" Errin was walking toward a car a few parking spaces away. "A black Charger! Just like Zenbe, eh?" As she neared it, she reached out to stroke the gleaming fender.

"You know, Errin, I wouldn't mess with that one. I really wouldn't." Cally looked around nervously and saw Ana glaring at them from the doorway of The Fountain.

Errin noticed her at the same time and snatched her hand back just before she touched the black car. "Oooh!" she said, rubbing her fingers as if they had been stung. "what is *she* doing here?"

"Same thing as the rest of us, I would guess," Cally said, not believing it for a second. "Witnessing the launch of a rock legend." She headed toward the open doorway. "Do you like burgers?"

40 - Very Metal

Ana had withdrawn back into the restaurant by the time Cally and Errin reached the door. Errin made a noise that sounded a lot like a horse snorting, but her cheerful demeanor returned when she saw Mima waving to her from the midst of the crowd around the bar.

Following Errin inside, Cally was overwhelmed by memories of the night she had come here with Ben, before she had ever imagined she might someday come to love him. The aroma of the pub's signature burgers filled the air, and the buzz of voices made her feel lightheaded, as if she were caught up in a dream. In a windowed alcove beyond the bar, a few tentative guitar chords crackled in the speakers on the stage where the band was setting up.

Errin wandered off to join Mima and her friends, and Cally was surprised and delighted to see Andi Kilmarten sitting at a small table near the stage. She wove her way through the crowd toward her.

"How did you get here?" she asked, meaning much more than people normally meant when they asked that kind of question.

"I caught a ride with Merv," Andi said, as if this were all the explanation that was required. "I wouldn't miss this for the world!" She patted the table in front of her. "Here, sit! We band-moms have to stick together!"

Cally sat down and looked over to where Brandon was setting up Ian's drums, now polished and gleaming in the colored lights surrounding the stage. Rosheen stood quietly near him, holding a bright blue electric bass. George was nowhere to be seen, but Cally knew he must be hovering near her somewhere. Rosheen had left the open bass case on the floor just in front of the stage, where she had seeded it with a couple of dollar bills to give the restaurant patrons a hint. Luke's keyboard was already set up behind it; Luke and Kurtis stood with Zenbe at the sound board, tuning each of several guitars in turn while Zenbe adjusted knobs on the amplifier.

"Hey!" Cally called to them. "Does it go to eleven?" Zenbe looked at her long enough to give her a tight-lipped grin before returning to the row of guitars.

"You must be the first person to *ever* make that joke!" Andi scolded her. Then she leaned across the table. "Did you see the ultrasound yet?"

Cally shook her head. "They came here straight from the clinic." She looked at the bag at Rosheen's feet on the stage, knowing her first glimpse of her grandchild was in there. "I'm sure they'll show us as soon as the show is over."

Merv could be seen wading through the crowd toward them, hands full. When he reached Cally and Andi, he set down three dewy, brown bottles and three paper trays containing thick fries and even thicker burgers. "I hope you like 'em rare," he said, taking a seat. "It's so nice to see Ian's old drums getting some use. I wish he could be here to see this." He heaved a great sigh, saluting with his bottle in the direction in which Woodley – theoretically – lay, and then took a long swallow. He looked at Cally as if he wanted to say something more, but then sighed and looked away.

"Oh! Hey!" Andi said suddenly, setting her purse on the table and digging through it. "Here." She pulled out a plastic bag, unzipped it, and held it out to Cally and Merv. It contained a dozen orange foam earplugs of the type Cally had seen Ignacio wearing whenever he mowed the lawn. "You'll need these." She tilted her head toward the young people on the stage. "Trust me. Even those guys are wearing them."

Cally accepted two earplugs from the bag, but she left them on the table beside her bottle. "I want to hear what they really sound like," she explained.

"Oh, you'll hear them just fine!"

Merv grinned and palmed two of the earplugs, himself. "Don't worry," he said. "This isn't my first rodeo."

"Suit yourselves." Andi squeezed orange foam into her ears as Kurtis shouldered one of the guitars and stepped up to the microphone.

"Welcome, everyone!" he said. "Thank you for being here for us. This is our first live performance together, and we are Jumping the Shark!"

Andi applauded wildly, but it took Cally several seconds to understand that "Jumping the Shark" was what the band had named itself. She had to admit that was kind of clever.

Then a shock-wave of sound exploded from the direction of the stage, and Cally barely had enough self-control to keep from putting her hands over her ears. She put in the earplugs Andi had given her, grinning as she watched Merv do the same. Andi saluted them with her beer bottle before turning to the stage to watch her son's band making its debut performance.

Even with the earplugs, Cally could barely hear herself think, but she had to admit the hard, grungy sound was also melodic, with clever twists of rhythm and rhyme. It was decidedly much edgier than the kind of music she preferred, but her heart swelled to see the way Brandon lit up behind the drums, coming alive as she seldom saw him do, laughing and using his entire body to become part of the music. Rosheen stood quietly at the back of the stage with the bass in her hands, doing a very convincing job of fingering the strings and frets, so that probably only Cally knew the notes coming from the speakers were not the ones she was playing.

In the dark corner behind the drum kit, Cally finally saw George. He danced, he jumped, he spun and strummed and thumped, but his hands were empty. The sound coming out of the speakers was a complex, melodic jazz bass line. Cally couldn't help but headbang in her seat like everyone else in the place, causing George to grin hugely at her. He did a high-kick and crashed the final notes of the song, landing in a split with his invisible bass held high over his head as the band wrapped up their first number.

Cally jumped to her feet to applaud, along with everyone else in the place. "Well!" She removed her ear plugs and shouted over the hubbub to her companions. "It's nice to see young people can still rock."

Andi gave Kurtis a thumbs-up and turned to ask Merv, "What did you think?"

He was applauding, but his smile was a little strained as he removed the foam plugs from his own ears. "It was certainly very...loud," he finally said.

Kurtis did a bit of patter about who was playing which instruments and about how everyone should be sure to tip their servers, then he said, "We're going to bring it down a little bit, now, and play a softer number for our moms, who are in the audience." Then the band launched into a Guns N' Roses cover.

Cally finished her burger, thinking it was good but just not the same as the one she'd enjoyed on that much quieter evening here, not so long ago, with Ben smiling gently at her from across the table. She offered the rest of her fries to Merv. He drew them over to his side of the table but continued to look at Cally as if he wished he could say something to her without having to shout. She acknowledged his gaze by nodding, and when the song ended, she asked, "How are Jud and Doc and the sheriff managing without you on the loading dock tonight?"

"Well, that's what I wanted to tell you," he said. "The sheriff got some unsettling news just before Ms. Kilmarten and I left tonight. Apparently, they are moving Ignacio to a different jail, down in Raleigh. They say his case requires a more secure facility."

Kurtis had invited Zenbe to step up to the microphone, and Zenbe had begun to strum a gleaming black Stratocaster, but all Cally could hear was the sound of blood pounding in her own ears.

"That can't be," she was muttering. "How can that be? That's..." She struggled to recall the Spanish epithet Katarina had used.

Zenbe strummed the opening bars to *"Green Grass and High Tides"* as Merv tried to continue telling her something about the detectives who had been working on Foster's case. Cally wasn't listening. She was imagining Katarina hearing this news, knowing that now it would be even harder for her to visit her husband who shouldn't even have been taken from her side in the first place. She was wondering how she could get her hands on the so-called detectives who were, apparently, taking dead Foster's old lies seriously. Her fist was pounding the table in time to the music, rattling it harder and harder with each beat.

Zenbe's voice drifted through to her consciousness, a snatch of lyrics about a place where one's soul was always free, and at that she jumped to her feet. She turned and walked to the bar, where Errin and Mima were laughing at a story Ana was telling. She didn't wait for a good moment to interrupt.

"I need to go to the Thing," she told them, and turned and walked out of the restaurant.

41 - Jump the Shark

People seated at tables outside the door were enjoying a less deafening version of Zenbe's five-minute guitar solo. Cally walked past them to the curb and stood beside her car. Errin and Mima did not take long to run out the door with Ana following, laughing in a particularly grating tone.

"Cally, don't!" Errin grabbed her by the elbow and tugged her back from the car. For a fleeting moment, Cally felt almost moved by the look of, quite possibly, concern on the girl's face.

"I need you to help me find my way there," Cally said. "I'll let you drive."

"No..."

"Fine, then. I'll find it myself, if I have to." She went around to the driver's side of the car.

Ana continued to laugh, and Cally threw her a look that would have withered a weaker being.

"No, it's just..." Errin's voice rose to a frantic pitch. "I mean, you probably won't find it anyway, but even if you did...well...you can't go in that!" She gestured toward the car. "That big hunk of iron. That would be very...offensive. The queen would turn you into a little lump of grease right there on the spot!"

"And that would totally mess up your car, right, Errin?" Ana walked past them to where her own car was parked, "You can come with me, if you want." She flashed Cally a grin and leaned her hip against the black car's hood. "I can get away with anything I want, being the queen's favorite granddaughter and all."

Cally might have considered accepting this offer, but for the glitter in Ana's eyes. She sensed instinctively that being in a car with Ana at the wheel would make traveling with Errin seem like an afternoon nap.

"I'll find my own way, thank you."

"It's your funeral." Ana slipped like smoke behind the wheel of the Charger and drove it away toward what, in a normal world, would have been Interstate 85.

"Great, great, okay," Errin was saying in a panicky voice. "I guess we can get you there. But, Cally, you'll have to..."

More people had come out to stand in front of the Fountain door. Cally looked across the hood of her car to see Andi, Merv and Rosheen watching her. Through the wall, she could hear Zenbe begin the second of his number's long guitar solos. George was doing a beautiful job with the bass line, perhaps not realizing Rosheen wasn't there to cover for him.

"Let me take care of your purse," Rosheen offered, reaching out her hand. "George can't finish the gig if you take you-know-what away with you."

The gig was the last thing Cally was concerned about at the moment, but she was thankful Rosheen had reminded her not to take George's zemi with her into the shadow lands.

Rosheen slipped Cally's purse from her shoulder so gently she didn't even try to resist. "Don't worry," she said. "I'll make sure the band gets their tip. It won't be too much." She grinned and winked, then, much more softly, added, "I'll make sure I get George home safely, and I'll put his zemi back in the desk."

Errin snorted. "It's just a Dumbo's feather," she said. "I keep trying to tell you!"

Zenbe's number had ended, and Rosheen, gesturing for Andi and Merv to follow, hurried back inside. "Right, then," said Errin, squeezing between Cally and the car to open the door. "And for my part, I'll get this car home safely." She started the engine (properly this time) and waved out the window to Mima.

Cally started around to the passenger side, but Errin was already pulling away from the curb. Cally had to step backward into the street to avoid being hit by her own car. As she watched the red Corolla moving away down the street, she shouted after it, "Errin, you are so dead when I catch you!

"Stop her!" she turned to implore Mima, but the blonde girl was no longer there. In her place, a magnificent white horse with glowing blue eyes stood pawing at the sidewalk.

"No," Cally said. "Oh, no, no, no."

As Kurtis's voice rang out once more inside the Fountain, singing something about a rose and a war, the people seated around the door tapped their feet and nodded their heads to the music. They didn't appear to think it at all strange that a white steed suddenly stood, without saddle or bridle, on the sidewalk next to them. By this alone, Cally was sure they were all, in fact, watching closely.

"Do we have to do it this way?" she asked the horse as quietly as she could manage. She had never imagined she would ever again have to repeat the wild ride she'd had, once before, on that white horse's back. "Just show me the way. I'll walk. I'm a fast walker!"

The horse shook its head, mane snapping like a white banner. "Don't make me say it," it said, and then said it anyway: "We don't have time for this shit." Mima moved closer and turned her broad, white side toward Cally.

The horse's back was level with Cally's chin. Resignedly, she looked around for something to use as a step, maybe an empty bistro chair. One of the people seated next to the door got up and came to her side. He was a slender, older man with a beatnick cap and trim, gray beard. "Would you like a leg up, My Lady?" he asked, stooping over and locking his hands together to form a step next to the horse's flank.

She wanted to ask the man who he was – who any of them were – but a flash of Mima's blue eyes let her know she was all out of time to stall. "Thank you," she said simply to the stranger, putting her foot into his linked hands and clinging to the white mane as she half clambered and was half lifted onto the broad, white back.

Once she was settled there, it all felt familiar and oddly comforting. At least it wasn't raining this time, she noted. The man tipped his hat to Cally as the horse swung away from the curb and began to canter down the street into the darkness beyond.

The town ended where the sidewalk did, as suddenly as if it had been written on a page that had just been turned. The horse's hoofbeats echoed in the dark woods that now surrounded them on both sides. The road curved away to the right, and Mima slowed to a trot.

"Why are we moving so slowly?" Cally wondered. "You were in such a hurry a moment ago." She found this slower gait to be much more uncomfortable than the flat-out gallop she remembered from the last time she'd been on this horse's back.

"We're about to make a sharp left turn. There is a time to run and a time to walk," Mima said, continuing to do something that was neither as she trotted around the bend she had foretold. Here the horse held her head high, swiveling her ears in all directions and making loud snuffling noises as she tested the air with flared nostrils. "It's a good thing you didn't try to do this on your own. You really don't know anything."

The terrain had changed around them. The road had faded from asphalt to packed dirt, running slightly downhill, and the trees had thinned considerably. The nearly full moon stretched the shadows of the bare trees so that they looked like crooked arms reaching across the road with long, grasping fingers. Cally sensed it was time to begin hanging on tightly to the horse's mane.

She was right. As they passed into the shadows, Mima lowered her head and shifted suddenly to the distance-devouring gallop Cally remembered. Even though the horse ran through the shadowy trees as if she feared they actually could reach down and grab her, or at least snatch Cally from her back, Cally found this faster gait much more comfortable than the jarring trot. She didn't feel like she had to hang on quite as tightly, and relaxed enough to glance down and see her own shadow flying beside her along the weedy ditch at the side of the road.

"There," said Mima. "Now you see it. Maybe you *can* be taught."

Cally heard the music, ahead, before she saw the light. The music was familiar: it sounded like a pre-school class experimenting freely with various hand-held rhythm instruments while their teacher tuned up a violin. Through the trunks at the side of the road she glimpsed a campfire. She was sure she recognized this place but, as Mima drew abreast of the fire and slowed once again to her annoying trot, it seemed different, somehow, from the last time she'd seen it.

The horse stepped off the road and paused beside a row of motorcycles parked just outside the circle of firelight. There were only a few people, this time. Several men and two or three women in long, flowered skirts sat on logs around the fire, passing jars of clear liquid between them. Mima nodded to them, and the fiddle player saluted Cally with his bow as Mima walked softly through the crackling leaves around the little gathering. As they passed, he began playing an old Irish ballad Cally thought she recognized.

She listened to the music fade behind her as the horse continued on slowly, down a gentle slope to the river bank. Then Cally realized what had been so different about the familiar riverside fire where she had once danced with Ben: there had been no aroma of Jerome's famous barbeque sauce. Jerome...well, Rum was, of course, at the Thing.

The slope before them leveled out at the bank of a broad, dark river. Ben had once told her this was called the Harmony River, and that it was the same watercourse that passed, as a creek, through Woodley. It curved, smooth and silent, through the woods in front of them, reflecting the lights of the little town on the other side.

"Seen's Mill."

"Very good," Mima said.

"There's no bridge," Cally observed.

"No, there isn't."

Mima started forward, but before she put her front hooves into the water, Cally called "Wait!" She pulled back on Mima's mane as if it were reins that could, conceivably, stop her. "Isn't this how kelpies kill people?" she asked in a voice that rose to a squeak.

The horse raised her head high, baring her teeth, and Cally looked at the ground, wondering how many limbs she would break when she jumped off. Then she felt the horse's ribs quaking beneath her, and she realized this was Mima laughing.

"Well," said the horse at length. "If I planned to drag you into the water so I can turn around and eat you, you wouldn't be able to dismount now, anyway, even if you tried." She turned her head and fixed Cally with a baleful blue eye. "Go ahead. Try."

Cally let out her breath. "Sorry," she said.

"As it is," said Mima, continuing into the shallows at the river's edge, "it will be far too easy for you to fall off, here, and if you do, and get washed downriver and drown, that's not on me. Just so we have that clear."

Cally watched the dark water rising above the horse's knees as she pressed forward. "Yes, Mima," she said, suddenly motivated to be just as polite as she possibly could.

The water was cold, as it rose above Cally's ankles, and she braced herself and shivered. She wanted to turn around and see how far they'd gone from the bank, but she didn't want to move, or do anything that might risk losing her seat. Winding her fingers tightly through the white mane in front of her, she took in deep gulps of air as if they might be the last she'd ever taste.

She bit back a scream as she felt the horse lunge forward, and frigid water washed up around her thighs as Mima let the river take their weight. Cally almost felt smug, then. She imagined Mima must be downright disappointed at having been deprived of the opportunity to tell her to shut up. Her teeth chattered, but she kept her mouth shut.

They moved forward much more quickly than Cally thought they should be able to with only four long, thin legs to propel them. She would not have been surprised, if she could have seen through the dark water, to see that Mima's hooves had turned into webbed flippers. She didn't try to look down through the water. She kept her eyes focused forward, instead, on the little town with its friendly lights glowing softly through the trees.

Then she saw the horse's white head plunge down, before her, into the dark water, and she felt herself pulled along behind it. Screams of panic and betrayal escaped her lungs in long streams of bubbles as her head plunged beneath the surface. She let go of the horse's mane and flailed, wishing only that she could take in one more breath to utter all the curse words passing through her mind. She opened her eyes to look for the surface, and saw, through the bubbles rising before her face, a great, white horse head reaching toward her with massive teeth as big as tombstones.

Mima fastened her teeth in Cally's hair and pulled, swimming backwards, until Cally felt her body being dragged along rocks and roots. When the horse let go, she pushed against the rocks and mud with both hands and raised her head into blessed cold air.

Gasping and spitting, she looked up to see the white horse standing on the bank, dark water flowing around its pale hooves.

"God damn it, Mima! You could have warned me!"

"Would you have come?" the horse asked, walking across the bank to the wooded hillside at the edge of the mud, not waiting for an answer.

Cally scrambled to her feet and followed, limping. Her jeans were torn in several places, where she had been dragged across the rocks, and she could feel bruises forming on her arms and legs. She reached down to brush mud and sticks off her clothes, and found that she was completely dry.

She caught up with Mima, realizing she was going to have to work hard to keep up, now, since there was no way she would ever be able to get back on the horse's back. She resisted her urge to put a hand on Mima' flank, to at least have contact with something warm and alive as they entered the dark, tangled woods cloaking the slope ahead.

"Thank you for pulling me out," she said. Looking up toward the top of the hill, she was dismayed to realize she could no longer see the friendly lights of Seen's Mill. She looked back, but couldn't see the river behind her anymore, either. At best, she could only make out a small stream, glittering in the moonlight between the roots of the trees below them.

She wasn't surprised at this, knowing how the landscape could change with every step in this shadow world, but she was disappointed. "I've always wanted to see Seen's Mill," she said. "It looked like a nice place."

She found that she had, indeed, put a hand on Mima's neck and wound her fingers through the horse's mane. In an uncharacteristically kind tone, Mima said, "Maybe someday you still will." She started forward again, and the two climbed in silence side by side through the shadows under the moon.

42 - And Then They Came Upon the Thing

The woods ended at the top of the hill, and where the ground leveled out, a wide, barren field spread out before them. Cally did not see the fire or the tree, here, that she had expected. Instead, the full moon overhead illuminated only another hill ahead, on the other side of the field, and this, also, was clad with dark, tangled trees. Mima stopped here, looking into the trees with ears pricked sharply forward.

Cally was grateful for the chance to catch her breath, until she realized this was not why Mima had stopped. From the shadows under the trees on the far hill, she began to hear what Mima was hearing: the sound of running hoofbeats, growing louder as they came nearer.

"Should we hide?" Cally wondered.

"No, it's only Errin. And a friend, I think."

Cally saw the rider long before she was able to make out the form of the dark red horse emerging from the trees. The rider was clad in a long, pale gown, like the ghost of the White Lady from Vale House who had turned out not to be a ghost, and her silvery hair streamed out behind her as the horse ran across the field many yards to their left.

"Who is that?" Cally asked.

"A petitioner," Mima said, "and she has got her answer, apparently." Mima reared up onto her hind legs in a salute as the red horse passed by them to plunge into the woods Cally and Mima had just climbed out of. The sound of hoofbeats faded as horse and rider disappeared back down the hill into the darkness. "I wonder how that went," Mima murmured before walking on across the field.

This second tree-clad hill was much steeper than the one previous. Cally apologized to Mima for having to hang onto her mane, letting herself be dragged up the slope in order to keep up, but Mima silently climbed onward. They were facing nearly straight up as they climbed, and through the bare branches above her Cally thought she could see the stars growing ever larger and brighter.

They emerged at last on a wide, grassy hilltop. At its center, many yards away, stood the tree, reaching into the sky like fire, with people gathered all around it. This was what Cally had been expecting to see. What she had not expected was the appearance of the sky above it. The stars were much larger than they should have been, no longer mere points of light. Here, they resembled flares, or swirls of light, against the dark blue background of space behind them. Even the full moon seemed dull and mundane amidst them.

"It looks almost as if Van Gogh painted it," she remarked.

"You say that almost as if you think he didn't."

Dozens of people, seated at tables or standing together in groups, surrounded the tree, and Cally could tell they were not all the same kind of person. The susurrus of their voices mingled with different strains of music from each group. She didn't see Ben anywhere.

"So where do I find this Queen person?" she asked. She turned back again, looking to Mima for guidance, and saw that Mima was no longer a horse. The blonde girl was walking away toward a distant, dark hill with a dim light near its top. "Wait!" Cally called. "I have no idea what I'm supposed to do next!"

Mima barely turned her head as she waved the back of her hand and called, "Oh, don't go getting all clingy on me, now, just because we had a moment."

Then Cally heard a voice at her side say, "Welcome to Thingol, the Thing Hill."

She turned and looked down, smiling because she recognized Rum's voice. He looked, now, like a shaggy stump with eyes, the manifestation with which she was most familiar. He bowed, a ridiculous sight to see because, in addition to being so short, he had no waist. He reached up to take Cally's hand.

"Come, I'll show you around," he said. "But it will be the Prince's place to introduce you to everyone."

Rum led Cally along the edge of the wavering circle of the light cast by the tree, gesturing with his walking stick toward the different groups seated at tables, on the ground, or in tall seats that looked like they were formed from the turf itself.

"You have met the People from the jewel city Shannish," he said. "They are here because of you. They do not ordinarily attend." The People recognized Cally and waved joyfully as she and Rum passed by. "And here is the Sluagh delegation." He didn't take her anywhere near this group of sullen, misshapen creatures seated on the ground, cowering away from the edge of the tree-light.

Instead, he led her a little further around the hilltop. "Here are the Aes Sidhe," he said, bowing toward a wide, turf-topped table surrounded by people who were only people in the broadest sense of the word: they were bipedal with, usually, two arms and legs each, but each bore distinct characteristics of various animals. The gathering looked like a child's tea party of chatting bears, wolves, goats, and others Cally couldn't quite place. She wasn't surprised to see Mr. Ennilangr seated at this table, his ponytail undone and curled ram's horns standing out from his blond locks. He was quaffing mug after mug of something with which he toasted her when he noticed her approach. "Didn't think you were gonna make it," he said heartily.

"I hadn't planned to," she said. "So, have you found Foster's murderer yet?"

She meant it sarcastically, but he answered frankly. "I'm getting warmer," he said. From a tall, wooden pitcher he poured a mug of whatever everyone at the table was drinking. This he offered to Cally, but she declined politely.

Rum led her counter-clockwise around the tree, rattling off the names of each group of people they passed. Most of them were Sidhe of one sort or another, though not all of these were tall or bright or beautifully terrible. Rum knew all their many different names: the Boccanach Sidhe and the Fir Bolg, the Gruka and the Ronin. The Fomorians were tall and beautiful, but shone with a dark light that made Cally's eyes hurt. They were gathered around a stone table with no food or drink, but many weapons and maps strewn across it. Cally looked anxiously over this group to see if she could spot the being she had once thought of as Eddie Teine, but she knew he had no reason to keep his human glamour here, and she realized with a sudden sense of panic that he would be able to spot her before she spotted him. She tugged at Rum's hand to urge him to continue on around the tree.

"There's a delegation from the Moruadh here this evening, as well," Rum said, leading her to what, under the stars she knew, would have been the east side of the hill to peer down into the darkness. Cally was sure she could hear surf roaring over rocks far below where no moonlight penetrated. In the black depths, she thought she could see a half dozen or so soft lights swirling in slow circles around one another. Rum drew her back from the edge before she could begin to feel dizzy, and led her around, once again, to the northernmost side of the tree. "Now, those are what we call the Uninvited." He laughed, pointing with his walking stick.

Dark hills stood all around the Thing Hill, but the next hilltop to the north was the only other one that had people gathered upon it. It, too, was crowned by a massive and ancient tree, but this tree had no light of its own. Harsh music emanated from a dim light beneath the tree. Cally squinted until she perceived that this emanated from the inside of a car: a black Charger was parked under the dark tree. Its doors stood open, letting the car's dome light, as well as tinny music from the car's radio, pour out. A handful of young faerie people of several types, including Ana and Mima, were gathered near it, laughing and passing cups and bottles among themselves.

"Looks like dear Ana has established her own presence here," Cally said.

"They won't let her near the Thingol with that iron vehicle of hers," Rum explained.

"She doesn't appear to be particularly upset about that."

"Look closer," Rum urged, and Cally peered into the shadows under the tree until she saw a lone silhouette sitting apart from the group. He sat with his back against the dark bole, looking up at the swirling stars above.

"Is that Michael Dawes?" she asked.

Rum nodded. "He's never far away from Rianwynn," he said. "She will not tolerate him coming nearer, or speaking in her presence even during a Thing, but he can still catch a glimpse of her from time to time."

Cally's heart broke for the man and she felt an urge to run across to the other hill to sit with him, but Rum was already tugging at her hand.

"Here at last," he said, "we have the Daoine Sidhe, the manifest rulers of this Vale." They arrived back at the west side of the hill, where Cally thought she remembered having first arrived, but it looked completely different, now. Elegant chairs, gilded with branching patterns and crusted with green and yellow jewels, stood in a semi-circle on a rise slightly higher than any other ground on the hilltop. These seemed to have sprung from the ground as if the tree had woven them from its own roots. Nobody was seated in them, but a group of people, mostly women, stood talking nearby. It was toward this group that Rum led Cally, stopping a short distance away.

That was when she spotted Ben. She was able to pick him out of the crowd because he was the only person who did not shine with golden light, and his darkness was as comforting as silence after leaving a noisy room. He was, however, clad in a flowing white robe embellished with gold thread and jewels that seemed to glow with an inner light of their own.

"Hah, he looks like Elvis Presley!" Rum observed, throwing his head back and laughing.

Cally didn't think so, but she did appreciate the way the fabric draped over Ben's shoulders and across his chest. She let go of Rum's hand and started to walk toward him, keenly aware of how starkly she stood out from the other people here, in her ruined jeans and *"Don't You Dare Turn Down That Bass"* t-shirt.

She squared her shoulders and walked, anyway, toward the little knot of Sidhe near the chairs. Astonishingly beautiful women surrounded Ben, three deep in places, attending to his every movement, unabashedly fawning over him. Cally wondered what they might look like without their glamour, if she could see them through Michael's glamour-busting talisman. She cattily imagined them turning out to resemble stick-insects or shambling mounds of compost.

Ben had not yet noticed her approach, but one of the women nearest her did notice. She was taller than the rest of them, with a black river of hair cascading over her silver circlet. She turned away from the group and passed like a bright cloud under the moonlight toward Cally.

"You're supposed to bow," Rum prompted quietly at Cally's

side. Cally guessed this must be Rianwynn, Ben's mother and queen the of the Sidhe.

"I notice you're not bowing," she muttered back.

Then she saw that Ben had spotted her. His smile was more of relief than surprise, and it spread ever wider as he endeavored to make his way through the press of women around him. She let out her breath, which she had not even known she'd been holding, and smiled back at him as she bowed deeply to his mother.

43 - Gold Dust Woman

"You took far too long to get here," the queen said while Cally's head was still bowed.

Cally straightened and did her best to look at the woman without averting her eyes. It was like trying to look into the sun. "I came to plead a case for a friend."

"Your case has already been brought, by the People of Shannish. Apparently, your story impressed them, and is now on the agenda of this Thing. In fact, several recent issues concerning your human city require resolution.

"Come into the light. Let us look at you."

Cally stepped away from Rum and followed the queen closer to the tree. All of the attendant ladies surrounding Ben shifted their attention to Cally, looking her up and down as breeders might look over a young racehorse for sale. She tried to tug her jacket closed over her grunge-metal t-shirt. When she tried to smooth her tangled hair, and her hand encountered leaves and sticks from the river. The light of the tree felt like a spotlight.

Ben had managed to maneuver through the crowd, at last, to arrive at her side. He looked at her, smile-crinkles radiating from around his eyes, as if she was the most beautiful thing he had ever seen. "I'm so glad you're here," he said, and then bent to speak quietly into her ear. "Stay close to me," he breathed.

Cally didn't want to think she needed his protection here, but the warmth of his breath on her cheek felt like a lifeline.

Putting an arm around Cally, Ben swept her around as he turned, himself, to face the queen. "Your Majesty," he addressed her, "I am more pleased than I can say, to introduce to you Callaghan McCarthy, the future Armadeur of the Vale, and the woman I have chosen, if she will have me."

The women surrounding them on all sides giggled or laughed at this in different levels of delight or disdain, but the queen did not laugh.

Setting her jaw, the queen said, "That is still to be decided." Then she turned her back to the tree and addressed the gathered peoples. "Now that our final attendee has deigned to arrive, we may resume our discussion of the matters at hand.

"Three items still remain to be discussed at this Thing. One is what to do about acquiring a mate for my son. Another concerns the impending end of the short, mortal life of the Vale's current Armadeur. And the third is the issue this human woman has brought, regarding her human friend and the murder of which is accused. Most of you already know, I would not have bothered with this topic at all, if it were not that our own people are also entangled in this matter. It must be handled delicately, as it impinges upon alliances we are bound to uphold."

The queen glanced at Rum, as she said this last, but he was already walking away from the hilltop, toward the light of the car atop the next hill over.

Cally started to say "I've had a feeling all along that whoever killed Foster was not human," but Rianwynn stopped her with a look.

"All remaining agenda items will be discussed in their proper order."

The queen and her women turned toward the semi-circle of chairs on the rise. Two chairs larger than the rest stood centered among these, at the highest point on the hill. Here everyone stood back while the queen took her seat on the centermost chair, and Ben looked back at Cally urgently as he sat down, himself, in the tall chair at the queen's right.

Suddenly, as the women around her maneuvered for position, Cally understood what Ben had meant when he'd said "Stay close to me." He had not been offering to protect her; he had been imploring her to claim her rightful place.

Quickly, before the other women could decide who among them

should do so, she sat down in the chair at Ben's right hand. A clatter of laughs and hisses went up all around as the other women seated themselves in the remaining chairs. Looking around, Cally noticed that Ben was the only male seated in this semi-circle. Any other men present remained standing, or seated themselves on the ground nearby, passing food and drink among themselves.

Beside her, she heard Ben let out a long breath. She glanced over to see him sitting stiffly in his chair, eyes shut and head pressed back against the headrest.

"Is that a glamour?" she asked, trying to ease the tension. "Are you wearing anything underneath it?"

He looked down at his gilded ivory robes. "Oh," he said. "Yes, it's a glamour. They like to dress me up in this sort of thing." A tilt of his head indicated the tittering women on either side of them.

Cally wasn't sure what she thought about the idea of beautiful faerie women dressing Ben up in anything. She risked a quick glance at the woman seated on her right. The woman was already looking at Cally and she smiled, unabashed, when Cally met her eyes. She looked like something straight out of a fashion magazine, with dark ruby-colored hair straight down to her lap, but she looked friendly and pleasant enough. Under less awkward circumstances, Cally thought she might even have liked to get to know her.

Across the distant hills to the northwest, Cally glimpsed lightning flashing upward into the sky at intervals, but she heard no thunder following, and the sky remained clear and starry. The men near the fire brought pitchers of drink and platters of food to everyone seated on the rise, and Cally was careful to politely decline these refreshments. She noted that Ben also passed any food or drink pressed into his hands to someone else. All the women, excepting the queen, to whom he handed cups or platters, giggled as they accepted them. Cally wondered when he'd last eaten.

Though his demeanor remained friendly and gracious, it seemed to Cally that Ben's entire body was stiff, his jaw set far too tightly. She reached over to lay a hand on his, and found he was gripping the arm of his chair as if he were clinging to the edge of a cliff.

Suddenly she laughed. "Do you know what this reminds me of?" she asked, leaning over to speak quietly to him. "It reminds me of dinners in the dining room at Vale House, when Joan used to play head-games with everyone at the table to try to manipulate them into doing things her way."

He spluttered as a most unprincely laugh escaped from between his clenched teeth, and his eyes were dancing when he turned them toward her. "Thank you, Cally," he said, taking a deep breath as he squeezed her hand. "Thank you. I know I have chosen well, and I'm so grateful you have chosen me back." His eyes closed again as he sat back in his seat, but his body was much less rigid, now.

Rianwynn had handed her goblet back to one of the attending men and now she stood, stepping between those seated on the ground and in chairs.

"This won't do at all!" she began abruptly, her eyes fastened on Cally. "You're too old!"

Cally nearly choked in surprise. "Excuse me?" She removed her hand from Ben's and leaned forward in her chair, stopping just short of standing, herself. That was the last thing she had expected to hear from a member of a race that was supposed to be far advanced over the human one. "I thought the Sidhe were supposed to be enlightened beings, but that is a positively primitive thing to say!"

Behind her, amid women's gasps and laughs, she heard Ben groan, but he didn't interfere.

Rianwynn's voice took the impatient tone of a parent speaking to a particularly obtuse child. "You know nothing about it. Your race is the one that still clings to the primitive practice of tracing parentage through the male line, which is the most ridiculous idea any race has ever pulled out of its...primordial ooze. And, you are the ones with the ludicrous idea that royalty is determined by parentage rather than through offspring."

Cally opened her mouth, but honestly couldn't think of what to say to that. She tended to agree with the lunacy of tracing inheritance through the male rather than the female line, but she couldn't imagine how anyone could determine royalty by offspring rather than parentage.

The queen shook her head and addressed Cally's unspoken question. "I will take the trouble to explain it to you quickly, because we need to move on and resolve other questions this evening. Understand: a king or queen is nothing if they do not produce heirs to continue the royal line. My son is the only reason I am Queen, for instance, though it would have been better if it had been my daughter who had joined us here instead, for obvious reasons." She cast a decidedly un-maternal look toward Ben. "If he does not produce an heir, he cannot be King. If I have not in actual fact produced a king or queen, then I am not Queen. The line would be broken and there would be chaos until a new royal line is established. And now, more than at times in the past, chaos would be extremely dangerous, for *all* the peoples living on this planet, including yours. I may not care about them, but I am charged with caring *for* them, and will do so regardless of personal considerations." The queen cast a quick, dark look toward the table where the Fomorians sat glowering at her, then she looked back to Cally. "Surely even one as primitive as you should be able to understand that."

Cally could hear her teeth grinding as she tried not to speak again before she had a chance to think. Well, she had used the word "primitive" first, so she deserved this.

"But I don't understand," she said. "I thought Ben had already...produced heirs, as you call it?"

Rianwynn threw back her head at this and let out a loud hiss. "*That* one!" She turned and called out toward the hill where Ana and her friends were having their little party. "She's too wild to ever be Queen, even if she wished to be. Which she has made it clear she refuses to ever consider in any case."

"Damn straight, Grandma!" Ana's voice called back from the darkness.

"Do not call me that." The queen straightened, standing ever taller as she leveled a gaze toward the car. Cally saw that Rum was now among the little group of people surrounding it, eating and drinking merrily.

"What should I call you, then?" Ana called back, completely unintimidated. "Granny, perhaps? Nana? I understand Me-Maw is popular in these parts."

Rianwynn didn't take the bait. "Until you begin to conduct yourself as someone who is part of my family," she said, "you may refer to me as Your Majesty." She waved the back of her hand toward the group on the hill. Beyond the tree where Ana was holding her little party, Cally again saw a flash of light stab into the sky.

"And the other one," she said, returning the sharpness of her gaze and voice to Cally. "We don't even know where that one is, where its mother and her cohorts are hiding, or even whether it is dead or alive. They have betrayed us all. That one is dead to all of us."

"Not to all of us," Ben breathed, and the edge in his voice caused the giggling all around him to abruptly cease.

The queen remained steadfast in her judgement. "No," she said. She stepped closer, and it was all Cally could do to hold herself still without cowering as the woman peered down at her.

"No," the queen said again, looking up and down the line of those seated there. "This one is unsuitable. My son must marry someone who is able to bear his offspring and ensure the continued security of my people and of this world."

The women on either side of Cally and Ben made affirmative noises and began discussing among themselves ways to solve this problem, occasionally glancing covetously over at Ben. Ben had resumed sitting rigidly with his eyes shut, his jaw set.

"However," the queen continued, "We can still discuss this one's suitability as the Armadeur of the Vale."

Ben did speak up, then. He leaned forward in his chair, hands gripping the ends of its jewel-encrusted arms. "That isn't ours to discuss," he said in a voice that was almost a growl. Cally had never heard him speak this way before. "Ian May has made it clear he has chosen Cally as the Armadeur, once he passes."

Before Cally could interject her own questions regarding this topic, she heard a number of women asking, "Cally? Who is this Cally you speak of? I thought Ian May had named a Callaghan McCarthy."

She stood up and turned to look at them all. "I am Cally. I am Callaghan McCarthy. My friends call me Cally."

"You may or may not have friends among us, Callaghan McCarthy," said Rianwynn, pressing her face so close Cally could see her shoulders rise and fall with her breath. Every bone in Cally's body screamed at her to back away, to sit back down, but she knew she dared not do that now. "But you will have to at least learn some decorum, before you can assume the position of Royal Guardian of this Vale."

Cally looked back at the queen's face and noticed for the first time that her eyes were violet, and that they reflected the swirling stars in the sky above. She spoke slowly to keep her voice from breaking, and she spoke truth to power. "I don't know why Ian May chose me. Honest to god, I don't even know what an Armadeur is, or is supposed to do. But I'll defend Ian's right to make that choice himself. You people have no say in the matter."

She resigned herself to her fate, waiting for the Queen of the Faeries to utterly destroy her on the spot. Everyone on the hill, those seated behind her and those in their different groups all around the tree, even the knot of partiers around Ana's car, fell silent, probably anticipating, Cally supposed, a fine show of fireworks.

A tiny smile crept slowly across Rianwynn's lips. "Well," she said. "Well, then. Perhaps Ian May chose right, after all."

She turned away and, in a rustling sweep of robes, took her seat again. "I always did like Ian, you know," she said, leaning across Ben and gesturing to Cally with one hand. "Tried to seduce him, once, many years ago, but he was too besotted with that fey human woman of his. Well."

Cally stepped backward to her seat, carefully because her legs, she realized, were trembling and she wasn't sure she had control of them anymore.

Before she could sit, though, a commotion arose from lower down on the hill, on the side where the Fomorian delegation sat gathered around their stone table. One ruddy figure had been seated with its back to them, but now it arose and turned around to glare balefully in the queen's direction. Cally wasn't sure whether this person's posture was naturally hunched or if he stood stooped in deference, but when he spoke, she guessed it wasn't the latter.

"I don't know what you think you are doing," it said in a deep, growling voice. "But you aren't fooling us. With all due respect, Your Majesty."

Rianwynn didn't bother to stand. "I am sure, in your humble opinion, that is a lot of respect, General," she said, and all the Daoine Sidhe on the hilltop laughed. "But, please, do indulge me. If, as you say, you don't know what I think I am doing, then what is your best guess as to what I am doing?"

"Don't trifle with me." He stepped away from his fellows, and they all stood as he went, heads held high in a show of support as their leader approached the seats on the hill. "You are dangerously close to voiding our truce. That one..." He turned and pointed a long, muscular arm at Cally, and when he did, she saw wide, yellow eyes and a mouth full of teeth just as Luke had described to her one night in an artist's loft in a small village long ago and far away (or so it seemed to her now.) She looked closer to see if she could discern any trace of the face of the Eddie Teine she had known, either recently or in her youth, but her gaze only made him draw his brow down and curl his lip. The lip curl, perhaps, was similar to the look of disdain she remembered from the high school lunch room.

He turned back to the queen. "We have been watching that one," he said. "She eluded our surveillance for many years, which was a neat enough trick in itself. Do not dream I would be fool enough to believe she could have done that without your help. And now here she is, just coincidentally arrived in the last place on where earth she should ever have turned up. Consorting with the prince, no less. And you are going to tell me you have not interfered in order to make all this happen? That you aren't conspiring to actually place this thing on the throne as soon as my back is turned?"

"I am indeed going to tell you that," Rianwynn said, but Cally thought her voice sounded more baffled than imperious. She was speaking the truth.

"I cannot even imagine what you must be thinking," the Fomorian general went on. "Do you seriously believe you could get away with placing a human on the throne? Let alone one who would be both Queen and Armadeur! The Fomorians have always known you for a traitor to all Fey people, and we do not stand alone. Even with all the authority of the Daoine Sidhe behind you, this you would not get away with. We have tolerated these mortals, against our will for three ages, but we will never bow to them. There is no star back to Inverness. Not anymore!" With a final grunt, he spun on his heel, casting one last withering look at Cally as he strode back toward his fellow delegates.

She had no idea what a *"star back to Inverness"* might be but, even in the monster's voice, the mere sound of the words brought tears to Cally's eyes. She gasped softly, feeling as if she were about to sob, and she heard the same soft gasp coming from the lips of people all around her. In the tree-light, she saw tears glittering in many eyes.

"Oh, do sit *down*, Eladha!" the ruby-haired woman beside Cally called out to the Fomorian, and that broke the spell. Laughter, albeit more tenuous than the laughter before, rippled along the row of chairs as the General returned to his stone seat. Cally had to sit down, then, herself, or she would have crumpled to the ground.

"He's always been such a prick," the woman confided to Cally, leaning across the arm of her chair.

"Don't let what he said go to your head," Rianwynn added, also leaning toward Cally. "You are not suitable to be a queen of any people." She reached toward the man who stood at the foot of her chair and accepted her goblet from his hand. "But the General does bring up an important point. Let us discuss this matter, concerning..."

Another commotion interrupted her, then, but not from the Fomorian delegation. This noise arose from beyond them, out amid the shadows between the moonlit hills. It sounded at first like a banshee screaming, but Cally slowly recognized the sound of a car engine laboring, as one might do if its tires were spinning on ice. A pair of lights could be seen cresting one of the hills, then descending the near side of it. Another car, apparently, was approaching the Thingol, across the hills where there were no roads.

"Everyone remain seated," the queen said sharply, and everyone, who had been rising from their seats, sat back down again. "Continue discussing the question of how to obtain a queen to succeed me, but do not to attempt to form a conclusion until I return."

Faerie men came and escorted Rianwynn away toward the pair of headlight beams. Something about the way the queen walked as she strode toward the intruding vehicle made Cally feel like she was carrying some kind of weapon Cally couldn't see.

The people seated on the hill resumed speaking to one another.

"More humans, it looks like," said one of the women seated beyond the queen's empty chair.

"They have the audacity to bring more of their iron machines," another observed.

"Not audacity. More like pure ignorance. Which is, of course, not an excuse."

"The human factor is proving to be a major nuisance. I wish it were not necessary."

"But it is," said the woman sitting at Cally's right. "And don't talk like that, or you could start to sound like a Fomorian!" She laughed.

Then the woman leaned across the arm of her chair, hair cascading over her alabaster shoulders like a river of garnets, and extended her right hand toward Cally. "Is this how you do it?" She shook her empty hand up and down. "Pleased to meet you, etcetera."

"Yes," Cally said, swallowing and grasping the proffered hand in mid-shake. The woman's hand felt smooth and cool, like polished bone. "I'm pleased to meet you as well. Call me Cally." She was gratified that at least one of these people was attempting to behave in a friendly manner toward a mere human.

"And please call me Aileen. Ana is my daughter."

Though Aileen's face remained nothing but friendly, Cally felt as if she had been slapped. "Then you're..." Cally swallowed, forgetting to release the woman's hand. She didn't dare glance over her shoulder at Ben, but she could guess he was probably squeezing his eyes shut and holding his breath again.

"When your young prince," Aileen continued, removing her hand from Cally's and tilting her head toward Ben, "was a younger and more impressionable lad, I seduced him and got a daughter from him." She said this in a completely frank and unapologetic tone, the way one might say, "I found a rib roast on sale at the supermarket last week."

"Well," Cally replied, feeling herself beginning to tremble, and then becoming angry at herself for this. "Then, according to the rules, as I understand them, that makes you the one who becomes the next queen."

"Oh, that was my intention!" Aileen's laughter rang over the moonlit hills as her hair spilled back over her shoulders. "Alas, my daughter has made it clear she intends to 'pursue a destiny of her own making.' She does, after all, come by her stubbornness honestly." She leaned forward and nodded past Cally to where Ben was sitting, and a quick glance showed Cally he was indeed carefully not looking at either of them. "Anyway," said Aileen, laying her hand companionably on Cally's arm, "the queen may well still decide to command her son and I to wed, should Ana someday come to her senses and outgrow this obstinate stage she's going through. But you needn't worry, even should he and I be wed." She gave Cally a conspiratorial wink. "I've heard all about you humans and your obsession with romance. You may still have him as your lover, whenever he gets a chance to visit you. I have no further use for him in that capacity. You may do with him as you like." Her smile was nothing but friendly, like that of any woman sharing a secret with a friend, as she patted Cally's arm. "I am sure the queen will find that to be an acceptable arrangement."

Before Cally could find words to assure this woman that she, herself, would not find it to be an acceptable arrangement at all, she heard Ben clear his throat.

"With all due respect," he said. And, when Cally looked, she saw that he was indeed regarding Aileen with respect (and with nothing else, that she could discern.) "I will not marry at all if I cannot marry for love. I have told you this, many times." He smiled congenially at the faerie woman.

The women seated on the rise (excepting Cally) all laughed at this. "How quaint," some tittered, and Aileen shook her beautiful head. "Too much human blood," she lamented, waving dismissively toward him.

"It's a shame his other child has disappeared from all knowledge," someone else said, from three or four seats away. "That one might have had the right balance of common sense and fertility, and we could begin discussing something else at last."

The queen had returned, and she came to stand before them again, trailing a small handful of dark figures who followed slowly, backlit by the tree's light.

"Let us table that topic, for the moment," Rianwynn said. To Cally's surprise, she seemed more than a little unnerved. "Someone has arrived with new information which may help us resolve at least one matter this night."

44 - Rosheen and the Queen

All seated Sidhe stood and gathered around the four dark figures that entered the circle of light. One of them was Rum, and Cally thought she saw him wink at her. Two humans followed him, and between them they helped a fourth, much smaller person, bent over and limping as it approached. When it drew near the queen, however, it straightened and shrugged off their help.

Bree Dawes hobbled forward to stand before the chairs and did not meet anyone's eyes when she spoke. "Sorry I'm late. I got lost."

Cally couldn't help jumping up and running to her, but she had to stop herself just short of hugging her. Bree was not the hugging type. She looked beyond Bree to see who had accompanied her, and there she saw Rosheen, smiling as sweetly and quietly as she ever did. Behind her stood Brandon, looking awkward and shy, but not alarmed by all that was going on. A quick gesture of Rosheen's thin hand warned Cally to hold her ground. Brandon gave them both a sheepish grin, waiting patiently.

"Found these two wandering," Bree was continuing, "and they never would have got here if I hadn't offered them a lift. Oh, by the way, brother, I got the car stuck in the mud. Sorry." She didn't really sound sorry.

Ben peered out into the darkness in the direction from which the three had come. Rosheen turned her smile toward the queen and bowed deeply, her long, dusk-colored hair sweeping the ground. As she bowed, she reached into the bag at her side and withdrew a small square of paper.

"I just wanted to show you something," she said, straightening and coming closer. She handed the paper to Rianwynn. "Now, what do you think of that, Grandmother?"

Rianwynn went stiff at her words and, in that moment, Cally could swear she ceased to shine like a Faerie Queen. She became, instead, as dull and dusky as the girl who stood before her. Her long, white hand, to Cally's astonishment, trembled as she took the paper from Rosheen's hand.

Rosheen, however, had ceased to look at the queen at all. Her eyes, wide and glittering with unshed tears, had turned to look past Cally to where Ben was slowly rising from his seat.

Cally heard Ben let out his breath as if he had been hit in the stomach, but she couldn't take her eyes from Rosheen and the queen. They were like mirrors, each reflecting one another, one reflection made of silver and the other of bronze, between them clasping the small white square of paper.

The queen looked at the paper for a long time. "How can this be?" she finally said, looking up and extending her free hand toward Cally. "Come," she said without the slightest trace of her previous haughtiness. "You should see this, also."

Cally walked forward as if in the kind of dream wherein she already knew what she was about to see.

"It's taken me all my life," she heard Rosheen saying, but the girl wasn't talking to Cally or Rianwynn. Her eyes were on Ben, and tears were spilling freely down her face now. "I've been looking for you all my life. I'm sorry it took so long, but I'm here now." She released the piece of paper and stepped back, allowing Cally to get near.

Cally looked down, and Rianwynn turned the paper so she could see it more easily as Rosheen stepped away. It was a print-out of an ultrasound, the ultrasound Rosheen and Brandon had gone to have done, earlier that day. The face of the infant nestled in the amniotic bow was directly facing the camera, smiling as if it knew they were looking at it. Cally recognized the huge eyes, the wide, foxlike grin, and she felt the hill beneath her feet begin to heave like a wave.

"Too bad it's a boy," Rianwynn was saying. "But it will do, for a few more millennia, anyway. Very well. The conditions are met, for now. The line is unbroken." She turned to speak to Ben, but he wasn't paying any attention to anything but Rosheen, who stood before him now with her hands on either side of his face. Her thumbs brushed away tears that were sliding down into his beard but she made no effort, herself, to stop the tears that poured over her own wide smile.

Her wide smile, her green eyes, her detached grace – everything suddenly clicked into place in Cally's mind as Brandon, taking Cally's hand, passed by and drew her with him. "We're going to name him Adam," he was saying, leading her toward Rosheen and Ben. "Apparently it's an old, family name on Rosheen's mother's side, or something."

Ben's arm went around Cally as she drew near. He tried to say something to her, but his voice was choked. Rosheen spoke instead.

"I was almost sure," she said. "I was almost sure he had to be somewhere in this Vale. I had tried so many other places. The day after Brandon and I arrived here, Ana came to call, and she had her suspicions right away. She asked me a lot of very interesting questions, and encouraged me to go to the store with her and I thought... Well, dear Bree certainly seemed to know something." She smiled affectionately toward the old woman, who stood staunchly facing away from the entire scenario. "It was when we ran into Auntie after the show this evening...well, actually she nearly ran over us. That's when she explained the rest of it.

"Now I am sure." She looked back up to Ben's face. "You are the father I have been searching for all my life."

Ana emerged from the shadows and shoved her way into the little knot of people standing around Ben. "Well, isn't this nice," she said, putting one arm around Ben and the other around Rosheen. She smirked at Cally. "Looks like you two have managed to become the progenitors of royalty after all, one way or another."

Bree's voice, behind them, croaked like a harsh night insect as she hobbled closer.

"Congratulations. I shall dance at your wedding. But let's celebrate later. I've come with information, myself, for you all. It's about the matter of who killed you-know-who, and about who is going to go down for it."

45 - Due Process

The chickens, Cally heard herself thinking, had certainly all come home to roost. At least, she hoped that was all of them, now. She was sure she wouldn't be able to handle any more, but Bree, whose presence here was surprising enough, had yet to explain why she had come.

Ben had turned back to his throne, but he had inexplicably folded, just before it, and sat now on the ground, facing the tree. His fingers were spread in the grass as if he hoped to draw strength from the Earth itself; his head was bowed, his eyes closed. Cally sat close beside him, supporting him with her presence as best she could, and Rosheen sat at his other side. The queen said nothing about this, standing to one side, herself, so that those seated, whether on chairs or on the ground, could see the bent, shadowy figure silhouetted against the fire.

"Few of you have met my daughter," said Rianwynn. "This is Brigid, whose human father's surname was Dawes, who has spent her entire life in the human realm."

The Sidhe bowed as Bree stood before them, hunched with age and what might have been rage, eyes glittering darkly as she looked up and down the line. The set of her chin was defiant as she looked squarely at each of them in turn, her face softening only when her gaze settled finally on Ben. She opened her mouth to speak, took a deep breath and let it out, closing her mouth again.

"Didn't you tell me you had something to share?" Rianwynn prompted. She reminded Cally exactly of a mother trying to coax a shy, little girl to recite a poem, and Cally struggled to remind herself that the queen was, in fact, Bree's mother. Bree looked ancient beside Rianwynn, reflecting no trace of faerie grace or beauty. Cally squinted, trying to imagine the young girl Bree had once been and, to her own surprise, perceived that she had once been every bit as beautiful as Ana.

Bree raised her chin and grunted. "There's something you all ought to know," she barked at last. Her stance was defiant, but her gaze clung to Ben as if to a lifeline. Cally wished she could hand the old woman a newspaper to glare at, as was her wont, to avoid looking at those around her as she spoke.

"I know who killed Foster Brentwood," Bree said at last. "It was me.

"I never intended to tell anyone," she continued, before the gasps and stirring all around her could resolve into words. "But now I understand: a good man might spend his life in prison if nobody else pays for the crime. And I have no intention of paying for something I feel I should have *been* paid for.

"Also," she added, turning to look up at the queen, "I have not, as you say, spent my entire life in the human realm. As some of you well know." She cast an accusing glare, dark as crows' eyes, around those assembled, particularly toward the men standing behind the queen. "I've been here once before." Ben stirred at last, looking up at his sister. This was, Cally realized, news to him. "That was when I committed a different crime or, more to the point, you all so *thoughtfully* stopped me from committing one." She said the word 'thoughtfully' as if it were an epithet. Ben stood.

"Wait." Cally couldn't stop herself speaking up as she stood as well. "Back up a second. Bree, that's nuts. You couldn't have killed Foster. How on earth could you have? I mean, I can believe you would! But the way he was killed, it would have taken a lot of strength, as well as sharp...claws or teeth or... something..." she subsided as people all around her, both sitting and standing, began to laugh. She heard several muttered remarks along the lines of "our queen's son has picked a bright one, hasn't he?"

There was a stir from the Fomorian delegation, as well. "So!" the General boomed as he stood and stepped closer. "Faerie hand has spilled human blood!" Despite the dark tone of his voice, he smiled and rubbed his hands together with delight at this news.

"Please note," he said, "that it was not one of us, as you all expected, who ended up voiding the Truce! But now that the Truce is void, I and my people are free. Nothing further stands in the way of taking back the lands that have always rightfully been ours." He bowed to the queen, then turned away toward the north, signaling to his cohorts to join him.

The queen directed the women on either side of her to intercept them. "You may not depart until the Thing is adjourned!" she reminded Eladha sharply. Then she turned to her own men. "Bring the creature," she said, and several of them headed off into the darkness.

Bree nodded to Rianwynn, then turned and glared at the General.

"Technically, human hand had already spilled faerie blood," she informed him.

This did not diminish his glee. He was practically dancing where he stood, licking his teeth in anticipation of being released to act on this news.

The faerie men who had departed now returned, dragging between them a dark and protesting figure. This they dropped unceremoniously on the ground between the queen and Bree. He pulled himself up into a crouch, cowering and shaking with silent sobs, until Rianwynn commanded him to stand. When he did so, he remained bent over, not looking up at anyone. Cally noticed, to her horror, that a dark, thick substance was dripping from his fingers like blood. Ben stepped closer, bending and trying to see into the man's face.

"Here is my proposal," said Bree. "I won't kill him, in return for which you can let him take the fall for my so-called crime. That should get everyone off the hook. Both human and faerie blood will be avenged, the Truce will remain intact, the human authorities will have their perp, and everyone can go skipping home singing Kum Bah Yah."

Rianwynn, to Cally's surprise, nodded as if she understood Bree's logic perfectly and agreed with it. It was Ben who asked the question, "What is going on?"

"This is the human to whom Bree was once married," Rianwynn explained. "We didn't let her kill him, back then, when she first discovered she had the power to do so. Instead we convinced her to let us take care of him, to keep him here, forever reminded of his crimes, but alive."

Ben peered again into the man's face, and finally he stood back. "Ware?" he asked. "I thought... Bree, you told everyone he abandoned you."

"He did that when he abandoned all decency," she said. "And that was long before he disappeared. Everyone knew John Ware was a wife-beater. But he didn't just hurt me. He also..." She stopped and looked up at her brother, unable to speak. She was clearly trying to finish her story, her jaw working up and down, but no sound came out.

Rianwynn finished for her. "She was expecting a daughter, and this creature..." She spat on the wretch crouched before her. "In one of his drunken rages, he killed the child before it was ever born."

The man sank once again to the ground, shivering, and Cally realized with horror that it actually was blood, continually dripping from his fingers, soaking into the grass all around him.

"I'd say, technically, that was the first blood spilled," Bree finally managed to say. "Faerie blood, at least in part, spilled by a human." The anger had gone out of her voice and had been replaced by a dead, flat tone. "And the blood of she who would have become Queen."

"I never knew." Ben's voice was nearly inaudible as he reached for his sister. "I never knew..."

"You weren't around." Ben winced at her words, but there was no blame in Bree's voice. "This happened during the years you were tricked into spending here. You didn't know so much time was passing. Remember? And I never wanted you to find out what had happened during that time.

"I wanted to tear his head from his body," she said to all the rest of them. "And once I had recovered, I finally understood that I could have done so all along. But by then, he had fled. I came here looking for him. I figured my mother's people would be happy to help avenge spilled faerie blood. I asked only for help in hunting him down. I got that, but when they found him, they wouldn't let me end his miserable existence. They said it would cause an international incident or some garbage like that. Instead, they promised to keep him imprisoned, and remind him every day of his crimes. I have to say, looking at him now, I almost think they did the right thing, after all." She aimed a kick at the wretched heap of humanity on the ground before her, but two faerie men drew her back.

Ben's head sank further with every word Bree said, until he looked almost as miserable as Ware. "I should have been there for you," he said. "I should have... Sister, I'm so sorry."

"Shush." Bree put a hand up to him. "You didn't know. And you've been there for me ever since."

He didn't seem to feel this excused him.

"I don't see how her proposal adequately addresses the conditions of the Truce," the General of the Fomorians said. "It doesn't change the fact that she..." he pointed an accusing finger at Bree, "did kill the other human, just a few days ago, with no respect for the due process of the laws of the country in which they live. Even as a human, she had no right to do that. If she isn't properly punished, there will be all manner of repercussions." Cally could almost hear him thinking, *At least, I hope so!*"

"Repercussions?" A voice boomed from the direction of the Aes Sidhe delegation. Ennilangr rose from the table, there, but he did not need to come closer for them all to hear his voice. "You mean, similar to the repercussions that will arise when it is revealed that you are the reason the deceased was out of prison, thanks to your interference, in the first place?"

"That's irrelevant," the General retorted. "What I did complied with the due process of the humans' law, and I did it for reasons of my own."

"I am sure you did," said Ennilangr. "It was still unlawful interference in international affairs."

While these two debated, the queen and her men and women stepped aside and quietly discussed the matter among themselves. Rianwynn finally returned with her decision.

"The Thing is adjourned," she said. "It's time to go to church."

46 - The Church of Logic, Sin and Love

Rianwynn turned toward the Tree, her beautiful head held high. Looking at her profile against the light, Cally suddenly understood why the Daoine, according to any legends that had drifted down to her human world, had always been considered the warrior class among the Sidhe. At a flick of the queen's hand, all the people on the hill began to move. Some of them cleared away the feast, while others began organizing into ranks. The tables and chairs disappeared as if they had been reabsorbed into the ground. The Fomorian delegation gathered around their General and departed, but not before Eladha formally assured the queen that, if she should attempt to stop him, war would almost certainly greet her by morning.

A tingle ran down Cally's spine as she noticed, from the corner of her eye, several lines of Sidhe men and women assembling in ranks behind her.

Rianwynn did not acknowledge Eladha's departure. Instead, she pointed at the crouched form of John Ware, and said to Ben, "Take him to the site."

Ennilangr left his group and came to stand beside Ben. Ben bowed to the queen, then straightened and looked at Cally. He said the words she had heard him say many times: "I'll see you in the morning." His voice was as earnest as it had ever been but, for the first time, Cally found herself wondering what the words even meant.

Then he turned and took John Ware by the arm. The man cringed visibly, as if he expected Ben to attack him, and Cally could tell by the knotted muscles Ben's arms that he was struggling to keep himself from doing just that.

Ben and Ennilangr flanked John Ware as they headed off toward the silver Daimler gleaming in the moonlight in a narrow space between two hills. The queen and her group, which included Bree and Ana, began to move in the opposite direction, their ranks curving around the tree on the hilltop in a clockwise spiral. Cally couldn't really call it marching; the Sidhe moved as silently as leaves blowing in a breeze, shining like torches being carried toward the flaming tree.

She looked around for Rum, or even for Mima or anyone who might know how to help her find her way home, but the car and the dark tree had disappeared from the hill to the north and the people around it had dispersed. Only Michael Dawes remained, standing in the moonlight, watching but coming no nearer. She thought she saw him place his hands over his heart and bow, but she couldn't be sure to whom this gesture was directed.

The Sidhe leading the ranks behind Cally urged her, almost gently, to follow the queen's regiment a little to the right and several steps behind. They ushered Rosheen, with Brandon close at her side, to a similar position at Cally's right. A formation of Sidhe almost as large as the queen's followed behind Cally, and another assembled behind Rosheen. As they all spiraled closer to the tree, Cally watched her son's eyes looking from Rosheen to the tree and back again. His expression was bemused, perhaps, but completely trusting as his eyes fell upon his beloved.

Cally was pretty sure she knew what would happen when they got close enough to the tree, but a more pressing matter occurred to her as she watched Brandon's face. She slowed her footsteps until Rosheen caught up to her, and then she spoke as firmly as she could manage while keeping her voice down to a whisper.

"I don't know what your intentions are," she said to the young woman. "But if you do what Ben's mother did to Michael Dawes, to the man who loved her, if you leave him once you have got your human child, if you break his heart, then trust me, I will find you. I will find you, and I will make you sorry you ever set eyes on my son."

At this, Rosheen threw back her head and let loose a clear laugh that echoed like music over the hills into the darkness. Everyone stopped to look at her, and she stopped, too. She laid her hands as lightly as bird's wings on Cally's shoulders and turned her so that both women looked into one another's eyes. Rosheen's smile was as gentle as the moonlight lying on the hills around them. "Remember who my father is," she said in a voice so soft only Cally could hear. "And my grandfather, as well. *I know how to love.*"

Still smiling, she turned to resume the march. As Cally stumbled back into place at the queen's right, Rosheen added with a softer laugh, "Besides, there isn't a whole lot about this child that is human."

It wasn't clear exactly when it had happened, but Cally found they were no longer walking through grass across the top of a hill. They were now walking along a broad, golden road. Cally looked down to see her feet treading over a shimmering surface patterned like fine bark. She had traveled this road before, on the back of a white horse. She thought she knew where it led, and that was the only thing that kept her feet moving, now.

The procession behind her quickened its pace and Cally had to speed up to keep the people behind her from walking over her. Only darkness lay on either side of the golden road. No, not utter darkness: Cally could also see stars at either side and she knew, somehow, that if she should step close to the edge of the road, she would be able to look down and see stars there, too, wheeling down and down forever into the depths of space. She tacked closer to the queen on her left and let her own retinue of people block her view of the edge of the road on her right.

They were all marching toward a forest, not far ahead, now, of long, thin trees radiating outward from the road. Cally had been here before, as well. She knew this forest wasn't a forest at all but the branches of the crown of the tree. She remembered that beyond the branches, at the heart of its crown, the tree would be cradling in its embrace a wide meadow.

Only, it wasn't the meadow this time. As Sidhe passed like ghosts through the forest of branches, only darkness lay ahead until they emerged into what felt to Cally more like an enclosed space, a vaulted chamber. Their footsteps, so silent before amid all the sounds of crickets and night breezes, now whispered like falling sand, echoing among the arches over the vast space. As the last of the people brought up the rear and stopped, the walls all around – or so it seemed to Cally – became more solid and drew in closer around them. Cally could, barely, perceive tall windows at either side, visible only because the night outside was brighter than the darkness inside. The faces of the Sidhe shone like cold starlight all around as they stopped, waiting, silently facing the queen in their ranks.

Cally broke position and walked to one of the windows, her footsteps echoing in the arches overhead. Peering out, she saw dark streets, and dark windows looking out of dark buildings that looked vacant. There was something unnervingly familiar about them – Cally felt so close to recognizing them, her brain itched.

Someone, somewhere in the echoing chamber, softly reminded, "Time is moving, now, your Majesty." Cally turned around and saw Rianwynn looking impatiently at her. The queen's pale arm pointed toward the opposite end of the building, where Cally perceived a tall, dark door.

"There isn't much time," said the queen." Come, this is what we brought you here for."

Cally didn't want to lead the way, but she did want to get out of this building, so she walked across the front of the assembled ranks and reached out to the dark door. Her hand encountered rough wood, covered with fine cracks and flaking paint. At about waist level, her questing fingers encountered cold iron, a handle with a thumb-latch. She pressed down on this, and it gave under her touch with a metallic click that resounded through the chamber as the door swung open.

At the sound, everyone in the chamber pressed forward. Cally stumbled out the door in front of them and found herself on a wide, concrete stoop enclosed by an iron railing. A wide set of steps descended to the street below. Faint light filtered around the corner of a building at the end of the street to Cally's left, and the familiar sounds and scents of an autumn evening filled the air: katydids, human voices, music, the scent of leaves...and of pizza.

Cally knew where she was, now. She turned her head and saw, as she knew she would, in the window of the building next door a piece of paper taped to the inside reading *"Lowest prices anywhere on all DVD players!"*

Daoine Sidhe were streaming out of the door, crowding together to avoid the iron railings, of the old church building on South Church Street in Woodley, USA. In the distance, from where a streetlight glowed softly through the space between two brick buildings, a few tentative guitar notes drifted to her on the breeze. A chill ran down Cally's spine when she heard what sounded like her own voice adding a strident comment to the conversation.

"You will go into your shop," the queen was saying to Bree. "You will leave the lights off, and you will stay there, quietly, in the dark until we come for you." Then, with one hand, she shoved Bree unceremoniously off the stoop. The old woman landed on her feet like a cat and, with an agility that belied her age, ran between the church and the empty storefront into the parking lot behind the News Store.

"There isn't much time." Cally, looking up to meet Rianwynn's gaze, heard herself repeating the words the queen had spoken earlier. Only, she was saying them to herself, under her breath, and she meant something completely different.

She understood now, quite clearly, where she was, and when. This was the night Foster had been killed and, judging by the song she heard the little band up on Main Street beginning to sing, he was still alive. She was frankly appalled by the idea that began forming in her head, astounded to hear herself thinking it, but once it occurred to her, she couldn't help but move. If she could get there fast enough, she realized, she could stop past-tense Bree from killing Foster. She could stop the whole thing from ever having happened in the first place.

Rianwynn seemed to realize what Cally was thinking as soon as she thought it. The queen waved a hand, directing her people to close in, but it was too late. Cally had already ducked under the iron railing and jumped down into the space between the buildings.

She ran, not the way Bree had gone but straight up Church Street toward its intersection with Main Street. She heard the queen shout "Stop!" Cally wished she could obey, but she only ran faster, ducking into the darkness beside the shop on the corner of Church Street and Main.

"This is nuts," she hissed with every breath as she ran. "This is nuts. Are you actually trying to save Foster's life? What is *wrong* with you?" She peered carefully across the street at the group of people on the loading dock, but looked away quickly when she saw her own back amid them. To her right she saw Ignacio, walking with his hands in his jacket pockets, back toward Vale House, and to her left she saw Luke, walking away with Andi, but looking right at her. He couldn't really see her, could he?

Doc strummed the refrain of *Friend of the Devil* on his mandolin and Luke looked away as Cally prepared to run across the street. She heard a soft rush of faerie feet, like leaves blowing over the pavement, behind her.

"Why are you doing this?" she whispered again, but she didn't give herself time to answer as she ran out into the street, dashing through the thin shadows to the far end of Church Street. It wasn't just because it would stop Ignacio ever having to go to jail in the first place. It wasn't just because it would wipe those tears from Katarina's eyes before they ever fell. It wasn't even because she hoped to avoid a Faerie Apocalypse without having to flout the due process of the laws of the United States. It was just – and she wished she didn't know it – because it was the right thing to do.

When she ducked into the darkness between the feed store and the other buildings along Church Street, she paused for breath. She could see at least one shadowy figure ahead of her. It was walking slowly, head hung low with shoulders slumped, silhouetted against the lights from the railroad yard at the end of the alley. She had no clear plan what she was going to do, now. She hadn't had time to make one. Never mind why she should save Foster – she had no idea just how she was going to stop some fey thing that could tear a man's head from his shoulders. It would be foolhardy to confront such a thing...

She resumed moving, more slowly now, toward the walking figure and, as she passed further into the darkness between the buildings, she could see out the end of the alley to the railroad yard beyond. She could see Danya Barry crouched at the other side of the tracks, checking her instruments; she could see the twinkling lights of the cottages along Bell's road. And then, in the shadows just inside the end of the alley, she could see another shadow, little more than a dark lump crouched against the building where the street emptied into the railroad yard. She was certain, by its size and hunched shape, that this must be Bree. She opened her mouth to call, but couldn't decide whether to call first to Bree or to Foster. She was expecting something huge and monstrous to show up at any moment.

All that appeared, however, was a horde of Daoine Sidhe in the moonlight at the end of the alley, assembling themselves into silent, watching ranks. Cally shrank against the rough wall of the feed store, looking right and left. There was another silent wall of Sidhe blocking the south end of the alley, as well, and this one included the queen, whose shining eyes were fixed on Cally as if they could pin her to the wall with the force of their glare alone. For a moment she almost thought they were doing just that. She clearly heard, inside her head, the queen's voice snarling: *Do not do what you are thinking of doing.*

"I'd go back if I were you." But that was Bree's voice, speaking to Foster, and Cally turned to see him stop, pivoting to face the old woman.

"Well, you're not me," he spat. "And which way would I go, if I were? My dear friends have already ordered me not to go along Main Street."

"That's not what I meant, and you know it." Bree straightened up and stepped toward Foster, who stopped as if he had run into an invisible wall. The old woman seemed to stand taller and straighter than she normally did. "I meant, you should go back to prison, where you belong. You'll be a lot safer there, trust me."

"Trust *you*, old hag? Trust any of you privileged snobs who have no problem taking away everything I own? I don't think so!" He tried to take a step toward her, but she put up a hand like a claw, and he stopped again, as if she had buried that claw in his chest.

"You never had anything to take away," she said. "All that you had belonged to Nell. You threw away everything you could have had. This always happens, when everything you have is never enough. Leave us now, while you still have a life to call your own."

"I will leave you and this pathetic town forever," he said, "as soon as I collect my dear wife."

"You don't have a wife anymore, either."

Foster's feet still seemed glued to the ground, but he leaned menacingly toward the tall figure. Cally wanted to shout to him to watch out, though she had no idea what he should be watching out for. Never knowing when to stop talking had always been Foster's biggest weakness, she thought.

"Nell is mine," he continued. "Even though you have all taken advantage of her illness to manipulate her into turning her back on me. It's your fault she's living all alone, when she needs someone to take care of her. She's been tricked by people she thought were her friends, but now she is coming with me!"

"You will not touch her." Bree's voice was lower, now, quieter yet somehow more menacing. Foster seemed to shrink before her, or was Bree standing ever taller and straighter? "You will not go anywhere near her."

"She belongs to me, and I will do whatever I wish with her," he affirmed with more courage – or was it stupidity? – than Cally would ever have given him credit for. He reached into his jacket. Bree stopped advancing, then, and perhaps spoke again, but all Cally could hear was a low, bubbling growl.

Foster drew his hand out of his jacket, metal flashing as he lifted it above his head. He took a deep breath to make some final, dramatic declaration, and then his gaping mouth finally snapped shut. As Bree took one last step toward him, her lips parted in a snarl and impossibly long fangs emerged from behind them. Pale claws, followed by vast hands at the ends of massive arms reached out of her black coat.

Cally couldn't move any more than Foster could, but she found her voice.

"Bree, don't!" she called. The old woman who was not an old woman anymore turned to glare at Cally, giving Foster a chance to break and run.

Without taking her eyes off Cally, Bree reached out one long arm and caught Foster by his collar so that his feet ran out from under him and he slammed onto his back on the pavement. Somehow, this broke the spell that had held Cally immobile, and she lunged forward and put herself between Bree and her prey. As Foster scrambled to his feet, Cally pushed her face as close as she dared to the face of the thing Bree had become. She searched desperately in the creature's china-blue eyes for some trace of the human being who had so recently stood there. "Bree, please! Don't do this! We can find some other way. We will! Bree, look at me!"

The deep growl rumbling up from the depths of the beast's chest let Cally know how close she was to feeling its pale teeth in her throat. She dared not back down now. To look away from that creature now would guarantee her death. "Bree," she said in a cracking voice. "Come on. Bree..."

A dark arm swept out, and ivory claws raked Cally's arm, tearing right through the sleeve of her jacket and sending her reeling backward into the wall. Her head struck the bricks and a burst of stars lit up the night inside her head; she slid slowly down to the sidewalk. Dizzy, she looked up in time to see Foster's lifeless body crumple to the ground.

"It is done, then." The queen stood over Foster with her retinue at her side. She reached out a hand and Ben appeared, dragging Ware along by the arm. At Rianwynn's nod, he positioned the man beside Foster where he sank to his knees, meek and unmoving, his fingers dripping blood onto the pavement. Cally had the odd impression he was actually glad to be left here, freed at last from the watchful care of the Daoine Sidhe.

"Time to go," the queen's men said, surprisingly gently, to Bree as they flanked her now shriveled and bent form, guiding her out the end of the street.

Cally heard Danya begin to scream. She heard her own voice laughing and saying, "Ghost hunters, am I right?"

"Time to go." This time it was Ben's voice, speaking softly in Cally's ear as he put a hand under her arm to lift her up. She bit her lip to keep herself from screaming in pain, and Ben looked at the three deep, bloody slashes on her arm. Shaking his head, he slipped an arm around her back to support her as they followed the Sidhe procession out the end of the street, turning east, passing through the residential back yards toward the meadow. The last thing she remembered was hearing herself shouting, "Hang on, Danya, I'm coming!"

47 - Ivory Tower

She awoke enveloped in softness, and looked up to see Ben standing in front of a window, holding a curtain to one side as he looked out into dim, gray morning light. All around her, the cream and green décor of the Dogwood Room slowly came into focus. She reached out to push the covers away, and cried out as searing pain shot from her right shoulder all the way down to her fingertips.

Ben dropped the curtain and came to sit on the edge of the bed. "We did the best we could for you," he said. "You've been asleep for three days. The venom is cleared from the wounds, but they will still take the normal amount of time to heal." He reached out and ran a gentle thumb over the bandages wrapped around her upper arm, where three thin lines of blood had begun to seep through.

"Venom..." Cally tried to sit up. Her memory of how she had been injured returned, slowly leaking through in patchy scenes, despite her attempts not to think about them. "It's over, then," she said, letting Ben tuck an extra pillow behind her back.

He looked over his shoulder, at the gray light coming through the window, and sighed. "It's not over," he said. Instead of explaining, he looked back at Cally and asked, "Did you really try to save Foster's life?"

Cally clenched her fists (though doing so made the torn muscles in her shoulder burn) and took a deep breath, preparing to defend her actions. But, meeting Ben's eyes, she saw no judgment in them. In his gaze lay only love and, quite possibly, admiration. He shook his head gently as his smile widened, and Cally realized she would never, ever have to defend herself to this man. Even as she unclenched her fists and relaxed back into the pillows, she wasn't honestly sure she would ever be able to get used to that.

"You are amazing," he said. And then his smile fell and he let out a heavy breath. "But no, it's not over."

He returned to the window and pushed the curtain aside again, looking down at the ground below. "And this isn't really Vale House," he added. "Mother and her ladies made this for us." He gestured behind himself at the room. "It's a glamour, for you to recover in. I'd like to think it's the queen's way of telling us we have her blessings, but it's probably just her way of keeping us out of the way while ..."

Waiting for him to finish, Cally looked around the room. She noticed, then, that many small details were not quite right. The dogwood wallpaper was just a wavy green and ivory pattern that didn't accurately portray any botanical that grew on the earth she knew; instead of the jumble of notebooks she had dumped there, the dresser was laden with generic hairbrushes and bottles such as might be seen in a home decorating magazine and, moreover, they looked fused to the wood of the dresser top, as if everything had been carved from one piece. The long mirror on the back of the door cast no reflection.

"Keeping us out of the way while she what?" Cally prompted when Ben didn't finish what he had been saying.

"We were unable to prevent the Fomorians from finding an excuse for their war," he said. "In fact, we may have accidentally unleashed it ourselves.

"When Foster got up and started to run, after you distracted Bree, one of Mother's men stepped in to block his way. Foster cut that man – didn't kill him, but he injured him badly, because the knife had iron in its blade. That prompted other Sidhe to attack Foster. They finished the job Bree had started. Faerie blood has been spilled by human hand, and human blood has been spilled by faerie hand. We left John Ware to take the fall, as planned, and the authorities think they have Foster's killer in hand, now. But the Fomorians know better. The Truce is broken; Eladha is free now to do as he has always wished."

There was no blame in his voice, but Cally knew many would even now be blaming her for this turn of events. Groaning, she slipped out of the bed to stand at Ben's side near the window.

The belvedere that should have been outside the window was not present, nor was the Vale House porch roof. Dizzy for a moment, Cally swayed and had to grasp the window frame for balance. She could see straight down to the ground far below – much farther below than it should have been. In place of the front porch, a circular stone balcony jutted out from the wall like a castle battlement, with no railing or parapet. From there, what should have been the lawn stretched out to what should have been the meadow. It was no meadow, now, and the land divided by the fence was equally gray and dead-looking on either side. Cally couldn't help but think of this as a battlefield – it was utterly without hue, and rolled on endlessly under a roiling leaden sky.

At a dozen different points along the plain, she could see fires burning, and people of different sorts gathered around them. The whole scene looked, to Cally, very much like the Thing, only with camp fires instead of tables, and with gray clouds instead of stars overhead. She thought she could tell, by the quality of the light of the fires, which kinds of Fey people were gathered near each one. Just slightly east of north, an especially large camp fire burned black and red like gory spears stabbing into the sky; dark silhouettes danced at its base like smoke. Cally knew that if she looked long enough, the vague shapes would, as always, resolve into individual forms and faces, and she looked away because she did not want to see.

"Today is October the twenty-fifth," Ben was saying. "And it is the final day of the Thing. Events have been different, in Woodley, since our little interference. And things have been different at the Thing, as well, because they remember both realities. Either way, Eladha is going to get his precious war. The battle will be joined when the sun sets tonight." He looked up at the colorless sky and shook his head. "Though, I don't think the sun is really going to rise today."

Cally gently turned Ben to face her, wincing as she put her hands up on his shoulders. "Just once," she said. "Just once, I wish I could wake up in my own bed with you there beside me."

He let the curtain fall and took her hands in his. "Go back to sleep, then," he said, drawing her toward the rumpled bed. "Let's see if we can make at least one of your wishes come true."

48 - This Side of the Fence

It was a while before Cally got back to sleep. When she awoke again, Ben was spooned behind her, snoring softly into the back of her neck, one arm draped around her. She tried very hard not to open her eyes. She didn't want to ever reach the end of this moment. But, through her closed eyelids, she could tell that the light in the room had changed. It wasn't the light of any sun Cally had ever known, but it had moved westward, behind the house (or what passed, here, as the house.)

She couldn't roll over to face Ben without rolling onto her injured arm, so she slid out of the bed and knelt beside it to look at him. He stirred and looked up at the sluggish light slouching into the room through the window, but when he saw Cally he smiled.

They arose and dressed without speaking. Though Ben was donning ordinary clothes again, rumpled jeans and the same blue oxford shirt he had been wearing when he had left for the Thing, something about the way he dressed himself gave Cally the uncanny impression he was putting on battle gear. In the closet she found, for herself, only a long, blue dress. She ran her hand over it and tugged at the seams. She sniffed the fabric and even tried it with her teeth. Ben laughed.

"It's real," he said. "Made of ordinary cotton. Aileen found it for you, the other day while you slept. Your clothes from the night of the...incident, were beyond repair." She bit her lip to stop herself crying out at the pain in her shoulder as he gently helped her slip the dress over her head. "I think I understand what you meant, now," he was saying. "When you said we are working together, even though our work is on different sides of the fence."

They stood side by side with their backs to the window, looking at the west wall of the faux Dogwood Room. There were two doors in this wall. One was the white-painted door that led – at least, in the real Vale House – to the upstairs gallery overlooking the dining room. The other, smaller door was varnished with a dark walnut lacquer, and stood slightly ajar to reveal the stairway which, under ordinary circumstances, should have led down to Cally's office. Now, however, the wall beyond this doorway was not the white-painted drywall Cally remembered. Instead, she glimpsed a gray wall of crude stonework encircling equally crude stone steps, and the smell of damp earth wafted up from the stairwell. Ben was steeling himself to enter this door.

He let out his breath and turned to face her. "When I go. Out there." He glanced quickly behind them at the window overlooking the not-meadow. "Please don't watch. I don't want you to see me that way. The way I'm going to be."

Cally couldn't imagine a way Ben could be that she wouldn't love. If his handsome exterior had been a glamour all along, if she were about to discover he had lizard skin and antlers, she was certain she would still want him as much as ever. She didn't press the issue – there wasn't any more time. She just smiled and nodded her promise.

"I'll see you in the morning," she said, shivering at the sound of her own words. She kissed him to make the chills stop. He returned her kiss tenfold, crushing her to his chest with both arms, then released her and, taking a breath as if he were about to plunge into deep water, strode toward the small doorway, disappearing almost soundlessly down the spiral stair.

Force of habit took over and Cally turned to the window, forgetting she had just promised not to watch him go. Craning her head to look down to the door at the bottom of the tower, she saw Ben emerge dressed in what definitely looked more like armor, complete with gauntlets, than what he had been wearing when he had left her side. She realized this must be a glamour, however, when he vaulted easily over the fence.

As soon as his feet touched the ground on the other side, all of the campfires across the plain went out as if snuffed by a giant hand.

Now the glowering sky lit the roiling masses of people below in a sickly glare, and all of them began to mobilize. Most of them – the groups to the east and southeast – seemed to be rallying to Ben. At the same time, the blood-colored mass of Fomorians in the northeast solidified into a wedge formation and began to drive like a spear across the field toward a point along the fence to Cally's left. There, in the world she knew, the stream crossed through the culvert under the railroad trestle. She remembered Melissa and... someone else... having tried to warn her about a portal, and she wondered if this was what they had been talking about.

Ben ran in a line that intersected the direction of the Fomorians' march and, when he reached high ground, stood with his back to the railroad trestle. The Daoine Sidhe and their various allies also appeared to be headed for this point, though it was not clear which group would reach Ben first. Standing with his feet planted wide apart, he drew a sword. Cally had no idea where he'd drawn it from – she hadn't seen anything like it when he'd been in the room with her. It was perhaps the most real and solid object in the entire scenario, now, and shone like the sun that would never break through the clouds above.

Despite the distance, Cally saw every detail with increasing clarity, just as she had always seen the City, before. It was as if the entire scenario were projected onto a movie screen unfolding inside her brain, and the longer she watched, the sharper the focus became.

She saw Ben lift the golden sword to hold it straight up before his face, like a scepter. At this, the mobilizing troops across the plain all stopped and dropped to their knees, so suddenly and in such perfect unison that Cally almost thought she could feel the earth shudder.

Even many among the Fomorian forces knelt, but as soon as they did, a shrill battle cry rose from behind them. The sound speared between Cally's collar bones as a single figure broke from the blood-red ranks, mounted on a steed that could only be called a "horse" in the broadest sense of the term. Riding from behind the ranks with its own dark sword, it cut down every Fomorian that had kneeled.

Still shrieking, the General pointed his own black blade in Ben's direction. Ben dropped his head, then, and lowered his blade, but just for a moment. When he looked up again, he held the sword differently, cocked over his shoulder, ready to do some cutting down of its own.

The Sidhe warriors rose to their feet and resumed their swift march to Ben's side. A small group, flying across the hills like a stray patch of sunshine, reached him first. Cally saw a figure who could only be Ennilangr position himself at Ben's right. Another warrior, who rallied to his left, appeared to have long, ruby hair flowing down her back.

While the united enemy horde advanced across the field, a handful of dark forms broke away like drops of black blood running ahead of the pack. They scattered into the shadows of the little valleys between the hills, while Ennilangr and Aileen turned their backs to Ben, watching to his right and left. The first of the Fomorian advance commandos to raise its head above the crest of the hill did not possess a head for very long – Ben's bright sword ran black as it shed the first blood of the battle.

Cally suddenly realized: this was what he had not wanted her to see. As he drew back his bloodied blade, before she could see him choose his next target, she turned her head away and stepped back from the window.

Even as she apologized to him under her breath, however, she was no longer sure she belonged on this side of the fence at all. Maybe she belonged at his side where Aileen was currently fighting.

She took a deep breath, much like the one Ben had taken when he left, and headed for the spiral stair, but when she reached the doorway her foot swung out into nothing. She managed to grab the door frame before she plunged into the dark pit that yawned below, echoing her stifled scream.

"Damn all Faerie Queens and all their goddamned glamour!" she hissed into the faux Dogwood Room. Slamming the door on the vanished spiral stair, she ran to open the other door that should lead, in an ordinary world, to the upstairs hallway of Vale House.

She nearly ran right through George.

"Being a musician means *'loading five thousand dollars' worth of equipment into a five-hundred-dollar car...'*" he was saying. He was not looking at her, but along the hallway to her left. Her breath turned to concrete in her chest. Even if she had wanted to, she could not turn her head to see who he was talking to. She did not want to, and she was grateful that the thunder of the rushing noise in her ears drowned out any reply that person made.

Sparks swam before her eyes so that she barely perceived George turning his head, for just the slightest moment, to look at her with a puzzled expression. Then he turned away again, and smiled and bowed and vanished.

She chanced a glance to one side, and found she could breathe again. The only other living thing in the hallway was Doctor Boojums sitting, with his back to her, at the gallery railing, peering between the balusters into the dining room below. He seemed more solid than he usually did, his fur tinged with the orange tones it had had in life, and somehow this helped her feel more solid again, herself. She reached a hand out to the railing, looking down to see what the cat was looking at. The rays of the sinking sun were casting long, windowpane-shaped swaths of light across the dining room table, and Katarina was passing through the room, carrying an empty dinner tray and humming tunelessly.

Cally took a deep breath to hold back tears. "I'm home," she whispered, and she knew in her bones it was true. This was the real Vale House, not some mock-up made of glamour by Sidhe women. "I'm really home."

The orange cat looked up at her and blinked, though what he meant to convey by this, she could not tell. She turned around and looked back into the Dogwood Room, the real Dogwood Room with the rumpled bed and the mess of notebooks and her computer piled on the dresser. For the first time, she loved this room, and was glad it was hers. She swore she would never give it up to a paying guest ever again.

If she ever got a chance to, anyway.

The ghost cat had stood up to rub against her ankles, something he had never done before. Ordinarily she would have appreciated this, even though it felt like cold fog pressing bodily against her skin. "I have to hurry," she told him by way of apology as she turned and walked swiftly to the stairs.

She could hear one side of a telephone conversation rising from the Hall.

"Oh, I know!" The sight of Bethany's back hunched over the telephone at the desk was so familiar and comforting, Cally almost burst into tears. "I won't say there's any love lost, there," Bethany was saying, "but still, it's always sad when a man dies." She didn't sound sad. "Excuse me." She put a hand over the receiver as Cally walked past the desk.

"I swear, the gossip just never stops! Cally, didn't you just leave for the concert?" Then she raised both eyebrows. "Oh! I see! You decided to put on a nicer outfit. Yes, that dress shows off your figure very nicely. Mr. Dawes will agree, I'm sure!"

Cally's heart melted inside her and she wanted more than anything to linger and chat with Bethany as she had always used to do, but she had no time. She could see, through the screen, a heavy dusk hanging over the meadow. The grasses beyond the fence swayed like tarnished bronze in a rising wind, with intermittent bolts of lightning flashing in the boiling gray clouds above. Even as she looked, the clouds tumbled closer and reached across the sky to close the gaps between them. In the distance, she heard a dull rumble that sounded like a drumbeat rolling toward Vale House, but she knew it wasn't thunder.

Doctor Boojums appeared in the middle of the Hall, crouching between Cally and the door. He was more solid and orange than ever, and he was glowering at her. She shivered, skirting the cat as Bethany resumed her telephone conversation.

"No, it really was!" she held forth. "John Ware, caught red-handed. Literally! Yes, Bree Dawes' ex. Yes, I know! We all thought so! Not that anyone would have blamed her, to be honest. But apparently he was alive all this time, on the lam somewhere. And completely insane, by all accounts, when they arrested him. Well, she may be eccentric, I agree, but Bree would never harm a fly."

Cally had a different opinion about that, but she didn't interrupt. She put up a hand to push open the screen door, despite Doctor Boojums, who had vanished only to reappear at her feet.

"So unusual to get a thunderstorm this time of year!"

This time it was Katarina's voice behind her. Cally turned to see her come into the Hall from the dining room, carrying a bundle of cloth in her hands. "But then," Katarina was saying, "it *is* October the twenty-fifth. Here." She held Cally's denim jacket up before her. "Ignacio managed to get all the blood stains out, but I don't know if we can salvage it. These three rips across the shoulder..." She hesitated, lowering the jacket and looking at it quizzically, as if she sensed, somehow, that this was not the way this conversation was supposed to go. "Well..." She swallowed, and her voice came out as if she were forcing it. "Maybe, if Ignacio is as good at sewing as he is at everything else..." She stopped again, unable to continue.

"Don't worry about it," Cally said, putting out her hand to take the jacket from Katarina's hands. "I think I like it the way it is. It looks kind of...intrepid." She put it on, wincing as she twisted her arm through the sleeve. The blood stains on her bandages showed through the slashes.

Katarina looked at these and blinked, as if she perceived them but couldn't really see them.

"Well it's appropriate for wearing to a rock show," she agreed provisionally. "And it goes very well with that dress. I've never seen you wear that before..."

Bethany hung up the phone and reached quickly to put the console into night mode. "I'd better not answer any more calls if I expect to get out of here at all tonight. Brr... feels like a storm coming!" Standing, she took her purse from the desk drawer.

Cally heard Ignacio's voice call from the dining room, "Ladies, it's past time to get out of here..." He paused in the doorway, staring at Cally as if she were a ghost.

His hair was unbound, falling loosely over his shoulders as it had when she had seen him in prison. He looked at her with wide, earnest eyes, his expression slowly shifting from one of confusion to one of realization. Somehow, then, Cally understood: he remembered. He knew, and remembered, somehow, both versions of what had happened to him over the past several days. She met his gaze and took a deep breath, and then they both nodded, agreeing wordlessly that they would never discuss this; they would never need to. As Katarina turned to join him, Ignacio closed his eyes and bowed deeply to Cally.

"*Mi reina, dios sea contigo,*" he said softly. "Be safe tonight." He put an arm around Katarina and, with one last backward glance, escorted her out through the dining room toward the kitchen.

Bethany explained again about making sure the porch light was off, and repeated as she went out the front door: "Make sure you don't come back inside the house until morning. Have a nice date!"

49 - Standing Up for the Lookout

Cally stepped around Doctor Boojums, who seemed to be in a particularly ugly mood this evening. He swiped at her ankles as she pushed open the screen door and went out into the wind whipping across the porch. She pulled the heavy oaken door shut behind her but she did not lock it. This wasn't just because she had no idea, now, where her purse and keys might have ended up. Mostly, she yielded to an irrational fear that if she did lock the door, she might not ever be able to come back.

The captain's ghost wasn't present on the porch, this evening. When the tail-lights of Bethany's car disappeared through the gate, the parking lot in front of Vale House stood completely empty even of Cally's own car. She didn't know where, or even in which timeline, her little red Corolla might be now, but that didn't concern her at the moment. She stepped off the porch and headed for the fence.

A cold wind moaned from south to north, flattening the grass in the meadow. The meadow appeared to be devoid of life, bird, insect, or equine. Cally could see lightning flashing all across the horizon, but the thunder preceded it, instead of following. This wasn't the lightning of this world, she knew. It flashed in different shades, colors matching the campfires of the battlefield where she had last seen the different faerie peoples clashing. To the south and east, bright white light jabbed westward and north. To the north, where the forested edge of the meadow met the horizon, angry red light intermingled with bursts of gold, and by this Cally knew where Ben was fighting. She ran in that direction, hiking up the ridiculous blue skirt so she could move more quickly. "Good lord," she thought. "I must look just like one of those ridiculous book-covers right now."

Doctor Boojums appeared before her once more and she tripped over him, feeling his claws scrape her ankle as she tumbled onto the lawn.

"What is *wrong* with you tonight?" she said, not even looking back at him as she stood, paying no mind to the bruised grass clinging to her knees. The orange tomcat leapt between her and the fence, back arched, fur standing on end as he hissed and raised a clawed paw, clearly threatening to scratch her again if she took another step forward. She ignored him and ducked between the fence rails.

Once on the other side, she could no longer see the cat. She continued to run unimpeded toward the north edge of the meadow, toward where the railroad trestle passed over the fence and under the blood-colored sky.

"You can't do that!"

The voice, muddled by the wind, called from the dimness to her left where the fence ran past the barn. Cally wondered if the cat had learned to talk now. Without stopping, she turned her head to tell whoever it was that she damn well could do that, and would do that, but when she saw who had spoken, she stopped so quickly she nearly tumbled into the grass again. She stared open-mouthed at the tall, hooded figure standing in the grass, but mostly she stared at the boy behind whom it stood.

She had seen the dark, hooded figure several times before. Local legends associated it with thunderstorms in and around Woodley. It and Ian May had some kind of arrangement to keep these storms from causing too much damage to Vale House, and its appearance was probably the only thing that could have stopped Cally from running straight to Ben's side on the battlefield. Even so, she was determined this would only be a short delay.

Usually the figure stood with a hand outstretched, but this time both its hands rested on Adam's shoulders. Adam looked alarmed, but not at the dark spirit behind him. "You can't do that!" he called again to Cally. "Please don't! You have to stay here! Please!"

Cally strode quickly through the whipping grass to where she could answer him without having to shout. He was standing partway down the slope above the creek, and behind him, behind the cloaked spirit, she could see the stone culvert beneath the railroad trestle. It appeared to yawn wider than ever, a rippling darkness emanating from it like some kind of inside-out light. Whenever lightning stabbed across the sky, growling thunder could be dimly heard from the other end of the tunnel. This, Cally understood at last, must be "the portal," where Eladha and his Fomorians could pass through the fence into her world if the Sidhe army did not succeed in stopping them.

"I'm sorry, Adam, I have to go," Cally said. "I can't just leave him to fight alone." She didn't mention that Ben was not exactly alone. "I may not be able to do anything, but I should at least be there beside him. Too much time has already passed!"

Adam stood with his hands at his sides, gazing at her with his wide mouth shut tight in a thin line. His distraught expression didn't seem to Cally like that of a frightened child, so much as that of a nobleman with cares much larger than his own life.

"If you go now," he said evenly, "I will never exist. That would be very bad. It would be very, *very* bad!"

As Cally feverishly debated whether to ask him why or just turn away and run toward the crimson lightning regardless, she heard a noise behind her. The wind whipping from the south carried the sound of a car door slamming shut. She, Adam, and even the hooded spirit turned their heads to look. Night had fallen over Vale House. The moon hung, now, above the roofline, and Cally remembered how, on the night she had stood in almost this same spot with Michael Dawes, she had understood how many more hours had gone by, in the human world, than had gone by on this side of the fence.

She saw the silhouette of her car parked, once again, in front of Vale House where it belonged. And then she saw the barn doors swing open, slamming back on themselves with a muffled boom. A red horse emerged from the barn and ran, with a pale figure on its back, south through the gates toward Gardens Road. Ian May stood alone in the barn's black, empty doorway, hand lifted in a salute as he watched the horse and rider go, and then he sank to his knees.

Cally's first instinct was to run to him, but then she heard more car doors slamming, house doors opening and shutting on Garden's Road, and a woman's voice on the wind, shouting something that sounded like "I'll just be a minute!"

Through the masonry gate Cally could just make out a figure running from the direction of Yellow House toward Main Street, long hair streaming out behind. It was Rosheen, carrying Cally's purse in her hand. Cally suddenly realized, to her horror, where Rosheen was going, and why.

"She's going to go into the house," Adam said.

"Oh, my god, it's my fault." Cally was talking to herself more than to him. "I sent her to put George's zemi back in the desk." She had completely forgotten, at the time, about the danger of entering Vale House on the night of the twenty-fifth *"What have I done?"*

She broke and ran, not to the battle in progress beyond the railroad trestle, but back toward the house. "Rosheen, stop! Wait!" The wind blew her words back into her mouth, and Rosheen continued across the parking lot to the porch steps. As the girl put her foot on the bottom step, Cally saw the porch light was on. She was sure she had left it off.

It wasn't the porch light at all, though, but a bright blue glow shining out from the parlor windows on the south side of the porch. It moved, as she watched, like a lantern being carried, from the parlor windows to the oval window in the middle of the front door, and then to the windows of Cally's office. As the light moved through the house, it seemed to be accompanied by a deep hum, almost a moaning noise, that Cally felt more than heard below the pitch of the wind all around her, resonating in her bones right up through the ground. She flung herself toward the fence, but was unable to make her feet move. Swearing, furious at herself, she tried again. Finally, she realized it was not her own fear incapacitating her.

Turning where she stood, she shook her fists at the hooded spirit behind Adam. "I don't have anything to give you!" she told it. "Let me go! We can work this out later!"

In response, it took a few steps away from the boy and raised its pale hand, palm upward. From the corner of her eye, she could see Ian May in the barn doorway, trying to struggle to his feet.

It had always been Ian, before, who would appease the spirit and calm the storm. Cally had no clear idea how he did this. Everyone at Vale House just thought he was exceptionally good at praying. None of them had ever seen the hooded figure, at least, none who ever admitted it out loud. Cally had always seen it, though, and had always watched Ian reach back toward it, almost in a salute, and when he did, the storm would be calmed. Now she understood that he had not merely been reaching. He had been offering a gift, and Cally had no idea what he had given or what she could give instead as Ian stood up, as best he could, and leaned against the doorframe.

Rosheen had reached the top step and was walking across the porch to the door. The blue light inside Vale House had moved to the northernmost front windows, those of the Magnolia Suite which had once been the Captain's quarters. As Rosheen crossed the porch and opened the door, Adam came and stood next to Cally, his expression completely un-foxlike, gazing sorrowfully at the house.

The hooded spirit remained where it had been, but now it turned and extended its hand toward Cally.

She glared back at it, filled to the brim with fury. "What do you want?" she screamed at the figure. "I don't have anything! What did Ian always give you?"

And then she understood. As she heard the front door of the house slam shut, muffling Rosheen's scream, Cally suddenly understood. She nodded, and reached out, and put herself in the goddess's hand.

Nothing changed, except that now she could clearly see the people fighting, far across the field, just as she had been able to do from the faux Dogwood Room tower. This time, however, she knew they could also see her. She turned and saw Ben and Ennilangr standing shoulder-to-shoulder as the Sidhe attempted to drive a wedge between the Fomorians and the culvert under the tracks. They were not losing ground, but they were not gaining any, either. She saw Aileen beside them, as covered in grime and gore as they were. And she heard the Fomorian General roar out from behind his troops the same words Adam had said to her earlier.

"You can't do that!"

He leaped like a sheet of flame over his troops, but Cally had already crawled between the fence rails and was heading up the porch steps. Wrenching open the screen door, she ran into the Hall and turned to slam the wooden door shut behind her. As she threw the deadbolt, red light leapt up like flame to fill the oval window in the door. It poured in to mingle with the blue light filling the Hall. The blue glow, now, and the moaning hum, came from the top of the stairs and from there, also, Cally heard Rosheen scream again.

The bones in her legs felt like water as she tried to force herself to climb the stairs toward the light, and she knew she could not blame the hooded goddess for this. She could hear her own trembling in every breath she dragged into her protesting lungs. In the end, she had to thank the Fomorian for motivating her to run, when he smashed the front door off its hinges. As he stepped over the door and entered the Hall, Cally found herself instantly at the top of the stairs.

There, beside the gallery railing, stood the blue specter of a man. It stood almost eight feet tall and its face, hair, and clothing were all blue, as if made wholly of nothing but dark blue light. The humming moan emanating from it was almost too loud, now, to hear.

Cally could see through it fairly easily, all the way to the end of the hall where Rosheen stood, illuminated in sickly blue hues, with her back against the butler's desk. The girl was clearly paralyzed with fear, and even if Cally had been able to move, if she had been able to make herself run through the specter, even if she survived that, she wasn't sure what she would be able to do to help, now.

To her consternation, George appeared beside Rosheen, and now Cally had two people to fear for. But George, though his face had gone ashen with terror, had a plan.

"Open that door!" he shouted, pointing past Rosheen to one of the doors along the hallway. "That one, the skinny one!" Rosheen reached out a hand to do so, but couldn't take her eyes off the blue ghost, which had begun to move, slowly and heavily, toward her.

"He's right!" Cally shouted to her through the blue glare. "Follow the backstairs down. I'll meet you at the bottom!"

This seemed to give Rosheen the courage, at last, to move, and she opened the door and ran through it with alacrity. George called "Close the door behind you!" as he crouched and vanished. When the door slammed behind Rosheen, the blue specter turned its attention to Cally.

It moved slowly, ponderously, but Cally felt like she was moving far more slowly, herself, as she turned to run back down the stairs. She kept missing steps, having to cling to the railing to keep herself from tumbling the rest of the way down. When she finally reached the bottom, swinging around the post with one hand, she nearly ran straight into the Fomorian General.

"What do you think you are doing?" he roared at her, swinging back his sword.

"For god's sake, Eddie!" His passive-aggressive questions were the last thing she had time for. "What is your damage, anyway? Get out of the way – run!"

He glowered down at her with his black blade cocked behind his head. Cally realized he could cleave her in half where she stood, but the thing behind her filled her with far more terror. "You don't understand how valuable you are..." Eladha began in his deep growl, and then Cally understood he really had no intention at all of killing her.

She couldn't say the same about the thrumming blue presence pressing closer at her back. Ignoring the sword, she ducked under the General's elbow and ran into the dining room. There she turned right and ran down the narrow back hall, while he bellowed behind her.

"You can't do... and who the hell are *you*?" His question was answered by a dull, crashing boom.

As commotion escalated behind her, Cally turned left where the hall ended in a T and found Rosheen, crouched with her back against the door at the bottom of the backstairs, sobbing uncontrollably with her arms wrapped around her knees.

Cally knelt beside her. "It's alright," she said. "You're alright now. Come with me." She urged to girl to her feet and tugged her toward the next door along the hall, the last one before the kitchen doors, which opened to the non-secret cellar stairs.

She never had found out where the light switch was, in this stairwell, but it turned out she didn't need it. Blue light was streaming down through several cracks in the floor above, moving from the front of the house toward the back as heavy crashes and thuds continued upstairs. The very timbers of the house shook and Cally had to cling to the crude railing with one hand, holding Rosheen with her other arm, to keep them from tumbling off the stairs. Dust sifted down, with each crash, through the shafts of light, and the light, wherever it struck the cellar floor, seemed to collect and spread, almost as if forming into puddles of indigo blood.

"This way." When they reached the bottom, Cally kept her arm around Rosheen and guided her between the pools to the only place where the ceiling was solid enough to stop the dripping blue ectoplasm: the little room under the stairs where Ian had once stored his drums. Here, she and Rosheen crouched with their arms around one another and listened to the tumult above. It sounded as if every piece of furniture in the house were being smashed to splinters as the commotion moved from the Hall through the parlor and then toward the south wing. The sub-aural hum remained constant. The only shouts, cries, and curses came in Eladha's voice.

"Shit," said Rosheen when her trembling subsided a little. "I thought I knew everything. My mother is a Moruadh, you know. My whole family is ... quite a motley crew. I thought I understood all this stuff. But *oh my god what the hell was that?"*

At this, Cally leaned her head back against the wall and let out a long laugh.

"What?" Rosheen peered at her through the dimness. "I don't understand. This isn't funny."

Cally got control of herself and wiped her eyes. She hugged Rosheen – a real hug, not just terrified clinging, this time – and said, "Welcome to my world."

The crashing noises above them continued interminably. The two women tried to converse, to ask questions of or give answers to one another, but eventually they succumbed, in spite of the noise, to fatigue. Cally drifted, both wrapped in Rosheen's arms and with her own arms wrapped tight around the girl, in and out of uneasy sleep filled with thunder and earthquakes.

By the time the cacophony faded to intermittent thumping and then to silence, the blue glow was slowly being subsumed by gray light peeking in to the cellar through foundation vents all around the house. Cally put her head out the doorway, and the last remaining traces of blue light winked out as if a switch had been flipped. Now, only a soft groaning could be heard from above, and it was almost a human sound.

Cally and Rosheen helped one another to their feet.

"Let's go this way." Wincing at cold stiffness in her joints, she picked a path through the boxes and trunks to the singed door of Sofie's old room, and through this to the little stair behind Ian's closet. They climbed out into the dim morning light to find the study in shambles, furniture disarranged and books scattered everywhere. The blue ghost was gone, but the Formorian general still sat, groaning, in the corner between the desk and the toppled book case. He was clutching his head, and his sword lay broken beneath him.

When he looked up at Cally, she thought he almost looked human, a cross between Eddie Teine and a handsome younger man with golden hair. "Never in all my days," he said. He shook his head, and then groaned, clutching at the pain this caused him. "I have never met anything like that."

He struggled to stand up, and Cally and Rosheen stepped back quickly. Cally looked around for any heavy object she could lay hands on. Footsteps could be heard, through the door at the other end of the room, running along the back hall, but Cally was unsure whether these reinforcements were arriving for her or for the Fomorian. She let out a sigh of relief when she heard Ennilangr's voice booming, "In here!"

Eladha mustered as much dignity as he could, even as he gave up trying to scramble to his feet. "Callaghan McCarthy," he said, resolutely. "You cannot be Armadeur and Queen at the same time. You don't understand..."

Cally let out a groan of exasperation. "Seriously, this again? What even makes you think I could ever do that? Anyway, I'm not either one!"

"But you are," said Rosheen. "You became the Armadeur just last night, out in front of the house. I felt it when it happened. That's the only reason Eladha would have left the battle."

Before Cally could think of an answer – or a question – to that, the door from the back hall burst open and six or seven armor-clad warriors shouldered their way into the room. Ben was at their head, followed closely by Ennilangr. All of them were covered in mud and blood, and when Ben saw Cally he pulled back into the crowd, awkwardly and unsuccessfully trying to hide his gore-covered sword from her.

Aileen strode across the room to stand over the Fomorian, who did not look up to meet her eyes. "Looks like little brother got his ass kicked," she said as she took him by the elbow and yanked him to his feet.

"No, wait," he said. "This isn't settled!" He raised his head enough to glare at Cally.

"Mr. Teine," said Cally. "Please be so kind as to remove yourself and your belongings from the premises. There is no vacancy at Vale House, today, and for you there never will be."

50 - I've Seen All Good People

"That was a legendary sword," said Nell. "It's a shame it got broken."

Doctor Boojums dozed on the sideboard with his paws tucked under his chest while staff, friends, and family of Vale House broke fast quite late in the morning. Sun streamed from the Hall into the dining room, but it was chilly in the house, with the front door lying on the floor and the torn screen door failing to keep out the cold morning air.

"We had our first frost, last night," Ignacio said, attempting to change the subject. "We'll be scraping our windshields in the mornings, from now on."

"The frost always comes and goes," Nell reminded him. "As does the dreaded spirit of the twenty-fifth, which actually ended up saving us, this time."

This was met with silence, not because anyone was ever surprised anymore at the things Nell tended to say, but because they didn't want to even consider that she might be right.

"That was quite a storm," Katarina remarked into the awkward silence. "But we've weathered worse." Cally didn't bother reminding her it had not been a storm at all.

"Well," Ennilangr offered, "I think without their General to keep reminding them, the Fomorians won't be able to remember why they're supposed to want to battle this world in the first place, when most of them already have perfectly good grudges against their own kin back home." He tipped back his head and poured a cup of coffee straight down his throat.

Katarina laughed and ran to the kitchen for a fresh pot.

Cally leaned across the table and asked Ignacio, "Does she even understand what we're all talking about here?"

"I think she does, deep inside," he answered. "But on the outside, she is going to keep telling herself and everyone around her it was all just a particularly bad thunderstorm." Far from seeming dismayed at this, his eyes shone with love as he watched his wife return and resume dashing around the table, refilling everyone's coffee cups.

Ignacio pushed his plate away and stood up. "Better get back to it, then," he said. "Lots of damage control to manage before guests arrive this afternoon." Ben stood and went with him out into the Hall. Cally, Ian, Sofie and Nell continued trying to eat their breakfast amid sounds of drilling and hammering. Doc sat with them, sipping coffee as Ennilangr quaffed his. He kept looking around behind him, into the Hall. Cally guessed he wasn't watching the door repairs so much as waiting for Bethany to arrive.

"Doesn't that sunshine feel good?" Sofie asked, smiling and nodding to everyone in turn before dipping her spoon back into her grapefruit.

"It does," Cally answered. "It feels wonderful." Sofie had rarely ever joined the household for meals, before, and when she had, she had usually hunched timidly at the table, picking at her food until Ian rose to go. Now she ate with gusto, and made eye contact with everyone between bites. "You are looking very well this morning, Sofie." Cally actually meant this as a question – a huge one – but she couldn't think of a sensible way to ask why two people who had so recently seemed to be at death's door were now eating breakfast as if they had never been sick in their lives.

"I *am* well!" Sofie said simply. "Johnny is, too!" She gave Ian a huge smile that made her brown eyes dance. "The Queen of the Faeries granted my wish!"

Doc coughed. He opened his mouth to say something, but then seemed to think better of it. Finally, he turned to Ian.

"You do look very well today. But I hope you will consent to letting me give you both a quick exam before I leave? For science. Please, finish your breakfast first!" he added as Ian laid his napkin on his plate and pushed back his chair.

"I am quite satisfied," said the old gentleman. He stood up at the end of the table and regarded them all with his gracious smile. "But I have a little announcement to make. I am retiring. Sofie and I would like to go sailing."

"Well, good for you!" Katarina said, applauding.

Cally wondered if this was actually good. Ian and Sofie did appear to be the picture of health, at the moment, but there had to be a catch somewhere. She patted the tablecloth beside her, trying to urge Katarina to sit down for once and have some breakfast, herself.

"Yes, there's a harbor just the other side of the meadow," Sofie explained, gesturing out through the Hall. "We're going to take the Pirate Ship. We've been invited by the queen herself!"

Doc and Katarina nodded and smiled politely at the disjointed ramblings of Sofie's gentle but broken mind, knowing the nearest harbor was at the Outer Banks, at least two hundred miles away. Cally knew otherwise, but kept her thoughts to herself.

"I trust Cally to take on the management of this bed and breakfast in admirable fashion," Ian continued. "I will be speaking to my lawyer tomorrow to arrange signing everything over to her."

"Well," said Nell. "While we're announcing life-changing plans, I have one, too. I am moving to Raleigh so I can go to medical school."

"Wow, Nell," Cally said. "You really weren't kidding, were you?"

"I'll be leaving Cyndi Lauper here, if that's okay with everyone."

"Oh, it's more than okay!" Bethany called as she came in through the Hall, stepping around the door and over the tools lying all over the floor. "I've missed having a cat around here!"

Doctor Boojums, from his seat on the sideboard, said nothing.

"Maybe Ms. May is right," Doc admitted as Bethany sat down beside him and reached for a muffin. "I can't keep putting off my own retirement forever. And Ms. May is uniquely qualified to take on the particular needs of this community." He made no mention of whether or not he felt Nell would be up to coping with the pressures of medical school.

As if in demonstration that there was nothing further to say on the matter, Ian reached down and urged Sofie to stand with him. Sofie waved as her husband escorted her to the back hall.

Doc gazed bemusedly after them. "The other day, I was looking into legal options for forcing them both into hospital," he said. "But today he shows no sign of pain, not even a limp. Maybe sleeping in the barn was what they both needed. Maybe there's some sort of fountain of youth out there."

"I'm sure you've seen stranger things around here," Cally said, "in your career as this town's physician." She gave him a steady look, but he did not reply.

"They say love is the best medicine," Nell pointed out.

"And is that your official, professional medical opinion?" Doc asked her, winking.

"It is," she said, nodding firmly. "Don't be smug. There is more in heaven and earth, Horatio. Etcetera."

He looked down at his crooked, blue-veined hands and said, "I guess you're right. And if anyone can take *proper* care of Woodley's citizens when I'm gone, it would be you, Ms. May."

"You'll be calling me Doctor May in a few years," she reminded him.

"I look forward to it." He looked up as Bethany stood to go to the reception desk. "Because I do need to pursue other...pursuits, in this life, myself. Life is too short not to spend it with the people we care about."

Bethany blushed. "Oh, it sounds like someone has left the TV on in the parlor again!" she said, rushing out of the room. Doc got up and nodded to everyone, then turned to follow her. Cally smiled after them, but she sighed at the same time. Life was, indeed, too short not to spend with the people one loved, but not everyone had the luxury of that choice.

She twisted in her seat to watch Ben through the doorway, where he and Ignacio were lifting the repaired door upright. Ben held it in place while Ignacio slipped shims underneath to align it with the shiny, new hinges attached to the doorframe. While Ignacio was changing the bit in his drill, a dark shadow filled the sunny glass oval in the center of the door, accompanied by a sharp and insistent rapping.

Bethany ran from the parlor to call through the door. "Just a minute!" Cally noticed she was still blushing. "Oh, dear. We weren't expecting guests to start showing up already!"

The knocking continued until Ignacio drove enough screws into the hinges to pull the door partway open.

Bree stood inside the screen door, yanking at her skirt, which was caught on some lumber Ignacio had left lying on the porch. Cally rolled her eyes. She had to bite her tongue to stop herself asking if the woman couldn't leave it alone just once, for just one day for god's sake.

The old woman grunted as she pushed her way into the Hall. She looked around until she spotted Cally in the dining room. Stepping over the tools and detritus on the floor, she hobbled to the dining room doorway. "That boy Brandon of yours is quite the enterprising young smarty-pants," she told Cally. "Starting today, I have hired him to open the store for me every morning. I will be retiring."

"There's a lot of that going around today," Ben commented, grinning at her.

Very pleased, at first, with the news that Brandon had found gainful employment, Cally said "Congratulations!" but then her smile froze on her face. Did this mean that, since Bree no longer needed him, Ben would now have to fulfill his obligation to return to the land of his mother's people? She couldn't recall anything that had been said or done, at the Thing, to alter that contract or release him from it.

Bree turned back to Ben and poked him in the chest with a pale, bony finger. "I won't be going in to work until noon, from now on," she clarified. "I expect to see you then, with bells on, and none of this horseshit about the position of the sun, either."

Ben wrapped a gentle hand around the old woman's jabbing finger and held her hand to his chest, smiling down at her. "I'll be there," he said. "Very clever, you. Only you could get away with bending the rules the way you do. You know that, right?"

"There's very little I don't know," she snorted. Turning to reach for the door handle, she said, "You're free until noon!"

"Thank you, Bree," said Cally.

"For what?" the old woman called over her shoulder, stepping back out onto the porch, letting the screen door bang shut behind her.

"Well, I'd better get on the road," said Ennilangr, tossing back one last hot cup of coffee. He had to duck to keep from hitting his head on the doorframe as he passed from the dining room into the Hall. "Ms. McCarthy, may I speak to you for a minute? Just a short minute," he added, nodding to Ben. "I don't want to take too much of your valuable time."

He went out onto the porch and Cally followed him to the steps, where they both sat down in the slowly warming morning sunshine. Cally's car, she noticed, bore a deep dent in its left rear fender. The three horses grazed serenely in the meadow, but Cally didn't see any foxes lurking about.

"As you might surmise," Ennilangr began, "now that Foster's murder is, ahem, solved, and Ignacio's bail is a moot point, my holdings are no longer tied up in bureaucratic red tape. The key players I have been watching are either neutralized or accounted for, and now I would like to find something else useful to do with my hoard."

"I'm afraid I've never been able to wrap my head around financial machinations," said Cally. "So I'm not sure how I could help you, there."

"No, this is a light request," he promised. "I would just appreciate it if you would keep your eyes open and watch for people who want to do something to help keep Woodley alive. Keeping this little town's economy strong is equivalent to keeping the gateway strong." He nodded toward the meadow fence. "People like Jake Lucas and Andi Kilmarten, they have some good ideas, but little money to act on them. Just point them in my direction, and I'll back them. How does that sound?"

"It sounds like you ought to talk to Jud Thornton!" Cally laughed.

"No." He shook his head so vigorously his ponytail rippled down his back. "No, I need you. You know what this place needs." He gestured with both arms, indicating the meadow and Woodley and everything around it.

"Alright," said Cally. "You do have a point. I know better than to encourage anyone to build a MallMart in Woodley, anyway. I'll keep an ear out."

"That's a good start," he said. "I won't be hanging around here as much as I have these past few days, though of course I'll still be making my normal deliveries. I just wanted to say, it's been an honor to meet you. You have given us many gifts."

"While I was just thinking," Cally said, "that last time I was in Faerie, I neglected to leave any gifts at all, and now I'm waiting for the other shoe to drop."

He gave her a steady look, as if lightning might shoot out of his brow.

"Don't say that," he said. "Don't ever say that. We are deeply in your debt. Don't ever let anyone try to tell you otherwise."

The way he fixed his gaze on her reminded her that he was not as human as he – mostly – appeared to be, that he was a very powerful being and might well have been some kind of god in the world from which he came. A shiver ran down her spine, and he did not look away until she nodded.

"I'll do my best to keep it in mind," she promised.

Postlude: I Had to Think About That Myself

Cold, gray wind buffeted the windows of the Law Offices of Johnston and Reid, Attorneys at Law. Someone behind Cally in the crowded room said, "Won't be surprised if we get snow by the end of the week."

"Well you know what they say," said someone else. "If you don't like the weather around here..."

"Just sign here, one more time," said Attorney Reid. Cally signed on the dotted line, and everyone in the room applauded.

"There you are, then." Jud handed Cally the set of keys with the yellow plastic fob. "You are now officially the owner of the Yellow House."

Cally turned and handed the keys back to Brandon and Rosheen. "And I will expect your rent to be paid in full to me on the first of every month," she told them.

"I still think you've set the rent too low," Jud told her, and she didn't bother to remind him that she had set it no lower than he had. "May I just pop over and put a 'Sold' sign in front of the house? It's been too long since I've had a chance to do that around here!"

"Please do," said Rosheen, "And then stay for the housewarming party. It will give us all a chance to pose for a picture around the sign." Rosheen had become very interested, lately, in collecting photos for her memory book.

As she walked, holding her collar closed against the wind, back up Main Street, Cally paused to peer through the front window of Dawes News. Ben was in the back, stacking boxes of Christmas decorations on a shelf. He didn't notice her, but Bree did, and glanced up from her paper just long enough to make sure Cally knew she was ignoring her. Cally smiled and waved.

She crossed the street to say hello to Merv. She'd been having to put her head inside the front door of the feed store for this, since the weather had become cooler. She saw that Luke was inside the store, as well, talking to Merv at the cash register. "You guys will be at the housewarming party, tonight, won't you?" Cally asked them.

"Don't worry!" said Luke. "The Moldy Blues will be there. After all, that's where all the pizza will be, tonight."

Merv gave him a look, then turned to smile at Cally. "I have to say, Ms. McCarthy, I'm impressed. You haven't even lived in this town a year yet, and already you own two major historical properties. What's next? Will you be opening a MallMart?"

"You know I would never do that," Cally said, wrinkling her nose at him. "Anyway, I don't own Vale House. I'm just the executive proprietor, or some nonsense title like that. And the bank, technically, owns the Yellow House. I'm still worried about being able to keep up the payments."

"I wouldn't worry about that," Merv said. "You have some powerful allies around here who, I am sure, will keep your, ahem, assets covered."

"Why, Mervyn Arkwright, I have no idea what you could possibly be talking about." She winked, and bowed, and stepped back outside. If he wanted to hear her secrets, she thought, he was going to have to start telling her some of his.

She passed under the bare oak branches along the residential stretch of town, smiling at the people she saw looking out from their front windows. As she drew closer to the end of the street, she could see someone waiting, watching her from where they stood with their back to the meadow gate. She knew it couldn't be Ben, and, though the figure had blond hair, he looked too tall to be Adam, of whom she hadn't had so much as a glimpse since the night of October twenty-fifth. She passed by the pineapple-topped Vale House gate and slowed as she approached whoever it was.

He was a congenial looking young man, tall and thin with sturdy shoulders and a crisp crew-cut. He leaned back against the gate with his arms spread, hands resting on the top rail. He looked very familiar somehow, but Cally couldn't quite place him.

"Afternoon, Ms. McCarthy," he finally said, reaching up to tip an imaginary cap to her.

"Captain?" It was the twinkle in his eye, more than his voice, that finally triggered her memory. "You look..."

"Young?" he suggested. "Taller? Solid?" He winked and laughed.

Cally laughed, too. "Well, I was thinking something more along the lines of really happy.'"

"And I am," he said. As he spoke, he looked south along Gardens Road to where a young woman, with dark curls and a flowered dress that did not look appropriate for the weather, skipped down steps of the Yellow House's porch and turned to walk toward them. When she reached the gate, the Captain reached out and put an arm around her, and they both turned to smile at Cally. "This is Barbara, the love of my life," the Captain said.

Cally could practically see through Barbara, but she held a slim, brown package in her hand that looked quite solid. This she held out to Cally.

Well, this is something new, Cally thought as she reached out to accept it. It really was a solid object, and Barbara laughed soundlessly when Cally took it in her hand.

"Go ahead, open it," the Captain encouraged.

Cally peeled back the brown wrapping paper to reveal a small, silver flask. A tiny, dancing stag was engraved on its front.

"We just wanted to thank you for making sure the Yellow House will have someone to look after it."

"Is that why you've been hanging around here, Captain?"

"Please," he said. "Just call me Doug. I never really rose above the rank of corporal, you know."

"You'll always be The Captain to me, sir," Cally told him. "But could you explain to me, please, about the..."

It was too late. He and the woman were already on the other side of the gate, walking arm in arm down the rutted dirt path until it, and they, disappeared into the distance.

Appendices

Questions

Emerald: So, who is going to take over as Queen of Faerie, now? Did they ever decide?

Cally: SMH. I'm sure they did. Their rules about who it should be are pretty clear, to them, anyway. As far as I can tell, it's Rosheen, but she says she has no plans to leave Woodley during Brandon's lifetime, so that's a problem. Maybe they're planning to wait for Adam to grow up, and will settle for a King instead. In which case, Rianwynn is still Queen, for now.

Emerald: You should ask Ben. He'll know.

Cally: I'm afraid to. He's likely to say it's me.

Nell finished realigning two of her paintings on the wall at the back of the coffee shop (someone had straightened them; she returned them to the tilt at which she felt they were best displayed) and came to sit down at Cally's table facing Main Street.

"It is you, silly," she said.

Cally expended considerable effort to ignore this, while Nell leaned over and scrolled the computer screen backwards to read what she had missed before she came downstairs. Cally and Emerald had been discussing the new television set which had been purchased for the Vale House parlor, since the screen of the old console set had been cracked during the fracas on the twenty-fifth. When he had delivered the new set, Ennilangr had – without help or even a hand-truck – moved the old set into Cally's office.

"Now you can finally get to know Melissa!" Nell happily told Cally.

Cally nodded – this was also what Emerald had been telling her. For both Nell and Emerald's benefit, she typed into the chat:

Cally: The first thing I'm going to do with the new TV is download "Dumbo" for Georgie.

Emerald: Why? Anyway, you'll have to move the TV closer to the door. George can only go about three steps into the parlor.

Cally: Right. He can't go more than a specific distance from his zemi. And that's why he's still back at Vale House, bound to the butler's desk in the upstairs hallway. Even though his zemi is here, with me, in my purse.

Emerald: Oh

"Oh," said Nell.

Cally: Right. He only thinks he's bound to a little wooden carving. It's all in his head. Or what serves as a head, for him.

Emerald: Why don't you tell him?

Cally: I only just figured it out myself this morning, when I cleaned out my purse. Rosheen never did get a chance to put the zemi back in the desk, that night, because of the blue ghost. I've had it in my purse ever since - I forgot it was there. If George were really bound to it, he would have been accompanying me everywhere I went since then, but he hasn't.

Emerald: So, in actuality, he could go anywhere he wants. You really should tell him.

Cally: I will... I freely admit I'm reluctant, but I will tell him.

"A ghost has got to leave the nest sometime," Nell said, nodding solemnly.

Cally: I think I'll just show him the movie and let him figure it out for himself. It might be less of a shock for him, that way.

Emerald: That's a pretty lame cop-out, Cally. :)

Cally and Nell looked up as the bell over the door jingled. Luke came into the coffee shop, wearing his usual friendly smile, but with a decidedly sly gleam in his eye. He placed a chunky black piece of computer equipment on the table before them – Cally recognized it as an old floppy disc drive. Luke turned it on its side to show Cally he had cobbled it to a modern USB connector.

"Merry Early Christmas!" he said.

The End

<h1 style="text-align:center">Playlist</h1>

George has selected the following songs from Cally's MP3 player and suggests that, played on shuffle, they would create a suitable ambience to this story, if you happen to have access to a music device such as Cally's and if you like - as humans often do - to read with earbuds in.

—

All You Need Is Love - The Beatles
Best Ever Death Metal Band in Denton - The Mountain Goats
Carry On Wayward Son - Kansas
Closer to Fine - The Indigo Girls
Dancing in the Moonlight - King Harvest
Desperado - The Eagles
Don't Bring Me Down - Electric Light Orchestra
Fields of Gold - Sting
Friend of the Devil - Grateful Dead
Gold Dust Woman - Fleetwood Mac
Green Grass and High Tides - The Outlaws
Hold the Line - Toto
Home - Edward Sharpe and the Magnetic Zeros
I Melt With You - Modern English
I've Seen All Good People - Yes
Jackie Wilson Said - Dexy's Midnight Runners
Lawyers, Guns and Money – Warren Zevon
Leather and Lace - Don Henley
Lights - Journey
Meet Virginia - Train
Nightbird - Stevie Nicks
Right Here, Right Now - Jesus Jones
Runaround - Blues Traveler
Seven Bridges Road - The Eagles
Seven Turns - The Allman Brothers Band
She Talks to Angels - The Black Crowes
Silent Lucidity - Queensryche
Solsbury Hill - Peter Gabriel
Sweet Child of Mine - Guns N' Roses

Thank God I'm a Country Boy - John Denver
The Church of Logic, Sin and Love - The Men
The Storm - Big Country
The Waiting - Tom Petty and the Heartbreakers
The Wind That Shakes the Barley -Loreena McKennitt
You Ruined Everything - Jonathan Coulton

ABOUT THE AUTHOR

Kim Beall started sneaking into the basement to read her parents' massive collection of Science Fiction, Fantasy, and Gothic Romance when she was nine years old, which resulted in her spending her teenage years writing dozens of novels. This might have worked out better for her if she had not written them during math class.

She sincerely believes every adult still yearns, not so deep inside, to find real magic in everyday life.

Other Books by Kim Beall

Seven Turns: A ~~Ghost~~ Love Story – May 2018
The Pizza Delivery Boy's Tale – September 2018
Rivers and Roads – Coming in 2020

—

www.kimbeall.com
www.kimbeall.com/blog
amazon.com/author/kimbeall
goodreads.com/author/show/18012965.Kim_Beall
facebook.com/kimbeallauthor
@KimBeallsGhost